AGENT to the Stars

AGENT to the Stars

John Scalzi

A TOM DOHERTY ASSOCIATES BOOK
NEW YORK

AGENT TO THE STARS

Copyright © 2005 by John Scalzi

A Tor Book
Published by Tom Doherty Associates, LLC
175 Fifth Avenue
New York, NY 10010

www.tor-forge.com

Tor® is a registered trademark of Tom Doherty Associates, LLC.

Library of Congress Cataloging-in-Publication Data

Scalzi, John, 1969–
    Agent to the stars / John Scalzi.—1st ed.
        p.   cm.
    "A Tom Doherty Associates book"—T.p. verso.
    ISBN-13: 978-0-7653-1771-1
    ISBN-10: 0-7653-1771-0
    1. Theatrical agents—Fiction.   2. Extraterrestrial beings —Fiction.
3. Human-alien encounters —Fiction.   I. Title.
    PS3619.C256A73   2008
    813'.6—dc22

                                                                    2008029701

Printed in the United States of America

0 9 8 7 6 5 4 3

DEDICATION

This book was originally dedicated to Natasha Kordus and Stephen Bennett, friends of old, and still is.

It's also now dedicated to Bill Schafer, friend and original publisher of this novel.

And to Irene Gallo, who (with help from John Harris, Shelley Eshkar, Donato Giancola, and Pascal Blanchet) has made all my books at Tor look so good.

Author's Note and Acknowledgments

Several of my novels have had strange journeys into print, but the journey of *Agent to the Stars* is probably the strangest. It began in 1997 as my "practice novel"—that is to say, the novel I wrote to see if I *could* write a novel (the answer: seems so). I had no intention of ever selling it or ever really doing anything with it. Nevertheless in 1999 I posted it on my personal Web site, offering it as "shareware," and encouraging people to send me $1 if they liked it. Over the next five years (until I told people to stop sending me money), I made about $4,000. It was a nice way to stay in pizza, but I didn't expect anything more out of it.

In 2005, Bill Schafer, publisher of Subterranean Press, wandered by the Web site, saw *Agent* there, started reading it, and then sent me an e-mail asking me if he could publish it as a limited edition hardcover. Well, I thought it would be cool to finally see it in print, so I said sure. Subterranean printed 1,500 copies, sold them all, and now people are asking (and getting) several hundred dollars for their copies on eBay. I think this is a little silly, and wish I had extra copies to sell. But again, after that, I didn't expect anything more out of it.

And now here we are in 2008, and the book has come 'round again, this time in a really lovely paperback edition, of which there are more than 1,500 copies, and I am officially done underestimating this book, because clearly, it doesn't know when to stop. I am delighted by this chain of events, and hope you, the reader, are enjoying this little book which *just won't quit*.

The book you have in your hands is substantially the same book I wrote eleven years ago now, but because the novel takes place in contemporary time, this version of the novel has been revised to update a number of cultural references, to bring it in line with the world as it exists in the latter half of the first decade of the third millennium. For example, a character who used to have a television show on the United Paramount Network now has it on Comedy Central, because UPN no longer exists. The age of a couple of characters has also been juggled to have the story make sense today. After this, the book is on its own, because barring it being made into a film or something (because it *just won't quit*), this is the last revision of the book I plan to make. Rumor is I have other books to write. This is what my mortgage tells me, anyway.

There are many people to thank for this book, and I'll begin with the folks at Tor: my editor Patrick Nielsen Hayden and art director Irene Gallo (to whom the book is co-dedicated) primary among them, as well as Liz Gorinsky and Dot Lin, and of course Tom Doherty himself. Also many thanks to artist Pascal Blanchet for the really wonderful cover, and to Arthur Hlavaty for his work in the copy editor mines. Copyediting is a thankless job, particularly when someone has to copyedit someone as sloppy as me. Er, *I*. Oh, whatever. You know.

Outside of Tor, these people have had a hand in the book, in its earlier incarnations: Bill Schafer, Tim Holt, Mike Krahulik, Jerry Holkins, Robert Khoo, Stephen Bennett, and Regan

Avery. My thanks to each of them for their work and/or encouragement and/or help.

I'd also like to extend a special acknowledgment to my wife, Kristine, who while I was writing *Agent to the Stars* was filled with trepidation, knowing that when I was done writing it, she would have to read it, and if she didn't like it, she would still have to live with me. So I think we were both glad when she finished that last page, turned to me, and said "Thank GOD, it's good." She's my first and most important reader, and I love her dearly, and I'm glad she's the one I get to be with.

Finally: Thank *you*. No, really. I still get amazed people want to read what I write. I'm really glad you do. Thanks.

CHAPTER
One

"*Fourteen* million and fifteen percent of the gross? For Michelle Beck? You're out of your fucking mind, Tom."

Headsets are a godsend; they allow you to speak on the phone while leaving your hands free for the truly important things. My hands were currently occupied with a blue rubber racquetball, which I was lightly bouncing off the pane of my office window. Each quiet *thock* left a tiny imprint on the glass. It looked like a litter of poodles had levitated six feet off the ground and schmooged their noses against the window. Someone would eventually have to wipe them all off.

"I've had my medication for today, Brad," I said. "Believe me, fourteen million and fifteen points is a perfectly sane figure, from my client's point of view."

"She's not worth anywhere near that much," Brad said.

"A year ago she was paid $375,000, flat. I know. I wrote the check."

"A year ago, *Summertime Blues* hadn't hit the theaters, Brad. It's now $220 million later. Not to mention your own *Murdered Earth*—$85 million for perhaps the worst film in recent history. And that's before foreign, where no one will notice that there's no plot. I'd say you got your one cheap taste. Now you've gotta pay."

"*Murdered Earth* wasn't that bad. And she wasn't the star."

"I quote *Variety*," I said, catching the ball left-handed for the briefest of seconds before hurling it back against the glass, " '*Murdered Earth* is the sort of film you hope never makes it to network television, because nearby aliens might pick up its broadcast signal and use it as an excuse to annihilate us all.' That was one of the nicer comments. And if she wasn't the star, why did you plaster her all over the posters and give her second billing?"

"What are you all about?" Brad said. "I remember you practically doing me for that artwork and billing."

"So you're saying you'll do anything I say? Great! Fourteen million and fifteen percent of the gross. Gee, that was easy."

The door opened. I turned away from the window to face my desk. Miranda Escalon, my administrative assistant, entered my office and slipped me a note. *Michelle just called,* it read. *Remember that you have to get them to pay for her hairdresser and makeup artist,* it read.

"Look, Tom," Brad said. "You know we want Michelle. But you're asking too much. Allen is getting $20 million and twenty percent of the gross. If we give Michelle what she wants, that's $35 million and a third of the gross right there. Where do you suggest we might make a profit?"

$14 million, she can pay for her own damn hair, I wrote on the pad. Miranda read it and raised her eyebrows. She left the room. The odds of her actually giving *that* message to Michelle were unimaginably remote. She's not paid to do everything I say—she's paid to do everything I *should* say. There's a difference.

"I have two points to make here," I said, turning my attention back to Brad. "First: Allen Green isn't my client. If he were, I'd be endlessly fascinated by the amount of money you're throwing to him. But he is not. Therefore, I could not possibly give two shits about what you're handing him. My responsibility is to my client and getting a fair deal for her. Second: $20 million for Allen Green? You're an idiot."

"Allen Green is a major star."

"Allen Green *was* a major star," I said, "When I was in high school. I'm about to go back for my tenth-year reunion. He's been out in the wilderness for a long time, Brad. Michelle, on the other hand, *is* a major star. Right now. $300 million in her last two films. Fourteen million is a bargain."

The door opened. Miranda popped her head in. *She's back,* she mouthed.

"Tom," Brad began.

"Hold on a second, Brad. The woman herself is on the other line." I cut him off before he could say anything. "What?" I said to Miranda.

"Miss Thing says she has to talk to you right now about something very important that can't wait."

"Tell her I'm already working on the hairdresser."

"No, it's even more important than that," Miranda said. "From the sound of it, it may be the most important thing ever in the history of mankind. Even more important than the invention of liposuction."

"Don't be mocking liposuction, Miranda. It has extended the career of many an actress, thus benefiting their agents, allowing them to pay your salary. Liposuction is your friend."

"Line two," Miranda said. "Let me know if fat-sucking is toppled."

I punched the button for line two. Ambient street noise filled my earphones. Michelle was undoubtedly careening along Santa Monica Boulevard.

"Michelle," I said. "I'm trying to make you very rich. Whatever it is, make it quick."

"Ellen Merlow got *Hard Memories*." Michelle said. "I thought I was in the running for that. I thought I had it."

"Don't feel too bad about it, Michelle," I said. "Everyone was up for that one. If you didn't get it, that puts you in there with Cate Blanchett and Meryl Streep. You're in good company. Besides, the pay wasn't that good."

I heard a short brake squeal, followed by a horn and some muffled yelling. Michelle had cut someone off. "Tom, I need roles like that, you know? I don't want to be doing *Summertime Blues* for the next ten years. This role would have helped me stretch. I want to work on my craft."

At the word *craft*, I mimed stabbing myself in the eye. "Michelle, right now you're the biggest female star in Hollywood. Let's work with that for a couple of movies, okay? Get a nice nest egg. Your craft will still be there later."

"I'm right for this role, Tom."

"The role is a fortyish Jewish woman victimized in the Warsaw ghetto and Treblinka, who then fights racism in the United States," I said. "You're twenty-five. And you're blonde." *And you think Treblinka is a shop on Melrose.* I kept that last thought in my head. No point confusing her.

"Cate Blanchett is blonde."

"Cate Blanchett also has an Oscar," I said. "So does Ellen, for that matter. One in each acting category. And she's also not twenty-five, or blonde. Michelle, let it go. If you want to work on your craft, we can get you into some live theater. That's craft. Craft up the wazoo. They're doing *Doll's House* over at the Geffen. You'll love it."

"Tom, I want that part."

"We'll talk about it later, Michelle. I've got to get back to Brad. Gotta go. We'll talk soon."

"Remember to tell him about the hair—" I clicked her off and switched Brad back on. "Sorry, Brad."

"I hope she was telling you not to blow this offer by asking for too much," Brad said.

"Actually, she was telling me about another project she's really passionate about," I said. "*Hard Memories.*"

"Oh, come *on,*" Brad said. "She's a little young and blonde to be playing Yentl, isn't she? Anyway, Ellen Merlow just got that part. Read it in the *Times* today."

"Since when does the *Times* get anything right? Michelle's a little young for the part, yes, but that's what makeup is for. She's a draw. Could get a whole other audience for serious drama."

Brad snorted. "She won't be getting fourteen million for *that,*" he said. "That's their entire budget."

"No, but she'll be working on her craft," I said. I popped the ball up and down on my desk. "The academy eats that stuff up. It's a nomination, easy. Like Charlize Theron in *Monster.*" Sometimes I can't believe what comes out of my own mouth.

But it was working. I could hear Brad weighing the options in his mind. The project at hand was the sequel to *Murdered*

Earth—called, in a burst of true creativity, *Earth Resurrected*. They had a problem: they killed off the hero in the first film. Which was just as well, since Mark Glavin, who played him, was a loser who was well on his way to replicating the career arc of Mickey Rourke.

So when it came to the sequel, they had to build it around Michelle, whose character managed to survive. The script had been written, the casting completed, and the preproduction was rolling along under a full head of steam. Stopping now to recast or rewrite was not an option. They were over a barrel—they knew it and I knew it. What we were arguing about now was the size of the barrel.

Miranda's head popped through the door again. I glared at her. She shook her head. *Not her,* she mouthed. *Carl.*

I set the ball down. *When?* I mouthed.

Three minutes, she mouthed.

"Brad, listen," I said. "I've got to get—I've just been told I have a meeting with Carl. He's going to want to know where we stand on this. *Hard Memories* has about wrapped up its casting. We have to tell them one thing or another. I have to tell Carl one thing or another."

I could hear Brad counting in his head. "Fuck," he said, finally. "Ten million and ten percent."

I glanced down at my watch "Brad, it's been a pleasure talking to you. I hope that my client can work with you again at some point in the future. In the meantime, I wish you and the other *Murdered Earth* producers the best of success. We're going to miss being a part of that family."

"You bastard," Brad said. "Twelve five, salary and percentage. That's it. Take it or don't."

"And you hire her hair and makeup people."

Brad sighed. "Fine. Why the hell not. Allen's bringing his people. It'll be one big party. We'll all put on pancake together and then get a weave."

"Well, then, we have a deal. Courier over the contract and we'll start picking at it. And remember we still need to wrangle about merchandising."

"You know, Tom," Brad said, "I remember when you were a nice kid."

"I'm still a nice kid, Brad," I said. "It's just now I've got clients that you need. Chat with you soon." I hit the phone button and looked at my watch.

I just closed the biggest deal of the year to date, earned one and a quarter million for my company and myself, and still had ninety seconds before the meeting with Carl. More than enough time to pee.

When you're good, you're good.

CHAPTER TWO

$\mathscr{I}$ came out of the bathroom with thirty seconds left on the ticker, and started walking briskly towards the conference room. Miranda was trotting immediately behind.

"What's the meeting about?" I asked, nodding to Drew Roberts as I passed his office.

"He didn't say," Miranda said.

"Do we know who else is in the meeting?"

"He didn't say," Miranda said.

The second-floor conference room sits adjacent to Carl's office, which is at the smaller end of our agency's vaguely egg-shaped building. The building itself has been written up in *Architectural Digest,* which described it as a "four-way collision between Frank Gehry, Le Corbusier, Jay Ward, and the salmonella bacteria." It's unfair to the salmonella bacteria. My office is stacked on the larger arc of the egg on the first floor, along with the offices of all the other junior agents. After today, a second-floor, little-arc office was looking somewhat more probable in the future. I was humming the theme to *The Jeffersons* as Miranda and I got to the door of the conference room and walked through.

In the conference room sat Carl, an aquarium, and a lot of empty chairs.

"Tom," said Carl. "Good of you to come."

"Thanks, Carl," I said, "Good of you to have the meeting." I then turned to the table to consider probably the most important decision of the meeting: where to sit.

If you sit too close to Carl, you will be pegged as an obsequious, toadying suck-up. Which is not all that bad. But it will also mean you run the risk of depriving a more senior agent his rightful position at the table. Which *is* very bad. Promising agency careers had been brutally derailed for such casual disregard of one's station.

On the other hand, if you sit too far away, it's a signal that you want to hide, that you haven't been getting your clients the good roles and the good money; thus you've become a drag on the agency. Agents smell fear like sharks smell wounded sea otter pups. Soon your clients will be poached from you. You'll then have nothing to do but stare at your office walls and drink antifreeze until you go blind.

I sat about halfway down the table, slightly closer to Carl than not. What the hell. I earned it.

"Why are you sitting so far away?" Carl asked.

I blinked.

"I'm just saving space for the other folks in the meeting," I said. Had he heard about the Michelle Beck deal already? How does he do it? Has he tapped my phone? I goggled frantically at

Miranda, who was standing behind me, notepad at ready. She shot me a look that said, *Don't ask me. I'm just here to take shorthand.*

"That's very considerate of you, Tom," Carl said. "But no one else is coming. In fact, if you don't mind, I'd prefer it if Ms. Escalon wouldn't mind excusing us as well."

This would be the point where I casually dismissed my assistant and turned suavely to Carl, ready for our executive pow-wow. What I ended up doing was staring blankly. Fortunately, Miranda was on the ball. "Gentlemen," she said, excusing herself. On her way out, she dug the spike of her shoe into my pinky toe, and snapped me back to reality. I stood up, looking for where to sit.

"Why don't you sit here," Carl said, and pointed to a chair on the far side of the table, next to the aquarium.

"Great. Thanks," I said. I walked to the other side of the table and sat down. I stared at Carl. He stared back. He had a little smile on his face.

There are legends in the world of agents. There's Lew Wasserman, the agent of his day, who went over to the other side of the movie business and thrived at Universal Pictures. There's Mike Ovitz, who went over to the other side and exploded, humiliatingly, at Disney.

And then there's Carl Lupo, my boss, who went over to the other side, took Century Pictures from a schlock-horror house to the biggest studio in Hollywood in just under a decade and then, at the height of his reign, came back over into agency. No one knows why. It scares the hell out of everyone.

"I'm sorry," I said.

"What?" Carl said. Then he almost immediately laughed. "Relax, Tom. I just want to have a little chat. It's been a while since we've talked."

The last time Carl and I had talked directly to each other in a nonmeeting setting was three years earlier. I had just graduated from the mailroom to the agency floor, where I shared a pod with another mailroom escapee. My client list was a former teen idol, then in his thirties and a semi-regular at intervention sessions, and a cute but brainless twenty-two-year-old UCLA cheerleader named Shelly Beckwith. Carl had dropped by, shook hands with me and my podmate, and blathered pleasantries with us for exactly two minutes and thirty seconds before moving on to the next pod to do the same thing.

Since then, the former teen idol strangled in his own saliva, my podmate imploded from stress and left the agency to become a Buddhist monk in Big Bear, Shelly Beckwith became Michelle Beck and got lucky with two hits in a row, and I got an office. It's a strange world.

"How are things going with Michelle Beck's negotiations?" Carl asked.

"They're done, actually," I said. "We're getting twelve five, cash and percentages, and that's before merchandising."

"That's good to hear," Carl said. "Davis thought you'd hit a wall at about $8.5 million, you know. I told him you'd top that by at least three and a half. You beat the point spread by a half million dollars."

"Always happy to overachieve, Carl."

"Yes, well, Brad's no good at bargaining anyway. I stuck him with Allen Green, of all people, for twenty million. How that film is ever going to make a profit now is really beyond me."

I chose not to say anything at this point.

"Oh, well, not our problem, I suppose," Carl said. "Tell me, Tom. Do you like science fiction?"

"Science fiction?" I said. "Sure. *Star Wars* and *Star Trek*, mostly, same as everyone. Watched a couple of those new *Battlestar Galacticas*. And there was a period when I was fourteen when I read just about every Robert Heinlein book I could get my hands on. It's been a while since I've really read any, though. I watched *Murdered Earth* once, at the premiere. I think that's killed the genre for me for a while."

"Which do you like better, movies with evil aliens or movies with good aliens?"

"I don't know," I said. "I haven't really ever given it much thought."

"Please do so now," Carl said. "Indulge me, if you don't mind."

Carl could have said *Please disembowel yourself and sauté your intestines with mushrooms. Indulge me, if you don't mind* and anyone in the agency would have done it. It's disgusting what sycophancy can do.

"I guess if I had to make the choice, I'd go with the evil aliens," I said. "They just make for better films. Put in a bad alien and you get the *Alien* films, *Independence Day*, *Predator*, *Stargate*, *Starship Troopers*. Good aliens get you, what? **Batteries Not Included*? No contest."

"Well," Carl said, "There is *E.T.* And *Close Encounters*."

"I'll give you *E.T.*," I said. "But I don't buy *Close Encounters*. Those aliens were cute, sure, but that doesn't mean they weren't evil. Once they got out of the solar system, Richard Dreyfuss was probably penned up like a veal. Anyway, no one really knows what's going on in that movie. Spielberg must have been downing peyote frosties when he thought that one up."

"The *Star Trek* movies have good aliens. So do the *Star Wars* movies."

"The *Star Trek* movies have bad aliens too, like the Klingons and those guys with the wires in their heads."

"The Borg," Carl said.

"Right," I said. "And in *Star Wars*, no one was from Earth, so technically *everybody* was an alien."

"Interesting," Carl said. He was steepling his fingers together. Apparently the revelation that everyone in *Star Wars* had a passport from some other planet had transfixed him like a particularly troublesome Zen koan.

"If you don't mind me asking, Carl," I said, "Why are we talking about this? Are we putting together a package for a science fiction movie? Other than *Earth Resurrected,* I mean."

"Not exactly," Carl said, unsteepling his fingers, and placing them, flat out, on the desk. "I was having a discussion with a friend of mine about this and I wanted to get another opinion on it. Your opinion on the matter is like his, by the way. He's pretty much of the opinion that people are more comfortable with aliens as a hostile 'other' rather than a group that would have friendly intentions."

"Well, I don't think most people really think of aliens one way or the other," I said. "I mean, we're talking about movies, here. As much as I like the movies, it's not the same thing."

"Really?" The fingersteeple was suddenly back. "So if real aliens dropped from the sky, people might accept that they'd be friendly?"

I was back to staring again. I remembered having a conversation like this, once before in my life. The difference was that *that* conversation was back in my deeply stoned college freshman days, in a room strung with Christmas lights and tin foil, lying on a beanbag. The conversation I was having now was with one of the few men on the planet who could have the president of the United States return his call. Within ten minutes (they roomed together at Yale). Having this conversation with Carl was profoundly incongruous, right up there with listening to your grandfather talk about the merits of the hottest new sports kayak.

"Maybe," I ventured. When in doubt, equivocate.

"Hmmmm." Carl said. "So, Tom. Tell me about your clients."

I have a little man in the back of my brain. He likes to panic in situations like these. He was looking around nervously. I kicked him back into his hole and started down the list.

First and foremost, obviously, was Michelle: beautiful, in demand, and not nearly smart enough to realize the dumbest thing she could do at this point in her life is not take the money and run. I blamed myself.

Next up was Elliot Young, hunky young star of ABC's *Pacific Rim*. *Pacific Rim* was second in its Wednesday 9 p.m. time slot and sixty-third overall for the year. But thanks to Elliot's tight, volleyball-player ass and ABC's willingness to have him drop his shorts to solve crime at least once per episode, it was cleaning up in the 18–34 female viewers category. ABC was selling a lot of ad time to yeast infection treatments and feminine products with "wings." Everyone was happy. Elliot's looking to expand into film, but then, of course, who isn't.

Rashaad Creek, urban comic, originally from the mean streets of Marin County, where they'll busta cap in your ass for serving red wine with fish. Rashaad wasn't nearly as neurotic as most comedians, which means on his own he's generally not as funny. Nevertheless, thanks to some nice packaging work, we'd sold his pilot *Workin' Out!* to Comedy Central. Rashaad's budding career was watched over like a hawk by his overbearing manager, who also happened to be his mother. We pause for a shudder here.

The unfortunately named Tea Reader (pronounced tee-a), singer-turned-actress who I inherited from my old podmate after his forebrain sucked inward. Tea, from what I can figure, contributed a good half of his stress—notoriously difficult and given to tantrums far out of proportion to her track record (three singles from one album, peaking at #9, #13 and #24, respectively, a second female lead in a Vince Vaughn flick, and a series of ads for Mentos). She was just this side (she insisted) of thirty, which made her a perfect candidate to host her own talk show or infomercial. Tea called about once a week and threatened to get other representation. I wish.

Tony Baltz, a character actor who was nominated for a Best Supporting Oscar a decade ago, and had since refused to consider anything that's not a lead role. Which was a shame, since the lead role market for fifty-something chunky, bald guys was pretty much already sewn up by James Gandolfini. We managed to get him the occasional Lifetime movie.

The rest of my clients were a collection of has-beens, never-weres, near-misses, and not-there-yets, the sorts of folks that fill out the bottom half of every junior agent's dance card. Someone has to play the second spear-carrier on the left, and someone has to represent them. Be that as it may, going over the list with Carl, I realized that if it wasn't for the presence of Michelle, my client roster was of the sort that makes for a lifetime of junior agenthood. I decided not to bring it up.

"So, to recap," Carl said, after I had finished, "One superstar, two average-to-mediocres, two marginals, and a bunch of filler."

I thought about trying to sweeten up that assessment, but then realized there wasn't a point. I shrugged. "I suppose so, Carl. It's no worse than any other junior agent's client list here."

"Oh, no, I wasn't criticizing," Carl said. "You're a good agent, Tom. You look out for your people and you get them work—and, as today proves, you can get them what they're worth and then some. You're a sharp kid. You're going to do well in this business."

"Thanks, Carl," I said.

"Sure," he said. He pushed back his chair a bit and plopped his legs on the table. "Tom, how many of your clients do you think you can afford to lose?"

"What?"

"How many can you lose?" Carl waved his hand. "You know, farm out to other agents, drop entirely, whatever."

The little man in my head had escaped from his hole and was running around frantically, as if on fire. "None!" I said. "I mean, with all due respect, Carl, I can't lose any of them. It's not fair to them, for one thing, but for another thing, I need them. Michelle's doing well now, but believe me, that's not going to last forever. You can't ask me to cut myself off at the knees."

I pushed back slightly from the table. "Jesus, Carl," I said. "What's going on here? First the science fiction, now with my clients—none of this is making much sense to me at the moment. I'm getting a little nervous, here. If you've got some bad news for me, stop twisting me and just get to it."

Carl stared at me for the fifteen longest seconds in my life. Then he put his feet down, and moved his chair closer to me.

"You're right, Tom," he said. "I'm not handling this very well. I apologize. Let me try this again." He closed his eyes, took a breath, and looked straight at me. I thought my spine was going to liquefy.

"Tom," he said. "I have a client. It's a very important client, Tom, probably the most important client we as an agency will ever have. At least I can't imagine any other client being more important than this one. This client feels that he has a very serious image problem, and I'd have to say that I agree with him there. He has a special project that he wants to put together, something that needs the most delicate handling imaginable.

"I need someone to help me get this project off the ground, someone that I can trust. Someone who can handle the job for me without my constant supervision, and who can keep his ego in check for the sake of the project.

"I'm hoping you'll be that someone for me, Tom. If you say no, it won't affect your role at the agency in the slightest—you can walk out of this office and this meeting that we've had simply won't have happened. But if you do say yes, it means you're committed, whatever it takes, for as long as it takes. Will you help me?"

The little man in my head was now pounding on the backsides of my eyeballs. *Say NO,* the little man was saying. *Say no and then let's go to TGI Fridays and get really, really drunk.*

"Sure," I said. The little man in my head started weeping openly.

Carl reached over, covered my hand like it was his computer mouse, and shook it vigorously. "I knew I could count on you," he said. "Thanks. I think you're going to enjoy this."

"I hope so," I said. "I'm in for the long haul. So who is the client? Is it Tony?" Antonio Marantz had been caught fondling a sixteen-year-old extra on the set of the latest *Morocco Joe* film. It was a bad situation made worse by the fact that the sixteen-year-old that *People*'s "Most Eligible Bachelor" was fooling around with happened to be a boy, and the son of the director. After the director's fingers were pried from Tony's throat, everything was hushed up. The director got a million dollar raise. The boy got a Director's Guild "internship" on the Admiral Cook biopic that was filming in Greenland for the next six months. Tony got a stern lecture about the effect that cavorting with underage boys would have on the asking price of his next role. The crew got lesser but still fairly rich favors. Everyone stayed bought; it didn't make the gossip sites. But you never know. These things spring leaks.

"No, it's not Tony," Carl said. "Our client is here."

"In the building?"

"No," Carl said, tapping the aquarium that was between us. "Here."

"I'm not following you, Carl," I said. "You're talking about an aquarium."

"Look in the aquarium," Carl said.

For the first time since I entered the room, I took a good look at the aquarium. It was rectangular and neither especially big nor small—about the size of the usual aquarium you'd see in any home. The only thing notable about it was the absence of fish, rocks, bubbling filters, or little plastic treasure chests. It was filled entirely with a liquid that was clear but slightly cloudy, as if the aquarium water hadn't been changed in about a month. I stood up, looked over the top of the aquarium, and got a closer look. And smell. I looked over the aquarium at him.

"What is this, tuna Jell-O?"

"Not exactly," Carl said, and then addressed the aquarium. "Joshua, please say hello to Tom."

The stuff in the aquarium vibrated.

"Hi, Tom," the aquarium gunk said. "It's nice to meet you."

CHAPTER
Three

"*How* do you do that?" I asked Carl.

"Do what?" Carl asked.

"Make it speak," I said. "That's a really neat trick."

"I'm not making it speak, Tom." Carl said.

"No, I know that. I realize it's not a ventriloquist thing," I said. "What I'm asking is, How does sound come out of it at all? Jell-O doesn't strike me as the most efficient medium for sound."

"I'm not really sure about the physics of it, Tom," Carl said. "I'm an agent, not a scientist."

"This is very cool technology," I said, touching the surface of the gunk. It was sticky, and resisted my fingertips a little. "I mean, I'm not going to rush out and buy Jell-O speakers, but it's still very cool. What is it? Something from a science fiction movie? Is our client doing a film about gelatinous aliens or something?"

"Tom," Carl said. "It's not about a movie. That," he pointed to the aquarium, "is our client."

I stopped playing around with the gunk and looked over at Carl. "I'm not following you," I said.

"It's alive, Tom," Carl said.

The stuff wriggled slightly under my fingers. I pulled them back so quickly I felt a seam on my suit jacket rip. An inside seam. Near the shoulder. I had paid $1,200 for the jacket, and it let me down in the first moment of crisis. I focused all my mental energy on considering that jacket seam, because the only other thing to think about at the moment was that thing in the tank. The jacket seam, that I could handle.

Finally, after a few minutes, the words came, something that, I think, covered the enormity of the situation and what I was experiencing in my head.

"Holy shit," I said.

"That's a new one on me," said the aquarium gunk.

"It's just an expression," Carl said.

"Holy Christ on a pony," I said.

"So's that," Carl noted.

"Ah," said the gunk. "Listen, do you mind if I get out of this box now? I've been in it all day. The right angles are killing me."

"Please," Carl said.

"Thank you," said the gunk. A tendril formed off the surface of the gunk and arched towards the conference table, touching down close to the center of the table. The tendril wobbled slightly for a second, then thickened tremendously as the gunk transferred itself out of the aquarium through the tendril. When the transfer was over, the tendril reabsorbed into the main body, which now sat, globular, on the conference table.

"That's much better," the gunk said.

"Carl," I said. I was keeping my distance from the gunk. "You'd really better catch me up on what's going on here."

Carl had put his feet back on the table. They rested not too far off from where the gunk was piled. That seemed a bad idea to me. "Do you want the long or short version?" He asked.

"Give me the short version for now, if you don't mind," I said.

"Fine," he said. "Tom, have a seat, please. I promise Joshua won't leap on you and suck out your brains."

"I won't," the gunk that was apparently called Joshua agreed. "I'm a good alien, not like those bad aliens that make for such good movies. Please, Tom, sit down."

I didn't know which was more fundamentally disturbing: that Jell-O was talking to me, that it had a sense of humor, or that it had better manners than I did. My body sat down in my seat; the man in my brain readied himself for a sprint to the door.

"Thank you," Carl said. "Here's the short version: About four months ago, the Yherajk, of which my friend Joshua is a member, contacted me. The Yherajk have been watching us here on Earth for a while, and they decided recently that, after several years of observation, it was time to make themselves known to humanity. But they have concerns."

"We look like snot," Joshua said. "And we smell like dead fish."

Carl nodded in Joshua's direction. "The Yherajk are worried that their physical appearance will present problems."

"We have seen *The Blob,* and it is us," Joshua intoned.

Another nod from Carl. "The Yherajk have decided that before they can appear to humanity, some arrangements have to be made—a way has to be made for them not to appear so ugly from the outset."

"We need an agent to get us the role of the friendly aliens," Joshua said.

"That's the short version," Carl said.

I sat there for a second, trying to process the information. "Can I ask a question?" I said.

"Shoot," said Joshua.

I looked at Joshua and for a moment I was frozen. I didn't know what part of it to address. It all looked the same. I dealt with it by looking straight at its center. "Dumb question first: Why didn't you just drop on the lawn of the White House? I mean, in the movies, that's pretty much how it was done."

"We thought about it," Joshua said. "Then we caught the presidential debates. The people you folks elect are sort of scary. And you Americans are the folks that do it the best on this entire planet. Besides, your president only speaks for Americans. American movies speak for your world. Who hasn't seen *Wizard of Oz*? Or *Jaws*? Or *Star Wars*? We've seen them, and we're not even from this planet." Joshua sprouted a tendril and tapped the table. "If you want to introduce yourself to the planet, this is the place to start."

"Okay," I said. I looked over at Carl. "The . . . Earjack—"

"Yherajk," Carl said, pronouncing it *yee-heer-aahg-k*.

"It's not our real name," Joshua said, "but you couldn't pronounce what we're actually called."

"Why not?" I asked.

"Well, for one thing, it's a smell," Joshua said. "Would you like to smell it?"

I glanced at Carl. He shrugged. "Sure," I said.

The room filled with a stench that resembled the offspring of a rotted sneaker and Velveeta. I gagged involuntarily.

"God, that's horrible," I said, and immediately regretted it.

"I'm very sorry," I said. "That was probably the first-ever insult to an extraterrestrial. I apologize."

"No offense taken," Joshua said, mildly. "You should come to a Yherajk get-together. It's like a convention of farts."

"I believe there was a question at the beginning of all this," Carl said.

"Right," I said, and looked back to Carl. "How many people know about the Yherajk?"

"Including you and me?" Carl said.

"Yes," I said.

"Two," Carl said. "Well, and a couple thousand Yherajk orbiting the planet. But among humans, it's just you and me."

"Wow," I said.

"It's not that hard to believe," Joshua said. "If you run out of here and say that you've just met an alien that looks like gelatin and smells like a cat in heat, who's going to believe you? All the really believable aliens have *spines*."

I ignored this. "Carl, why me?"

Carl tilted his head at me, and regarded me like a favored child. Which, perhaps, I was. "What do you mean?" he asked.

"I mean, I'm flattered that you picked me to help you to do . . ." I waved my hands around, "whatever it is that we're going to be doing here. But I don't know why you picked me."

"Well, it's like I said," Carl said. "I need someone who's smart and that I can trust."

"I appreciate that," I said. "But Carl, you don't even *know* me. I've worked here for five years, and every other time we've spoken, it was in meetings, about our clients and how we were going to package them. And that wasn't that often."

"Do you feel neglected?" Carl asked. "I wouldn't have pegged you for that."

"No, that's not it," I said. "It's never bothered me. That's not what I mean. What I mean is that I don't know why you feel you can trust me, or why you think I'm smart. You can, and I am, but I wouldn't have thought I'd be an obvious choice. I'm surprised you even thought of me."

Carl smirked, looked off for a second, as if communicating to an unseen audience, and then turned back to me. "Tom," he said, "give me *some* credit for knowing something about the people who I employ."

I straightened up slightly. "I didn't mean to offend you, Carl."

"You haven't," he said. "My point here is simply that I've been aware of you and your work for this company. Your work speaks quite a bit as to the person you are, and as for the rest of it . . ." he shrugged. "Sometimes you take a chance."

"Thanks," I said.

"Also, to be blunt," Carl continued, "you're just a junior agent here. You're flying under the radar. If any of the senior agents suddenly divested himself of his clients and started sneaking around, it would be noticed. There would be gossip. In-fighting. Stories in *Variety* and the *Times*. No one's going to notice or care if you do the same thing."

It was my turn to smirk. "Well, my mother might be concerned."

"Does she write for the *Times?*" Carl said.

"I don't think so," I said. "She lives in Arizona."

"Well, then," Carl said. "That's fine with me."

"I'm still confused as to why you need me," I said. "Certainly you don't need me to put something together."

"But I do," Carl said. "Because I can't."

"Tom," Joshua said, "If it would throw the company in

turmoil if one of the senior agents here dropped what they're doing to start working on a secret project, how much more suspicious is it going to look if Carl did it?"

"I can't even take a vacation without someone here attempting a palace coup," Carl said. "There's no way I'm going to be able to stop running this place to look after this. No, someone else has to deal with this thing. You've got the job."

"Carl, I don't even know what the job *is*," I said.

"Make me beautiful," Joshua said. "I'm ready for my close-up, Mr. DeMille."

"The Job," Carl said, implying the capital *J* with his voice, "is to find some way to prepare the planet for the presence of the Yherajk. They're ready to show themselves to humanity, Tom. *You* have to make humanity ready for them."

The words hung out there in the air for a minute, not unlike, I suppose, the fragrance of a Yherajk conversation—invisible, but very hard to ignore.

"I'm just guessing here," Joshua said, "but I'm thinking this is probably where you say 'Holy shit' again, Tom."

CHAPTER
Four

Miranda was being monopolized by Ben Fleck, another junior agent, when I returned. She glanced at me pointedly as I walked by. The glance had a double meaning. The first was *What the hell happened in there?* The second was *Rescue me.* Ben was a first-class jerk who had been trying for eighteen months to get into Miranda's pants; it would have constituted sexual harassment except that Ben was so obviously inept at it.

"Miranda," I said. "Could you please come to my office?"

"Hey," Ben said. "I'm discussing a client with Miranda at the moment."

"That client is in your pants, Ben," I said. "And he's never going to get the job. Miranda?" I held the door open for her as she took her notepad and walked by me into my office.

"Thank you," she said, as I closed the door behind us. "Though you shouldn't be so rough on Ben. He's sort of sweet, in his own lecherous, oafish way."

"Nonsense," I said. "I'm not going to let him get away with anything I'm not allowed to get away with."

"But Tom," Miranda said, "you're neither lecherous nor oafish."

"Thanks, Miranda," I said, and leaned against my desk. "I'll put that on my gravestone. 'Here lies Thomas Stein. He was neither lecherous nor oafish.'"

"Enough chitchat," Miranda said. "Do you still have a job, or are you just putting on a brave face for your devoted staff?"

"Miranda, did anyone pay attention to where we were going when we went to the meeting?"

Miranda sat in the chair in front of my desk and thought for a moment. "Not that I could tell. You nodded to Drew Roberts as we walked past him, but I don't think he noticed. You're a junior agent. You don't rate a nod back."

"Good," I said. "Did anyone ask where I was?"

"In the office? No. Michelle called again," Miranda crossed her eyes slightly at the word *Michelle*, indicating in her own subtle way that she believed Michelle to be less intelligent than the average protozoan, "but I just told her you were in a meeting. Other than that, my attention was monopolized by Ben, who loathes you and would not ask about you even if he could get a promotion out of it. Why?"

"If anyone asks, I was just out to get a bagel, okay?"

"You're killing me," Miranda said. "I don't normally threaten my bosses, but if you don't tell me what happened in there, I may have to hurt you."

"I *can't*, Miranda. You know if I could tell anyone, I would tell you." I gave her my best I'm-utterly-helpless look. "I just can't. Just trust me for now, please, and just forget that meeting ever took place?"

Miranda looked at me for a minute. "Okay, Tom," she said, finally. "But if we're not going to talk about the meeting that didn't take place, why did you call me in here?"

"I need you to get my files on everyone I represent. Also, give me the names of the latest agents up from the mailroom, and their client lists, if you can."

Miranda jotted on her notepad. "All right," she said. "Anything in particular I should look for in the new agents?"

"I want someone who is so new that he still could do his mail route with his eyes closed. Someone who doesn't know anything. Me, about three years ago."

"Young and naive. Got it, Tom. Actually, I know just the person."

"Great. Give me about an hour with my files and then have them come for a visit."

"Fine. Anything else?"

"Yes. I'm going to need one of those watercooler bottles. And a dolly."

Miranda looked up from her notepad. "A watercooler bottle?"

"Yeah. One of those Arrowhead Water bottles. The five gallon ones."

"And a dolly."

"If you can find one. They have them in the mailroom, I think. You can have the new agent retrieve it."

I could see Miranda debating with herself whether or not she wanted to ask what the water bottle was for. She finally decided against it. What a pro. "Do you want the water bottle empty or full?"

"Doesn't matter," I said.

"It does to me," she said. "I have to lug the damn thing to your office."

"Empty, please."

She stopped writing. "Okay," she said. "You'll have your files in just a minute." She stood up and walked over the two steps to where I was. I stopped leaning on the desk and stood up. "Tom," she said, "you can trust me; I'll never speak of that meeting in front of anyone. But whatever happened in that meeting, congratulations." She reached over and tousled my hair. It was an old-fashioned and matronly move from someone who was my assistant, and a year younger than I was. It made me grin like an idiot.

Miranda dropped the files on my desk. It was now time to play everybody's favorite game: ditch the clients.

"This thing is going to take up all of your time from now on," Carl had warned, right after I had signed up for the ride. "You're going to have to formulate a plan and execute it. You're going to have to be an aide to Joshua, as well. Which reminds me: he needs to stay at your place."

"What?" I said. Visions of slug slime coating my upholstery leapt, unbidden, into my mind.

"Tom," Joshua said, "it's not exactly an easy commute between here and the ship."

"We can work out the details later," Carl said, getting back on track. "But what you need to do now, Tom, is go through your client list and as quietly as possible, offload as many as you can. Joshua is your full-time job now."

I stared at the files and had a weird tingling in my head. On one hand, this was an agent's dream—get rid of the truly annoying clients! Cut the dead weight! Unload the ballast! Every agent who was not running an agency had clients they'd rather be without—and here I was being told to eject them. On the other hand, as an agent, you're only as good as your client list. Better bad clients than none at all. I was understanding intellectually that my new "client" was an opportunity that comes along—well, that's *never* come along before, now that I thought of it. Emotionally, however, it still felt like I was taking the ascending 747 that was my agentorial career and aiming it into the Pacific, while all the passengers, my clients, were screaming in the coach seats, their little emergency plastic airmasks waving in the turbulence.

Enough thinking, I decided. I grabbed the first file.

Tony Baltz. Gone. He was on his way down anyway, since he was too proud to take the roles that had made him famous in the first place.

Rashaad Creek. Keep. I could work through his mother, who was doing most of the heavy lifting in that partnership, anyway. The unsettling Oedipal overtones to Rashaad's situation had always disturbed me, but now I could finally use them to my advantage.

Elliot Young. Keep. Elliot, bless his heart, was not the brightest of studs. I could sit down with him one afternoon and convince him that by buckling down on the series for a season, it would make the transition to films much more profitable in the long run. Who knows, it might even be the truth.

Tea Reader. Gone. Thank the Lord almighty.

Michelle Beck. Keep. Of course. Michelle Beck was my cover: when a client can rake in twelve million per film, an agent can't be faulted for wanting to spend more time concentrating on that client. Also, flying under the radar or not, dropping Michelle after today's paycheck would be noticed by someone. Michelle and I were bound together for life, or until she pulled a hissy fit and got new representation. If I didn't have her, I would be, as my father liked to say, walking through a thick shag carpet of shit. The ambivalence I felt about this fact was staggering in its depth.

The undercard folks were all toast. It didn't really matter who agented them, anyway.

I was finishing up my client triage when Miranda buzzed me. "Mr. Stein," she said. I could count the times she called me *Mr. Stein* on one hand, without having to use my thumb or index finger. "Amanda Hewson is here."

"Accompany her in, please, Ms. Escalon," I called Miranda *Ms. Escalon* even less than she called me *Mr. Stein*.

Miranda walked in, followed by a gawky blonde who looked like she wasn't old enough to see R-rated films without accompaniment. Amanda Hewson had graduated from the mailroom just over a month before. Her two clients were a former Mexican soap opera star who wanted to make it big in Hollywood, but didn't want to learn the English language, and an actor who administered first aid to her after she fainted on mile four of the LA Marathon. She represented him, apparently, largely out of gratitude.

She was perfect.

"Amanda," I said, motioning to the chair in front of my desk. "Please sit down." She did. I regarded her the same way Carl regarded me earlier today. It's fair; the distance, career-wise, was not dissimilar.

Amanda was looking around. "Nice office," she said.

My office is a dump.

"It is, isn't it?" I said. "Amanda, do you know why I asked you here?"

"Not really," Amanda confessed. "Ms. Escalon"—Unseen by Amanda, Miranda crossed her eyes; she didn't appear to cotton to all this formalness—"said that it was important but didn't say what it was."

I did some more regarding. It was making Amanda nervous. She looked behind her briefly to see if I was actually looking at something behind her, then turned back, tittered nervously. Her hands, restless in her lap, spasmed lightly.

I looked at Miranda. "You think she's the one?" I asked.

Now it was Miranda's turn to regard Amanda. I have to admit, she did a much scarier regarding. Amanda looked about to wet her pants. "I think so," Miranda said. "At least, she's much better than the other possibles."

I had no idea what Miranda was talking about. Then again, she didn't know what I was talking about either. We were making this up as we went along.

"So, Amanda," I said. "Where'd you go to school?"

"UCLA," she said. "In Westwood," she added. After she said that I could see the thought travel through her head: *Moron! We're in LA! He KNOWS where UCLA is! God! I'm an idiot!* Panic can be truly endearing when it's done right.

"Really," I said. "I'm a Bruin myself. How's the high-speed life of an agent treating you these days?"

"Well, really well," she said, with obvious fervor. "I mean, I'm just getting started, so it's a little rough. I think it'll be a few more months before I really get my legs." She smiled brightly. She was so new that she didn't realize that admitting weakness was a mortal sin among agents. I wondered how she got past the screening process. Beside me, I could feel waves of pity emanate from Miranda. Now I knew why she had suggested Amanda—she was trying to keep this clearly noncynical young woman from having the stuffing kicked out of her by her more vicious compatriots.

"Well, I hope your legs are ready now, Amanda," I said. "The officers of this corporation"—I always thought that phrase sounded dramatic, and I was right—"have instructed me to inaugurate a pilot mentor project for our newest agents, a sort of helping hand to get them up to speed more quickly. Now, I have to emphasize that this is just a pilot program, and highly experimental. In fact, it's a secret—"

Amanda's eyes actually widened. If I were just ten percent less jaded, I think I might have fallen in love.

"—so you'll have to keep it that way. It's officially unofficial. Understand?"

"Sure, Mr. Stein."

"Call me Tom," I said. "Amanda, what do you think of Tea Reader?"

Her eyes got even wider. Make that five percent less jaded.

Two hours and a Starbucks latte each later, the Officially Unofficial Mentor Project was underway. Under my "supervision," Amanda would take over the day-to-day representation needs of Tea Reader, Tony Baltz, and my undercard clients. For the first month, Amanda would make detailed weekly reports on "our" clients, which I would read and comment on. That would decrease to twice monthly the second month, and monthly thereafter. During this time, any money made from representing these clients would be split between mentor and student. After six months, pending mentor approval, Amanda could represent up to six of these clients full-time, with all commissions and fees going to her from that point forward. To myself, I figured that any clients she didn't want to keep after six months I would drop in any event.

Amanda was happy because even with a reduced commission rate, she stood to make far more money over the next six months than she could have off her own clients, and would get an automatically expanded client list at the end of it. Plus, of course, my invaluable mentoring services. I was happy because I off-loaded my clients. The only one who might not be entirely happy with it was Miranda, because she knew that the reports I was supposed to read and comment on were actually going to be read and commented on by her. But she didn't say anything about it. I was going to have to get her a raise soon.

Amanda went off in a haze of blissfulness and promises to "get right on it." She was like a Mouseketeer on "Let's Represent Someone" day. I could almost see her skip to her pod. I hoped her first experience with Tea Reader would not send her too much into shock.

"That was a dirty trick," Miranda said to me.

"What do you mean?" I said. "Look at her. What are her chances of getting a decent client list on her own?"

"Not to her," Miranda said. "To me. Now I'm going to have to add babysitting to my list of things to do."

"She'll be fine," I said. "And anyway, I thought you liked her."

"I *do* like her," Miranda said. "And she *will* be fine. Eventually." She put her face closer to mine. "But in the short term, I might as well be a crossing guard, for all the hand-holding I'm going to do. Now, I'm off to get your water bottle." She walked out of the office.

I was going to have to get her a raise *very* soon.

I knocked on the conference room door. It was unoccupied. I entered the conference room with the water bottle and the dolly, closed the door, and locked it behind me.

"You have *got* to be kidding," Joshua said.

Joshua had slipped back into the aquarium, which stayed in the conference room after our meeting was done. My job had been to find an unobtrusive way to get him from the conference room to my place. Carl wouldn't tell me how he had gotten Joshua into the building unnoticed, and he wasn't giving me any tips on how to get him out. *Think of it as your first challenge,* he said. Were I palming off the first known extraterrestrial on a subordinate to take care of, I think I'd be a little more concerned.

"We give you three hours to come up with something, and this is the best you can do," Joshua said. "I'm not scared yet, but I'm getting there."

"I'm sorry," I said. "I had to improvise." I wheeled the bottle over and sat it next to the tank. I had figured that a five-gallon water bottle would be big enough to fit Joshua in. Now I wasn't so sure.

Neither was he. He extended a tendril out of the aquarium and sent it down into the bottle and waved it around, as if to check it for roominess. "How long will it take to get to your place?" he said.

"Probably an hour, maybe more," I said. "I live in La Canada. The 405 will be jammed up, but once we get over to the 210, it should be pretty quick. Is it going to be a problem?"

"Not at all," Joshua said. "Who *doesn't* enjoy being crammed into a five-gallon plastic bottle for an hour?"

"You don't have to stay in the bottle once we get to the car," I said. "Once we're out of here, you can spread out." This wrinkle in the plan was as new to me as it was to him. I had assumed he'd stay in the bottle the whole trip. But my car upholstery was a small price to pay for interplanetary peace. I'd just have to remember to get one of those little pine tree air fresheners.

"Thanks, but no thanks," Joshua said. "The conversation where you try to explain to a highway patrolman why you have forty pounds of gelatin in your passenger seat is one I think we'd both rather avoid."

I laughed. "I'm sorry," I said. "I'm sort of amazed you know what a highway patrolman is."

"Why?" Joshua said. "You've been beaming *CHiPs* into space for decades." He wiggled his tendril again, and then sighed. He must have picked that up purely as a sonic affectation because he had no lungs from which to exhale. "All right, here I go," he said, and started putting himself into the bottle.

He came dangerously close to filling up the bottle. In the last few seconds, a thought popped into my skull: *I'm going to need another bottle.* It didn't occur to me to question the logic of that thought. He was gelatinous, he should be able to divide up. It became academic when he topped out about three millimeters from the top of the mouth of the bottle.

"Comfortable?" I asked.

"Remind me to stuff you into a medium-sized suitcase and ask you that same question," Joshua said. His voice was diminished and tinny, no doubt due to the relatively tiny amount of surface area he had to vibrate.

"Sorry," I said. "Listen, do you need this open? I'm thinking it might be better if I put the top back on this thing."

"Are you out of your mind?" Joshua said. "Keep it open."

"Okay," I said. "I didn't know. I suppose you need to breathe."

"It's not that," Joshua said. "I'm claustrophobic."

"Really?"

"Look," Joshua said. "Just because I come from a highly advanced alien species doesn't mean I can't be intensely neurotic. Can we go now? I already feel like I want to scream."

I hiked the dolly up on its wheels, wheeled over to the door, unlocked it, and headed out into the hallway. It was still early enough in the day that the office was still busy. I was worried that someone might ask me why I was wheeling a five-gallon water bottle around until I remembered that I was on the second floor, the land of senior agents. A senior agent would naturally assume it was my job to wheel water bottles around. I was probably safe until I hit the lobby.

Which is in fact where I got noticed. As I passed the receptionist's desk on the way to the parking lot, some guy at the desk turned around. "Tom Stein?" he asked.

The *Just Keep Moving* command left my brain a tenth of a second after the *Look Around* reflex kicked in. By then, of course, it was too late; I had already stopped and looked back. "Yes?"

The man jogged the short distance over and extended his hand. "Glad I caught you," he said, as we shook. "Your assistant said you had already left."

"I had," I said. "I just had to stop elsewhere and pick something up."

"I can see that," he said, glancing down at the water bottle. "I guess you've gone past office supplies."

"Who are you?" I asked.

"I'm sorry," he said. "Jim Van Doren. I write for *The Biz*."

The Biz was a magazine written in a snide, knowing sort of tone that implied the folks who slapped together *The Biz* were just coming from lunch with movie company heads, who couldn't wait to slip them the latest gossip. Neither I nor anyone I knew knew anyone who had ever actually spoken to anyone at the magazine. No one knew how the magazine got written. No one knew anyone who would actually pay to read it. Blogs should have killed it by now, but it just kept going.

Van Doren himself was about my age, blond and balding, sort of pudgy. He looked like what happened to former USC frat boys about three months after they realize that their college days were never, ever coming back.

"Van Doren," I said. "No relation to Charles, I assume."

"The guy from *Quiz Show*? I wish," Van Doren said. "His dad won a Pulitzer Prize, you know. Wouldn't mind getting one of those myself."

"You'd probably have to work for a magazine that didn't devote six pages to an illustrated article about fake porn on the Internet," I said. "You remember, the one where big stars' heads were Photoshopped on to pictures of women having sex with dogs and glass bottles? The one that just about every movie studio in the city sued you over."

"I didn't have anything to do with that story," he said.

"That's good," I said. "Michelle Beck is my client. She was rather unamused by the picture that had her taking it up the back door from George Clooney while eating out Lindsay Lohan. As her agent, I'd be required to break your nose on her behalf. Of course, I'd take my ten percent, too." I started walking towards the lobby door.

Van Doren, who was not taking the hint, followed. "Actually, Tom, I knew you were Michelle Beck's agent. It's sort of why I came here. Heard that you got her twelve and a half for *Earth Resurrected*. That's not bad."

I opened the lobby door with one hand and propped it open with my foot as I maneuvered the dolly through the entryway.

"The agency hasn't made an announcement about that to the press, much less *The Biz,*" I said. "Where did you hear about it?"

Van Doren grabbed the door and held it for me. "I got it from Brad Turnow's office," he said. "They faxed out an announcement to the press, and I got the figure from his receptionist when I called to follow up."

I made a mental note to have Brad fire his receptionist. "I can't comment about my client's affairs," I said. "If you're looking for something, I'm not going to give it to you."

"I'm not here to do anything on Michelle Beck," Van Doren said. "I'm hoping to do a story on you."

"On me?" I said. "Really, Van Doren. I'm not that interesting. And there are no pictures of me on the Net having sex with anyone."

"Look, we know we lost a lot of goodwill on that story," Van Doren said. This statement was on the same level as the captain of the *Titanic* saying, *I guess we've taken on a little water.* "We're trying to get away from that sort of thing now. Do some real journalism. The story I'm doing, for example, is 'The Ten Hottest Young Agents in Hollywood.'"

"You getting ten agents to talk to you?" I wheeled over to my car, a Honda Prelude.

"I've got six so far," he said, "including one of your guys here—Ben Fleck. You know him?"

"I do," I said. "I wouldn't call him one of the ten hottest young agents in Hollywood."

Van Doren grimaced. "Yeah, I know," he said. "Frankly, none of the really good young agents want to talk. That's why I'm really hoping to do something on you. I mean, twelve and a half million! I'd say that makes you the hottest agent in Hollywood at the moment, period. You're the money guy, in all senses of the term. This is cover story material, Tom. You need help getting that in the trunk?" he gestured to the water bottle.

I just did *not* want this guy here.

"No thanks," I said. "It's going up front."

"Well, here," he said, stepping around to the dolly. "I'll hold this while you get the door open."

What could I do? I gave him the dolly and went to open the passenger side door. As I opened the door, I realized I was on the wrong side of it; Van Doren would have to put the bottle in. I felt a mild stirring of panic.

Van Doren realized this as well. "I'll get it," he said, and walked around to pick it up. "I don't suppose you have a cap for this—if you hit a bump, you're going to get it all over your interior."

"Nope," I said.

Van Doren shrugged. "Your car." He reached down and picked up the bottle, wobbled it slightly, provoking a spike of fear to my mild stirring of panic, turned and maneuvered it onto the passenger seat. As he stood up, his face was red and blotchy. "Out of shape," he said. "Tom, don't take this wrong, but that water smells a little off. You're not planning to drink it, I hope."

"No," I said. "It's from a sulfur spring one of our agents just got back from. You heat it up and soak in it. Good for the skin. But stinky."

"No kidding," Van Doren said. He leaned against the door, effectively blocking my ability to shut it. "So, Tom, how about it? I think you'd make a great profile. In fact, if everything goes well, I might be able to persuade my editors to drop the other nine hottest young agents out of the story. A cover story, Tom."

On a normal day of my life, I would have wanted to be on the cover of *The Biz* about as much as I wanted to run my tongue over a cheese grater. Today, with an alien in my passenger seat and no clue as to my future in the agency, I wanted to be on the cover of *The Biz* even less than that.

"Thanks, but I'm going to pass," I said. "I'm not much one for the limelight. I save that for my clients."

"Do you hear yourself?" Van Doren said. "You talk in perfect pull quote nuggets. Come on."

I decided to lie. "I'm late for dinner with my parents," I said, nodding to the door.

He reluctantly backed away. "And concerned about family, too. You're screaming to be made famous, Tom."

I smiled, thought about saying something, thought better of it. "I don't think so, Van Doren. Make Ben famous instead." I closed the door and walked over to the driver side.

"Think about it, Tom," Van Doren said, as I got in the car. "I'll be around when you want to talk."

Is that a promise or a threat? I wondered. I waved, started the Prelude, and got the hell out of there.

I got a ticket from the California Highway Patrol, for speeding on the 210.

"That cop was not at all what I expected," Joshua said. "Neither Ponch nor John had breasts. I'm going to have to revise my expectations."

No kidding.

"*All* right," I said. "Question and answer time."

"Gasp," Joshua said. "Torture me all you want. But I'll never tell you the location of the rebel base."

Joshua and I were sitting at my dining room table. More accurately, I was sitting at the table; Joshua was sitting on it. Between us was a Pizza Hut carton and the remnants of a large pepperoni pizza. Joshua had eaten four slices. They lay, haphazardly, near the center of his being. I could see the slices slowly disintegrating in an osmotic haze. It was vaguely disturbing.

"You going to eat that last piece?" Joshua said.

"No," I said, turning the carton towards him. "Please."

"Great," Joshua said. A pseudopod extended, folded around the crust edge, and withdrew back into his body. The slice was surrounded and joined its brethren. "Thanks. I haven't had anything all day. Carl thought it might be upsetting to you to see food rotting away in the middle of something that looked like dried glue."

"He was right," I said.

"That's why he's the boss," Joshua said. "Okay. Here's the rules for the question and answer period: you ask a question, then I ask a question."

"You have questions?" I asked.

"Of course I have questions," Joshua said. "From my point of view, you're the alien."

"All right."

"No lying and no evading," Joshua said. "I think we can be pretty safe with each others' secrets, because, really, who are we going to tell? Fair enough?"

"Fair enough," I said.

"Good," Joshua said. "You go first."

"What are you?" Might as well get the big one out first.

"A fine question. I'm a highly advanced and organized colony of single-celled organisms that work together on a mac-rocellular level."

"What does that mean?" I asked.

"Wait your turn," Joshua said. "How did you get this place? These are nice digs."

He was right. They *were* nice digs. Far better than I could have afforded on my own (until today, that is)—a four-bedroom ranch on three-quarters of an acre, overlooking the valley and abutting Angeles National Forest in the back. Occasionally I woke up and went out back to find a deer in the yard or a coy-ote digging through the trash. That passes for nature here in LA. It was just above the smog layer, too. Such are the advan-

tages of having prosperous parents. My mother left it to me after my father died and she retired to Scottsdale, to be closer to
her mother's nursing home.

The only thing that could be held against it was that it was
in the wrong valley—San Gabriel, where the "real" people
(read: not in the movie business) lived. Every once in a while
one of the other agents would mock me about that. I would
smile sweetly and ask them what the rent was on their one-
bedroom condo in Van Nuys.

"I've lived here all my life," I said. "My mom gave me the
house when she moved. What does 'highly advanced and organized colony of single-celled organisms' mean?"

"It means that each of the cells in my body is a self-contained,
unspecialized organism," Joshua said. "How did you decide to
become an agent?"

"My dad was an agent—a literary agent," I said. "When I was
a kid, he'd bring his clients over for dinner. They were weird but
fun people. I thought it was cool that my dad knew such weird
people, so I decided I wanted to be an agent. I must have been
about five. I had no idea what an agent really did. If you're actually a bunch of smaller creatures, how do you get them all to
move and act the way you want them to?"

"I don't know," Joshua said. "Do you know how you make
your heart beat?"

"Sure," I said. "My brain sends a message to my heart to
keep beating."

"Right," Joshua said. "But you don't know the exact
process."

"No," I said.

"Neither do I," Joshua said. "Do you have a game console?"

"What? No," I said. "I had a Nintendo when I was younger, but that was a long time ago. Do you have any organs, like a heart or a brain?"

"Not exactly," Joshua said. "The cells take turns performing functions, based on need. Right now, for example, the cells on my surface are collecting sensory information. Other cells not otherwise occupied are performing cognitive functions. The cells around the pizza are digesting it. Like I said, I don't think about doing these things, they just get done. What about cable?"

"Basic plus HBO and Playboy Network."

"Naughty boy."

"I wanted Showtime. They screwed it up. I never got around to fixing it."

"I believe you," Joshua said. "Really I do."

"Are you male or female?" I asked.

"I'm neither," Joshua said. "My cells reproduce asexually. Spice Channel will do nothing for me. Do you have a computer with an Internet connection?"

"I have a Mac and DSL," I said. "Why are you asking about these things?"

"I don't know if you've noticed, but I'm a gelatinous cube," Joshua said. "It's not like I'm going to be getting out of the house much. The neighbors would talk. So I want to make sure I'm going to be able to keep myself amused. Got any pets?"

"I had a cat, but he ran away about two years ago. I say 'ran away,' but I think he was hit by a car or eaten by coyotes. The Escobedos next door have a retriever, Ralph, that will occasionally get out of the yard and come over for a visit. I don't think you need to worry about Ralph, though. He's fifteen years old. He might be able to gum you, but that's about it.

Anyway, he never comes in the house. So, if your species repro-
duces asexually, that means you're a clone of some other Yherajk,
right?"

"Eeeeeeh . . ." Joshua sounded suspiciously like he was
trying to evade the question. "Not exactly," he said, finally.
"Our cells are asexual but we have a way of creating new . . .
'souls' is probably the best word for it. I'd have a really difficult
time explaining it to you."

"Why?"

"You're out of turn."

"You're evading."

"Oh. Well, in that case, let's say it's a sort of societal taboo.
Asking me to talk about it would be sort of like me asking you
to describe in graphic detail the sexual encounter between your
parents that resulted in your conception."

"It was during their honeymoon in Cancun," I said.

"What position did they use? How many thrusts did it
take? Did your mom bark in pleasure?"

I reddened. "I think I see what you're saying."

"I thought you might," Joshua said. "Speaking of which—
any brothers or sisters?"

"No," I said. "Mom had complications during the preg-
nancy and nearly died. They thought about adopting for a
while but they decided against it. Can you die?"

"Sure," Joshua said. "More ways than you can, too. Individual cells in this collection die all the time, like cells in your
body die. The whole collection can die, too—I'd say we're
probably less prone to random death than your species is, but it
happens. The soul can also die, even if the collection survives.
You in a relationship?"

"No. I had a girlfriend at the agency for a while, but she

took a job in New York about six months ago. It wasn't very serious, anyway—more of a tension release thing. How long do you live?"

"Three score and ten, just like you," Joshua said. "More or less. It's actually a very complicated question. Do you like your job?"

"Most of the time," I said. "I don't know. I think I'm good at it. And I don't know what else I'd do if I wasn't doing this. What's your spaceship like?"

"Crowded. Smelly. Poorly lit. What do you do when you're not working?"

"I'm pretty much always working. When I'm not, I read a lot. Got that from being the son of a literary agent. When my mother moved out, I made my old room into a library. Other than that, I don't do too much. I'm sort of pathetic. How do you know so much about us?"

"What do you mean?" Joshua said.

"Your English is as good as mine. You know about stuff like video games and cable television. You make references to fifties horror films. You seem to know more about us than most of us do."

"No offense, but it's not *that* hard being smarter than most of you folks," Joshua said. "Your planet's been broadcasting a bunch of stuff for the better part of the last century. We've been paying attention to a lot of it. You *can* actually learn English from watching situation comedies several thousand times."

"I don't know how to feel about that," I said.

"There are some gaps," Joshua allowed. "Until I actually got down here, we were under the impression 'groovy' was still current. It's all those *Brady Bunch* reruns. Stupid Nick at Night. For the longest time it never really occurred to us that they

weren't live broadcasts. We thought that the repetition had
some ritual significance. Like they were religious texts or something."

"I'd think the fact that the Brady Bunch never aged might
have been a tip-off."

"Don't take this wrong," Joshua said. "But you all pretty
much look the same to us. Anyway, we figured it out eventually. My turn."

The question-and-answer session went on for another couple
of hours, with me asking larger, cosmic questions, and Joshua
asking smaller, personal questions. I learned that the Yherajk
spaceship was a hollowed-out asteroid that traveled at slower-
than- light speeds, and that it had taken them decades to travel
from their home planet to here. Joshua learned that my favorite
color was green. I learned that Yherajk-to-Yherajk communi-
cation most often took the form of complex pheromone "ideo-
graphs" launched into the air or passed on through touch: the
"speaker" was identified with an identifier molecule—his own
personal smell. Joshua learned that I preferred Eurotrash dance
music to American guitar rock and roll.

At the end of it, I knew more about the Yherajk than any
other person on the planet, and Joshua knew more about me
than any other person on the planet. I ended up thinking that
Joshua had somehow gotten the better end of that bargain;
there was only one other person who knew about Joshua, after
all. But presumably a lot of other people knew about me.

Only one question remained unanswered: how Joshua got
his name. He refused to tell me.

"That's not fair," I said. "You said no lying or evading."

"This is the exception that proves the rule," Joshua said.

"Besides, it's not my story to tell. You need to ask Carl how it came about. Now," he executed a maneuver that looked very much like a stretch after a long bout of sitting, "where is that computer of yours? I need to sign in. I want to see how much spam I have."

I led him to my home office, where my computer was; he slithered onto the seat, glopped himself onto the keyboard, and shot out a tendril to the mouse. I was mildly worried that parts of him might get stuck in my keyboard. But when he moved from the table on the way to the office, he didn't leave any slime trails. Chalk one up for my upholstery. I figured my keyboard would be okay. I left him to clack away online and headed out to the back porch.

My backyard was sloped up into the mountainside and heavily wooded in the back. It was on slightly higher ground than the adjoining houses' backyards—something I appreciated greatly when I was thirteen and Trish Escobedo next door would lay out next to her pool. I settled into my usual chair, which looked out onto the Escobedo backyard—Trish was now married and hadn't lived there for nearly twelve years, but old habits died hard. On the way out, I had pulled a beer from the fridge; I twisted off the top and sat back to look up at the stars.

I was thinking about Joshua and the Yherajk. Joshua was an immediate problem—very smart, very amusing, very liquid, and, I was beginning to suspect, very prone to boredom. I was giving him a week before he went off his rocker in the house. I was going to have to figure some way of getting him out of the house on an occasional basis; I didn't know what a bored Yherajk was like but I didn't aim to find out. Priority one: field trips for Joshua.

The Yherajk were a less immediate but infinitely more complicated problem—alien globs who want to befriend a humanity that, if asked, would probably prefer to be befriended by something with an endoskeleton. The only thing that possibly could have been worse was if the Yherajk looked like giant bugs: that would have turned the half of humanity already afraid of spiders and roaches into insane gibbering messes. Maybe that was the way to go: "The Yherajk—At Least They're Not Insects." I glanced back up at the stars and wondered idly if one of them was the Yherajk asteroid ship.

I heard a scratching at the side gate. I went over to unlatch it; Ralph, the World's Oldest Retriever, was on the other side, huffing slightly. His tail was wagging feebly and he was looking up at me with a tired doggie grin as if to say, *I got out again. Not bad for an old fart.*

I liked Ralph. The youngest Escobedo kid, Richie, had graduated from college and moved out about two years ago, and I suspected since then Ralph didn't get that much notice; Esteban, who owned a mainframe software company, didn't have the time, and anyone could tell that Mary just wasn't a dog person. He was fed but ignored.

Richie used to drop by every now and then with Ralph; he was only a few years younger than I was, and for a while had been thinking about becoming an agent before he got nervous and went pre-law instead. After Richie moved out, Ralph would keep dropping by. I think I reminded him of times when someone was around to pay attention to him. I didn't mind. Ralph didn't want anything other than to be around somebody else. He's like a lot of old folks that way. Eventually Esteban or Mary would realize he was gone and would come over to get him. Ralph would look at me sadly and follow the one or the other home. A week later he'd get bored and the cycle would repeat.

I headed back to the patio. Ralph shuffled along at my feet and sat next to me when I got to my chair. I knuckled him on the head gently, and returned my thoughts to the Yherajk situation.

For some reason, a memory of my childhood popped into my head: my father, Daniel Stein, sitting at the dining room table with Krzysztof Kordus, a Polish poet who had been sent to a concentration camp during World War II after he, a Catholic, had been caught trying to smuggle Jews out of Poland. Late in life he had emigrated to America, and he hoped that he would be able to publish his poems in English.

I eventually read the poems when I was in college. They were terrible and beautiful: terrible in their themes of Holocaust and death, beautiful because they somehow managed to find moments of hope in the shadow of that terrifying destruction. I remember feeling the need to go out into the sun after reading them, crying because for the first time I was made to understand what happened.

I had had relatives who had died in the Holocaust: great aunts and uncles on my mother's side. My own grandmother had been in a work camp when the war ended. But she would never talk about it while I was growing up, and then she had a stroke that took away her ability to speak. It wasn't until Krzysztof's poems that the story was brought home to me.

The night Krzysztof and my father sat at our dining room table, however, Krzysztof had received yet another rejection letter for his book. He sat raging at my father, for not being able to sell the book, and at the publishers, for not buying the book.

"You have to understand," my dad said to Krzysztof, "hardly anyone buys books of poetry anymore."

"I understand *shit*," Krzysztof said, thumping the table. "This is what I do. These poems are as good as any you will find in the bookstore. Better. You must be able to convince someone to buy these, Daniel. That is what *you* do."

"Krzysztof," my father said. "The bottom line is that no one is going to publish these poems right now. If you were Elie Wiesel, you could sell these poems. But you're nobody here. No one knows you. No publisher is going to throw money away publishing poems that no one's going to read."

That set Krzysztof off for another ten minutes on the stupidity of my father, the publishing world, and the American people in general, for not recognizing genius when it sat arrayed before them. Dad sat there calmly, waiting for Krzysztof to take a breath.

When he did, my dad jumped in. "You're not listening to what I'm saying, Krzysztof," he said. "I know these poems are masterworks. That's not in dispute. The problem is not the poems, it's you. No one knows who you are."

"Who cares about me?" Krzysztof said. "The poems, they speak for themselves."

"You're a great man, Krzysztof," my father said. "But you know diddly about the American public." And then my father told Krzysztof a plan that would thereafter be known as The Trojan Horse.

The plan was simple. In order to sell Krzysztof's poems, people had to know who Krzysztof was first. Dad accomplished this by convincing Krzysztof, after much arguing and protestations of humiliation, to take a lullaby that he had written decades earlier to amuse his daughter, and publish it as a children's book. The book, *The Dreamers and the Sleepers,* sold millions, much to Krzysztof's horror and my father's delight.

During the publicity tour for the book, Krzysztof's Holocaust story was splashed across the features pages of every large and midsized daily in the country. From that, my father was able to wrangle a made-for-television movie on Krzysztof's story out of TNT. It was the most widely watched television show that month on cable. Krzysztof was embarrassed (he was played by Tom Selleck) but also both rich and famous.

"There," my dad said. "*Now* we can sell your book of poems." And he did.

I needed a Trojan Horse. There had to be some back door way to slip the Yherajk through, like my dad did with Krzysztof. But I had no idea what it was. It's one thing to sell a book of poems. It's another thing entirely to introduce a planet to the thing they've hoped for and feared for the last century.

The doorbell rang. Ralph looked at me sadly. His owners had come for him. I patted his flank gently, and then we went to answer the door.

CHAPTER
Six

I glanced through the window into my office. "Tell me that's not Tea Reader I see in there," I said.

"All right," Miranda said. "That's not Tea Reader you see in there."

"Thank you for conforming to my reality," I said.

"Not at all," Miranda said. "It's an honor and a privilege."

I grabbed my doorknob, took a deep breath, and went into my office.

If nothing else, Tea Reader was heart-stoppingly beautiful; half Hawaiian, half Hungarian, five feet ten inches, and naturally possessed of the sort of proportions that most women insist exist only on foot-high plastic dolls. Her record company publicist once drunkenly confided in me that his company estimated at least forty-five percent of Tea's record sales were to boys aged thirteen through fifteen, who bought them for the CD insert that featured Tea rising from the waters of the Pacific, clad in a thin T-shirt and a thong bikini bottom, both a particularly transparent shade of tan.

I drunkenly confided to him that, when I had inherited her from my former podmate, I held the poorly masked hope that she might be one of those actresses who occasionally slept with their agents. Then I got to know her. I learned to be glad that she was not.

"Hello, Tea," I said.

"Hello, Tom, you miserable fuckhead," Tea said.

"Always a pleasure to see you, too, Tea," I said. I walked to my desk and set down. "Now," I said. "How can I help you?"

"You can explain to me why I suddenly seem to be represented by Little Miss Hysterical over here." Tea motioned to the far chair in the corner, where Amanda Hewson sat, crying. At the mention of her existence, Amanda let out an audible sob and lifted her feet, in an attempt to curl into a fetal position while still sitting. The chair was getting in the way.

"Amanda is a full agent here at the company," I said. "And she's quite good."

"Bullshit," Tea said. Amanda gave another sob. Tea rolled her eyes dramatically and shouted over her shoulder at Amanda, "Could you *please* shut the fuck up? I'm trying to talk to my *real* agent over here, and it's hard enough without you crying a fucking river."

Amanda exploded from her seat like a flock of birds flushed out of the underbrush, and attempted to flee the room. She grabbed at the door, pulled it, and whacked herself on the side of the face. I winced; that was going to leave a mark. Amanda wailed and sprinted towards her pod. Tea watched the scene and then turned back to me. She had the expression of the cat who ate the canary and then threw it up in her owner's favorite shoes.

"Where were we?" she said.

"That wasn't very nice," I said, mildly.

"I'll tell you what's not very fucking *nice,* Tom," Tea said. "It's not nice to get back from Honolulu, where I've been visiting my family, and having a message from *Mandy,* telling me how excited she is to be working with me." From her sinister stretch, Tea straightened up, preternaturally perky. Her voice became a dead-on ringer for Amanda's Girl Scout–like tone. "'I have your album! I love to listen to it while I'm exercising!'" Tea slouched again. "Great. Add that to the half that are whacking off to my picture on the cover, sister."

"It's actually only forty-five percent," I said.

Tea's eyes narrowed. "What?"

"Forty-five percent are whacking off," I said. "Your record company's own estimate. Tea, Amanda's working with me. She's my assistant."

"I thought Miss Bitch back there was your assistant," Tea said, jerking a thumb towards Miranda's desk. "She almost didn't let me in to your office today. I was getting ready to smack her."

Before getting her act together and working her way through college, Miranda spent a reasonable portion of her teen years gang-banging in East LA. One night, at a company party, Miranda showed me her collection of scars, inflicted by razors in a number of cat fights. *The other girls got it worse,* she said. I didn't suspect Tea realized how close to death she had gotten this morning.

"Miranda is my administrative assistant," I said. "Amanda is working with me with some of my clients."

"Well, *I* don't want to work with her," Tea said.

"Why not?"

"Hello? Tom? Did you not see Miss Mandy in here today? What a fucking crybaby."

"How did she get that way, Tea?" I asked.

"Beats me," Tea said. "We were just sitting here, waiting for you, and I was just telling her that there was no fucking way on the planet she was going to be my agent."

"How long were you in here before I got here?"

Tea shrugged. "A half-hour, forty-five minutes."

"I see," I said. "And you don't think being shat on for three-quarters of an hour is a good reason to get upset."

"Hey," Tea sat up again and jabbed a finger at me. "*You're* the one that put her in that situation. Don't get angry at *me* because I went off on her a little."

"Forty-five minutes is not *a little,* Tea," I said.

"What the fuck does *that* mean? I'm the one getting screwed here." She slumped back, sullen.

I was getting a headache. "Tea, what do you want from me?" I asked.

"I want you to do your fucking *job*," Tea said. "I'm not giving you ten percent so you can palm me off on Mandy, the Teenage Agent. I can think of about ten agents in town who'd get on their hands and knees to represent me. You're not doing me any favors, Tom."

"Really," I said. "Ten agents."

"At least."

"Fine," I said. "Name one."

"What?"

"Name one," I said. "Give me the name of one of those agents."

"Hell, no," Tea said. "Why should I tell you who your competition is? Stay nervous."

"Nervous? Hell, Tea, I want to call them up," I said. "If they're so gung-ho to have you, I'll let you go. I don't want you to be unhappy. So let's do this thing. Let's get it over with. Unless you're running off at the mouth."

That got her. "Alan Finley at ACR," she said.

I buzzed Miranda. She came to the door. "Yes, Tom?"

"Miranda, would you call Alan Finley over at Associated Client Representation, and put him on the speaker when you get him?"

"Sure, Tom."

"Thanks," I said. "Oh, one other thing. After you get Alan, would you mind bringing me Tea's file?"

"Not at all," Miranda said. "Do you want the whole file?"

"Just the clippings, please, Miranda."

Miranda smiled slightly and glanced at Tea. "Delighted to, Tom. Tea," she said. Tea fairly snarled at Miranda as she closed the door.

"Fucking bitch," Tea said. "Did you see that look she gave me?"

"I must have missed it," I said.

Miranda's voice clicked in over the speakerphone. "Alan Finley at ACR, Tom," she said, and left the line.

A male voice piped up. "Tom? You there?"

"Ho, Alan," I said. "How are things over there at ACR these days?"

"The land of milk and honey, Tom. We're giving away Bentleys as party favors. You want one?"

Two weeks ago, an ACR internal memo made its way to *Variety*; in it, ACR's CEO Norm Jackson offered a Rolls-Royce to the agent who stole the most A-list clients from other agencies in the next three months. Jackson first declared it a forgery, and then tried to chalk it up as an inside joke. Nobody bit. Longtime clients were offended that they, by implication, were not A-listers, and started jumping ship. Clients in the process of being wooed by ACR stopped returning calls. *Variety* suggested that the second-place winner get Norm Jackson's job.

"I'll pass for now, Alan, but I hope you remember me during the holidays," I said. "Listen, Alan. Got a question for you."

"Shoot."

"I have a client who has recently become, shall we say, dissatisfied with the quality of representation she's receiving here. She's thinking of going over there."

"Well, aren't you just the helpful one, Tom," Alan said. "Is it Michelle Beck? You can send her right along. I'll get that Rolls after all."

I laughed. He laughed. Tea glared at the speakerphone.

"Sorry, Alan. The client is Tea Reader. You know her."

"Sure. I bought her CD. For the picture on the inside, mostly."

Tea looked like she was about to say something, but I put my finger to my lips. "Right," I said. "So are you interested? Want to take her on?"

"Jesus, Tom, you're actually serious?"

"Sure am, Alan. Serious as a heart attack."

"She wouldn't happen to be there at the moment, would she?"

"Nope," I said. That, at the very least, would keep Tea quiet for a few minutes. "Just you and me. You want her?"

"Fuck, no, Tom," Alan said. "I hear she's a harpy."

Tea looked like she'd been slapped.

"I hear she drove her last agent insane. You knew him, right?"

"Yeah," I said. "We were podmates."

"That's right. Cracked up like Northridge in a quake is what I heard. Became a Moonie or a Scientologist or something like that."

"Buddhist, actually."

"Close enough," Alan said. "No offense, Tom. I have enough clients who make me want to get religion, so I could be assured that there was a Hell for them to be sent to. I could look at Tea for hours. Wouldn't want to be in the same room as her, though. Certainly wouldn't want to represent her. How do you manage it, anyway?"

"Just a saint, I suppose," I said. "Well, look, Alan, you know anyone over there who might want to have her?"

"Not off the top of my head. I think everybody's perfectly happy to let you represent her for as long as you want, pal. I'll remember you in my prayers, if it will make you feel any better."

"It does, it does," I said. "Thanks, Alan."

"Sure, Tom. Be sure to let me know when Michelle gets bored with you. Her, I'd put up with." He hung up.

"Well," I said. "That was certainly instructive."

"Fuck you," Tea said, and stared off out a side window. Miranda came in, dropped a file on my desk, and left.

"What is that?" Tea asked.

"This is your clipping file," I said. "Our clipping service scours the trades and the magazines and the blogs for a reference to any of our clients and sends them on to us. So we always know what people are thinking about the people we represent."

I separated the clips into two piles. One was very small. The other was not. I pointed to the smaller pile. "Do you know what this is?" I asked.

Tea looked over, shrugged. "No."

"These are your positive notices," I said. "They're mostly about the fact that you're built like Barbie, although there's one here that says you were the best thing about that Vince Vaughn flick you were in, with the further admission that that is a text-book example of damning with faint praise."

I thumped the other, much larger pile with an open palm. "This," I said, "is your pile of negative notices. We have an office pool here, you know. We've got bets on how thick this pile is going to get by the end of the year. Right now, it's a modest three inches. But it's early yet, and TMZ *loves* you."

Tea looked bored. "Is this going somewhere?"

I gave up. "Tea, I've been trying to find some way to put this delicately. Let me make it simple: *Nobody* in town likes you. No one. You're monstrously difficult. People don't like working with you. People don't like being seen with you. People don't even like being in the same room with you. Even the thirteen-year-old boys who fantasize about you know enough not to like you as a person. In the grand pantheon of legendary bitches of Hollywood, it's you, Shannon Doherty, and Sean Young."

"I'm not anything like them," Tea said. "*I* still have a career."

"You sure do," I said. "And you have *me* to thank for it. Any other agent would have written you off long ago. You're good looking, but that's not exactly a rare thing around these parts. I have to *fight* to get you work. And every time I *do* get you work, I hear back about how everybody on that crew would rather chew glass than work with you again. Everyone.

They have craft service workers who won't cater a set you're on. My best estimate is that you have about another eighteen months before we run out of people who'll work with you. After that you'll have to find some nice, eighty-year-old oil tycoon you can marry and screw into a coma."

Tea was dumbstruck. It couldn't last. It didn't. "Gee, Tom. Thanks for the vote of confidence."

"The vote of confidence isn't for you, Tea. I'm giving you two choices here. The first choice is to sit here, shut up, and do what I tell you. We may have an outside chance of saving your career if you do. The other is *not* to sit here, shut up, and do what I tell you. In which case, I'm dropping you and you can get the hell out of my office. It really doesn't matter to me which you do. Actually, I'm lying. I'd prefer it if you left. But it's up to you. What's it going to be?"

Tea sat there with a gaze of pure, unadulterated hate. It was unnervingly arousing. I ignored it and went on.

"All right, then. The first thing you're going to do is apologize to Amanda."

"Fuck, no," Tea said.

"Fuck, yes," I said, "or we have no deal. I realize you didn't notice this while you were dismantling her, but Amanda may have been the only person in the entire Los Angeles metropolitan area who actually genuinely liked you. There are seventeen million people in the LA basin, Tea. You need her."

"The hell I do," Tea said.

"Tea," I said. "Two words. 'Boinking Grandpa.'"

"Fuck," Tea said. "All right."

"Thank you," I said. "The second thing you're going to do is trust me. Amanda isn't much to look at at the moment, but she's going to devote more of her brain to you than she does to herself. Work with her. Try to be nice. In the comfort of your own home, you can stab life-sized dolls dressed up to look like her, for all I care. But give her something to work with. Understand?"

"Fine," Tea said. She was hating this.

"Great," I said. "Off you go, then."

"What, you want me to apologize now?" She was genuinely shocked.

"No time like the present, Tea. She's in the building, you're in the building. It's more convenient that way."

Tea got up, gave me one last glare, and exited the office, slamming the door on the way out. I sat there for a good fifteen seconds, and let out a tremendous *whoop,* and began spinning my desk chair around.

Miranda came into the office. She had something in her hand. "Tea left looking like she was going to implode, Tom. You must have done a number on her."

"Oh my *God,*" I said, stopping the spin cycle. I felt pleasantly dizzy. "I've been wanting to do that for *years.* You have *no* idea how good that felt."

"Sure I do," Miranda said. "You left the speakerphone on."

She extended her hand to me. In it was a digital voice recorder.

"What's this?" I asked.

"A memento of your special Tea time," Miranda said. "Sorry. I just couldn't resist."

Michelle speared a sliver of chicken from her salad. "I'm thinking of dyeing my hair," she said, and popped the chicken in her mouth.

"Blue hair only looks good on Marge Simpson, Michelle," I said.

She wiggled her hand at me. "Ha ha, funny guy. No, I'm going to dye it brown. You know, for the part."

"What part are we talking about, if I may ask?" I said.

"Hard Memories," Michelle said.

Now I knew why I was sitting inside the Mondo Chicken in Tarzana. Michelle and I had met there years ago, when she was a waitress named Shelly, looking for an agent, and I was a newly minted agent looking to get laid. She turned out to be the more determined one; I never did have sex with Michelle, but she got me as an agent. She took it as a lucky omen (the getting the agent part, not the part about not having sex with me); since then, any time Michelle had a special occasion to mark or an announcement to make to me, she did it at Mondo Chicken.

So far it had included six movie decisions, one double funeral when her parents died in a car accident, three engagements (and subsequent breakups), two religious epiphanies, and one pet euthanization. There were a lot of memories between us, packed into one moderately overpriced eatery in the Valley. The fact that Michelle decided to tell me about wanting *Hard Memories* here was a very bad sign. It meant that she was determined, and that there was going to be little I could do to change her mind.

But, of course, I had to try. *"Hard Memories* is already taken, Michelle," I said. "Ellen Merlow's been signed for the part."

"Not yet," she said. "I called. It's only an oral agreement. I think I can make them change their minds."

"By dyeing your hair?"

"For a start," Michelle said. "I mean, it would at least signal that I'm serious. And if I look more like the part, maybe they can see me in the role. Brown hair would change my entire look." She stabbed at her salad again.

I set down my own fork and massaged the bridge of my nose. "Michelle," I said. "If you had brown hair, you still wouldn't look a forty-year-old Eastern European Jew. You'd look like a twenty-five-year-old Californian Aryan with hair dyed brown. Look at yourself, Michelle. You're blonde. Naturally. You have Newman Blue eyes. And you have a body shape that wasn't even *invented* until the late nineties."

"I can plump out," she said.

"You throw up in panic when you have dessert," I said.

"I stopped doing that a long time ago, and you *know* that," Michelle said. "That was a cheap shot."

"You're right," I said. "I'm sorry."

Michelle relaxed. "I'll even have dessert today," she said. "I think they have nonfat yogurt here."

"It's not just how you look, Michelle," I said. "Don't take this the wrong way, but you're just not ready for that part. It's a part that's meant for someone much older."

Michelle pointed her fork at me. "*Summertime Blues* was meant for someone older, remember? When we first got the script, it called for a thirty-year-old woman to seduce those two teenage brothers. When I got the part, it got kicked back to a twenty-two-year-old. That's what re-writes are for, you said."

"*Summertime Blues* was a comedy about two kids losing their cherry," I said. "*Hard Memories* is about anti-Semitism and six million people dying. I think you could agree there's a slight difference in tone there."

"Well, of course," Michelle said. "But I don't see what that has to do with the main character."

I sighed. "Let me try a different tack," I said. "Why do you want this role so badly?"

Michelle looked puzzled. "What do you mean?"

"I mean, what is it about the role that makes you so passionate about it? What is it about this role that's getting you so worked up?"

"It's a great role, Tom," she said. "It's so dramatic and filled with feeling. I want to do something like that. You know, something with emotional baggage. I think it's time Hollywood started taking me seriously."

"Okay," I said. "Now, how much do you know about the Holocaust?"

"I know a lot," Michelle said. "How can you not know about the Holocaust? It was terrible, everyone knows that. I saw *Schindler's List*. I cried."

"All right, crying at *Schindler's List* is a good start," I said. "Anything else?"

"I've been thinking of going to that museum here about hatred," she said. "I forget what it's called at the moment. Simon something. The Norton Simon?"

"Simon Wiesenthal," I said. "The Norton Simon is an art museum."

"I knew it was one of the two," she said.

"Did you ever read that book of poems I gave you?"

"The ones by that Christmas guy?"

"Krzysztof," I said.

"I started them, but I had to stop," Michelle said. "I had to put my dog to sleep around that time, and reading those poems just made me depressed. I just kept thinking about my dog and crying."

"Right," I said. "Look, Michelle, I think it's great that you want to do dramatic roles. I think you'll be great in them. I just don't think that this is the right one. *Hard Memories* isn't just going to take technique, it's going to take knowledge. I know you think you know about the Holocaust and about this woman's life, but I don't think you do. If you were to take this role without knowing anything about it, it's going to come back to haunt you. Melanie Griffith once did a movie called *Shining Through* and on the press junket she said 'There were six million Jews killed in the Holocaust. That's a lot of people!' It didn't help her film any."

"Six million *is* a lot of people," Michelle said. "I don't see why people would be so upset that she said that."

"I know, Michelle," I said. "That's why I think you should skip this role."

Michelle glared at me angrily and appeared to be winding up to a tirade when her eyes slipped into her skull, leaving only the whites visible. Her mouth dropped open slightly. She dropped her fork onto the table. I stared, panicked—I had made her so angry I caused her to stroke out. I was in the process of yanking out my cell phone to dial 911 when she snapped back.

"That's better," she said.

"Jesus Christ, Michelle," I said. "What was that all about?"

"I've been going to a hypnotherapist," she said, "to help me handle my stress. He placed an autosuggestion into my subconscious so that every time I get angry or stressed, I sort of float away for a couple of seconds. It's really helping me deal with my issues."

"Let's hope you don't have any issues while you're on the 405," I said.

"Well, I usually stress out in traffic jams, so it's not a problem," Michelle said. "I'm not moving anyway. Listen, you just made me very angry back there."

"I know that now," I said.

"You're supposed to be my agent, you know," she said, "and that means helping me get the roles I want."

"Yes, but I'm also your friend," I said, "and that means looking out for you. And also, as your agent, I have to look out for the longevity of your career. If *Hard Memories* flopped, it wouldn't stop you from making movies, but it would make folks think twice about hiring you for another drama. And then you *would* be stuck doing *Summertime Blues* and *Murdered Earth* sequels. Very profitable in the short run, but not what I think you want to do all your life."

"I don't even want to do this *Murdered Earth* sequel," Michelle said, sullenly. "Any way I can get out of it?"

"Afraid not," I said. "We've gone beyond the oral agreement stage. Besides, you've got twelve million plus back end. You're unbelievably rich now. Enjoy it."

Michelle poked at her food. "The only reason I got the first film was because Brad wanted to screw me."

"There was more to it than that, Michelle," I said, and that much was true—at the time, she had also been cheap to hire. "But look at it this way: now you get to screw him. To the tune of twelve mil."

Michelle shrugged and looked down at her plate. "All I'm saying is sometime soon I'd like to get to do something where the reason I got it wasn't because someone wanted to get in my pants."

I remembered why I had started representing Michelle. I felt unbelievably filthy.

"You ready to go?" I said.

She looked up at me. "What?"

"Let's go," I said. I pulled out my wallet and set down a couple of twenties.

"I haven't ordered dessert yet," Michelle said.

"I believe that you would have eaten it," I said. "Now I want you to come with me. I have an idea."

Across the strip mall from the Mondo Chicken was a Barnes & Noble. We went in.

"What are we doing?" Michelle asked.

"Getting research materials," I said, and sat her down in one of the store's chairs while I went shopping. I picked up Hannah Arendt, Primo Levi, Elie Wiesel, and Simon Wiesenthal. I grabbed *Hitler's Willing Executioners, Denying the Holocaust, Shoah,* and *Why Did the Heavens Not Darken?* I went to the graphic novel area and fished through costumed superheroes until I found *Maus.* On the way through the fiction I spotted *Sophie's Choice.* I grabbed it. Couldn't hurt.

I had no illusions—these books were enough to confuse graduate students, let alone Michelle, who was, at the very best, a middleweight in the intelligence arena. I couldn't even imagine what she was going to make of the concept of "The Banality of Evil." But we had eaten at Mondo Chicken, and that meant something. She'd kill herself slogging through all these. And who knows. It could take. Stranger things have happened.

Twenty minutes later, we stood at the checkout while the overawed cashier rang up our purchases.

"You want me to read all of these?" Michelle asked.

"Try," I said. "Start with *Maus* or *Sophie's Choice.* Convince

me that you're serious by reading some of these and I'll do everything I can to get you that part. Fair enough?"

Michelle squealed like the cheerleader she was and gave me
a bear hug and a smack on the cheek. The cashier nearly fainted
with envy.

CHAPTER
Seven

"*When* I said I wanted to get out of the house, this wasn't what I was thinking of," Joshua said.

Joshua, Ralph and I were at the edge of the Big Dalton Canyon reservoir, a tiny, out-of-the-way clot of water in the foothills. It was a weekday, so no one was likely to be around during the day. I had a fishing rod. I didn't know if the reservoir had been stocked with fish, but I figured today was as good a day as any to find out.

"What were you thinking of, Joshua?" I asked.

"I don't know," he said. He had a pseudopod half-in, half-out of the water, as if testing how cold the water was. "I was thinking maybe a drive-in movie."

"There's a drive-in over in Azusa," I said. "I don't know if they still show movies, though. I think it's all a flea market now."

Joshua finally slid all the way into the water, and floated on the top like an oil slick. "Well, let's try it, anyway. Get a big tub of popcorn, too. Get really sick on the artificial butter flavoring."

I zinged the fishing line into the reservoir. "As if you know anything about artificial butter flavoring."

"Hey," Joshua said. "I'm open to the experience. I've never vomited. It could be fun. So can we go?"

"Sure," I said. "We'll have to go after it's already dark, though. I don't want anyone to see you."

"If I understand it correctly, people don't actually go to drive-in movies to watch the movies," Joshua said. "If they're not watching the movies, what's the chance they're going be to watching us?"

Ralph, who had been pacing the edge of the water, barked towards Joshua. Joshua quivered for a second, then shot an arc of water at Ralph, who took it broadside on the flank. He reared up slightly, barked again, and then charged into the water after Joshua. They splashed around with each other for several minutes. It was the happiest I'd seen Ralph be in years.

Ralph and Joshua became friends earlier in the week. The day I had taken a sledgehammer to Tea, I had come home and opened the front door to find Joshua and Ralph having a tug-of-war with one of my dress shirts in the front corridor. Ralph was winning due to the fact that he had both teeth and paws; Joshua, lacking much in the way of traction on the waxed hardwood floor, was skidding around like a large gelatin fruit cup. Ralph was about to take off out the door, Joshua in tow. I shut the door quickly.

"What are you doing with my shirt?" I had said.

"I'm sorry," Joshua had said. "It wasn't your favorite, was it? We were just playing."

"How did Ralph get in?" I had asked.

"I went out back, and then he showed up and followed me in," Joshua had said. "Can we keep him?"

Ralph, winded, barked once and collapsed happily on the wood.

I sent Ralph home later that night but he came back almost immediately, and went looking for Joshua. It was kind of a cute scene: a dog and his gelatinous boy. When Esteban came to get him again, I told him I wouldn't mind looking after Ralph for a few days. Esteban went away, looking palpably relieved. I hadn't seen him since. I had the vague suspicion I had just assumed ownership of a dog.

Personally I would have assumed that the sight of a mobile lump of goo would have blown Ralph's little doggie mind, but watching him goof with Joshua in the water, it was clear he was handling it pretty well, better than most humans would. I mentioned that to Joshua.

"That's because Ralph and I speak the same language," Joshua said, oozing back towards the shore with Ralph.

"What do you mean?" I said. "I'm not hearing any barking coming out of you."

"I'm talking about smells," he said. "Ralph's wired for that sort of information, you know. He's a retriever. It took me about an hour to figure out what smells he pays attention to. Now we've got a pretty good working vocabulary."

"So you can actually talk to Ralph?" I said.

"Of course not," Joshua said. "He's a *dog*, Tom."

"But you just said you had a working vocabulary with him."

"Sure, but so do you. I've heard you talk to him. He understands a few of those words. Doesn't mean you're talking nuclear physics. But I do speak better to him than you do. He understands smells better than words. And since that's the way I usually talk anyway, it's easier for me to speak to him than it is to you—isn't that right, Ralph?"

Ralph, back on shore, barked.

"What's that you say, Ralph? Little Timmy's fallen down a well and needs help?"

Ralph barked again.

"Good boy!" Joshua said. "Hand him a snack, Tom."

"Right away, oh globulous one," I said. I rummaged through the cooler next to me and fished out one of the sandwiches I had made, and gave Ralph a piece of the ham inside. Ralph accepted it gravely and then lay down next to me.

Joshua slid over and held up a tentacle. "Hey, look," he said. "I found me a frog." Inside the tentacle a terrified amphibian kicked, slowly, through the gunk that was Joshua.

"Jesus, Joshua," I said. "You're killing that thing. Give it some air."

Joshua created an air pocket and slid it up the tendril to the frog, who now sat inside it. It hopped a couple of times, trying to escape, before settling down and sitting there placidly. Joshua showed the frog to Ralph, who sniffed at the proffered tendril politely before laying his head down for a nap.

"We have these where I come from," Joshua said.

"Frogs?" I said.

"Well, obviously not frogs, exactly," Joshua said. "More legs, for one thing. And much, much larger. But the same concept— amphibian, not very smart, all that. We used 'em sort of like you used horses and other big animals. Beasts of burden."

"Hi-ho, Silver."

"I get that," Joshua said.

"I'm not surprised," I said.

"I wasn't trying to kill it when I was surrounding it, you know," Joshua said. "I was just trying to check something. I was seeing if I could control it like we control the frogs back home."

"I don't get that," I said. "What do you mean?"

"Back home, we get into their brains," Joshua said. "We extend a very thin tendril into their skulls, connect into their nervous system, and use them for what we need."

I pictured Joshua slopped on the head of a horse, filling the animals ears with himself. It was a disturbing image, to say the least. "That's terrible," I said.

"Why?"

"It's just creepy," I said. "Invading someone's brain to have them do your bidding." I did an involuntary shudder. "It's like a mental rape or something."

"Tom, they're big *frogs,*" Joshua said. "It's certainly not any worse than whipping some dumb animal to get it to do what you want to do. Anyway, it's not like we take over the brains of anything that can think. That's a—" He stopped for a second and waved the tendril, as if to imply trying to think of a word; the frog shifted uncomfortably within. "—sin. A really big sin. Like murder or incest would be for you."

"What a relief," I said. "Because, you know, people *never* murder each other or commit incest around here," I said.

"Don't blame me for the shortcomings of your own species," Joshua said. "Here, look. While we were talking, I got into this guy's head. Now watch." He dropped the tendril to the ground and slid it back into himself. The frog sat there, not doing much.

"Where's the tendril?" I said.

"The operative phrase here is 'very thin,' Tom," Joshua said. "You're not going to see it. Here we go."

The frog sat there some more. After a couple of seconds it nudged itself forward. Then it sat there some more.

"There," Joshua said.

"That's it?" I said.

"Let's see *you* do that, smartass," Joshua said.

"Do what?" I said. "The frog moved. Big deal. The frog would have moved anyway."

The frog lifted up on its hind legs and did a hoppy little samba. Its front legs moved in time.

"All right," I said. "That, I don't see very often."

"Thank you," Joshua said. The frog made an awkward bow and then tipped over. They're not exactly designed to be on two legs. It sat for a few minutes, then aimed itself towards the water and hopped away.

"You still controlling it?" I asked. I was imagining microscopic tendrils spieling out of Joshua like the fishing line in my rod.

"No, I let it go," Joshua said. "I wasn't doing a very good job. Your wiring is different here on Earth than it is back home. Even getting it to hop around was a bit of trouble. I'm sure if I worked at it, I could figure it out. But it's hard to do on the fly."

"You'll have to teach me to do that," I said.

"You'll have to become a blob first," Joshua said.

I patted my stomach. "Give me time," I said. "On another, not-entirely-unrelated note, I hope you weren't expecting fish for dinner. They don't seem to be biting."

"I don't think you're going to find any," Joshua said. "I'm pretty sure there aren't any fish here."

"So am I," I said. "But you never know."

"Well, when I was in the frog's head, I didn't feel any fish memories," Joshua said. "If there were any fish here, the frog would have been likely to have some record of it. At least, I don't think I felt any fish memories. Like I said, the wiring is different."

I sat looking at Joshua for a couple of minutes. Then I started reeling in the line. "You know," I said, "I hate the way you do that."

"Do what?"

"Just casually drop stuff like that in the conversation," I said. " 'Oh, look. Here's a frog! Watch me make it dance like Danny Kaye! Incidentally, did you know I could read its mind, too?' It really bugs me."

"I'm sorry," Joshua said. "I'm not trying to hide anything. You could have asked me about it earlier—when we were having that little Q&A."

"I didn't *know* to ask," I said. "Look, Joshua, I'm not really upset, but you have to understand. I need to know all about you. In the space of five minutes, you've shown me that your species has the ability to get into someone's head and read their thoughts—"

"Some*thing*, not someone," Joshua said.

"That's a distinction that's going to make a lot of difference to the ninety percent of humanity that doesn't know the difference between astrology and astronomy," I said. "This is a power that bothers *me* immensely, and I understand exactly what you're saying. How the hell am I going to find a way to make the rest of the world get it?"

"If it bothers you, I just won't do it," Joshua said.

"You're missing the point, Joshua," I said. "It doesn't matter if you choose not to do it. It's the fact that you *can* do it. It's alien and it's scary. It's something that we're going to have to work with. And *that's* my point. You know more about us than we know about you. If you know you can do something that humans can't, you really have to let me know. Don't wait for me to ask about it. And don't just bring it up in conversation. We *can't* have any surprises. *I* can't."

"You were lying just a second ago," Joshua said. "You *are* upset."

I started to refute that, but I stopped myself and gave Joshua a little grim grin. "I'm sorry, Joshua," I said. "You're right. I am upset. I've been thinking about this thing for over a week now. But I have no idea what to do. And it really bothers me."

"A week's not that much time," Joshua said.

"No, it's not. But by this point I should have at least some idea of a plan," I said. "Even a bad idea would be better than nothing. But I'm drawing blanks. I think I'm having performance anxiety."

"If it will make you feel better, I'll still respect you in the morning," Joshua said.

I grinned more widely. "That's the problem, you know," I said. "When I was a kid, I remember seeing this 1950s science fiction movie. These guys went to Venus and discovered it was populated by women. One of the Gabor sisters was the ruler. Here was humanity's first contact with life on another planet, and they all looked like fabulous dames. And of course the guys from Earth were having no problems with it at all. It would be much simpler if you looked like that."

"I don't know if I'd want to look like a Gabor sister," Joshua said. "Although it could have interesting ramifications. 'People of the Earth! Surrender now, or we will slap your policemen!' "

"Maybe not a Gabor sister," I said. "But not a blob, either. If you looked like Ralph," I motioned to the sleeping dog, "then we'd be set. Everyone loves dogs."

"We know about this problem," Joshua said. "That's one of the reasons we came to you."

"I know. That's what I'm saying. By now I should have some idea of how to get away from this or work around it. But I'm having a hard time. I know I probably shouldn't tell that to you, but there it is. You've got me stumped at the moment."

"You'll figure it out," Joshua said. "Maybe while you're doing that, I'll take some lessons on dog behavior. As a backup. There are worse things than being a dog. Right, Ralph?"

Ralph cracked an eye open at the sound of his name.

From beside the cooler, my cellular phone rang. I sighed and picked it up. "Miranda, I'm busy with a client right now," I said. Miranda was the only person that had the number to this particular cellular phone (I had two), so I didn't worry about who it would be on the other end.

"Tom," Miranda sounded upset. "You remember Jim Van Doren?"

"Yeah," I said. During the last week Van Doren had been calling every couple of hours trying to get an interview with me. I eventually told Miranda to tell him whatever it was, I was not available for comment. "What about him?"

"Where are you?" Miranda said. "Are you in LA?"

"I'm in Glendora," I said. "It's about forty-five minutes out."

"This week's edition of *The Biz* just came out," Miranda

said. "You need to get back to LA and pick it up. You're on the cover. And you're not going to be happy with the story."

"Why?" I asked. "What's it about?"

"Here's what it says on the cover," Miranda said. " 'Tom Stein is the hottest young agent in Hollywood. So why is he acting so damned weird?' "

Chapter Eight

Secretive Agent

Tom Stein is the hottest young agent in Hollywood.

So why is he acting so damned weird?

By James Van Doren

At first glance, Tom Stein doesn't seem like your typical Hollywood millionaire. Maybe it's because he's lugging a five gallon bottle into his car. The bottle is filled, he says, with sulfurous waters from an out-of-the-way desert spa the agents at Lupo Associates go to whenever they're feeling a little stressed out. The fact that Stein is hauling this into his car tells you two things: first, he's stressed out. Second, he doesn't have time to feel stressed out right now.

And who can blame him? Last week, Stein pulled the biggest coup of his young agentorial career, when he managed to pull a $12.5 million paycheck out of the hat for client Michelle Beck, for her return to the Murdered

Earth *series. There have been larger paychecks for an actress, but not many, and certainly not so soon: Michelle's most recent paycheck for a supporting role in the just-wrapped* Scorpion's Tail, *was a mere $650,000—a twentieth of her next. Or, to put it another way, Stein's 10% is worth almost twice as much as his client's previous highest salary.*

Stein's success is another example of hard-nosed Hollywood capitalism—but the question becomes: at what price? For shortly after Stein's magic trick with Michelle Beck, friends and colleagues started noticing the normally affable Stein has become more closed and secretive. And his clients are discovering the oddest behavior of all: without warning, Stein has dropped them onto a subordinate agent, whose inexperience and (some allege) incompetence could send their careers into cinematic limbo. What have they done to deserve this, they ask? And what secret is gnawing away at Tom Stein? Is his red-hot career over just as it begun?

(Continued on page 65)

The story itself would have been funny, if it had been written about anyone else. Van Doren, in the absence of reality, spun out a fascinating tale of stress and paranoia that speculated that I was suffering from everything from conflicted sexuality to drug use to a "late-blooming Oedipal conflict," with my agent father—my making my first million apparently being a way to "claim my father's crown" in my chosen field, according to what the psychologist Van Doren managed to dig up.

The Biz being the pariah magazine it is, the quotes about me from colleagues and friends were unusually skimpy—the attributed quotes coming largely from high school acquaintances and college dorm-floor residents who generally described me as "friendly" and "driven,"—nothing to get worked up about, since they were true, and blandly nonspecific; these folks could have been describing a ski rescue dog with the same words, with equal results.

The unattributed quoters, of which there were two, were not that hard to figure out. The first, the "Lupo Associates Insider," was obviously Ben Fleck. Ben, no doubt relishing a chance to take a whack at me, described me as a "shark with Brylcreem" who was "insanely secretive, to the point of forbidding his assistants to even talk with other agents." The latter I found amusing, the former, inscrutable—I don't put anything in my hair, much less Brylcreem. I suspected Ben didn't actually know what Brylcreem was. I had Miranda send him a tube with my compliments.

The second was a "strongarmed client" who described Amanda as a "shrieking virgin" and myself as a "fucking over-lord of ego," and then went from there. It was pretty clear that Van Doren got more than he expected from Tea Reader, since by the end of it, even he noted that it seemed this particular client "was on her own personal vendetta against the universe, and Tom Stein happens to be the closest moving object."

Be that as it may, Van Doren took Tea's grudge against Amanda and ran with it, taking a bat to the poor girl. Van Doren dug up the Mexican soap star, who complained, through an interpreter, that Amanda had found her no work in the big Hollywood productions. The actor who revived her at the marathon described how they met, which made Amanda appear both sickly, for passing out in the first place, and then flaky, for representing the first passing jogger who happened to administer mouth-to-mouth.

Ben Fleck then reappeared in his Lupo Associates insider guise to make dismissive comments about the practice of bringing up agents from the mailroom (Ben got his job through nepotism: his stepfather was a senior agent before keeling over, corned beef in hand, at Canter's Deli), and mentioned, darkly, that I had come up from the mailroom myself. Obviously we mailroom types were looking out for each other, like frat brothers or Templars.

Amanda read the story and burst into my office, flinging *The Biz* onto my desk and then collapsing into the chair, moody. "I want to die," she said.

"Amanda, no one reads *The Biz*," I said. "And those that do generally know enough to realize that it's full of shit."

"My mom reads *The Biz*," Amanda said.

"Well, all right, *almost* everyone knows it's full of shit," I said. "Don't worry about it. Next week they'll find some more naked pictures of celebrities and they'll forget all about it. Don't be so upset."

"I'm not upset, I'm pissed off," Amanda said, whispering the words *pissed off* like she was worried about being punished. I wondered again how she ever managed to become an agent. "I know who talked to *The Biz*. I know who that unnamed source is. It's that bitch Tea." She stumbled over *bitch,* and then she gave me a bitter smile. "You know, I just got her a part in that new Will Ferrell film, too. A good part. Guess it doesn't matter."

"I'm sorry, Amanda," I said. "I shouldn't have unleashed Tea on you unawares. I should have let you know she's a high-riding bitch. It's my fault."

"No, it's all right," Amanda said. "It's okay. Because I know something Tea doesn't know."

"What's that?"

"That she got a part in a Will Ferrell movie."

"Amanda," I said, genuinely surprised. "You star. And here I was beginning to worry about you."

Amanda smiled like a five-year-old who had gotten her

first taste of being naughty and realized it was something she would enjoy doing. A lot.

Amanda ended up getting the best of it; the worst of her problems were over with Tea right then. My problems with my clients had just begun. For the next week, I was in Agent Hell.

"*Mind* the light," Barbara Creek said.

The light she was referring to was a huge klieg light, which lay on the set of her son's sitcom, *Workin' Out!* The light casing was heavily dented and the lens was shattered and strewn like jagged jewels across the floor, nestled up to the weights and exercise equipment that made up the health club locale set.

"I'm guessing that light's not supposed to be on the set," I said.

"Of course it's not," Barbara said, and then raised her voice so everyone on the set could hear her. "It's on the set because some damned fool UNION light hanger doesn't know how to do HIS DAMN JOB! And he wouldn't HAVE a JOB unless HIS DAMN JOB was protected by his DAMN UNION!" Barbara's voice, a commanding boom in normal conversation, reverberated through the set like the aftershock of a particularly nasty quake. From the corners and the rafters, members of the crew glared down at her. Something was telling me this was not going to be a frictionless set.

"Shouldn't someone come and pick this up?" I asked.

"Hell, no," Barbara said. "It's staying where it is until the union president gets here. I want him to see what sort of job his IDIOT UNION BROOM PUSHERS"—once again Barbara pitched her voice to the cheap seats—"have been doing around here. No one here is going to do a DAMN THING until he gets here."

That much was true. There were forty people on the set, mostly crew, ambling around aimlessly. The cast seemed to be missing, with the exception of Chuck White, who played Rashaad Creek's best friend on the show. Chuck was working out on one of the set decorations.

"How long have you been waiting?" I asked.

"Six long, unproductive hours," Barbara said. "And I'm going to keep waiting, and everyone here is going to keep waiting, until the union president gets here. Anyone who leaves before he gets here is fired, UNION OR NOT."

Directly behind Barbara, one of the cameramen gave her the finger.

"But I didn't ask you here to talk about the lights, Tom," Barbara said, strolling over to the audience seats. "I want to talk to you about the future of Rashaad's representation."

I followed Barbara. "Has there been a problem, Barbara?" I asked.

Barbara took a seat on a bleacher. "Not as such, Tom—here, sit down a minute," she patted the seat next to her, "but I have to tell you, I'm hearing some very disturbing things."

I took a seat. "This wouldn't have anything to do with that article in *The Biz,*" I said.

"It might," Barbara said. "You know, that reporter Van Doren gave Rashaad and me a call. Asked us if we've been noticing if you've been acting strangely lately. And then he told us that you had dropped so many of your clients. As you might imagine, we found this *very* disturbing. *I* found it *very* disturbing."

"Barbara," I said, "you really have nothing to worry about. Yes, I transitioned a number of my less important clients, but I certainly have no intention of doing that with Rashaad. He's on his way up, and I intend to keep him going there."

"Tom," Barbara said, "are you on drugs?"

"Excuse me?"

"Are you on drugs?" she repeated. "That reporter mentioned something about a health spa and sulfur treatments. To my ear, that sounds like rehab. You know how I feel about those drugs. I won't have them anywhere near my boy. You know I had everyone here on the set take a urine test before they could work here. If they had the slightest hint of anything in their system, they're gone."

After *Workin' Out!* was green-lighted, Rashaad threw a little party for himself and thirty of his most geographically immediate friends at the Four Seasons hotel in Beverly Hills. One of Rashaad's "pals" arrived with more cocaine than was in the final scene of *Scarface*. But then, Rashaad wasn't the one having to pee in a cup.

"I'm clean, Barbara," I said. "The last time I smoked anything illegal was my junior year in college. You don't have to worry about it."

"Then what is wrong, Tom? I—" she stopped as someone approached us. It was the assistant producer of the show. "What do you want, Jay?" she asked.

"Barbara, we really have to get a move on. Another forty-five minutes and we have to start paying overtime. And we still haven't shot half of the episode. We're going to be here all night if we don't start now."

"Then we'll be here all night," she said. "Nothing's happening until that damned union man gets his lazy ass over from Burbank."

"Barbara, we have to get this show in the can. We're already two days behind schedule."

"I don't give a damn about the schedule," Barbara said, building up a head of steam. "What I give a DAMN about is that my son's show is being held hostage by MORONS WHO CAN'T SCREW IN A LIGHT BULB. And if these boys think they're getting overtime, they are seriously mistaken, Jay. It's their fault we had to stop. If anything, at this point, they ought to pay me."

Jay the assistant producer threw up his hands. "You're the boss, Barbara."

"That's RIGHT," Barbara said, looking around. "I AM the BOSS. You'd all do VERY VERY WELL to remember who's signing your DAMN PAYCHECKS. Now leave me alone, Jay, I've got to talk business."

Jay split. Barbara turned back to me. "Do you see what I have to put up with around here? Now I know why Roseanne was so hard on her crew. You have to be. These folks are nothing but a bunch of lazy assed slackers. Do you know, that light almost killed me. Another two feet and it would have landed right on my head."

"That's awful," I said.

"Now, enough about this," she said. "What's your problem, Tom? Something's up with you, and it has us worried. How can you be my son's agent if you're falling apart over there?"

"I'm not falling apart, Barbara," I said. "*The Biz* piece had nothing to it. Everything is fine. Really."

"Is it?" Barbara said. "I wonder. I've been thinking about where my son is at, and I truly wonder if this is where he should be at this juncture of his career."

"Well, hell, Barbara," I said. "He's got his own show on a national network. I say that's pretty good for a twenty-three-year-old."

"At twenty-three, Eddie Murphy had made *48 Hours, Trading Places,* and *Beverly Hills Cop,*" Barbara said, "and his show was on a *real* network."

"Not everyone can have Eddie Murphy's career," I said.

"See, *this* is what I'm worried about," Barbara said. "*I* think Rashaad can have Eddie's career. *You* think he can't."

"I didn't say that," I said. "But now that you mention it, I don't want Rashaad to have Eddie Murphy's career. It includes *Harlem Nights* and *The Adventures of Pluto Nash,* too, you know."

"But this is all academic, isn't it?" Barbara said. "Because the fact is, Rashaad's not even in film at *all*. All he has for himself is one little show on one little network."

I started to reply, but there was a rap on the railing. We both turned to see Rashaad, in a hooded sweatshirt, surrounded by his lackeys. Someone had apparently forgotten to tell Rashaad that gangsta went out when Notorious BIG got perforated in Los Angeles.

"Say, yo, ma," Rashaad said. "The boys and I are going to get something to eat. You want we should, you know, bring you something or something?"

Rashaad finished in the top fifth of his private boarding school, with a verbal SAT of 650. He majored in English at the University of California, Berkeley, before dropping out in his second year to become a standup comedian. Back then, his name was Paul.

"Rashaad, honey, where are your manners?" Barbara said. "Say hello to Tom."

"Hey, yo, Tom," Rashaad said. "What's the word?"

"The word is 'abrogate,' Rashaad." This was an inside joke between us, my reminder to him that I remembered his GPA. He'd ask me what the word is, and I'd give him the most obscure one I could think of at the moment. Then he'd give me the definition back in street talk.

Except this time he looked surprised and shot his mother a quick look. Barbara gave him an almost imperceptible shake of her head. He turned back to me. "Good to see you, Tom. I'll catch you later." He and his stooges slunk out, followed enviously by the eyes of the trapped crew. I watched him until he slipped out of the studio.

"So, Barbara," I said. "Who did you get to replace me?"

"What?" Barbara said.

"After you decided that you were going to can me," I said. "You must have had someone in mind to get your son's career into high gear. I can't imagine you'd fire me without having someone else already lined up."

"I didn't say you were fired, Tom," Barbara said.

"'Abrogate—to annul, or repeal,'" I said. "Your son knows what it means, of course. That's why he looked so surprised when I used it. It's sort of funny, because I didn't use it to mean anything—it was just the first word that came into my head. But his reaction says to me that you didn't really call me over here to express your concerns about your son's career. You had me come over here to fire me. Right?"

"I'm looking out for the best interests of my son," Barbara said. "I don't know what it is you're going through at the moment, Tom, but you need to work out those issues, and my son can't wait for you to do that."

"Really?" I said. "Did you actually *ask* Rashaad if he wanted to drop me? Or did you just tell him after the fact? For that matter, did you ask him if he wanted to wait for the union boss, or if he wanted to just get someone to sweep up with a broom? It *is* his show, after all."

Barbara bristled. "*I'm* the producer. And I'm his manager. These things are my job—to look after this show and to look after him. I don't make any apologies for that, Tom, not to you or to anybody."

"One day, you might have to make an apology to *him,* Barbara. But I bet you didn't think about it that way."

Barbara glared at me but said nothing.

"So," I said, "who did you get to replace me?"

"David Nolan at ACR."

"He's not bad," I said.

"I *know* that, Tom." Barbara said. She got up and walked back towards the set. She began yelling at the assistant producer before she even got off the bleachers.

I sat there for a few moments, watching her go. One of the crew came over.

"Hi," he said. "You wouldn't have been talking to her about when we could leave, right?"

"Nope, sorry," I said. "I just came to get fired."

"Wow," he said. "Some guys have all the luck." He started off.

"Hey," I said. The guy turned. "Next time, don't miss."

He grinned, gave me a salute, and went backstage.

The next day, on the way to the *Pacific Rim* set, I got a phone call on my cellular. It was Joshua.

"Ralph and I are going on a hike," he said. "Ralph smells something interesting out back of your house, and I'm worried about him if he goes alone. He's pretty old."

"Joshua," I said, "think about what you're saying, here. If Ralph has a little doggie stroke, it's not like you're going to be able to rush to the nearest street and flag down a passing motorist. Why don't you guys wait until I get home? Then we can all go together."

"Because I'm bored, and so is Ralph, and you're no fun anymore," Joshua said. "Ever since that article came out. It's like living with a cardboard cutout of a formerly interesting person. Remember the good old days, when we'd have fun? It was just three days ago. Boy, those were times. Let me tell you."

"I'm sorry, Joshua," I said. "But I need these guys."

"Tom, I respect and admire you greatly, but I think you may have your priorities slightly out of order," Joshua said. "You're representing an entire alien culture. I think you shouldn't sweat the occasional television actor."

I pulled into the set and waved at the security guard, who let me through. "Thanks for the tip, Joshua. But I'm already here. Might as well go for the save."

"All right, fine," Joshua said. "We'll try to be back before you get home, then."

"Joshua, don't go. It'll only be a couple of hours. Really."

"La la la la la la la," Joshua said. "I'm not listening. Bye."

"At least take a phone," I yelled, but he had already hung up. Which was just as well. I didn't know how he would carry a phone, anyway. Probably the battery would leak into his insides. I parked, got out, headed towards the set.

Pacific Rim was nominally supposed to take place in Venice Beach, but the majority of it was filmed in Culver City. One day a week, the cast and crew decamped to Venice Beach for location shots. Today was one of those days. It made for an interesting set, if only because the vast majority of extras were in bikinis and Rollerblades. On one end of the set, a blocked-off section of the Venice boardwalk, an assistant director was blocking a shot with a pair of buxom Rollerbladers—apparently Rollerblading was harder than it looked. On the other end, Elliot Young had his script out and was conferring with the director, Don Bolling. Their conversation became more intelligible, as it were, the closer I got.

"I don't understand what I'm doing here," Elliot was pointing to a page in the script. "See, look. I'm running after the girl, screaming, 'Helen! Helen!', right? But Helen's dead. She was killed in the aquarium scene on page five. Isn't that a continuity problem?"

"Elliot," Don said, "I *know* that Helen gets killed on page five. The reason you're running after this woman, screaming Helen's name, is because you think she's her. And, as it happens, it's not Helen, but it *is* her identical twin sister. Which you would know, if you ever bothered to read the script before we shot it."

"But don't you think that's confusing?" Elliot said. "You know, this identical twin sister thing."

Don let out an audible sigh. "Yes, I do. That's the point, Elliot. It's called a plot twist."

"Well, that's just it," Elliot said. "It's a plot twist, but now *I'm* having a hard time following the plot at all. I want people to be able to follow what I'm doing on the show when I'm doing it."

"All right, Elliot," Don said, "what do you suggest?"

"Well, it's obvious," Elliot said. "When he chases the other woman, the other woman shouldn't look like Helen. It clears up the confusion."

"If we do that," Don said, "then it doesn't make any sense that you're running down the street, calling her Helen. She would just be another woman."

"They could still be sisters," Elliot said.

Don looked pained. "What?" he said.

"Sisters. They could still be sisters. Sisters look a lot alike. They're related. They could even still be twins, just not the kind that look alike. What are those called?"

"Fraternal," I said. They both looked at me. I waved, cutely.

"Yeah, fraternal," Elliot said, turning back to Don. "Personally, I think that makes a lot more sense."

"Tom," Don said, "please help me out here."

"I don't even know what's going on," I said. "Except that it involves sisters."

"In this episode, a marine biologist named Helen that Elliot's dating witnesses a mob hit and gets killed," Don said.

"She's thrown in with the electric eels," Elliot said.

". . . Right," Don said. "So Elliot's despondent, and then several days later, he sees another woman who looks just like Helen. So of course he's *confused*,"—Don whipped the word at Elliot, who took no notice—"since he knows she's supposed to be dead. It turns out to be her twin sister."

"Who is of course also seen by the mob killers, so he has to protect her from them, and during the process he falls in love with her as well," I said.

"How about that, Elliot?" Don said to his star. "Your agent figured out what was going on, and he didn't even have to read the script. My count shows him two up on you."

"You don't find that confusing at all?" Elliot asked me.

"It *is* confusing," I admitted. "But it's a good kind of confusing. It's the sort of confusing that viewers actually like, especially as I assume it gets explained at some point during the action. I'm right about that, Don?"

"It happens not far past the place where you stopped reading the script, Elliot," Don said.

"Well, there it is, then," I said. "It works out well for everyone."

From the other end of the set there was a wail followed by a crash. One of the buxom Rollerbladers had careened out of control and impacted against a Steadicam operator. The resulting collision managed somehow to dislodge her bikini top. The Rollerblader appeared momentarily flummoxed, deciding whether to cover her nipples or to grab at the rapidly swelling knob on her forehead, where her skull connected with that of the cameraman. Her right arm switched between both locations, dealing with neither very effectively. In the wash of pain and embarrassment, she seemed to have forgotten that she had a whole other arm that she could deploy.

The Steadicam operator lay sprawled on the pavement, out cold. None of the predominately male crew was paying even the slightest bit of attention to him.

"Oh, look," Don said. "An actual legitimate crisis." He turned to Elliot. "When I get back, I would really like to shoot this scene. Please try to have all your philosophical problems with it resolved by then." He sauntered toward the scene of the accident, angling towards the girl rather than the cameraman.

"Exciting day," I said, to Elliot.

He was gnawing on a thumb, still looking at the script. "Are you sure that this isn't going to be a problem with this? I'm still sort of lost."

"It'll be fine, Elliot. Stop worrying about it. And stop gnawing on your thumbnail. You're going to make your manicurist miserable. Look, you said you wanted to talk. Here I am."

"Yeah, okay," Elliot said. He seemed distracted as we went back to his trailer.

As we entered his trailer, I was greeted by a life-size cutout of Elliot in his "beach volleyball" costume and shades, grinning toothily and holding a bottle of cologne. I had a brief flashback to my earlier conversation with Joshua. "Who's the handsome guy?" I said.

"Oh, that," Elliot said. He bent down to get a bottle of water out of his refrigerator. "The production company thinks we ought to branch out into other markets. So we're making a *Pacific Rim* cologne."

"Well, if *Baywatch* did it, so can you," I said.

"Ours is different than the *Baywatch* cologne. It's made with real human pheromones."

"You're kidding," I said.

"No, man, really." Elliot reached up into an overhead compartment, grabbed a sample-sized cologne bottle, and handed it to me. "They're actually *my* pheromones, too."

I unscrewed the top and took a whiff. It smelled like I expected Joshua would smell if he were left out in the sun too long. "Powerful," I said. "How did they get your pheromones, if you don't mind me asking?"

"They put me on a treadmill and then collected my sweat," Elliot said.

"Sounds delightful," I said.

Elliot shrugged. "It wasn't so bad. They let me watch movies while I exercised. Listen, I think we should see other people."

"What?" I said.

"I think we should see other people," Elliot said.

"Elliot, we're not going steady," I said, putting the top on the cologne and placing it on the near table. "Shucks, we've never even dated."

"You know what I mean," he said. "I've been thinking a lot about my future recently, and I sort of want to explore my options. See what else is out there. Tom, you know there's a lot of wild rumors going around about you at the moment."

"Great," I said, flopping into a chair. "The one week everyone reads *The Biz* is the week I'm on the cover."

"*The Biz?*" Elliot said.

"Yes, Elliot," I said. "You remember, the place where you read all those wild rumors."

"I didn't read anything about it," Elliot said. "I heard about most of it from Ben."

I sat up. "Who?"

"Ben," Elliot said.

"Ben *Fleck*?" I asked.

"Yeah," Elliot said. "You know him?"

"I can't believe this," I said. "I've been cherry-picked by Ben Fleck."

"He said that you've cracked up lately," Elliot said. "That you've been handing all your clients to other agents because of the stress. So I figured, if you're doing that anyway, might as well at least stay in the same company, where they know me."

"Elliot," I said. "I'm not cracking up. I'm fine. And I still want to be your agent. Look where you are now, Elliot. You're doing pretty well for yourself. Which means that *I* did pretty well for you. You don't just chuck that away because Ben Fleck calls you up and tells you I'm cracking up. You don't even *know* Ben, Elliot. He's an incompetent agent. Trust me on this one."

"Yeah," Elliot shrugged again. "Well, he says that he can get me into film, that I'm ready for the big film roles."

"Of course he would say that, Elliot. He knows that's what you want. That's what everybody wants."

"Well, what do you think? You think I'm ready for film roles?"

"Sure, some," I said, conveniently ignoring my previous plan to keep him strictly on television for the next season. "But you still need to build your base. You remember what I told you about David Caruso. Jumped out of TV too soon. He had two flops and then it was ten years before *CSI Miami*."

"Uh-huh," Elliot said. "Look, Tom. I know you don't think I'm a rocket scientist, but I'm not totally dumb. I'm thirty-two years old. I'm only making $50,000 an episode. I've got another four seasons on my contract. Where does that leave me?"

"With five million dollars?" I said.

"I can make that off of *one* movie, man," Elliot said. "Thirty-two is prime time in the movie business. I've got to strike now. Ben's ready to back me up on this, and I think I ought to take him up on that. You're right, it *is* what I want. I'm sorry, Tom."

There was a knock on the door. "We're ready, Elliot," Don said, through the door. "Put down that Mensa test and get on the set."

"Elliot," I said. "Think about this, all right? Don't decide anything right now."

"I got to go," Elliot said. "No hard feelings, Tom? It's just business."

It was my turn to shrug. I could see where this was going. "Sure, Elliot. No problem."

"Great," he said, and opened the door. "You know, you can keep that bottle of cologne."

"Thanks," I said. He smiled, closed the door behind him. I

picked up the bottle of cologne and stared at it for a minute before I threw it against the far wall of the trailer. It shattered quite nicely.

Ben's administrative assistant, Monica, beamed at me prettily as I strode up.

"Hi, Monica," I said. "Ben wouldn't happen to be in at the moment, would he?"

"He is, but he's with a prospective client."

"Really," I said. "Anyone I know?"

"Do you know any Playmates on a personal basis?" Monica asked.

"Afraid not," I said.

"Then you don't know her," Monica said.

"I'll learn to get past the disappointment," I said.

"That's the spirit," Monica said. "You want me to tell him you dropped by?"

"That's all right," I said. "This will just take a minute." I stepped past her desk and walked into Ben's office.

Ben was sitting at his desk with the aforementioned Playmate in the guest chair. He smiled expansively at me. "Tom," he said. "What a surprise. Have you met Leigh? She's a Playmate."

"Not yet," Leigh piped. "Not until November."

"Something for us boys to look forward too, then," Ben said.

"Hello, Leigh," I said, shaking her hand. "It's a pleasure to meet you. Excuse me for just one second, please." I turned, leaned over the desk, and sucker-punched Ben in the nose. I turned back to Leigh, who sat, stunned, watching as Ben yodeled in pain at his desk, holding his bleeding nose in his splayed fingers. I sat on the edge of Ben's desk and smiled winningly.

"So," I said. "Found an agent?"

Leigh ran screaming from the room. I turned back to Ben. He had fingers jammed into his nostrils to staunch the bleeding.

"You fucker," he said. "You broke my fucking nose!"

"You cherry-picked Elliot Young from me, Ben. I don't appreciate that very much. I also don't appreciate what you said about me in *The Biz*. Those were hurtful words. I was bothered. Since you don't have any clients I want, and I'm not planning to talk to the press, I had to do something to even up our ledgers. I think we're about even now, don't you?"

"You're totally fucking insane," Ben said. "Enjoy your last day as an agent, you asshole."

"Ben, let me make this clear to you," I said. "If you ever stick your nose in my business again, I'm going to work you over with a sledgehammer. I don't mean that figuratively. I literally mean that I will walk into this office, lock the door behind me, pull out a sledgehammer and work on you until your bones resemble gravel. Are we clear?"

"You're out of your fucking mind, Tom," Ben said.

"Ben, are we clear?"

"Yes," Ben glared at me through the beginnings of bruises. "Yes, we're fucking clear, already. Get out of my fucking office, Tom. Just get out."

I walked to the door. A crowd was waiting on the other side. I stared at them.

"Congratulate Ben," I said. "He's the proud father of a bouncing baby nosebleed."

Ben started screaming for Monica. I walked the short distance to my office.

Miranda followed me in. "Are you okay?" she asked.

"No," I said, "I am in *so* much pain. I think I broke a finger."

Miranda slipped her notepad under her arm. "Let me see," she said. She reached over. I gave her my hand. She palpated my middle finger.

"Ouch," I said.

"It's not broken," Miranda said. "It's not even sprained. But you clearly don't know how to throw a punch."

"I'll do better next time," I said.

Miranda pinched down hard on my finger. I screamed.

"Don't you *ever* do something like that again," she said, "or I'll kill you myself. I like my job, and I'm not going to have you risk it just because you're my boss. Got it?"

"Yes!" I said. "Let go." She did.

"Now," she said, pulling her notepad back out. "Messages. Jim Van Doren called."

"The hell you say," I said.

"No lie," she said. "He says he's working on another story and wanted to see if you wanted to comment this time."

"I can't comment," I said. "I already promised you I wouldn't punch anyone else."

"That's my boss," Miranda said. "Amanda called. She says she wanted you to know she made Tea 'grovel like the she-dog she is' for the part in the Will Ferrell film. Says that she and Tea have come to an understanding and that she doesn't expect too many more problems."

"And here you thought you were going to have to do a lot of hand-holding," I said.

"No kidding," Miranda said. "I think we created a monster. Carl called. He wants to know if you're available for lunch tomorrow."

"This is a question?" I asked.

"That's what I thought you might say," Miranda said, "so I told him you'd be free at 12:30. Meet him at his office."

"Got it," I said.

"Last message," Miranda said. "Someone I've never heard of, but says he knows you. Didn't leave his last name."

"Joshua?"

"That's him," Miranda said. "Sort of cryptic message. Said you'd understand."

"What is it?"

"He said, 'Something happened. I'll be late.'"

Chapter Nine

Carl leaned on the railing of the Santa Monica Pier, happily munching on a corn dog. I had a corn dog of my own, but I was somewhat more somber. I was figuring out how I was going to tell my boss that the alien he had entrusted to my care had mysteriously disappeared into the Angeles National Forest.

The good news was that Joshua *did* take one of the cell phones with him; it was from that phone that he had called my office and left the message. The bad news was that after leaving the message he wasn't answering the phone. As soon as I got his message, I began calling his phone at five-minute intervals until I got home. There was no answer.

When I got home, I changed into sweats, a T-shirt, and my long-neglected hiking boots, and hauled my carcass out of the backyard. Between a fifteen-year-old dog and pile of goo, I figured the chances were slim that the two of them had gotten very far. I picked the direction that I figured they might go in and went thataway.

When I was thirteen, I knew every tree, every slope, every large rock in the woods out back of my house. Every once in a while, I'd drop a book, several candy bars, and a couple of Cokes in a backpack, leave a note for the parents, and head into the hills. I'd come back several hours later in pitch darkness, unconcerned that I might get lost or misdirected. This was Los Angeles, after all; just point yourself in the direction of the lights, and ten minutes later you're on one suburban street or another. More to the point, however, was the fact that I knew my way around—it was as unthinkable for me to get lost in those woods as it was for me to get lost in my own backyard.

In the fifteen years between my thirteen-year-old self and my current one, someone went into the woods and switched the trees and rocks around. Five minutes in, I was utterly lost.

Three hours later, scratched, bruised, and limping from where I jammed my foot into a rabbit hole, twisting my ankle, I resurfaced from the Angeles National Forest miles from where I had entered. I would have been completely disoriented if I hadn't had the luck to emerge from the brush two hundred yards from my high school; as it was it took me nearly another hour to get home because of my ankle.

Later, as I soaked in the tub, I formulated a plan: when Joshua came home, I would discover if it were possible to strangle protoplasm. It was a good plan, and I congratulated myself for coming up with it on my own.

Joshua, however, stayed one step ahead. He simply didn't reappear.

At 2 a.m., I gave up and headed to bed. The rational portion of my mind figured that a creature that had crossed trillions of miles of hard vacuum would be able to keep himself alive for a night in the suburban woods above Los Angeles. The crazy little man in my head, however, was convinced that Joshua had already been eaten by the coyotes. I briefly considered trying to get my cellular company to triangulate the phone's position, but I suspected that the phone had to be receiving for that. There was the other small matter of Joshua being an extraterrestrial; it would be hard to explain to search teams what my phone was doing immersed in a puddle of sentient mucus. The best I could do was leave the patio door unlocked and hope Joshua and Ralph made it home.

I got to sleep at six. Neither Joshua nor Ralph had made an appearance. When I finally left the house at eleven for my lunch with Carl, the two of them were still missing.

The one space alien on the entire planet, and I had managed to lose him. I was fired for sure.

"God," Carl said, holding his half-eaten corn dog in front of him. "I love corn dogs. Who would have thought that hog snouts could taste so good if you just rolled them into a tube, shot them up with nitrates and breaded them in corn paste? But there it is. How old are you, Tom?"

"I'm twenty-eight," I said.

"When I was in my twenties, Tom, I'd come out here with Susan, my first wife, and we'd get a couple of corn dogs and then we'd walk to the end of the pier and watch the sunset. This was in the late seventies, when the smog was so bad breathing the air constituted a health hazard."

"I remember the bad smog," I said. "I got out of a lot of P.E.

classes that way. We had to stay inside and watch filmstrips. I learned all about the California missions that way."

"I don't really miss all the smog, mind you," Carl said, staring off. "But they made for some beautiful sunsets. The late seventies were a horrible period in the history of the universe, Tom—you had stagflation, the American hostages in Iran, and some terrible, terrible apparel. And smog. But the sunsets weren't so bad. It doesn't make up for anything, but it goes to show not everything can be bad all at once."

"I didn't know you had been married more than once," I said. "I had thought Elise was your first wife." Carl's wife Elise was the scariest person you'd ever want to meet—a terrifyingly intelligent trial lawyer who also had a doctorate in psychology. She was thinking of running for Los Angeles District Attorney. From there it would be a short hop to mayor. Between the two of them, Carl and Elise would be running southern California within the decade.

Carl glanced over. "Elise is my second wife. Susan died in '81. Car accident; some drunk idiot came up the wrong way on an on-ramp and plowed right into her car. They both died instantly. Pregnant at the time, you know."

"I'm terribly sorry," I said. "I didn't mean to bring up any painful memories."

Carl waved it off. "No reason you should know. I never talk about it and no one ever talks about it around me. One of the advantages of being the sort of boss that scares the hell out of the subordinates. Susan was a wonderful woman—but so is Elise. I've been very lucky."

"Yes, sir." We ate our corn dogs in silence.

"Come on," Carl said, after he had finished his dog. "I haven't walked on the beach for weeks. We can chat while we walk." We walked off the pier, stopped off at Carl's car to drop off our shoes and socks, and then walked into the sand towards the surf.

"So," he said, when we walked to the water. "How is Joshua doing?"

I swallowed and saw my career flash before my eyes. "He's missing at the moment, Carl," I said.

"Missing? Explain."

"He and Ralph—my neighbor's dog—went out for a walk in the woods yesterday, while I was off seeing Elliot Young. When I got back into the office, Miranda had a message from him, saying that something had happened, and that he'd be late. That's the last I've heard of him. I went looking for him last night, but I didn't find him. I stayed up until six this morning, and he hadn't returned."

"Where would he go?" Carl said. "He's not exactly inconspicuous."

"The Angeles National Forest starts more or less in my backyard," I said. "They went into the woods."

If I were Carl, this would have been the point where I would have fired me. Instead, Carl changed the subject. "I hear you flattened Ben Fleck's nose yesterday."

"I did," I admitted. "He pinched Elliot Young off of me. He's also the 'Lupo Associates insider' in that damned story in *The Biz*. Punching him seemed the only alternative to breaking his neck. Although I'm feeling guilty about it now. I think I may have broken his nose."

"It's not broken," Carl said. "We had some X-rays done at Cedars Sinai. It's merely 'severely bruised.'"

"Well, that's good," I said. "I mean, relatively speaking."

"It is," Carl agreed. "Be that as it may, Tom, I would prefer in the future that you find some less dramatic way to resolve your issues with Ben. Ben may have been asking for it, but that sort of thing isn't very good for company morale. Also, all things considered, it's drawing unwanted attention to you at the moment."

Carl was referring to the blurb in the *Times'* movie industry column—one of the office spectators had leaked to the paper, and the paper did the legwork and found out that Ben had snaked one of my clients. It also mentioned the article in *The Biz* as a contributing factor, giving the article credence in the process. For even more fun, the *Times* had called my office this morning as well, looking for a comment on *The Biz* and its editorial practices. It felt like the media had pried up a floorboard looking for a bug, and that bug was me. I just wanted to fade back into the darkness.

I laughed. Carl look at me oddly. "What's so funny?" he asked.

"I'm sorry," I said. "I was just thinking about it. This week I was ditched by two of my clients, was labeled insane by a magazine, assaulted a colleague, and let an alien walk off into the woods, where he's probably been eaten by a coyote. I'm trying to imagine how this week can get any worse. I don't think it can."

"We could have an earthquake," Carl said.

"An earthquake would be wonderful," I said. "It would give everyone else something to think about. A nice big one, seven or eight on the Richter scale. Major structural damage. That'd work."

Carl stood there a moment, seemingly preoccupied. I followed his line of sight down to his toes. He was busily squelching sand through them. After a few seconds of this, he stepped out of his footprints and let the tide wash into them, partially erasing them. Then he put his feet back into them.

"Tom," Carl said. "Don't worry too much about Joshua at the moment. He'll be fine. The Yherajk are pretty much indestructible by our standards, and I doubt that the coyotes or whatever are going to get a bite out of him. Joshua can make a skunk seem like a bed of roses. He and . . . Ralph?"—He looked for confirmation; I nodded—"are probably just roughing it or something. You didn't tell me that he had made friends with a dog."

"They get along great," I said. "They're the solution to each other's boredom. I think Joshua likes Ralph better than he likes me."

"Well, that's good news, at the very least. Anyway, I expect Joshua will be back soon enough. Try to relax a bit."

I snorted just a little. "Now if I could just get *The Biz* off my back, I'd be set."

"Some of that's been taken care of," Carl said. "The *Times* is doing a story on *The Biz,* you know."

"They called me this morning," I admitted, "I've been sort of dreading calling them back."

"I've already talked to them," Carl said. "Gave them a nice long chat about how *The Biz* took our company's innovative mentoring policy and made it look like you were having a nervous breakdown. I said that if you were having a nervous breakdown, then I and several of the senior agents were also having them, since we've also started mentoring some of our newer agents."

"Thanks," I said. "You didn't have to do that."

"Actually, I did," Carl said. "It keeps the bad press to a minimum. I'm not blaming you about it—this Van Doren character was already working on something, and you just happened to be in the wrong place at the wrong time with him. Anyway, the mentoring idea is not a bad one; we've been a sink-or-swim agency long enough. It might do some good to do things the other way for a while."

"I'm surprised you found out about it," I said.

"I asked Miranda," Carl said. "She seems to think highly of it and you."

"I think highly of her as well," I said. "Actually, I'm hoping to get her a raise."

"Give her a ten percent hike," Carl said, "but tell her to keep quiet about it. We've been cracking down on raises recently. But I figure she deserves it, or will by the time this whole thing is through. Which reminds me, since you thought of the mentoring program, you've won our Annual Innovation in Agenting Award. Congratulations."

"That's great," I said. "I've never heard of this award before."

"It's the first annual," Carl said. "Don't get too excited. I've already told the *Times* you've donated the cash award to the City of Hope."

"That was very nice of me," I said.

"It was," Carl agreed. "The point of all this is that now, rather than being looked upon as someone who is cracking up, which is interesting and creates press, you look like someone whose eye is on the ball and whose heart is in the right place, which is boring and no one gives a damn about. *The Biz,* properly, looks like a rag filled with poor reporting. And Ben Fleck looks to have gotten his. Everything works out."

"Wow," I said. "I thought I was fired for sure."

"Well, I'll be honest with you, Tom," Carl said. "It's not exactly the way I wanted it. We've cleared most of these distractions away this time. Now do me the favor of not requiring me to pull another *deus ex machina*. I don't really like it, and it brings more attention to us than I want. Fair enough?"

I sensed the extreme irritation that lay directly under Carl's placid statement. He may not have been blaming me for anything that had happened, but that didn't mean that it didn't reflect on me. I was now going to have to work twice as hard to keep from pissing him off in the future. I figured, sooner or later, given the way things had gone so far, I was doomed.

"Fair enough," I said.

"Good," Carl said. He clapped his hands together. "You like ice cream? There's this place nearby that has the best soft-serve ice cream in LA. Let's go get some."

The ice cream was as good as Carl promised; first it spiraled out of an ice cream maker, then it was dipped into chocolate that formed a hard candy shell. We sat outside the shop and watched rollerskaters and gulls go by.

"You know what I'd really like to know," I said.

Carl was wiping off his chin from where some chocolate had smudged it. "I'm sure you'll tell me," he said.

"I will indeed," I said. "I'd like to know how you met up with our smelly little space friends in the first place. And I'd like to know how Joshua got his name."

"Lunchtime is almost over," Carl said. "I don't know that I have time to go into it right now."

"Oh, come on," I said, risking a little familiarity. "You're one of the most powerful men on this half of the continent. If you have a meeting, they'll wait."

Carl bit into his ice cream. "I guess that's true. All right, then. Here it is."

CHAPTER Ten

You think of the human race meeting the first alien species, and you think of *Close Encounters* or maybe *The Day the Earth Stood Still:* big production numbers involving scientists, government officials, and a lot of background music. The fact of the matter is the first human contact with aliens happened on the phone. It's a letdown if you're into grand scale entrances, but in retrospect, I find it comforting, and, now that I think of it, indicative of the Yherajk: they were dying to meet us, but they're polite enough to make sure they're wanted.

At the time, though, I thought it was a crank call. Of course; who thinks aliens are going to use the phone?

The phone call came at about a quarter past eleven. I'd just gotten back from the premiere of *Call of the Damned;* I skipped the after-party because I didn't want to have to tell anyone what I had really thought of the movie. Elise was in Richmond, Virginia, on her book tour—I remember her leaving a message and telling me she was thinking we should get a horse farm out there for when we retire. I mean, really—what the hell am I going to do with horses? But she's a horsey type. Never got over it as a girl.

I was sitting in my lounger with my second beer, listening to Fritz Coleman talk about one of those annual meteor showers. Perseids or Leonids. Can never remember which is which. Fritz was going on about it when the phone rang. I picked it up.

"Hello," I said.

"Hi," the voice on the other end said. "My name is Gwedif. I'm a representative of an alien race that is right now orbiting high above your planet. We have an interesting proposition, and we'd like to discuss it with you."

I glanced over to the LED readout on the phone, which displays caller ID information. There wasn't any. "This doesn't involve Amway products, does it?" I asked.

"Certainly not," Gwedif said. "No salesmen will come to your door."

Thanks to the beer, I was just mellow enough not to do what I usually do with crank calls, which is hang up. And anyway, this one was sort of interesting; usually when I get random calls, it's some wannabe actor who's looking for representation. I was bored and Fritz had given way to commercials, so I kept going.

"A representative of an alien race," I said. "Like one of those Heaven's Gate folks? You following a comet or something?"

"No," Gwedif said. "I'm one of the aliens myself. And we passed by Hale-Bopp on the way in. No spaceships that we could see. Those people didn't know what they were talking about."

"*Actually* one of the aliens," I said. "That's new. Tell me, does this bit work with other folks? I mean, I'm loving it, personally."

"I don't know," Gwedif said. "We haven't called anyone else. Mr. Lupo, we know it sounds unbelievable, but we figured this was the best way to go—cut the ooh-ah Spielberg stuff and get right to the point. Why be coy? We know you like to get right to business. We saw that PBS documentary."

You remember that thing, Tom—they had a film crew from KCET follow me around for a week about a year ago, when I was putting the *Call of the Damned* package together over there at Sony. They actually ran it in a theater before they ran it on TV, so it'd be eligible for Oscar consideration. I'm pretty sure they can write off any votes from the Sony suits; the documentary makes it look like I rolled them. Well, maybe I did.

Anyway, the "aliens" saw it, and thus, the upfront phone call. And now they wanted to arrange a meeting. By this time I had drained the second beer and had gone to the fridge for a third. So I figured, what the hell.

"Sure, Gwed—you don't mind if I call you Gwed, do you?" I said.

"Not a bit," he said.

"Why don't you come on over to the office sometime next week and we'll set up a meeting. Just call the front desk and ask for Marcella, my assistant."

"Hmmmm, that'd be sort of difficult," he said. "We were kind of hoping we might have a chat tonight. There's a meteor shower going on."

I didn't really understand that last part, but I figured it was par for the course when you're talking to 'aliens.' "All right," I said. "Let's chat tonight."

"Great," Gwedif said. "I'll be down in about fifteen minutes."

"Swell," I said. "You going to need anything? A snack? A beer?"

"No, I'm fine," he said, "though I'd appreciate it if you'd turn on your pool light."

"Well, of course," I said. "Everyone knows to turn on their pool light when aliens drop by."

"See you soon," Gwedif said, and hung up.

I hauled myself out of the lounger, clicked off the TV, and went to the sliding glass door that leads to the pool area. The pool's light switch is right by the door, so I clicked it on as I headed out the door. You've never been to our place, Tom, but we have a huge pool—Olympic-sized. Elise was a swimmer at UCSD and still uses it to stay in shape. I wade around in the shallow end of the pool, myself—I float better than I swim.

I plopped down into a patio chair and sucked on my beer and thought about what I had just done. I never invite strangers over to the house, even sane ones, and now I had just invited someone who said he was a representative of an alien species over for a chat. The more I thought about it, of course, the more stupid it seemed. About ten minutes of this, I had become convinced that I had just set myself up for some sort of ritual Hollywood murder, the kind where the newscasters start off their stories by saying "The victim appeared to know his assailant—there was no struggle of any kind," and then pan to walls, which are sponge-painted with blood. I stood up to go back into the house and phone the police, when I noticed a meteor streaking across the sky.

This in itself was no big deal. There was meteor shower going on, after all, and my house is high up enough in the hills that the light pollution isn't so bad; I'd been seeing little meteor streaks the entire time I was sitting there. But most of them were small, far off, and lightning quick; this one was large, close, and dropping its way through the sky directly towards my house. It looked like it was moving slow, but as I stared at it, I realized that it was going to impact in about five seconds. Even if I hadn't been paralyzed, staring at it, I doubted I could have made it into the house. It looked like I wouldn't have to worry about being murdered by psychopaths, after all—I was going to be struck down by a meteor instead. At this point, some absurdly rational chunk of my consciousness piped in with a thought: *Do you* realize *the odds on getting hit by a meteor?*

About two seconds to impact, the meteor shattered with a tremendous sonic boom, the tiny pieces of the rock vaporizing in the atmosphere like a sudden fireworks display. I stared dumbly at the point of the explosion, blinking away the afterimages, when I heard a far-off whistling sound, getting closer. I saw it a fraction of a second before it hit my pool—a chunk of meteor that had to be the size of a barrel, whirling end over end. The explosion of the meteor must have acted like a brake on its momentum, because if something that size had hit my backyard at the speed the meteor had been going, neither I nor any of my neighbors would have been around to tell the tale.

As it was, it hit the pool like a bus, and I was hit by a tidal wave of suddenly hot pool water. Steam fumed from where it dropped, in the deep end. I regained enough of my senses to wonder how much the pool damage was going to cost me, and if meteor strikes were covered by my home insurance. I doubted they were. Several pool lights had been extinguished by the impact; I went back to the door and turned them off, so as not to have electrified water, and then turned on the main patio lights to get a closer look at the damage.

Miraculously, the pool seemed in good shape, if you didn't count the broken pool lights. The pool water was still bubbling where the meteor had gone in, but even so, I could see enough through the water to see that the concrete appeared to be un-cracked. The meteor chunk had come in at just the right angle into the pool; the mass of the water, rather than the mass of the concrete, absorbed the impact. The water level of the pool was a good foot lower than it had been pre-impact, however.

If my neighbors heard anything, they gave no indication—or at least, I never heard them if they had. The walls around the backyard are twelve feet high; I had had them built around 1991, when my next-door neighbor was a heavy metal drum-mer. I had gotten sick of listening to his parties and watching him and his women having cocaine-fueled orgies in the hot tub, and it was easier to build the walls than to get him to move. As it turns out, I needn't have bothered; about a week after the walls were up, his wife filed for divorce and he had to sell the house as part of the settlement. George Post lives there now. Plastic surgeon. Nice neighbor. Quiet.

After the water settled down for a few moments, I heard a small *crack*, and looked into the pool in time to see a thick liq-uid oozing out of the meteorite remains and floating to the top of the water. The stuff was mostly clear but oily-looking. Space phlegm. After a couple of minutes of accumulating, the phlegm did something surprising: it started moving toward the side of the pool. When it got to the edge, a tentacle shot out onto the patio concrete and the rest of the phlegm hauled up through it. When it was totally out, it launched up another tentacle that waved around for a second, then stopped and shot back down into the rest of the phlegm. It began to slide over towards me.

I can't even begin to tell you what was going through my mind at that moment, Tom. You know those dreams where something horrifying is coming at you, and you're running as fast as you can, but you're moving in slow motion? It was like that feeling: disassociated horror and utter immobility. My brain had stopped working. I couldn't move. I couldn't think. I'm pretty sure I stopped breathing. All I could do was watch this thing work around the patio to where I was standing. For the third and final time that night, I was utterly convinced I was going to die.

The thing stopped short two feet in front of me and collected itself into a compact Jell-O mold shape. A bowling ball–sized protuberance emerged from the top and launched itself up to eye level, supported by a stalk of goop. And then it *talked*.

"Carl? It's Gwedif. We talked on the phone. Ready to take a meeting?"

Tom, I did something I've never done before. I fainted straight away.

I was down for just a couple of seconds; I woke up to find Gwedif looming over me. I caught a whiff of him: he smelled like an old tennis shoe.

"I'm guessing that wasn't planned," he said.

I rolled away from him as quickly as I could and reached for the nearest dangerous object. My beer bottle had broken, so I grabbed it and held it in my hand, jagged end out.

"Eek," Gwedif said.

"Stay away," I said.

"Away put your weapon," he said. "I mean you no harm."

The line floated in my head for a second before I attached it with what it was from: it was a line of Yoda's in *The Empire Strikes Back*. It knocked me off kilter just enough that I relaxed just a little. I lowered the beer bottle.

"Thank you," Gwedif said. "Now, Carl, I'm going to move toward you, very slowly. Don't be frightened. All right?"

I nodded. Slowly as promised, Gwedif moved over to reaching distance.

"You okay so far?" Gwedif asked. I nodded again. "All right, then. Hold out your hand."

I did. Slowly, he pulled a tentacle out of his body and wrapped it around my hand. I was surprised not to find it slimy; in fact, it was firm and warm. My brain looked for a concept to relate it to and came up with one—those Stretch Armstrong dolls. You know, the one where you pulled on the arms and they stretched out for a yard. It was something like that.

My hand wrapped in his tentacle, Gwedif did the unexpected. He shook it.

"Hi, Carl," he said. "Nice to meet you."

I looked at Gwedif, dumbfounded, for about twenty seconds. Then I started to laugh.

What can you say about the experience of meeting an entirely new, wholly alien, intelligent species of life? Well, of course, Tom, you know what it was like; you've done it, too. But I think by now you may have noticed that I plowed you right through that first meeting with Joshua, and I did it for a reason. I wanted to give your conscious brain something relatively familiar to work on, while your subconscious was grinding its gears on the existence of an alien. I don't know if it was fair to do it that way; it might have been a sort of *coitus interruptus* for appreciating the wonder of the moment. What? Well, it's good to know it doesn't bother you, then.

Personally, it took me a good hour before I finally calmed my brain down enough that Gwedif and I could start having a real conversation. During the interim he answered my semi-coherent questions, allowed me to touch him, literally sticking my hands *into* him on one occasion, and otherwise talking me down back into a rational state of mind. I was like a kid with a new toy. You're looking at me like it's hard to believe, Tom. And it is, I suppose; you folks at work only see me in control, and that's also for a reason.

But there's no way that I could contain my enthusiasm and excitement! Only one person on the planet gets to be the first person these aliens would meet, and it was *me*. I didn't yet understand why, or for what purpose, but at that moment I didn't care. The answer to one of the biggest questions humanity had ever asked—are we alone in the universe?—was sitting, globular and stinky, in the living room of my house. It was . . . indescribable. A boon of monumental proportions. About half an hour in, as the implications sank in, I wept with joy.

We talked all through the night, of course; I was too excited to sleep and Gwedif, apparently, doesn't need it. When nine o'clock rolled around, I called Marcella and told her I was taking a sick day. Marcella was concerned; she wanted to send a specialist over. I told her not to worry, that I could take care of myself. Then I went to sleep, but woke up two hours later, too excited to stay in bed. I found Gwedif outside, by the pool.

"I'm just admiring my work," he said. "I don't know if you can appreciate it, but *this*"—he produced a tentacle and motioned at the pool—"took some doing. *You* try to shoot a pod into a swimming pool from fifty thousand miles out. And not have it do major damage. *And* have it look like a natural meteor on the way down."

"It was a nice touch," I said.

"It was, wasn't it?" Gwedif agreed. "A pain in the ass, you should pardon the expression, as I obviously don't have an ass to have a pain in. But we have to do it that way if we want to land near a city. You can fool some of the Air Force all of the time, and all of the Air Force some of the time, but you can't fool all of the Air Force all of the time. Better this way than shot down by a Stealth fighter. Of course, there *is* the problem of getting back. *That* thing"—he pointed to the detritus at the bottom of the pool—"isn't moving anywhere it's not hauled."

"So how are you getting back?" I asked.

"Well, we've scheduled a rendezvous near Baker for later tonight. There's nothing out there in the desert, so we don't have to worry about rubberneckers. Even so, we'll probably light up the radar something fierce. It's going to have to be quick in, quick out. I was hoping I could get you to drop me off."

"Of course," I said.

"And also that you'd come with me," Gwedif said.

"What?"

"Come on, Carl," Gwedif said. "You can't possibly think I came this far just for a quick hello. We have serious stuff to talk about, and it will go much, much faster if you come to the ship."

Even though I had known Gwedif for a very short time, I could tell that he was holding back on something. He wanted to have me come to the ship, all right, but I had a feeling it was for more than just a chat. I had the immediate brain flash to the alien abduction cliché, strapped down to the table while a blob of Jell-O readied the rectal probe. But that wouldn't have made any sense. You don't act all friendly with someone just to get them for lab experiments. They would have just grabbed me.

And anyway, I *wanted* to go. Are you kidding? Who wouldn't?

That morning, I phoned for a taxi and went to a used car lot in Burbank to get a cheap, nondescript car. I paid two thousand dollars and got a twenty-year-old pickup. I then went to a pick-a-part place and pulled the license plates off of a wreck. Finally, I pried the Vehicle Identification Number off the dashboard. I didn't know if Gwedif was right about the radar being lit up when they came to pick us up, but I didn't want my own car there if anyone came to investigate.

At about eight o'clock we set off down the 10, towards the 15, out to Baker in the middle of nowhere. Gwedif spread himself out under the bottom of the truck seat and popped a tendril over the back to see and talk. The truck wasn't worth nearly what I had paid for it; it almost died twice on the way out, and once I did an emergency stop into a gas station to add water to the radiator.

About five miles to Baker, Gwedif had me exit the 15 and take a frontage road for a few miles until we came to an unmarked road heading south. We drove along that for another four or five miles, until literally the only lights I could see were my headlights and the lights of the stars above me.

"All right," Gwedif said, finally. "This is the place."

I stopped the pickup and looked around.

"I don't see anything," I said.

"They're on their way," Gwedif said. "Give them another three seconds."

The ground shook. Thirty yards to the left of us, a black,

featureless cube twenty feet to a side had dropped unceremoniously from the sky. The ground cracked where it landed.

"Hmmm . . . a little early," Gwedif said.

I peered over to the cube, which, disregarding the fact it had just fallen from the heavens, was severely lacking in grandeur. "Doesn't look like much," I said.

"Of course it doesn't," Gwedif said, transferring from behind the seat. "We'll save all the pretty lights for when we want to have our formal introduction. For now, we just want to get up and out without attracting attention. Ready?"

I started to open the door.

"Where are you going?" Gwedif asked.

"I thought we were leaving," I said.

"We are," Gwedif said. "Drive into it. We can't very well leave this car in the middle of nowhere. Someone might find it. That's why I had them send an economy-sized box."

"I wish I'd known," I said. "I would have brought the Mercedes."

"I wish you had," Gwedif said. "Air conditioning is a good thing."

I turned the wheel and drove gingerly towards the black cube. When the bumper nudged against the cube's surface, I lightly tapped on the gas pedal. There was a slight resistance, and then almost a tearing as the cube's surface enveloped the pickup.

Then we were inside the cube. The inside was dimly it, from luminescence coming off the walls. The space was utterly nondescript, the only architectural feature being a platform ten feet up that I couldn't see onto, since we were underneath it.

"When do we leave?" I asked.

Gwedif stretched out a tendril to touch the nearest wall. "We already have," he said.

"Really?" I said. "I wish this thing had windows. I'd like to see where we're going."

"Okay," Gwedif said. The cube disappeared. I screamed. The cube reappeared, transparent but visibly tinted.

"Sorry," Gwedif said. "Shouldn't have made it completely clear. Didn't mean to freak you out."

I gathered my wits, rolled down the window, and stared down at the planet, which was tinted purple by the shaded cube.

"How far up are we?" I asked.

"About five hundred miles," Gwedif said. "We have to go slow for the first few miles, but once we're up about ten miles, nobody's looking anymore and we can really pick up speed."

"Can I leave the truck? I mean, will the floor support me?"

"Sure," Gwedif said. "It's supporting the truck, after all."

I opened the door and *very* carefully placed a foot on the cube floor and added weight to it. It felt slightly spongy, like a wrestling mat or a taut trampoline, but it indeed held my weight. I stepped fully outside, leaving the truck door open, and walked away from the pickup. I looked up, and I was able to see through the platform; on the other side of it were two other blobs, also with tendrils extending into the walls—the pilot and copilot, I assumed.

After a few minutes of walking around, I had Gwedif make the cube totally transparent. For the briefest of seconds, I felt a surge of panic again, but it was immediately replaced by the most astounding sense of exhilaration—a God's-eye view of the planet, unencumbered by spacesuit or visor. I asked Gwedif if there was artificial gravity in the cube and he said that there was; I asked him if we could cut it off so I could float, but he demurred. He said he'd prefer not to have the pickup floating around aimlessly. They did decrease the gravity to match the spaceship that we were going to; suddenly I was forty pounds lighter. After a few more minutes I asked them to retint the cube—my forebrain had accepted I was safe, but the reptile regions were having trouble with it.

The flight was a little under a half-hour long; we slowed appreciably as we approached the spaceship although I of course didn't feel the deceleration. But I *saw* it—one moment I was staring at the blackness of space, and the next a huge rock came hurtling at me, not unlike the meteor had the night before. I cringed involuntarily, but suddenly it appeared to stop, hovering what seemed a few miles away.

"There it is," Gwedif said. "Home sweet home."

It was impossible for me to judge how big this asteroid-turned-spaceship was. As we got closer, I guessed that it must be close to a mile in diameter, a guess that was confirmed by Gwedif to be in the right ballpark. The asteroid appeared to have no nonnatural features, but as we approached, I saw featureless black streaks dotting the surface. We were heading towards one.

"Does the ship have a name?" I asked.

"Yes," Gwedif said. "Give me a second to translate it." He was quiet for a moment, then, "It's called the *Ionar*. It's the name of our first sentient ancestor, like an Adam or Eve for you. It also means 'explorer' or 'teacher' in a loose sense of those words, in that Ionar, realizing he was the first of his kind, learned as much as he could about the world so that his"—another pause here—"*children* could know as much as possible. His exploration is our culture's first and greatest memory epic. We thought that his name would be a good one for this ship. Provident. That reminds me, we should plug your nose before we go out into the ship."

"Excuse me?" I said.

"We communicate with smells," Gwedif said. "When I said I had to translate, I meant that I had to translate the smells that we associate with a concept into an auditory analogue. But only a few of us know this translation as yet—and obviously the rest of us will be speaking our 'mother tongue.' But I don't think that you'll find our conversation very appealing to your senses."

"I wouldn't want to be rude," I said.

"Well, here," Gwedif said. "Here's how we say *Ionar*." A smell erupted from Gwedif like fart from a dog. "And here's how I say my name." The fart this time came from a larger dog than the first. My eyes watered.

"Now, keep in mind that there's a couple thousand of us in this ship," Gwedif said.

"I see your point," I said.

"I thought you might. I'll make arrangements. Look, we're about to dock."

Our cube was coming to rest on the edge of one of the black surfaces, about a hundred yards long and half as wide. Underneath the surface of the cube, the black surface thinned out and cleared away, leaving what seemed to be an airtight seal around the outside of the cube. The cube dropped slowly through the seal. As we cleared the skin, I could see that we were dropping into a cavernous hangar about a hundred feet deep. The hangar was dimly lit, and as far as I could see there weren't any other cubes or anything else that might resemble a ship.

I thought about asking Gwedif about it, but then there was

a gentle thump and we landed. Almost instantly the cube began to melt; a circular hole started in the center and became wider, with the residue sliding down the walls of the cube, which were themselves sliding away. The Yherajk on the piloting platform slid down the walls a fraction of a second before the walls dripped away like wax; the platform itself sucked into the wall and disappeared. The mass of the cube lay in huge mounds on the floor of the hangar; then were suddenly absorbed, leaving me, the three Yherajk, and the pickup. The whole process took less than a minute.

"Interesting," I said.

"Yup," said Gwedif. "We grow 'em when we need 'em. Making a cube, though, takes slightly longer than breaking one down."

From a near wall a door appeared and a Yherajk stepped out and approached us. It was carrying what looked like cotton wads in a tentacle. It came up to Gwedif, touched him briefly, and presented the cotton wads to me.

I took them. "Do I eat these?"

"I don't think you'd want to," Gwedif said. "Stuff them in your nose instead."

I did and immediately felt the 'cotton' expand, totally blocking my nasal passages. I suppressed the urge to sneeze.

The Yherajk who presented me with the wads exited, as did the pilots, after briefly touching Gwedif.

"Now," Gwedif said, after we were alone. "Oewij, who came with the nose plugs, tells me that the ship-wide meeting has been arranged at our communion hall, and that our presence is requested immediately. However, I feel that it is only fair and courteous to allow you some time to collect yourself or even sleep if you so desire. I know you've haven't had much rest since we've met. Or, if you'd like, I can arrange for the tour of the ship. It's up to you, really."

"I'm not tired," I said. "I'd love a tour of the ship, though. May I have a tour after the meeting?"

"Of course," Gwedif said.

"Well, then," I said. "Let's go have a meeting."

Gwedif and I entered the *Ionar* through the same door that the other Yherajk disappeared into. I had to duck to get through the door and then had to hunch down as we walked down several corridors; the ceiling was about an inch shorter than I was tall. I suppose that this would make sense: the Yherajk are not exactly tall. These corridors must have seemed roomy to them.

Gwedif sensed my discomfort. "Sorry about this," he said. "I should have gotten us a transport so that you could sit. But I thought you might want to experience a little of the ship on the way to the communion room."

"It's all right," I said, looking around. The corridors appeared carved out of the rock of the asteroid, and didn't have ornamentation of any sort, like the hangar we had just been in. I mentioned this to Gwedif.

"You're right," he said. "The Yherajk have never been much for visuals. While we see quite well by your standards, it's not our primary sense to the world, like it is to you. But the walls here have scent guides, which function in the same manner. And this isn't to say we have no artistic impulses. Later on, when we tour the ship, I'll take you to our art gallery. We have some *tivis* there which are really quite nice."

"What are *tivis?*" I asked.

Gwedif stopped for a second, suddenly enough that I braked myself, reflexively straightening up and bumping my head in the process. "I'm trying to think if there's a human analogue, and I'm not coming up with one," Gwedif said. "I guess the closest words in English to what they are would be 'Smell Paintings,' but that's not quite right, either. Oh, well," he started off again, "you'll get it when you see them—or more accurately, smell them." I hurried off after him.

A few more corridors, and then we stopped outside a door. "Here we are," Gwedif said. "Now, Carl, nearly every Yherajk who is on the ship is in here now. I want to know if you're prepared."

"I think I can wrap my mind around it," I said.

"I'm not talking about *that*," Gwedif said. "I just wanted to make sure your nose plugs are secure. It's pretty stinky in there."

"I feel like my nose is filled with cement," I said.

"Okay. Let's go in, then." He extended a tendril to the door. At his touch, it opened inward.

Two things struck me immediately as we stepped through. The first was that the Yherajk tradition of visual monotony continued unabated—the room consisted of an unadorned dome over a large circular floor that sloped downward to where a small central dais jutted up modestly, itself unadorned. On the floor, large clumps of Yherajk assembled here and there, pretty much like humans do before a meeting gets down to business.

The second thing was that even through my nose plugs, the smell of the room slammed into me like a rocket in the chest. It was as if someone had fermented an entire horse stable. It was unbelievably strong. I leaned back against the wall.

"You all right?" Gwedif asked.

"I think I'm getting a buzz from the smell," I said. "And not in a good way."

"It's because everyone's talking at the moment. It'll get better when we start the meeting and everyone shuts up," he said. "For now, just take deep breaths."

In the middle distance, a Yherajk broke from the clump and approached us. It briefly touched Gwedif—I was beginning to think this was their way of greeting or saluting each other—and then extended a tendril at me. I looked at Gwedif.

"Carl, this is Uake," Gwedif said. "Uake is the *Ionar's ientcio*—our leader in both ship's operations and social interactions. A captain and a priest. He welcomes you and hopes that you have had an interesting visit so far. He'd like to shake your hand."

I extended my hand, let Uake's tentacle envelop it, and shook. "Thank you, ientcio. It has been a very interesting visit, and I thank you for allowing me the honor to make the visit to begin with." I directed my comments directly to Uake, assuming Gwedif would translate, without prompting.

He did. "I've passed the message on and added my own comment that we should start the meeting soon, before you pass out from the fumes. To you, Uake says that the honor is ours, that you would visit. To me, he says that if we will accompany him to the dais, we will begin the meeting and get the rabble under control. Shall we?"

Uake, Gwedif and I walked through the crowd to the dais. As we arrived, three Yherajk also arrived, carrying a block of something, and set it on the dais.

"I thought you might like to have something to sit on," Gwedif said. "We don't have any chairs, but this should work just as well." I thanked him and took my seat. Uake took up a position on the far side of the dais from me, and Gwedif sat between us.

Some signal scent must have gone up, because the Yherajk on the floor broke up their clumps and encircled the dais, forming concentric rings. The room became noticeably less smelly; everyone must have shut up.

"The ientcio is about to begin his speech," Gwedif said. "He has asked me once again to translate for him so that you will understand what is being said. The translation will not be exact, I'm afraid—Uake will be using a lot of High Speech, which we use to quickly pass along large amounts of information. But I'll be able to give you the gist of it. If you have any questions, let me know—our talking isn't going to disturb the speech." He fell silent for a few minutes and then started speaking again, starting and stopping as Uake made his statements.

"The ientcio welcomes all to the meeting, with the hope that this moment of our journey finds them all well and at peace with themselves. He asks us all to look back on that moment, over seventy years ago now—your years—when the first faint signals of intelligence from this world were picked up by our scientific arrays, and the confusion, turmoil, joy and fear that those signals, first sound, then picture, brought to our race.

"He asks us also to remember the day when this ship began its journey to this place, our people's emissary to a people so strange and unlike ourselves. The ship was to serve two purposes: to learn about those people, to find if they could be communicated with; and if they could, then to make contact, with the hope of joining our two peoples in friendship and comity.

"The ientcio now recounts the difficulties of the journey—its length, both in distance and time, a number of accidents that diminished the number of the crew and caused damage to the ship, and the mutiny attempt that resulted in the soul death of

Echwar, our first ientcio, and the loss of a tenth of the crew. This recounting is made to remind us even in this moment of happiness that we must not lose sight of all that this journey has required of us.

"Now, the ientcio says, our journey comes to the cusp, in which we learn if our efforts form a memory epic for all Yherajk, to be told in the days when our race is old and the stars red with age, or if they disappear into darkness. We have made contact with one of the humans, one who we believe will be wise, and whose actions will determine our path. It is difficult to assign our fates to the will of one who is not one of us, but that is the way of such encounters as these—though we prepare for the moment, the moment itself is not a thing we can control."

Tom, I was dumbfounded by what I was hearing. These creatures had traveled across the stars, over unimaginable distances. And if what I was hearing was correct, the success or failure of their trip was being placed into *my* hands. It was a burden that I didn't want or even frankly that I understood. I asked Gwedif if I was comprehending correctly what was being said.

"Oh, yes," Gwedif said. "Your actions in this meeting will determine what happens to us and to our journey. It's something that we've known for a long time, and something that is characteristic of the Yherajk—the surrender of control in the hope that the moment germinates into something greater. This is that moment."

"Wait a minute," I said, becoming angry. "I didn't come up here to play God for you. You're asking me to do something I don't know that I can do. I don't even *know* what it is that you want me to do, much less if I can do it. I feel like I've been tricked."

Gwedif sprouted a tentacle and placed it on my hand.

"Carl," he said, "you're not being asked to play God. Your part is about to be explained. If you refuse it, then we go back home, and our people plan a new way to try to contact your people. That's all. We're not going to launch our ship into the sun if we fail—the drama you hear is part of the formal nature of High Speech. You've been around me enough to know we don't usually talk like that. But we *do* need your perspective on this. You know your people like we could never know them. We need to see through you whether we can make contact with humans here and now. Do you understand a little better now?"

I nodded.

"All right," Gwedif said. "The ientcio is speaking to you now. He formally welcomes you to the *Ionar,* wishes you happiness at this moment in your journey, and presents to you the host of the ship, the crew of the *Ionar,* and hopes that you will acknowledge them thusly."

"How do I do that?" I asked.

"Got me," Gwedif said. "No human's ever done it before. Try waving, and I'll wing the speechifying."

I stood and waved. Two thousand Yherajk sprouted tentacles and waved back.

"I have said that you acknowledge the host of the ship and wish them happiness at this moment of the journey," Gwedif said. "It's more or less the correct response and doesn't commit you to anything further. Was that all right?"

"Yes," I said, sitting back down.

"Good," Gwedif said. "Uake is now speaking to you about the journey, and what we have learned of your people through your radio and television transmissions. What he's saying is completely untranslatable due to the complexity of the High

Speech structures he is using, but the upshot of it is that while your transmissions point to a rich and fascinating culture, we also have found them contradictory and confusing at the same time. There is no structure to your planet's transmissions into space."

"Well, it's *television*, you know," I said. "It's meant to be understood by humans and not intended for anyone else. You're just getting the leakage. I do believe that we have a scientific program that is beaming messages for alien cultures into outer space, but that's the only thing that's intended for nonhuman audiences."

"The ientcio wishes to inform you that we have indeed received those messages from SETI and have found them . . . amusing is probably the best word. Television is much more interesting."

It was a good thing Carl Sagan wasn't alive to hear those words. Gwedif continued. "The ientcio says that we have found that we have been able to learn something of you from television and radio. Some of us, and I am obviously being referred to here, have learned English, and have begun to piece together something of a world and cultural history of your planet.

"But we have become aware that we have been quite unable to make a clear distinction between what is factual and what is fictional—what represents your true culture and what constitutes your imaginings. We understand the distinction, for example, between your news reports and your entertainment programs. But we lack the context to tell which is the exaggeration of the other. This is a source of frustration for us—to the Yherajk, you can at times seem to be a culture of pathological liars, unable yourselves to tell the difference between truth and falsity. You can see how that can make us nervous to initiate contact. We need someone to help us create a context, so we can separate the truth from the lies and make an accurate reckoning of the status of your planet.

"This is of specific interest to us as it relates to your planet's tendencies towards the idea of alien contact. The SETI program implies that your planet is actively seeking contact with other peoples, but your entertainments show you to be hostile to the idea, full of the fear that the peoples you encounter will try to subjugate your planet. Moreover, when you do show aliens as friendly or benevolent, they tend to be humanoid in appearance. When they are hostile or violent, they tend to appear like us. Obviously, this is very worrying."

"I think you are underestimating the influence of special effects budgets on that particular question," I said.

"The ientcio agrees that this might be the case," Gwedif said. "Again it comes to a question of context and knowledge of the culture. He hopes that now you may understand our predicament.

"You are one of the most powerful men in the industry that creates the programs that are beamed off of your planet, and have become so because of your character and intelligence. You are in a unique position to help us understand the distinctions between what is real and what is fanciful, between the things that your planet hopes for and the things that your planet fears. It is his hope, and he wishes to stress, the hope of every Yherajk on this ship, that you would be able to help us in our efforts to understand your people, to give us a grounding in the reality of humanity that only a human can."

I blinked. "Is that it? You want *advice*?"

"For starters," Gwedif said.

"Well, of course I'll help you with that any way I can," I said. "But I don't know how much help that will be. You understand that even humans don't understand humanity most of the time. I could tell you everything I know, but it would only be my opinion. And it would take years to get it all down at that."

"The ientcio understands that you are just one man among billions. Nevertheless, of those billions, you are one whose skills and mind lend themselves most favorably to our needs. As for taking years to know what you know—" Gwedif stopped for a moment, seemed to collect himself.

"As for taking years," he continued, "we have another way."

Tom, did Joshua ever tell you how the Yherajk reproduce? No? Well, I'm not too surprised about that; it's an immensely personal event. On the cell level, all Yherajk are the same—massive colonies of asexually reproducing, single-celled organisms. But their experiences are different and unique to each Yherajk. Think of them as a race of identical twins, sharing the same genetic information but obviously separate people, divided by their individual experiences.

When humans learned about genetics, they began arguing whether people are the way they are due to genetics or environment; what our genes are versus our experiences. With the Yherajk, this isn't even a debate—since they're all the same genetically, who they are is all about experiences. Personality is all.

Yherajk personalities are remarkable things. For example, once they are formed, they can be transferred. Their personalities don't have to stay in a particular body. That personality and set of experiences can go from one body to another—if, for example, that body were dying of disease or something else of that nature. Yherajk do a much simplified version of this when they transmit information; a single Yherajk can go off and have a set of experiences, and when it comes back, it connects with an entire group and "downloads" its memories to the whole group. Then all the Yherajk there know what that one knew.

But it requires physical contact and takes a great deal of time. The Yherajk High Speech, which is an even more simplified version of this, performs the same function by encoding a concept as an aromatic molecule, which is then set aloft and automatically decoded by the Yherajk who come in contact with it. It'd be like having an entire memory created in your head simply by someone saying a word. Fascinating stuff, Tom.

In Yherajk reproduction, the personalities do something else entirely—they *meld* with another personality. The Yherajk join together into one mass, and, rather than simply transferring information or even a "soul" from one body to another, the individual souls interact over the entire mass of their combined body. Some portions of one personality end up being dominant, and other portions from the other personality end up being dominant.

After those personality traits are figured out, the mass splits into two parts. One of those parts splits again and becomes the original Yherajk that had melded, with its own personality traits and memory intact, but physically smaller than it was before. The other part is an entirely new personality: it has the memories and intellect of its parents, but it comes with a brand new "soul," if you will, made of the new, melded personality, and it's ready to go—there's no childhood, per se, with the Yherajk.

This melding isn't easy—it requires the Yherajk in question to surrender its will and allow another entity, another soul, to mingle freely with its own. This other soul surrenders to you and you to it—complete communion. But with the ultimate risk: a Yherajk's defenses are down—the other Yherajk, if it has been insincere in the joining, can attack the other's personality and destroy it, replacing it totally with its own. This is a "soul death," and causing it to happen is the worst crime a Yherajk can commit against another Yherajk. A large part of the reluctance of the Yherajk to speak about their reproduction comes from its potential to change in an instant from an act of perfect union to one of the ultimate rape.

But it's rare—far more rare than murder is with us. Most of the time, it is a joyous experience—and apparently better for them than sex is for us.

The interesting thing is that while nearly all reproductions occur between two Yherajk, there is no theoretical barrier to having the melding occur between three, four, or even more. It's vastly more complicated, and it takes longer for the personality traits to suss out, but it can be done. Gwedif told me that one of the great memory epics of the Yherajk involved an exploring colony, under siege from attackers, who all melded together in the desperate hope of birthing a hero who could save them from destruction. The colony numbered four hundred. It worked—of course. Otherwise it wouldn't be an epic. For millennia, partially out of respect for the epic, that had been the record.

The ientcio of the *Ionar* was planning to break that record.

He proposed two thousand—the entire crew of the *Ionar*. And one human as well.

"*I'm* not following you," I said to Gwedif, after he translated the ientcio's proposal.

"The ientcio implores you to meld with us," Gwedif said. "Pool your knowledge with ours and help us birth a new Yherajk—one that has an intimate understanding of humanity, who can help us learn, quickly, easily, whether our two people can be joined in friendship. It would be a great gift—and you would be remembered not only as our first human friend, but also a parent, the most important parent, of the greatest Yherajk in our race's long history. As he will be—one that two thousand of us have surrendered our wills to create. It is a powerful event."

I looked out into the mass of Yherajk, and got the distinct impression that two thousand of them were waiting for me to say something. Anything. Tom, I got stage fright. But there was nowhere to go.

I stalled for time. "I don't know if you noticed this," I said, "but I'm not a Yherajk. I don't meld very well."

"With your permission, the ientcio says," Gwedif said, "I will act as your conduit."

"What does that mean?" I asked.

Gwedif paused for a moment. "Aw, hell," he said at last. "Uake has just sent some High Speech crap that I'm not even going to try to translate. Carl, what it means is that I'd stick tendrils into your brain, read your memories, and transmit them to the rest of the crew. Bluntly speaking, I'll be rooting around your skull, looking for the good stuff."

"It sounds painful," I said.

"It won't be, I promise," Gwedif said. "But you're going to feel stuffed-up like you wouldn't believe. Carl, don't misunderstand, I'll be effectively downloading your brain to the group. In the melding union, there are no secrets—and the offspring of this melding will know what you know. We know we're asking a lot of you, more than has been asked of any of us. If you don't want to do this, then don't."

"What will happen if I say no?" I asked.

"Nothing," Gwedif said. "We would never try to compel you to a melding."

I looked out at the crew. "And every one of you is willing to do this?"

"We are."

"What if one of you tries to take over the rest? Isn't that possible? What would happen to me?"

"You'll be connecting to the group through me," Gwedif said. "If one of us tried to overtake the entire crew, I'd disconnect before he could overtake you. I'd *probably* have time." That qualifier disturbed me, but Gwedif went on. "But I'd say it's highly unlikely that someone will do that. For one thing, it'd wipe out the entire crew; whoever did it would never get back home. For another thing—Carl, this is *epic* stuff. If this works, this is going down in our history as one of the defining moments of our people. We'll be famous forever. Believe me, none of us wants to be the one that screws *that* up."

"Will I be able to read all your crew's thoughts?" I asked.

"No," Gwedif said. "I'm going to be translating your thoughts—I won't have time to translate the other way. You'll experience all our thoughts, they just won't make a lick of sense. It will be the weirdest trip you'll ever take, my friend."

"Well," I said. "When you put it that way, how can I refuse?"

"Then you'll do it?" Gwedif asked.

"If you will be my conduit, Gwedif, I'll be honored. Translate that exactly to your ientcio," I said.

Gwedif apparently did—the room became filled with the odor of distilled dumpster juice. I asked Gwedif what was going on.

"The crew is applauding, Carl," Gwedif said. "They're relieved and happy. They didn't just spend half of their lives traveling here for nothing. I lied a little to you, Carl—if you hadn't accepted, it would have been a crushing disappointment for us all. But I didn't want to burden you with that sort of guilt. Sorry to be sneaky."

"That's all right," I said. "I don't mind. It'll help me to recognize your thoughts during the melding—I'll look for the sneaky ones."

"I won't be able to meld myself," Gwedif said. "I have to manage your thoughts. That requires me to remain fully alert during the whole thing. In fact, of all the crew, I'll be the only one that won't be melding."

I was dismayed. "I'm very sorry, Gwedif," I said. "If I had known, I'd have asked for someone else to act as the conduit. I don't want you not be part of it."

"My friend," Gwedif said. "Please. I am honored that you have chosen me as your conduit, more than you know. In doing so, you have allowed me to be the only one truly conscious during the melding—the only one who will see the event as it happens. When this story becomes our memory epic, the eyes that it will be seen through are mine."

Gwedif sprouted a tendril and waved it at the crew. "This crew will be *in* the memory epic. But I will *write* it—and thus I will live forever through it, the Homer of this, my people's greatest Odyssey. You have given me a great gift, Carl, and for it, I cannot thank you enough, you, my friend, my great and true friend."

"Well," I said. "You're welcome, then."

"Great," Gwedif said. He sprouted another tendril, and wiggled both of them at me. "Now, you have to take out those plugs—I've got to stick these up your nose."

"You're kidding," I said.

"Not at all," he said. "This might sting a little."

I won't try to describe the melding, Tom, except to say—try to remember the most vivid, wild, erotic dream you have ever had. Now try to imagine it entirely as a clutch of smells, colliding, sliding, fading into each other. Now imagine it going on for a lifetime. That's what it felt like.

I woke up, still on the dais, with three Yherajk around me. I asked for Gwedif. The one to my right waved a tentacle.

"Did it work?" I asked.

"It did," Gwedif said, and motioned to the Yherajk near my feet. "Carl, please meet the progeny of two thousand Yherajk—and one human."

"Hello," I said to the Yherajk.

"Hi, Pop," he said.

"The ientcio"—Gwedif indicated the final Yherajk—"wishes to thank you once again for your great help and understanding, and assures you that you will undoubtedly become one of the great heroes of our race, something which *I* can tell you is already taken care of."

"Thank him, and thank *you*," I said to Gwedif.

"No problem," Gwedif said. "The ientcio also wishes you to know that the honor of naming this newborn Yherajk belongs to you, as the Initiating Parent."

"Thanks, but it was Uake's idea," I said. "I can't claim credit."

"Sure," Gwedif said, "but your acceptance of the proposal in this case has been agreed by all the parents to be the initiating act. So it's back to you. However, the ientcio, anticipating your reluctance, does indeed have a name picked out, which will be given to the newborn if you agree."

"What is it?" I asked.

"We wanted a name that reflected the importance of this Yherajk to us, and hopefully his eventual importance to your own people, one that was immediately recognizable. What do you think of 'Jesus'?"

I laughed unintentionally.

"See," The Yherajk Who Would Be Jesus said. "I told them it wasn't going to fly. But what do *I* know? I'm a *newborn*." The sarcasm in his statement was unmistakable.

"It would be a very bad idea," I said. "About half the folks on the planet would get very touchy about it."

"Nuts," Gwedif said. "Can you give us something else?"

I could. "Jesus" is the Latinized version of "Joshua"—a name that's still in use, of course, and without the same religious overtones. It was also the name of my father, and, incidentally, of the baby that Sarah was carrying when she died—we found out it was a boy the month before. Elise and I aren't planning to have children, Tom. So this Yherajk, which was only the smallest fraction of me, and only of my thoughts at that, was nevertheless the only "child" I was likely to have. The name "Joshua" had long been with me, and I was happy to finally give it a new home. Joshua was happy with it, too. Of course he would be—he would know what it means to me.

After I had named Joshua, Uake excused himself to attend to ship's duties. As we shook "hands," I managed a glance at my watch. It was 11:30 in the morning.

"Uh-oh," I said. "I have to go."

"You haven't had a tour of the ship," Gwedif said.

"Don't bother," Joshua said. "These people just do *not* know how to decorate."

"I'd love to, but I'm late," I said. "I already missed a day yesterday. By now my assistant Marcella has called my house looking for me. If I don't show up at the office today, she's going to file a missing persons report."

"Well, there's a problem," Gwedif said. "It's daytime now. We can't really risk being seen doing a drop."

"So don't do a drop," Joshua said. "Make it a one-way trip."

"We could do that," Gwedif said. "But there's a problem with that, too."

"What's that?" I asked.

"It depends," Joshua said. "How well can you control your sphincter muscles?"

Gwedif explained it as we headed to the hangar. They could build an unmanned cube the size of the pickup, launch it, and have it land near where we had departed. But, as with the "meteor" and the black cube, it would have to arrive full-speed to avoid being picked up on radar for any length of time. Another thing: the cube would have to be transparent.

"Why?" I asked.

"Black cubes in the daytime sky are suspicious," Gwedif said. "Red pickups in the daytime sky are merely unbelievable. Even if someone saw it, no one would know what to think of it. And that's not a bad thing."

"Good thing you haven't had anything to eat in a while," Joshua said.

A few minutes later, as I prepared to get behind the wheel of my pickup, I said my good-byes to Gwedif and Joshua. I asked Gwedif when or if I would see him again.

"Probably not for a while," Gwedif said. "When we send someone again, it will be Joshua. But even he will stay here for a few months, to benefit us with your knowledge—now his—as to how to approach humanity. We probably won't see each other until the day our race makes its debut. But I look forward to that day, Carl. I will be happy when it arrives. We'll finally take that stroll through the tivis gallery."

"I can't wait," I said, and then turned to Joshua. "I look forward to seeing you again, then."

"Thanks, Pop," Joshua said. "It'll be soon. Get a better car by then."

I got into the pickup; immediately a cube began to grow around the truck. It indeed took longer to make a cube than to break it down, but not by much; within five minutes I was entirely enclosed. Then the cube became totally transparent, and it was as if it wasn't there at all. I looked at Gwedif and Joshua and waved. They waved back.

Suddenly I was flung into space, the *Ionar* receding behind me like a fastball thrown by a titan. The large blue plate that was the planet Earth began to grow at a distressing rate.

It didn't get bad until the last minute, as the pickup showed no signs of slowing down and the surface of the planet became ever more sharply defined. The last five seconds I couldn't even watch—I covered my eyes and sobbed out the Lord's Prayer.

And then I was just off the unmarked road I and Gwedif were picked up from. I didn't feel the landing, but when I opened my eyes, dust was swirling around and there was cracked earth underneath my pickup that matched the cracked earth on the other side of the road.

I started the pickup and went home. Then I went to work. Marcella said that if I hadn't arrived in those last ten minutes, she had been planning to call the FBI.

CHAPTER
Eleven

Carl looked at his watch. "Damn," he said. "I've missed my 4:00."

"The *Call of the Damned* premiere was four months ago, Carl," I said. "What have they been doing between now and then?"

"Grilling Joshua, I'd imagine," Carl said. "Remember, he's got my memories—it's better than having me there, really, since I don't know that I'd be up for a daily brain-sucking. It's with Joshua that the Yherajk came up with the idea of using us to be their agents."

"I don't get that," I said. "If they have all your knowledge, I don't see why they would need you or me to do anything for them."

"Well, they *are* still gelatinous cubes," Carl said, "which does limit their ability to blend in. But I think there's something else to it. I think they have a plan already, but they wanted to see what I, and now you, would come up with. For them, it's not simply a matter of the most efficient way of doing something, otherwise Joshua would be addressing the UN right now. But there's that notion the Yherajk have of surrendering to the crucial moment, burned right down into their reproductive strategies. I think that once again, they're surrendering the moment to us—they're saying, here, we trust you to take this, the most important moment in the history of both our races, and make it work."

"That's a lot of trust," I said.

"Yes, well, frankly it's also annoying," Carl said. "I'm not saying that we should refuse the responsibility, not at all. But we're carrying the entire load—if it gets messed up, the failure is entirely on our shoulders. All the pressure is on us. On you, actually, Tom, since I foisted it on you. Have you, since we started this, *really* thought on what we're doing here?"

"I've tried to avoid doing that," I said. "It just makes me sort of dizzy. I try to concentrate on the smaller things, like hoping that Joshua will turn up sometime today."

"That's probably the right attitude to have," Carl said. "Now, *I* think about it quite a bit. It's monumental and exhilarating—and I wish it were already done with."

"It's going to work out fine, Carl. Don't worry about it," I said. I was taken aback by Carl's comment—it didn't sound like the Carl Lupo we all knew and feared.

Carl must have realized it, because he suddenly gave a wolf-like grin, true to his name. "I can tell you these things, Tom, because we're both in on the biggest secret anyone's ever had—no one else would believe me. Or you. Who else are we going to tell these things to?"

"That's funny," I said. "Joshua once said the very same thing."

"Like father, like son," Carl said, and stood up. "Now, come on, Tom. We have to head back. I can't keep Rupert waiting much longer. He gets testy when he's stood up."

"*Three* and a half hours for lunch?" Miranda said, as she followed me into the office. "Even by Hollywood standards, that's a little extravagant. Your boss would kill you, if it weren't for the fact you had lunch with him."

"Sorry, Mom," I said. "I'll do all of my homework before I go out tonight."

"Don't get fresh," Miranda said, "or you'll get no dessert. Would you like to hear your messages, or do you want to give me more lip?"

"Oh, I'd like messages, pretty please," I said, sitting.

"That's better," Miranda said. "You have six, count them, six messages from Jim Van Doren. In one two hour-period before your lunch. I think that qualifies as stalking by California law."

"I should be so lucky," I said. "What does he want?"

"Didn't say. Didn't sound particularly happy, however. I suspect if he hasn't been raked over the coals by his editors at *The Biz,* he may be in the process of being torched right now. Carl called me this morning to get some information on the mentor program of yours. He mentioned that he was planning to rip Van Doren and *The Biz* new assholes in the *Times.* Not promising for either of them, if you ask me."

"God," I said. "That's just going to make them both more annoying. Anyone else?"

"Michelle called. She's apparently having some sort of difficulty with the *Earth Resurrected* folks. She said something about a latex mask. It didn't make much sense to me. She also said that Ellen Merlow is definitely out of *Hard Memories*, and that she now felt she was up to the role, because she read 'Iceman in Jerusalem.'" Miranda looked up at me, confused. "She can't possibly mean *Eichmann in Jerusalem*."

"Give her a break, Miranda," I said. "She got two-thirds of the title."

Miranda snorted. "Yeah, well, and I bet she's averaging that for the rest of the words, too. Anyway, she'll be calling back later. Last message, from your mysterious friend Joshua. He says he's fine now, and not to call, he's busy at the moment but he'll be there when you get there, whatever that means. Dealing with shady characters again, Tom?"

"You have no idea," I said. Why wasn't I supposed to call? Despite Joshua's reassurance, I was worried. I fought the urge to grab the phone right off. I decided to think about another entirely futile task instead. "Miranda, could you get Roland Lanois on the horn for me?"

"Absolutely. Who is he?"

"Miranda," I said, pretending shock. "You're so low-class. He's the director and producer of the Academy Award–nominated motion picture *The Green Fields,* and also of the upcoming *Hard Memories.* His production company is on the Paramount lot, I believe."

"What?" Miranda said. "Tom, you can't be serious. You're not really going to try to get Michelle that part."

"Why not?" I said. "It's not totally outside the realm of possibility that she could get the role, you know."

Miranda rolled her eyes and looked up, with upturned palms. "Take me now, Jesus. I don't want to live here no more."

"Oh, stop it, and get Roland for me."

"Tom, the gods of common decency implore me to stop you from making this call."

"There's a ten percent raise in it for you if you get Roland on the phone for me, right now."

Miranda blinked. "Really?"

"Got it approved by Carl at lunch. So you have a choice. Common decency or a raise. Your call."

"Well, I've done my part for humanity for today," Miranda said. "Time to cash in."

"That's what I love about you, Miranda," I said. "Your firm bedrock of moral values."

Miranda did a little step as she exited the office. I smiled. Then I grabbed the phone and made a quick call to Joshua's cell phone.

No answer.

Roland was in a meeting but his assistant said that he'd be happy to chat if I wouldn't mind dropping by the offices in an hour. "Roland hates talking business over the phone," the assistant said. "He says he likes to have people within stabbing distance." It was already past 4:30; if I was going to make it to the Paramount lot in an hour, I'd have to leave at that moment. I left instructions with Miranda to call me immediately if Joshua called, and then headed out.

About halfway there, on Melrose, I realized that I was actually being tailed. A decrepit white Escort three cars behind me remained three cars behind me constantly; whenever one of the cars between us changed lanes, the Escort would swerve dangerously into another lane, let another car pass, and then swerve dangerously back into the lane, properly spaced. The constant honking that these maneuvers caused were what brought the car to my attention in the first place. In a way it was a relief—if it had been the government, or Mafia hit men, they wouldn't have been so inept.

I was coming up at a light; I purposely slowed down to miss the yellow—the first time that I could recall ever doing *that*—and when the light turned red I took the car out of gear, set the parking brake, popped the trunk, switched on my hazard lights and got out of the car. I reached into the trunk just as the driver behind me, in a rusted-out Monte Carlo, started yelling at me in Spanish. He stopped when he realized I pulled out an aluminum softball bat, left over from last season.

The guy in the white Escort didn't even see me coming; as I walked down the road, he was furtively talking into a cellular phone. The guy's white, pudgy features became recognizable as I got closer. It was Van Doren, of course.

I stopped at the driver-side window, flipped the bat around so I was holding the thick end, and rapped hard on the window with the handle end. Van Doren jumped at the noise and looked around, confused. It took him about five seconds to realize exactly who it was banging at his door. He spent another three seconds trying to figure out how to make a break for it before he realized he was boxed in. Finally, he smiled sheepishly and rolled down the window.

"Tom," he said, "isn't this a small world."

"Get out of your car, Jim," I said.

Van Doren's eyes made a beeline for the bat. "Why?"

"As long as you're following me, you're a danger to other motorists," I said. "I can't have anyone's death but yours on my conscience."

"I think I'll stay in my car," Van Doren said.

"Jim," I said. "If you don't get out of the car in exactly three seconds, I'm going to take this bat to your windshield."

"You wouldn't dare," Van Doren said. "You've got a whole street full of witnesses. With cameras on their phones."

"This is LA, Jim," I said. "No one's going to whip out their phones unless I'm wearing a badge. One. Two."

Van Doren hastily opened his door and undid his seat belt.

"All right," I said, once he had gotten out of his car. "Let's go. We'll take my car."

"What about my car?" Van Doren said. "I can't just leave it here."

"Sure you can," I said. "The police will come by any minute now to pick it up."

"Please," Van Doren said. "I *can't*. It's a company car."

"Should've thought of that earlier. Come on, Jim. Less talk. More walk. The light's changed already." I nudged him with my bat. He went. We got in my car and made it through the tail end of the next yellow, thus restoring my traffic karmic balance.

Van Doren watched as his Escort faded in the distance. "I want you know, this qualifies as kidnapping," he said.

"What are you talking about?" I said. "There I was, at a light, minding my own business, when you open my passenger side door and plop yourself into my car. You started asking me harassing questions. A real pain in the ass. But, of course, you've done this before. You left six messages at my office just today, in fact. I'm driving you around just to humor you. After all, you *are* acting erratic. If anyone's in danger here, Jim, it's me."

"You're forgetting the witnesses again," Van Doren said.

"Oh, come *on*," I said, getting into a left turn lane. "Anyone who *was* there has now gotten out from behind your car and driven off into the sunset. The only thing anyone's going to see is a deserted car in the middle of a major traffic artery. If I were you, Jim, I'd start making up a cover story right about now. Normally, I'd suggest saying you were carjacked, but no one's going to believe that. You were driving an *Escort*."

Van Doren stared at me for a few seconds, then buckled himself in, almost as an afterthought. "I think I was right," he said. "You *are* completely off your rocker."

I sighed and turned north. "No, Jim, but I *am* tired of you. Your story about me was a tissue of lies from start to finish. It caused two of my most important clients to bolt. There's not a single thing in it that's true, and you caused my career a lot of damage. I could probably sue you and *The Biz* for libel and get away with it."

"You'd have a hard time proving malice," Jim said.

"I don't think so," I said. "After all, you did come looking to profile me, and then, after I refused, this thing came out. Given the amount of utter bullshit that floats to the surface of your magazine each week, I think a good lawyer could probably convince a jury you were gunning for me. Bet our lawyers are better than your lawyers."

"Why are you threatening me?"

"Simple. I want you to leave me alone. I haven't ever done anything to you, or anything other than try to be the best agent for my clients. I don't use crack cocaine. I don't have sex with little boys. I don't cut up animals for fun. There's no story, Jim. Just leave me alone."

"Well, there's one problem here, Tom," Van Doren said. "I don't believe you. Maybe you're not losing it, though I doubt that at the moment. But you *are* up to something, and something weird." He held up a hand and started ticking off points.

"First, my boss got a phone call from the *Times* this morning about your 'mentor program.' They say Carl Lupo said that this program has been in place for a while. But I know for a *fact* that this isn't the case—my guy inside your company told me so."

"This wouldn't be the same 'inside guy' who used your story to snake one of my clients, would it?"

"I don't know anything about that," Jim said. "Though I have heard you broke another agent's nose the other day."

"It's not broken," I said. "Merely bruised."

"Second," Van Doren continued, "you had lunch with Carl Lupo today for over three hours. Three hours, Tom. The last time Carl Lupo did lunch for three hours, he joined Century Pictures as their president. Something is definitely up between the two of you."

"You watched us for three hours, having lunch?" I said. "Jim, you need to get a life."

Van Doren cracked a smile. "This may be so. Or maybe I have a life, chasing the biggest story in Hollywood, one that will actually get me away from writing lousy little pieces about agents that no one really cares about. You could just make it easy for me and tell me what it is, and then I'll leave you alone."

"Fine," I said. "Carl and I are laying the groundwork for an encounter between humans and space aliens. He even went up to their ship. I've got one of them boarding with me at home. His best friend is a dog."

"Uh-huh," Van Doren said. "I'm buying that one. A spaceship. Was Elvis there with Jim Morrison and Tupac Shakur?"

"Of course not," I said. "That's just plain silly."

"Right. I don't mind if you don't tell me, Tom," Van Doren said. "Just don't expect me not to follow it up. Something's going on and I'm going to find it out. I work for a shitty magazine, but I'm not a shitty journalist. I'm actually good at what I do, whatever you might think."

"If you're so good, how come you did such a bad job of tailing me just now?"

"Oh, that," Van Doren said, smiling again. "I'm just a really bad driver."

I pulled over. Van Doren looked around. "Where are we?"

"The place where you get out of my car," I said.

"You're just going to leave me here?" he asked.

"Well, you didn't think I'd actually take you where I was going, did you?" I said.

"Man," Van Doren said. "You're just plain evil." He got out of the car, then turned around and held onto the door for a minute. "By the way, Tom. There are no sulfur spas around here. And your father is dead and your mother lives in Arizona, which would have made having dinner with them difficult in one case and impossible in the other. If there's no story here, why did you start lying to me from the beginning?"

I didn't answer. He closed the door, put his hands in his pockets, and walked away.

Roland Lanois poked his head out of his office. "Sorry, Tom," he said, "I ran a little late on that last one, and I had to finish up some paperwork."

"No problem," I said. "I was running late myself. I had to drop someone off."

"Well, then," Roland said, opening his office door. "We're both forgiven. Come into the sanctum, Tom."

Roland Lanois, Montreal-born, Eton and Oxford–educated, was cultured, sophisticated, and witty; had great taste and an industry-wide reputation for being the most polite producer in the business. Most people who met him assumed he was gay. In fact, he cut a swath through his leading ladies like a harvester through a wheat field. Hollywood folks just aren't used to heterosexual men having any sort of culture.

"Can I get you anything, Tom?" Roland said. "A drink? I was just sent a very nice eighteen-year-old Glenlivet from Ellen Merlow's people. I'd be honored if you'd help me break it in."

"Thanks," I said, settling on Roland's couch. "Neat, please. With a touch of water, if you would."

"Ah," Roland said, cracking open the bottle. "A man of refinement. I have some Evian that should do the job. Ideally, of course, you'd have a bit of the water that the scotch is made from, but we must make do. Anyway, most people in this town put ice in their scotch. Savage, really." Roland poured the scotch.

"Why did Ellen's people send you the scotch?" I asked.

"Oh, come now, Tom," Roland said, glancing over with a slight smile. "You wouldn't be here if you didn't already know that Ellen's dropped out of *Hard Memories*. It appears she's going to be taking on a more regular—and lucrative—gig on television." Roland said *television* like it hurt his teeth to form the word.

"I hope you know I am sorry to hear about that. She would have been great for the role."

"Yes, indeed," Roland had gotten out the Evian and was delicately administering a drop to both our glasses, "she was perfect. Brilliant actress of course, the right age, and she appeals to the core audience we were going for. But she's going through that divorce of hers, and it doesn't look like her prenuptial is going to withstand scrutiny. She's worried about whether her postnuptial worth is going to allow her to maintain her lifestyle choices. A working horse farm apparently takes more money than you or I would suspect."

Roland handed me the scotch and took a seat in the other side of the couch. "And as you know, we're not working with a very large budget for *Hard Memories*. So she's jumping ship to play a suburban mother whose butler is an alien. She's getting $250,000 an episode. NBC has committed to a forty-four-episode buy. She keeps her horse farm, and I'm left with my project's arse hanging in the wind. Cheers." Roland reached over to clink his glass. We sipped.

"Damn, that's good scotch," I said.

"Yes, quite good," Roland said. "Which is why it was sent along to soften the blow. Oddly enough, it came along with a Hickory Farm sausage assortment. Strange, isn't it? I suspect they have a new assistant over there who's not quite used to how these things work. At least it didn't come with one of those fruit baskets with a balloon and a stuffed animal. I think I might have killed myself."

"Balloons aren't that bad," I said.

"No, it would be the stuffed animal that would send me over the edge," Roland said. "Now, Tom. You didn't come over to commiserate with me over my project, though you have been very gracious to do so to this point. What's on your mind?"

"Well, I'll get right to it," I said. "I have a client who is very interested in pursuing the role Ellen Merlow's vacated in *Hard Memories*. Michelle Beck."

"Oh, yes, right," Roland said. "She's been calling here nearly every day, following up on it. Become quite good friends with my assistant Rajiv, in fact, up to the point where the poor lad is practically falling over himself to tell her all the things that are supposed to be production secrets. Really a problem, but you're aware of the effect someone like Miss Beck will have on young males. He's probably impressing the hell out of his old friends from university. I haven't the will to fire him for it."

"You're a good man, Roland Lanois," I said.

"Thank you, Tom. I don't hear that nearly enough." We clinked glasses again, and then Roland sat back, hand to his chin. He looked as if he was considering something weighty, and actually had the intellectual wherewithal to do it. "Tell me, Tom. What do *you* think of Michelle Beck for the part?"

"I guess that depends if you're asking me as an agent or as a lover of film," I said.

"Really," Roland said, an amused glint in his eye. "I'd like to hear the agent response first."

"She'd be great," I said. "She's hot, she's a draw, she'll absolutely guarantee you a $20 million opening weekend plus strong foreign openings."

"And as a lover of film?"

"You'd have to be out of your mind to give her the role," I said.

"Well," Roland said, sounding impressed. "That's something you're not going to hear out of the mouth of every agent."

I shrugged. "I'm not telling you anything you don't already know," I said. "And I'd look like an idiot if I said anything else."

"What I find interesting," Roland said, "is that you think I'd be mad to give her the role, and yet here you are, about to ask me to do just that. It's a near-Orwellian example of double-think. I'm fascinated to hear how you are going to reconcile the two."

"There's no need for reconciliation," I said. "I think she'd probably be no good for the role. I'll be honest about that. But—and here's something you're not going to hear an agent say much of, either—I could be wrong, and wrong in a big way. I can name you any number of actors and actresses that no one suspected would be able to take on a role, who have turned around and made it work. Sally Field was Gidget for years. Now she's got two Oscars. Hell, Ellen Merlow's first film role was a straight-to-video horror flick."

"I didn't know that," Roland said.

"*Blood City III: The Awakening,*" I said. "It also features Ellen's first and currently only nude scene."

"Really. I'll have to find that."

"Now Ellen has two Oscars as well. My point here is, just because *I* think Michelle is wrong for the part, doesn't mean she *is.*"

"All right, point noted," Roland said. "But there *is* the complication of Miss Beck not being the right age or, let's put this as delicately as possible, having the right amount of intellectual stamina."

"We have forty-year-old actresses who move heaven and earth to make themselves look twenty-five," I said. "I think we have the cosmetic technology to go the other direction as well. We might have to reel back the age of the character half a decade or so, but that's not going to make a real impact on the thrust of the story. As for the intellectual end, it may surprise you to know that Michelle has recently been reading Hannah Arendt."

"It does surprise me," Roland said.

"She and my assistant Miranda were discussing the book just this afternoon," I said. I left out the part about Michelle mangling the title of the book.

Roland put his arm on the top of the couch and sipped his scotch, thoughtfully. Then he shook his head. "I'm sorry, Tom," he said. "But I just have a very hard time seeing any way that Michelle Beck could work this role. I wouldn't want to give it to her, just to have it be a fiasco for both her and me. You can see the position I'm in."

"I'm not asking you to *give* her the role," I said. "All I'm asking is that you give her a reading. If she flubs it, fine. But she'll know she had a shot at it. She'll know I made the effort for it. Knowing Michelle, it'll make her work harder for the next thing that she does. And again: we could both be wrong about this. It couldn't hurt to cover the bases. Roland, what's the status of the movie right now?"

"It's been pushed back, of course," Roland said. "We were in the process of hiring crew and now we've had to let them all off. It's damned inconvenient—I'm going to lose Januz, my cinematographer, to another project. Some child's film. About *primates.*" He grimaced. "Those things never do well. I don't know what he's thinking."

"Do you have any other actresses lined up?"

"Not any of the really good ones," Roland said. "Once we selected Ellen, they all went off to other commitments. The earliest we'll have any of our A-list choices open is nine months from now. We have some B-listers who could do it, but this isn't the sort of film that will succeed without an established name."

"Well, then," I said. "You've got nothing to lose."

Roland did his thoughtful thing again. "Even if Michelle confounded our expectations," he said. "I don't see how we could afford her. You know that the studios don't throw any sort of money at all to these things."

Inwardly, I did a victory dance. When a producer starts

talking about money, it means he's cleared off any philosophical problems he might have with your client. We were now moving through the final steps of the dance. Outwardly, of course, I showed no change in emotion. "Michelle's not looking to do this picture for the paycheck," I said. "I think that, should she confound us, we could come to an accommodation concerning salary."

One more minute of the thoughtful thing. "All right, fine," Roland said. "I don't suppose it could hurt to give her a look. And if, God forbid, she pans out and we get this production on track, all the better. To tell you the truth, Tom, I was thinking of abandoning *Hard Memories* altogether for another project, which is actually along the same lines—Holocaust drama, that is."

"Really," I said.

"Yes. Well," Roland ducked his head in what I suspected was his version of a shrug, "it's not really a project yet. It's just a script—came into our slush pile by a student at NYU, but it's marvelous. It's about a Polish poet, a Catholic, who is put in a Nazi concentration camp for helping Jews during World War II."

"Krzysztof Kordus?" I asked.

Roland looked surprised. "Yes, right, that's the man. Again, Tom, I'm impressed. Most people in this business don't know about anything they didn't read in *Variety*. Anyway, this script is brilliant, really moving. They did a thing on this Kordus fellow a couple decades back on *television*,"—again, the word was almost spat—"but this script is far beyond what they did with that. The problem now, of course, is getting clearance to use the man's works in the film. I'm going to have Rajiv chase down who's in charge of Kordus's literary estate, and see what we can come up with. Probably will charge us an arm and a leg for clearance. That's the way these things work."

"You don't have to have Rajiv track anything down," I said. "I can tell you who administers Krzysztof's literary estate. You're looking at him."

Roland slipped his arm off the couch and leaned forward. "Get out," he said. "You can't be serious."

"I am," I said. "My father was Krzysztof's agent. When Krzysztof died, he named my father administrator of his literary estate. When my father died, I inherited the role. I tried to place Krzysztof's estate with a real literary agent, but his family asked me to continue on. They wanted to keep it in the family, as it were. I couldn't very well say no, so I stayed with it. It's really not very difficult, since the deals for his books are already in place. All I do is sign off on the current arrangements and mail his daughter a check every three months."

"Tom," Roland said. "I am so *very* glad you dropped by. Hold on a moment, and I'll get you the script for this project. Read it and let's talk."

"Two scripts, if you don't mind," I said. "Remember why I came here in the first place."

"But of course," Roland said. "By all means, let's set up the screen test. Will a week from today be good? Say, noon?"

"That would be just fine."

"Brilliant," Roland said, and got up. "Don't go anywhere. I'll be back in a flash." He went out to get the scripts from his assistant. I finished my scotch. It was very good scotch.

I called Michelle with the good news as soon as I got home. She squealed like a happy pig, which in my mind didn't bode well for her chances for the role.

"Thank you, Tom, thank you, thank you, thank you!" she said. "I'm so happy! I can't believe it!"

"Settle down, Michelle," I said, not unkindly. "All you're getting at this point is a reading. You haven't got the film yet. You could go in only to find out they hate you." This was my subtle way of getting her ready for the disappointment.

It wasn't working. "Oh, I don't care," she said. "I'm ready. I've been doing my reading. They're going to be surprised. You'll see. You'll be there, right, Tom?"

"Uh . . . ," I said. "Oh, what the hey. I'll be there."

"Tom, I could just kiss you," Michelle said.

"Let's not try to ruin our client-agent relationship," I said. Michelle giggled. I cringed inwardly and changed the subject. "Miranda tells me you called earlier with a problem with the *Earth Resurrected* folks. Something about a latex mask?"

"Oh, *that*," Michelle said. "Tom, they want to pour latex on my head so they can make a stand-in dummy, or something. I don't want to do it."

"Michelle, it's not that bad. They have to make those masks so they can get shots of your head doing things it doesn't normally do, like having veins pop out or your eyes explode. Things like that. It's a little old school, but it's not unusual. All the great action stars have to have them made. Arnold Schwarzenegger did it before they made him governor. Really, you're not an action star *until* you have one made."

"But they pour goo on your head, and then you sit there for hours." Michelle said. "How do you *breathe* through that?"

"As I understand it, they stick straws up your nose," I said.

"No way," Michelle said.

There was a scratching at the back door. I looked over and saw Ralph the retriever standing on the other side of the door.

"Michelle, hold on a second, I have to let my dog in," I said.

"Tom, I can't do the latex mask thing," Michelle said. "I don't want straws in my nose. What if I have a cold? What if they fall out? How am I going to breathe?"

"Michelle, let me just, oh, just hold on a sec." I placed the phone down, ran over to the door and slid it open. I ran back to the phone. Ralph walked through the door.

"Michelle, you still there?" I asked.

"I'm not going to do it, Tom," she said again. "I'm claustrophobic. I can't even put a blanket over my head without freaking out. I don't care if they fire me or not."

"Don't say that," I said. "Listen, when are you supposed to have your mask made?"

"A week from today," she said. "Three in the afternoon. I have to go to Pomona."

"Damn," I said. "That's the same day as your reading."

"Well, then," Michelle said. "I can't get the mask made."

Ralph walked over to me and sat. I started knuckling his head, absently. "How about this," I said. "I'll go with you to both. I'll pick you up, we'll go to the reading. Once the reading is done, we'll go to have the mask made, and I'll make sure the straws stay in place. Okay?"

"Tom . . . ," Michelle began.

"Come on, Michelle," I said. "We'll go to Mondo Chicken afterwards. I'm buying."

"Oh, all right," Michelle said. "You always know the right thing to say, Tom."

"That's why you love me, Michelle," I said. I hung up, set the phone down, and knelt down to rub Ralph's ears and coat.

"Hey, there, Ralph," I said, in the goo-goo voice you use with dogs. "Where's your little friend Joshua? Yeah? Your little friend? The one that I'm gonna kill for heading off into the woods when I told him not to go? Huh? Where is the little bastard, Ralphie?"

"Why the hell are you asking me?" Ralph said. "I'm just a dog."

I screamed for a really long time.

CHAPTER
Twelve

"Eeyow," Ralph said, after I stopped hollering. "That hurt. I would have been happy with a simple 'Welcome back.'"

"Joshua?" I asked.

"Of course," Ralph/Joshua said. "But I'm also Ralph now, too. Ralphua. Joshualph. Take your pick."

"Joshua," I said. "What have you done?"

"Tom, snap out of it," Joshua said, irritably. "It's obvious what I've done. Look, I'm a dog!" Joshua barked. "Convinced? Or do you want me to hump your leg?"

"I know *what* you are," I said. "Now I want to know why you did it. I thought you liked Ralph. I thought he was your friend, Joshua. And now look what you've done." I gesticulated, looking for the right words. None came. I used the next best. "You *ate* him, Joshua!"

Joshua laughed, which sounded unbelievably bizarre coming from a dog. "I'm sorry, Tom," he said, finally. "Now I know what you're getting at. You make it sound like I was waiting for the right moment to body-snatch Ralph. It didn't happen that way. I told you before that the Yherajk don't do that sort of thing. Tom, Ralph was dying. And this was the only way to save him."

"I don't understand," I said.

"Well, if you promise not to yell at me anymore, I'll tell you. All right?"

"All right," I said.

"Good," Joshua said. "Let's go into the living room. Could you do me the favor of getting me a beer?"

"What?"

"A beer, Tom. You know. A brew. Oat soda. Suds. I don't have any tendrils to open things with anymore. And just because I'm a dog doesn't mean I couldn't use a drink every now and then. I'll meet you in the living room." He padded out. I went to get him a beer, a bowl to drink it out of, and a couple of aspirin for myself, and then joined him in the living room, taking a seat in my lounger.

I downed the aspirin, took a slug of the beer to chase them down, and put the rest of it in the bowl. Joshua lapped it up. I reached over to pet him, but then I stopped. It didn't seem appropriate anymore. You don't pet thinking things.

"That's better," Joshua said. "Thanks, Tom."

"You're welcome," I said. "Now, what happened out there?"

"Ralph had a heart attack," Joshua said, and I watched his mouth as he spoke. His mouth hung open as the words came out—it was like he had swallowed a radio. "We were a couple of miles from here, going up a hillside. Ralph had been fine up until then. But on the way up the hill, I heard him give a little whimper. I looked back and he had collapsed. I went back to see if there was anything wrong, but I didn't see any cuts or bone breaks. So that's when I entered his brain, and found out he had a heart attack."

"How could you tell?"

"I could read where he was feeling pain," Joshua said. "His whole chest felt like it was being squeezed. Ralph was confused, of course; he's just a dog, after all. He didn't know what was going on."

"Why didn't you call me then?" I asked. "I would have come back and taken Ralph to the vet."

"Think about it, Tom," Joshua said. "You were in Venice Beach at the time, remember? By the time you got back here and hiked out to where we were, Ralph would have been long gone. And even if you *had* got back in time and had taken him to a vet, the vet would've just told you there was nothing to be done. And besides, he's not really your dog. You couldn't have done anything."

That stung. Joshua must have picked up on it. "I don't mean to imply that you had done anything wrong, Tom," he said, gently. "Just that there wasn't time. Even if there was, this was a better way. Ralph deserved better than to die on a vet table with strangers over him."

"So Ralph had a heart attack," I said, my voice slightly husky. "What did you do then?"

"The first thing I did was I cut off the pain," Joshua said. "I didn't want him feeling any pain. I also cut off his motor control, so he wouldn't go bounding off because he was feeling better. Then I sent a tendril into his chest to see how bad it was, and whether or not we could make it back to the house. As it turned out, it was pretty bad. Ralph was old and his heart was in bad shape.

"By this time, Ralph was pretty much out of it—his little brain was blipping all over the place, Tom. I didn't want him to die, so I did two things. First I called your assistant and told her that we'd be late. And then I inhabited Ralph."

"What does that mean?" I asked.

"Well, look at me," Joshua said.

"I mean, how it that different from Ralph just dying?" I said. "After all, it's not Ralph in there, Joshua. It's you."

"Not quite accurate," Joshua said. "All of Ralph's memories and feelings are still here. I distinctly remember being a dog and doing doggie things."

"But you're *not* Ralph," I said.

"No," Joshua admitted. "But on the other hand, Ralph didn't die. His personality just . . . melded into mine. From Ralph's point of view, he suddenly became a lot more intelligent. He's the dog with the 180 IQ. On my end, I now know the world from a dog's-eye point of view. I, being Joshua, am obviously going to be dominant. But don't be surprised when I do something that reminds you of Ralph. It's all here, in one big package. Which is why I said, 'Ralphua.' "

"What did Ralph think of this, if you don't mind me asking?"

"He was good with it," Joshua said. "Though not in any way you'd understand. I basically let him know not to worry, and he basically let me know that he trusted me. Then he and I became we. Which then became me. And *I'm* pleased to be alive, so there you have it."

I leaned back in my chair. "This is making my head hurt."

"Have some more aspirin," Joshua suggested.

I looked back down at Joshua. He sat there like a typical retriever. "What did you do with your old body?" I asked. "Did you leave it up there on the hillside? Do we need to go find it and bury it or something?"

"Nope," Joshua said. "It's in here. Timesharing, as it were. Right now my old body is in Ralph's digestive system and in his blood vessels. He's not eating anything that I'm not eating, obviously, and my cells are doing the role of blood, transferring oxygen to his cells. See, look at my tongue," Joshua's doggie tongue rolled out, an albino sort of pink, "not nearly as red as it used to be. Anyway, this is only a short-term solution— controlling two bodies is a lot of work, even when I have my old body more or less on autopilot."

"What's the long-term solution?"

"Well, eventually my cells will take the place of all his cells," Joshua said. "It's more efficient, especially since I won't have all these damned specialized organs to deal with. The only thing I'll need to be concerned with is maintaining my shape and appearance, which won't be that difficult. It'll take about a week."

"What happens to the old cells?" I asked.

"I digest them."

"Oh, *man*," I said. "You *are* eating him."

"Tom," Joshua said. "It's not nearly as gross as you think. And anyway, it needs to be done—I can't keep controlling both bodies, and my Yherajk body is more flexible."

"And none of this,"—I waved my hands—"conflicts with your 'don't take over other life-forms' thinking."

"Hmmmm, well," Joshua said. "It's a borderline case. The limitation is 'sentient life forms.' We could argue whether or not Ralph, character though he was, truly qualified as sentient. Now, *I* think he was—a low-grade variety, you know, but that's a matter of degree, not of kind. But I also feel that he gave me consent. Sort of. It's something that could be argued. But I don't feel wrong for having done it. Besides, I *like* being a dog. I marked every tree on the way here, you know. It's all my territory now."

"Good thing my cat's not still alive," I said. "I think you and he may have had words about that."

"Hey, that reminds me," Joshua said. "Was your cat a striped tabby?"

"He was," I said. "Orange. Big."

"Don't know about the orange part, but I've got a memory of chasing a big tabby down the road a couple of years back and seeing it get squashed by a big truck." Joshua squinted, which is a funny look on a dog. "A Ford Explorer, it looks like."

"Great. Ralph is a cat murderer. Just what I needed."

"He was just playing around with the cat, Tom," Joshua said. "He felt really guilty about it afterwards."

I slapped my hands on my legs and stood up. "On that note, I'm going to get another beer. I think I could use it."

"Could you bring me another one, too?" Joshua asked. "Can't open one myself, you know."

"Now wait a minute," I said. "If you can't make tendrils anymore, how did you make the call earlier today?"

"The cell phone has a 'redial' button, Tom. And believe me, it was a pain in the ass to try to hit it."

"Where *is* the cell phone?" I asked.

"Uh. . . ." Joshua hung his head. "I left it out on the hillside. Sorry. I didn't want to have to carry it in my mouth for two miles."

"Joshua, you're a *retriever*," I said. "That's what you *do*."

"That's what I *did*," Joshua said. "I'm in another line of work now."

The next morning, Joshua and I visited Carl.

"Well, isn't that just the most adorable puppy!" Carl's assistant Marcella said, leaning over her desk to look at Joshua.

"Only on the outside," I said.

"Why, Tom, what a terrible thing to say," Marcella said. "You know that dogs can pick up on what you're saying about them."

"I have no doubt whatsoever about that," I said. "Is Carl in? I'd like to speak to him, if he has a moment."

"He's in," Marcella said. "Let me see if he can see you." She motioned us over to the waiting area. As we sat, Joshua put his paw on my foot, our signal for when he had something he wanted to say to me. I leaned down, very close to his mouth. "What?" I whispered.

"I just want you to know, I'm having a rough time of things at the moment," Joshua said, his voice barely above a whisper itself. "My dog nature is getting the best of me."

"What do you mean?" I said.

"I mean I have this *incredible* urge to stick my nose in every crotch that goes by," Joshua said. "It's driving me insane."

"Try to control yourself," I said. "After this meeting I'll take you to the park and you can sniff some other dogs' butts. Good enough?"

"You're mocking me, aren't you," Joshua said.

"Maybe," I said.

"Tom?" Marcella looked over to us. "Carl will see you now." She crinkled a smile and wiggled her fingers at Joshua.

Joshua surged, as if to make a beeline for her lap. I held him by his collar and dragged him into Carl's office. Carl was at his desk, glancing at a *Hollywood Reporter.* He set it down as I closed the door.

"Tom," Carl said, and then glanced down at Joshua. "Is this Joshua's friend?"

"Not exactly," I said, and turned to Joshua. "Say hello, Joshua."

"Hello, Joshua," Joshua said.

Carl was momentarily startled but recovered quite a bit quicker than I did. "Cute," he finally said.

"Thanks. I love that joke," Joshua said.

"Would one of you mind telling me how Joshua got in there?" Carl said.

"His dog friend was old and had a heart attack, and Joshua decided to inhabit the body," I said.

"I've also melded with the dog's personality," Joshua said.

Carl furrowed his brow. "You mean your personality is part *dog*?"

"If you throw a stick, will I not fetch?" Joshua intoned. "If you scratch my backside, will I not jerk my leg? If you show me a cat, will I not chase? Sorry, Tom."

"It's all right," I said.

"Tom," Carl said, "I'm hoping this isn't your idea of how to bring our peoples together. Joshua appears happy to be a dog, but I don't think that's the form that we want the Yherajk to take for their grand debut."

"Believe me, it's not," I said. "But I think letting him be a dog for a while has some interesting aspects."

"Explain," Carl said.

"Well, for one thing, it finally allows him to interact with humans besides you and me," I said. "I can take him places now. He's not going to get the full human experience, to be sure, but he's going to see more of the place than he would trapped in my house all the time. And maybe the interaction will give us some ideas to go on for how we finally do introduce the Yherajk."

"Joshua?" Carl said.

"Being a dog isn't optimal for observation," Joshua said. "But it's better than what I was doing, which was watching cable television and going into online chat rooms. And I'm having fun. I am the Alpha Dog of the Universe. It doesn't get much better than that."

Carl turned his attention back to me. "What is your plan?"

"I don't have one at the moment," I said. "I thought I'd just take him places and let him look around. You know, be a professional dog walker for a while."

"He's good at it," Joshua volunteered, "and he needs the exercise."

"Quiet, you," Carl said to Joshua. Joshua immediately looked like a dog who knows he's taken a dump in the wrong place in the house. I never would have told Joshua to be quiet. But then, I'm not his dad.

"I can't have you wandering around with a dog," Carl said. "That Van Doren character is still floating around out there. We have to keep you busy." Carl thought for a few moments, then turned back to Joshua.

"Can you act?" Carl asked Joshua.

"I'm pretending to be a dog, aren't I?" Joshua said.

Carl buzzed Marcella. "Get me Albert Bowen, if you please, Marcella," he said, and clicked her off. He turned to me. "You have anything going on in the next few days?"

"Not really. I got Michelle Beck a reading for *Hard Memories,* but that's not until next week. Amanda's handling all the rest of my clients. I'm free," I said.

"Good," Carl said. "Albert Bowen and I went to college together. He's a vet and a trainer, and handles animal casting for commercials and television. Let's see what we can do with this."

Marcella's voice came over the speakerphone. "Albert Bowen holding for Carl Lupo," she said, and clicked off.

"Hey, Al," Carl said.

"Wolfman!" Bowen said on the other end. Carl twitched slightly at the nickname. College familiarity was probably the only reason Carl let him get away with it. "Haven't heard from you in a while, my friend. What can I do for you?"

"I got an interesting potential client, Al," Carl said. "Animal trainer from the Yukon Territory. Trains dogs. One of my agents did a trek up the Pacific coastline about a year ago and found this guy doing a show outside of Whitehorse. Smartest damned dogs you ever saw. The agent managed to convince the guy to ship one of the dogs down for a week, to see if they might have a future in commercials and films. I think they might, and if it works out, we're going to represent the trainer."

"The trainer shipped one of the *dogs*?" Bowen said. "He didn't come down himself?"

"Said he didn't need to. Sent the agent a manual with hand signs. Said that's all he'd need, the dog would understand. I told you these were smart dogs, Al."

"Hmmph. I'll have to see it before I believe it," Bowen said.

"Well, Al, that's my plan. I'm going to send the agent over with the dog. The agent's name is Tom Stein, and the dog's name is Joshua. You want to give the dog a look-see and tell me what you think? And if you can use him in any commercials over the next week or so, that'd be good with us. The trainer has given us free rein for this week only."

"Who is this guy?" Bowen said.

"Not going to say, Al," Carl said. "Company secret until we have a deal signed. But if you like what you see, I think we can work out an exclusive contract for your casting company. Work for you?"

"Hell, yes, Carl," Bowen said. "Have them come up today around one. We'll put the dog through the paces and I'll get back to you by tomorrow morning. You know where my ranch is?"

"Valencia, if I'm not mistaken," Carl said.

"Right you are," Bowen said. "Take the Magic Mountain exit, go left, and head into the hills for five miles. Can't miss it. We'll be looking forward to seeing them." Carl and Bowen did their good-bye pleasantries and hung up.

"Yukon Territory? Whitehorse?" I said.

Carl smiled broadly. "I'd like to see anyone check up on *that* whopper," he said.

Al Bowen met us in the driveway of his ranch, clearly eager to meet Joshua. That is, until he saw him.

"*This* is the dog?" Bowen said, after we made our introductions. It was clear that he didn't think Joshua was any great prize. But the same could be said of him; Al Bowen was one of those guys who looked like he had spent far too much of his life being a roadie for the Grateful Dead.

"That's him," I said. "He's really more intelligent than he looks."

"I hope so," Bowen said, and knelt down. "He's not a biter, is he?"

"Not that I know of," I said.

Bowen held out his hand to let Joshua sniff him. Joshua declined. Bowen took hold of Joshua's snout and took at look at his gums, then felt down Joshua's body.

"How old is this dog?" he finally asked.

"Eight years, I think," I said.

Bowen snorted. "He's twice that if he's a year, Tom," he said, straightening up. "I have to tell you, if Carl hadn't vouched for this animal, I'd turn you around right now. Come on, let's go this way." He led us past the ranch house, into the back.

"Nice place you've got here," I said.

"Thanks," Bowen said. "It's nothing big, just a couple thousand acres. Family land, you know. Been in the family since the 1800s. Thought I might have to sell it in the seventies, but then I got my vet degree and started doing this. Pays the bills. Got quite a menagerie here—dogs, cats, pigs, horses, even some llamas. We had a herd of cattle we'd rent out for stampede scenes, but there's not much call for that recently. Had to turn most of them into cat food." We stopped at an enclosed yard that looked like an obstacle course.

"What is this?"

"Well, this is a training track," Bowen said. "If we want to have an animal do something complicated, like run through a house and open a window, we'll sort of create that here and run them through it until it gets hardwired into their brains. I figure that dog of yours has a repertoire of tricks. Tell me what they are, and we'll set up the track and run him through a couple."

"That's not the way he was trained," I said.

Bowen looked at me like I was a bad peyote flashback. "What do you mean?" he said.

"Well, as I understand it, he's sort of trained the other way. Set up the track the way you want it, and tell him what to do, and he'll do it." I was making all this up, and this sounded reasonable to me.

But apparently it didn't sound that way to Bowen. "Look, Tom," he said. "I don't know what fool chase Carl has you running, or if you've pulled a fast one on Carl. But every dog has to be trained for specific tasks. I love and respect dogs, but even the smartest ones can't just be told to do something brand new and then do it. That's just not the way their brains work."

"Mr. Bowen, before you say it can't be done, why don't we try it first?" I said. "I think you'll be surprised."

Bowen looked irritated, and then he laughed. "Fine, then," he said. "Give me a minute to prepare the track." He went into the enclosed area and began moving things around.

" 'Is he a biter?' " Joshua said, under his breath. "I almost nipped off his nose, just for that one."

"Behave yourself, Joshua," I said. "You think you can handle this?"

"Deep in the bowels of my intellect, I have the knowledge necessary to pilot an interstellar spacecraft," Joshua said. "I think I should be sufficiently competent to walk and jump."

"No need to get testy," I said.

"Sorry," Joshua said. "Personally, I think I'm a fine dog. Remind me to pee on this guy's shoes before we go."

Bowen came back to our side of the enclosure and opened it to let us through.

"Let me walk you through this," he said.

"You can just tell me," I said. "That should be fine."

Bowen smirked. "All right, then. Here's what I want. I want your dog to leap over that plastic fence over there, come back around this way to this"—he motioned to a window with a shade on it—"and grab the blind string in his mouth to open the blind. Finally, I want him to go all the way back there"—He pointed to what looked like a kid's playhouse—"there's a door-bell button on the right side of the door that he should be able to press. Have him press it, turn around, sit, and bark back at us."

"Is that all?" I said.

"Son," Bowen said. "It would take the better part of a year for a dog to learn something this complicated. If your dog can get just one of these things on the first try, he qualifies as the smartest dog in the history of dogs."

"Joshua," I snapped my fingers as if to make him heel. He sauntered over and sat, looking at me. I pointed to the plastic fence.

"Jump!" I said. I then moved my arm over to the blind.

"Pull!" I said. I then moved my arm over to the playhouse doorbell.

"Press!" I said. I then made a spinning motion with my hand, and mimed my hand sitting.

"Bark!" I said.

Joshua shot me a look that clearly said, *give me a fucking break.*

"Go!" I said. He sprinted off.

"Mary mother of God in a lobster bib," Al Bowen said, roughly twenty seconds later.

"I thought he was a little sloppy about the blinds," I said. They were, in fact, slightly crooked.

"Listen," Bowen said. "I've got a Mighty Dog commercial scheduled here for the day after tomorrow. Tell me you can make it."

"Sure," I said.

"We start shooting at ten-thirty," Bowen said. "Try to be here by seven. This is smartest dog I've ever seen in my life, but he's still going to need a lot of grooming work." He shook his head and walked away.

Joshua walked up. "Well?" he said.

"You're going to be in a Mighty Dog commercial," I said.

"Well, all right, then," Joshua said. "I would hate to be associated with anything that wasn't one hundred percent pure beef, you know."

CHAPTER
Thirteen

On September 1, 1939, Nazi Germany began World War II by bombing the hell out of the Polish capital of Warsaw. By September 27, the Germans were dipping their feet in the Vistula river, which bisects the city; shortly thereafter, the Jews of Warsaw were herded into the Warsaw Ghetto—500,000 of them, initially, in an area roughly one mile square. In July of 1942, the Nazis began deporting the Jews *en masse* from the ghetto. Between July 22 and October 3, 300,000 were deported to the various concentration camps—Treblinka and Chelmno were the closest to the city of Warsaw—and exterminated. In April of 1943, the 40,000 or so Jews who remained in the ghetto were attacked by the Nazis. They fought back, heroically, for three weeks. And then nearly all of them were killed.

One who survived was Rachel Spiegelman. In pre-War

times, Rachel and her family were well-to-do professionals; the daughter and granddaughter of physicians, Rachel herself had studied law and worked as the office manager of her husband's law firm. In addition to Polish and Yiddish, she spoke German and English, and had even been to America as a child, to visit family members who had emigrated there. She was a daughter and wife of privilege, and the fall from having servants and summer homes to living six to a room in the ghetto was a long one.

And yet, inasmuch as one can in the circumstances, Rachel thrived. She was tough-minded and sensible—and also formidable. When the Nazis informed the ghetto residents that they were to form Jewish councils that would oversee housing, sanitation, and manufacturing production, she forbade any member of her family from joining the councils, declaring that those who worked with the Germans were leading the rest to the slaughter. When her husband disobeyed her and served on a council, Rachel threw him out of the room that they shared with Rachel's parents, her brother, and her brother's wife.

She then organized her neighborhood to operate around the councils and clashed with them repeatedly over their edicts. With a young Pole who was rumored to be her lover, she operated a black market, somehow finding meat and sweets when the Germans allowed only turnips and beets to be sent into the ghetto. When the Nazis ordered the Jewish councils to find "volunteers" for deportation, Rachel, working desperately, found her neighbors work in armament plants or hid them, delaying but ultimately failing to stem the death flow out of the ghetto. She fought alongside the remaining Jews during the ghetto uprising for two weeks, one of the very few women left in the ghetto to do so; in the third week, against her better

judgment, she attempted to escape the ghetto with her young
Pole. They actually did it, only to be turned in by one of the
Pole's "friends." He was shot and killed; she was sent to Tre-
blinka.

From April until the beginning of August, Rachel slaved in
the camp; on August 3, it was decided that she was no longer
needed. She was sent a mile up the road to Treblinka II, where
the "bathhouses" were. These bathhouses were connected to
huge diesel engines that pumped in carbon monoxide—deadly,
but not very efficient. It typically took nearly a half hour before
the hundreds crammed inside the "bathhouses" died. It was a
long and terrifying death, and between 700,000 and 900,000
people died that way, in that camp.

On August 3, however, there were some surprising deaths
at Treblinka II; namely, an SS officer and several guards. They
were killed by some of the Jews who worked at the camp, performing the executions, excavating the corpses for gold teeth
and other valuables, and transporting the bodies to mass graves.
The Jews chose that day to attempt a revolt, and while it was
not successful, over two hundred Jews escaped the camp during
the chaos. Rachel was one of them. Most of the escapees were
eventually recaptured or killed. Rachel was not. Rachel went
north, eventually finding passage to Sweden. After the war
ended, she emigrated from there to the United States.

Rachel's story would be remarkable enough if it had ended
there. But it did not. Once Rachel arrived in the United States,
she was outraged to discover that her adopted country, the one
that had fought for the freedom of Europe, was dealing with
Black Americans like the Germans dealt with the Jews. Even
some of the laws were effectively the same—no intermarriage,
segregated schools and services, and violence either ignored or

actively condoned by those whose job it was to keep the peace. "There are black shirts beneath those white robes," she would later write.

So she did something about it. She went back to law school and got her J.D.—and the next day got on a bus to Montgomery, Alabama, the heart of Dixie. She passed the bar and set up shop: a female, Jewish lawyer, offering legal services to black sharecroppers and factory workers. Her office was firebombed twice in the first month. The next, someone drove by and put a bullet through her window. It ricocheted and struck her in the leg. She went to the hospital to have it removed, and was denied medical help by the emergency room resident, who refused to work on a "nigger-loving Jew." Rachel responded by prying out the bullet herself, right there, slamming it down on the resident's clipboard, and walking out under her own power. Then she sued the hospital and the resident. She won. Her office was firebombed again.

She stayed on—on through the Montgomery Bus Boycott of 1955, when she bought her first car to avoid riding the buses and ferried black friends to and from work. On through the Birmingham protests of 1963, when she was arrested twice by white policemen and bitten three times by their dogs. On through Martin Luther King's 1965 march from Selma to Montgomery, when she and King walked arm-in-arm as they strode past her offices, now staffed with partners—half of them black.

Just before she died in 1975, she wrote in *Time* magazine, "I feel the work I have done was the work I was destined to do. I know what it is to lose my rights and to be told that I have no right to exist, to see my family, my friends and my humanity stripped away from me. These are hard memories, couched in sorrow and anger. But I also know what it is to see others begin to gain their rights and their humanity, to be told, yes, you are our brothers and sisters. Come join us at the family table, and be welcome. My work, though such a small part of a larger whole, has helped to make this a reality. It makes those hard memories a little easier to bear, because *these* memories—they are glorious."

This is the woman that Michelle Beck wanted to portray. Could she do it?

Well, she was the right sex.

By the time Michelle and I waited in Roland Lanois's anteroom, however, any hint that I felt Michelle to be utterly wrong for the role had vanished. After a certain point as an agent, you simply stop worrying about the far-reaching implications of what you are doing and deal with the at-the-moment details. Some would call it enforced amorality. But it's really just a matter of being there for your client, and doing what needs to be done. At the moment, I was trying to keep Michelle from hyperventilating.

"Breathe," I said. "Respiration is a good thing."

"I'm so sorry, Tom," Michelle said. She was gripping both sides of her chair so hard it looked like she might dent the metal. "I'm just so *nervous*. I didn't think I would be. But I am. Oh, God," she said. She started thumping her chest with her fist. "Oh, Tom, I'm sorry." She sounded like a helicopter.

I grabbed the fist before she could break her ribs. "Stop apologizing. You haven't done anything wrong. It's okay to be nervous, Michelle. This is a pretty big role. But I don't think you need to bruise yourself over it. Have you read the scene Roland wants you to do?"

"Yes," she said, and then grinned sheepishly. "I actually memorized the whole thing. All the parts. I didn't want to blow it. Isn't that stupid?"

"No, not really," I said. "You know, when Elvis started work on his very first film, he memorized the entire script. All the parts, not just his own. No one told him there was any other way to do it."

Michelle looked at me, confused. "Elvis was an actor?"

"Well, I don't know that I'd go *that* far," I said. "But he was in movies. *Jailhouse Rock. Love Me Tender. Blue Hawaii.*"

"I thought those were songs," Michelle said.

"They are songs," I agreed. "But they're also movies."

"Oh, great," Michelle said. "Now Elvis songs are going on in my head." She stood up and started pacing. Watching her was making me tired.

Rajiv, Roland's assistant, came out of Roland's office. "Okay," he said. "We're setting up the video camera, so if you want to come on in, we'll get started right away."

Michelle took in a sharp intake of breath; it sounded like she was trying to inhale the ficus plant on the other side of the office. Rajiv jumped slightly at the noise.

"Give us just a minute," I said.

"No rush," Rajiv said, and closed the door.

"Oh God," Michelle said, wringing her hands. "Oh God oh God oh God oh God."

I went over and started massaging her shoulders. "Come on, Michelle," I said. "This is what you wanted."

"God, Tom," Michelle said. "Why am I so nervous? I've never been this nervous about an audition before."

"It's because you're finally using a script that has words longer than two syllables," I said.

Michelle wheeled around and pushed me, semi-hard, in the chest. "You're a jerk," she said.

"Noted," I said. "On the other hand, you're not hyperventilating any more. Now, come on. Let's do this thing." I took her hand, walked her to the office door, and opened it.

Inside was Roland, his assistant Rajiv, and a woman that I did not recognize. Roland and the woman were sitting comfortably on the couch; Rajiv was standing over a video camera, fiddling with something.

Roland got up and strode over to us as we came through the door. "Tom," he said. "A pleasure to see you again. I hope you are well."

"I am, Roland, thanks," I said, and motioned to Michelle. "This is my client, Michelle Beck."

"But of course. Miss Beck. The woman who has driven my poor assistant to traitorous activity. It is a pleasure." Roland took Michelle's hand, and in a playfully dramatic fashion, kissed it. Michelle smiled uncertainly and glanced over to me. I gave a shrug that said *go with it*.

"And now, if you'll both allow me to make introductions of my own," Roland said. "First, Miss Beck, I should like to introduce you to Rajiv Patel, my assistant, with whom you have had many long and interesting phone conversations. I believe somewhere in the office he may have erected a shrine to you."

Rajiv was dark-skinned enough that it was somewhat astonishing to be able to see his blush. "Hello, Michelle," he said, and went back to fooling around with the video camera.

"And this," he said, turning to the woman on the couch, "is Avika Spiegelman, who is one of the assistant producers of the film."

I walked over to shake her hand. "A pleasure," I said. "Are you related to Rachel Spiegelman?"

"She was my aunt," she said. "Actually my second cousin, or cousin twice removed, or whatever you'd like to call it. But we all called her 'Aunt Rachel.' It was simpler that way."

"In addition to being one of our producers, Ms. Spiegelman is acting as an advisor to the film, giving us insight into the real Rachel Spiegelman," Roland said. "As such, I thought it might be prudent to have her give us her thoughts."

"I loved you in *Summertime Blues,*" Avika said to Michelle. "You were perfect for *that* role."

Roland and I caught the subtext of that statement; Michelle did not. Instead she smiled brightly. "Thank you," she said. Avika smiled thinly. It was going to be a tougher crowd than I had expected.

"All right, we're ready," Rajiv said.

"Splendid," Roland clapped his hands together and turned back to Michelle. "My dear Miss Beck, if you wouldn't mind sitting in the chair in front of the video camera. Ms. Spiegelman will be feeding you lines while Rajiv records you. Do you have a copy of the script?"

"She memorized the scene, Roland," I said.

"Really," Roland said. "Well, that's certainly a point in your favor, my dear. Let's have a seat, shall we?"

Michelle sat in front of the video camera. Rajiv fixed the focus on the camera and then stepped back. Avika opened up her script. Roland sat back down on the couch. I stood back by the door.

Roland looked at Michelle. "Are we ready, then?"

Michelle nodded. Roland glanced over at Avika and nodded. Avika scrolled down her page until she found the line she was looking for. " 'How dare you tell me what I can and cannot do?' " she said, tonelessly. " 'You are my wife, not my master.' "

Michelle blinked, opened her mouth as if to say something, and then closed it again. "I'm sorry," she finally said. "Could you say the line again?"

" 'How dare you tell me what I can and cannot do?' " Avika repeated. " 'You are my wife, not my master.' "

Michelle stared at Avika, then stared over to me, panicked.

"Is something wrong, Miss Beck?" Roland inquired.

"I . . . uh . . . I," Michelle began, and placed her hand on her chest. Eventually she got out the words. "That's not the scene I memorized," she said.

"It's Scene 29," Avika said, peering over the top of her script.

"I memorized Scene 24," Michelle said. "I thought we were doing scene 24."

Roland looked over to Rajiv. "Rajiv, did you tell Miss Beck we were going to be doing Scene 24?"

"I don't think so," Rajiv said. "I'm pretty sure I said Scene 29."

"I must have read it wrong after I wrote it down," Michelle said. "My nines and my fours look a lot alike."

"As do mine," Roland said. "It's a common mistake, I'm sure. Why don't we just do Scene 24, then."

Avika was already there. "This scene only has four lines in it," she said. "Three of them are spoken by other characters."

"What's Rachel's line?" Roland asked.

Avika looked down at the page. " 'Yes,' " she said.

"Hmmm," Roland said. "Not a lot to work with."

"Now we know how she memorized the scene," Avika said. Even Michelle couldn't miss that one. She blushed and began taking in sharp breaths.

Roland clapped his hands together again and stood up. "Why don't we do this. Rajiv will go get a copy of the script for Miss Beck, and we'll spend a couple of minutes preparing Scene 29, and then we'll be ready to give it a go. Sound good? All right. Rajiv, if you wouldn't mind getting that script and working with Miss Beck for a couple of minutes, then. I'm going to go for a little walk." He wandered out of the room, distracted. After a moment, Avika Spiegelman followed him. Rajiv hovered, and then went out into the main office to get another copy of the script.

I went over to Michelle. "Don't panic," I said.

"What was I thinking?" Michelle said. She ran both her hands through her hair.

"You just memorized the wrong scene, that's all," I said. "It's nothing to worry about."

Michelle rolled her eyes at me. "Tom, the scene has *four lines,*" she said. "Don't you think I should have figured out it was the wrong scene?"

"Well, I think that the fact you're only line was 'yes,' should have been a tip-off," I admitted.

Michelle looked restless. I quickly held my hand up. "But— even so. It was an honest mistake, Michelle. You need to roll with it, and do the scene right." I took her hand and clasped it, lightly. "You can do it, Michelle. Just be calm."

"Did you see how that woman looked at me?" Michelle said.

"I get the feeling that Avika Spiegelman doesn't get many thrills out of life," I said. "Think of her as an object of pity, not of fear."

"She made me feel like an idiot, Tom. Like I'm back in grade school and the nuns are out to get me."

I grinned. "That's a pretty good simile, Michelle," I said.

"A what?" Michelle said.

Rajiv came back in the office with scripts in hand.

"Listen," I said. "Practice the scene with Rajiv. I'll track down Roland and schmooze the man. It's what you pay me the big bucks for."

Michelle smiled wanly as I exited.

Roland's office was tucked into a corner of the studio lot; to the left were huge sound sets. To the right was a little park in the center of a collection of offices. Roland was in the little park, standing. Avika Spiegelman stood next to him. As I got closer, it became clear that Avika was chewing Roland out over something. Before I could hear what it was, however, she saw me approach, clammed up, shot Roland a look, and walked away from him. He stood there, a rueful little grin on his face, as I came up.

"Looks like you two had a nice chat," I said.

"Lovely," Roland said, watching Avika walk back into the office. "It reminded me of some of the more painful dental experiences of my life."

"Up the anesthesia," I suggested.

"Or simply get defanged," Roland said. "Which is, now that I think about it, the process I'm undergoing at the moment. Tom, would you mind terribly if I had a smoke?"

"Not at all," I said.

"Thanks," Roland said. He fished out a Marlboro, and lit up. "I'm trying to quit," he said. "But I'm afraid now's not a good time."

"The audition is that bad?" I said.

"Well, Tom, we haven't really had the audition yet, have we?" Roland said. "We have to actually have lines read to see if they're being done properly."

"Ouch," I said, on behalf of my client.

Roland picked up on it. "Sorry about that, Tom," he said. "I don't mean to run Michelle down. She's a lovely girl. And I'm afraid I haven't been straightforward with her or with you about this reading."

"What do you mean?" I said.

Roland took a long drag on his cigarette before answering. "To be brief," he said, "I have less than a month left on my option for *Hard Memories*. If I don't have the lead cast by that time, I'll lose the option. The buzzards are already circling, you know."

"I didn't know," I said.

"Yes. Well, that's why Michelle is having a reading today, not because of your own work last week. In fact, once it became clear Ellen was going to drop, I told Rajiv to do whatever he could to encourage Miss Beck to read. I don't really expect her to be brilliant, mind you. But if she was passable, I thought I might convince Ms. Spiegelman to let us make the attempt. Michelle is, as you say, quite a draw at the moment."

"Not to be rude, Roland," I said. "But why does it matter what Avika thinks? You're the director and producer."

"Funny about that," Roland said. "One of the conditions the Spiegelman family put on my optioning the official biography was the right of refusal for the lead actress. At the time, when I had everyone from Ellen Merlow to Meryl Streep interested in the script, I considered it the least of my worries."

"I take it that Avika isn't impressed so far," I said.

Roland used his cigarette as a pointer towards the office. "In our conversation prior to your arrival, Ms. Spiegelman declared that she's met pets who are smarter than Miss Beck."

"Well, so have I," I said, truthfully. "But they haven't brought in $300 million with their last two films."

"And I wish you the best of luck convincing Ms. Spiegelman with that argument," Roland said.

"I didn't realize you had so much riding on this audition," I said.

"That's why I said I was sorry, Tom," Roland said. "I wasn't entirely honest with you on the matter. I don't know that it would have changed anything if I had been; still, I try to be more honest than the typical Hollywood producer."

"You have other projects in the pipe, I'm sure," I said.

"No, not really," Roland said, and brought back the rueful smile. "I'm a prestige producer, Tom. One of those fellows you hire when your studio has been cranking out one too many action films, and you need to throw in an Oscar contender to prove you still care about the art of filmmaking. None of my films actually make money. Even *The Green Fields* only broke even, and that after video. So I tend to work one project at a time. I've been thinking about that Kordus project, but you know where we are on that one. Which reminds me, have you looked at that script yet?'

"I did," I said. "It's very good." Actually, it wasn't just good, it was astonishingly good. And written by a twenty-three-year-old film student. Reading it, I had made the mental note to myself to get him to hire me as his agent, or steal him away from whichever one he currently had.

"It is, isn't it?" Roland puffed a final puff on his cigarette and threw it to the ground, snuffing it out. "If I don't manage to pull this project's chestnuts out of the fire, I'll have a nice long time to fiddle with it. Come on, Tom. Let's get back for the second act." We headed back.

Back in the office, Rajiv had pulled up a chair and was sitting with Michelle, going over Scene 29. Avika, upon seeing

Roland and me enter, pointedly looked at her watch and then at us both. "Well," Roland said. "Are we ready to begin again?"

Michelle looked at me, uncertain. I smiled back at her and gave her a thumbs-up signal. Rajiv rolled his chair back and took his position behind the video recorder. Roland sat down again and nodded to Avika. Avika recited her line.

My phone rang.

"Sorry," I said, after everyone glared at me. I ducked out of the office.

It was Miranda. "Carl wants to know when you're getting into the office," she said.

"Probably not long now," I said. "Michelle is self-destructing at the moment. Did he say why?"

"He mentioned something about someone needing a dog ASAP, and that Marcella would have details," she said. "I have no idea what that means. It sounds like code, and I've lost my secret decoder ring."

"I know what it means," I said. "But I can't. I have to be with Michelle this afternoon. I promised her I would go with her to have to her latex mask made."

"I'm just passing along messages," Miranda said. "I can't give you permission to defy the orders of your CEO."

I sighed. "Is Carl in right now?" I asked.

"Let me check," Miranda said, and put me on hold. My hold music, I was shocked to discover, was Olivia Newton-John. I was going to have to have someone drag my Muzak out of the eighties. Before it became thoroughly intolerable, Miranda came back on the line.

"Marcella says he's in a meeting right now but can schedule three minutes for you if you really need it. She also notes that his tone indicated that you probably don't want to need those three minutes."

The door to Roland's office opened up and Roland popped his head out. "Tom," he said. "I think you'd better come in here. We've had a development."

"Gotta go, Miranda," I said, and snapped the cell phone shut.

In the office, Michelle was lying on the floor. Rajiv, panting, was placing ice cubes on her forehead. He had sprinted to the bar to scoop up the cubes, proving chivalry was not dead, merely out of breath. Avika sat on the couch, not knowing whether to look concerned or outraged.

"I don't know what happened," Roland said. "She was very nervous about doing the lines, but she seemed all right. And then her eyes rolled back in her head and she fell off her chair."

"You're kidding," I said.

"She's out cold on the floor, Tom," Roland said, his gentility cracking just for a second. "I don't generally brain the actors at readings. I usually wait until we're actually on the set."

"What a fucking nightmare," I muttered, and then turned to Roland. "It's her autosuggestion," I said.

"What?" Avika said, from the couch.

I sighed again. "She's been going to a hypnotherapist," I said. "The damned fool put in an autosuggestion that blacks her out every time she gets too stressed out."

"That's the stupidest thing I've ever heard," Avika said.

I ignored her. "Give her a few seconds and she'll be good as new," I said to Roland.

"What a relief *that* is," Avika said, and stood up. "Well, I've wasted enough time for one day. When she comes to, thank her for her time and then show her the door. She's not getting the role."

Roland looked at Michelle sadly. "Yes, right, all right," he said.

"I don't think you're giving her a chance," I said. "You haven't even heard her do a reading yet."

"Who has the time?" Avika said. "Between the wrong scenes and the fainting, by the time we run through the scene, Roland's option will be up, anyway. As if it matters. Frankly, Mr. Stein, I don't know what Roland was thinking. Your client is good for roles that require teenagers to be deflowered. But this role is something else entirely. Michelle Beck has about as much in common with my aunt as David Hasselhoff has with Gandhi. After today, I'd rather give the part to a golden retriever than to her."

"I could arrange that," I said.

Roland jumped in before Avika could respond. "Thank you for coming, Ms. Spiegelman," he said, showing her to the door. "And don't worry. We'll find someone for the role."

"No offense, Roland," Avika said, "but if this is where we are in the casting process, I seriously doubt it." She nodded to me and walked out.

Roland turned to me and slumped slightly. "Scotch?" he said.

"No, thanks," I said. "I have to be driving back soon."

Michelle moaned slightly as she worked her way back into consciousness.

"Well, then," Roland said. "I'll have a double for the both of us."

"*Bad* day?" Miranda asked, when Michelle and I arrived at the office.

"You have no idea," I said, and walked Michelle into my office to lie down on my couch. Michelle's reaction to her incredible imploding reading had passed beyond mere depression and moved into the region of pharmaceutically untreatable mental states. I urged her to take a nap before she went to have latex splotzed all over her face.

"That's terrible," Miranda said, after I recounted our little adventure. "I mean, I didn't think she was going to be good for the role, but what a way to flame out."

"If I were her hypnotherapist, I'd lie low for a couple of weeks," I said. "I don't think their next session is going to be very pleasant. Listen, did you find out anything more about what Carl wants?"

"I did," Miranda said, reaching for her notebook. "I went over to Marcella's desk and got the message. Here—apparently a stunt dog they have on this Bruce Willis film contracted a nasty case of mange, and they need a replacement for some shots they're doing this afternoon." She tore the page out of her notebook and handed it to me. "You're going to have to spend a lot of time in makeup, Tom."

"Hardy har," I said, taking the note. The film was shooting in Pasadena, which was helpful—it wasn't far from where I lived, and not all that far from Pomona, where Michelle was to have her face done. "It's not me. It's Joshua, the Wonder Pup."

"Isn't that the name of your friend that's always calling?" Miranda said.

"It is. Oddly enough, they look a lot alike, too. When am I supposed to be at the set?" I asked.

"You're supposed to go as soon as you can," Miranda said. "Which, I'd guess, means right now."

"Fine," I said. "Miranda, I'm going to need you to do

something for me. You need to take Michelle to have her face done."

"I'm kind of busy here," Miranda said.

"Really," I said. "Doing what?"

"Answering phones?" Miranda ventured.

"Who's going to call? Carl isn't going to call, because I'm transporting his dog to the set. Michelle isn't going to call because she's going to be wrapped in latex. The only person who might call is Van Doren, and I don't want to talk to him, anyway."

"Hmrph," Miranda said.

"Is there a problem here, Miranda?" I asked.

Miranda scrunched up her face. "No. It's just that now that she's all depressed, I feel guilty for not wanting her to get the part. I forget that she's a real person sometimes, and not just this thing that makes $12 million for being perky. It annoys me to have pity for someone who makes more in a day than I'm going to make in a year."

"Try," I said. "I'm supposed to go with her, but I can't. You saw her, Miranda. She's definitely not in any condition to be by herself at the moment. She's certainly not in any condition to drive. I'm afraid in her state she'll zonk out on the 60, drive into opposing traffic, and mangle herself on a semi. Look, as soon as I'm done with this other thing, I'll be there. And anyway, Michelle likes you. Thinks you like her too, for some strange reason. Could be a big bonding moment for you two."

"Hmrph," Miranda said again.

"Come on, Miranda." I said. "You're my assistant. Assist."

"Can I expense lunch?" Miranda asked.

"By all means. Expense dinner, too."

"Whoo-hoo," Miranda said. "Taco Bell, here I come."

"So," Joshua said. "Can I have my own trailer yet?"

"Not yet," I said, "but look, you have your own water bowl."

"Man, that's the problem with being a dog," Joshua said. "The perks are just *not* there."

Joshua and I were waiting as the second unit crew of Bruce Willis's latest action spectacular set up their next shot. The first unit crew was in Miami, shooting on location with Willis and his costars. The second unit crew, meanwhile, was roaming around Los Angeles, shooting all the scenes the first unit didn't want to deal with: cut scenes, establishing shots, and, of course, scenes with dogs. Joshua was, in fact, the biggest star on the set that day.

In the space of less than one week, Joshua had become the most requested dog in Los Angeles film. It was the Mighty Dog commercial that did it: Joshua nailed it on the first take, no small feat in an industry where thirty seconds of animal action is often stitched out of twelve to fifteen hours of raw footage. This so stunned the director that he filmed the commercial twice just to cover his ass. Even with the extra take, the commercial was wrapped in two hours flat, saving the ad company about $200 thousand in fees. The ad company tried to lock Joshua down to an exclusive contract before the commercial was done. I politely declined. Joshua peed on the company rep's shoes.

By the time we got back to the house, Al Bowen had gotten ten phone calls asking to get Joshua for a commercial. We let Bowen pick and choose the assignments; I got the distinct feeling that Bowen was using the opportunity to rack up some long-term favors. He wasn't such a genial hippie after all. Not that it bothered either Joshua or me. Joshua was having fun and I didn't mind hanging around a set, grazing off the craft service table and catching up on my reading.

Joshua especially liked hanging around with dogs now that he was one—when we weren't at a commercial set, we'd go to the beach or a park where he could go off, tail wagging, to meet and greet other members of the species. I suspected that his enthusiasm for other dogs probably came from poor Ralph, who had spent most of his life not in the company of other dogs, and was now making up for lost time. But then, since Joshua had been on Earth, most of his time had been spent alone as well. So maybe they were both making up for lost time.

The tendency for vicious gossip, however, was pure Joshua. "See that dog over there?" Joshua pointed out a German shepherd with his muzzle. "It's my understanding that he was almost fired off the last set he was on because he just would not stop licking his genitals on camera."

"Stop it," I said. "What a horrible thing to say about your costar."

"Hey, I didn't *start* the rumor," Joshua said. "And anyway, it's true. I heard his trainer talking about it to another trainer while I was on set. From what I hear, off-camera, he runs through his paces perfectly. You couldn't ask for a better-trained dog. As soon as he hears the cameras running, though—bam, nosedive into the crotch. It's the sound of the cameras, I think. Such a good-looking dog too, you know. It's a real shame."

"You know, your gossip would be much more interesting if it were actually about human beings," I said.

"Maybe for you," Joshua said. "But I'm in the canine universe, Tom. It's a whole different ball game down here. See that poodle? She's a tick carrier. Saw one on her when we were doing that scene near the trees. It was the size of a Jeep, Tom. I was scared for myself."

"I don't think any of the other dogs would like you if they knew how you talked about them behind their backs."

"Well, that's just the point," Joshua said. "I can't very well tell any of them, now, can I? Language capability is a bitch, Tom."

"Pun intended, I'm sure."

"But of course."

Al Bowen picked that moment to walk up. "You sure spend a lot of time talking with that dog," he said.

"Well, I see you talking with your dogs, too," I said. "And with your other animals."

"I'm talking *to* my dogs," Bowen said. "You, on the other hand, talk like you're having a conversation. I can see you jabbering at Joshua from the other side of the set. I don't know how to break this to you, Tom. You may have the smartest dog in the world, but he still doesn't speak."

"Doesn't speak?" I said, feigning incredulousness. "Doesn't speak? Joshua, what's on top of a house?"

Joshua barked a bark that could have sounded like "roof," if one had enough to drink.

"And what's the bottom of a tree?"

This time, it could have been "root."

"And who's the greatest baseball player of all time?

The bark, with a little help, could have been a "Ruth."

"There you are," I said. "A talking dog."

"Very cute," Bowen said. "Could you please bring your talking dog to the set? It's the last shot of the day. We need him as the strong, silent type, if you don't mind." He walked away.

"Hmmmm," Joshua said. "Guess I should have said 'DiMaggio.'"

"I can't believe you actually knew the joke," I said.

"Between my brain, Ralph's brain, and Carl's memories, you'd be amazed at the stuff I've got up here," Joshua said. "Now, let's go. I do so love those tasty liver snacks I get whenever I do a scene right." He bounded off to the set, towards the German shepherd he had been backstabbing mere moments before. The German shepherd, oblivious to Joshua's treachery, greeted him with a sloppy canine grin.

It was a happy moment. As much as anything else, I remember that fact.

I answered the cell phone on the second ring. "Michelle can't possibly be done with her latex job," I said. "It's barely five o' clock."

"Tom, you have to get out here," Miranda said. Her voice odd, strained. "We have a problem. A big problem."

"What's the problem?" I asked.

"It's not something I think you'd want me to talk about on a cellular phone," Miranda said.

"It's a digital phone, Miranda," I said. "Virtually snoop-proof. Now what is it?"

There was silence on the other end of the phone.

"Miranda?" I said.

Suddenly Miranda was back. "Michelle's in the hospital, Tom. It's bad. It's very bad. They think she has brain damage. They think she might die. They have her on a respirator right now, and they're trying to figure out what to do next. You have to get out here now, Tom. She's at Pomona Valley Hospital. It's right off the 10. Hurry up."

"All right," I said. "I'm on my way, Miranda."

"Hurry up, Tom," Miranda said.

"I will," I said.

"Hurry," she said again, and then hung up.

After she hung up I realized her voice sounded odd because she'd been crying.

CHAPTER
Fourteen

This much we knew.

Michelle and Miranda arrived at the workshop of Featured Creatures, Inc., one of the special effects houses working on *Earth Resurrected*, at 3:15. Miranda said that she and Michelle barely talked on the way out to Pomona, or during the brief lunch they had at the El Loco Taco drive-in before heading out. Michelle would answer questions asked her, but that was about it; after about ten minutes of this, Miranda stopped trying to converse and switched the radio on to a light hits station.

They were met at Featured Creatures by Judy Martin, the technician who was going to plaster goo over Michelle's face. Miranda said that Martin looked somewhat dazed right from the beginning. As it turned out, Martin's husband had picked that day to announce to his wife that he was divorcing her, and that he intended to marry her younger sister Helen, who, if she really had to know, was the one he'd always been in love with, anyway. Martin had spent most of the day on the phone with her lawyer, her traitorous sister, her mother, and the Ford dealership at which she and her husband had just jointly purchased an Explorer. She wanted to send it back.

Martin took Michelle and Miranda back through the workshop to a room where the latex was to be applied. The room, fairly small to begin with, was stuffed to the ceiling with monster body parts, motor equipment for creature models, and two-gallon cans of latex. In a corner of the room was what looked like a dentist's chair, in which Michelle was to sit as the latex was applied to her face. Michelle sat in the chair and was ready to go, when the workshop intercom paged Judy to the phone. It was the Ford dealership. Martin went to the phone in the room, punched the flashing line button, and immediately began screaming into the receiver. Miranda looked over at Michelle to roll her eyes. Michelle was just staring out, blankly.

Ten minutes later, Martin slammed down the phone, hollered an obscenity at no one in particular, and stalked back over to the chair to prepare Michelle. As she was doing so, she spoke to Miranda.

"You're going to have to leave," she said. "You're going to get in my way."

"I'd rather stay," Miranda said.

"I don't care," Martin said "Get out."

Miranda flushed, a bad sign for whomever it was who caused the reaction. But before she could fully get her dander up, Michelle spoke. "I want her to stay," she said.

"This isn't a committee," Martin said.

"How about we do this," Miranda said. "You stay. We leave. We explain to the producers that we left because of you. The producers fire your company from the film. And then your company fires you."

At this point, Miranda swears, Martin actually snarled. Miranda grabbed a stool from one of the work benches and took a seat. Michelle reached over for Miranda's hand. Miranda gave it.

About five minutes later, as Martin applied the latex, Miranda spoke up again. "How is she going to breathe?" she asked, to Martin.

"What?" Martin said, spackling Michelle with a frosting knife.

"You're about to cover her nose with latex." Miranda said. "Once you do that, Michelle won't be able to breathe. Shouldn't you be thinking about these things?"

"Don't tell me my fucking job," Martin said, but went to find a couple of breathing straws for Michelle. As Martin covered Michelle's nose and eyes with latex, Michelle squeezed hard on Miranda's hand. Miranda squeezed back.

After Martin finished, she stepped back and turned to Miranda. "That's going to take about three hours to dry," she said. "She can't move between now and then."

"Where are you going?" Miranda asked.

"I have to make some phone calls," Martin said.

"You should stay here," Miranda said.

"Why?" Martin said. "You're here, aren't you?" She looked at Michelle again. "You know, she's my husband's favorite actress. He's such an asshole." And she walked out.

Over the next half hour, Miranda slowly became aware that the chicken burrito she had at El Loco Taco was doing terrifying things to her digestive tract. At first she ignored it, but near the end of the half-hour, Miranda felt the line between discomfort and peritonitis had become tissue-thin.

"Michelle, I have to find a bathroom," she said.

Michelle's grip on Miranda's hand suddenly became vise-tight.

"I'll go as fast as I can," Miranda said, pried her hand loose, and went to find the bathroom.

It was back near the reception area. On the way there, she saw Martin in an office, screaming into another phone. She thought about asking her to go back and check on Michelle. Then Martin grabbed the phone and hurled it furiously across the room. Miranda decided against it. In the bathroom, Miranda discovered just exactly what the burrito did to her; it was about ten minutes before she was done.

Miranda was walking back to the latex room when she saw Martin standing outside of it, with the door open. As she got closer, Martin heard her steps, turned around and yelled. "It's not my fault!"

"What are you talking about?" Miranda said. Then she looked into the room and saw.

Michelle was out of a chair and sprawled on the floor for the second time that day. This time, however, things were much worse. There was creature debris all over the floor. A can of latex lay on its side, its contents flowing out. Miranda looked up and saw the wreckage of a set of shelves; they had collapsed. Miranda's gaze went back down to the floor and she noticed a glint of red on the bottom of the latex can. Then she noticed the small pool of blood near Michelle's head.

"Oh shit," she said, and pushed Martin out of the way to get to Michelle.

Michelle sprawled face down; Miranda checked quickly to see if she had broken any bones, and then turned her over. That's when she saw that Michelle's breathing straws had fallen out and the latex had closed up over Michelle's nostrils. Michelle was suffocating.

Miranda immediately dug her fingers into the latex and began tearing it off of Michelle's face. Her lips were blue when Miranda ripped the latex away. Miranda got down in the latex and blood, reached a hand underneath Michelle's neck to lift it up, then began mouth-to-mouth.

"She wasn't supposed to move!" Martin said.

"Damn it," Miranda said, and checked for Michelle's pulse. It was there, faint and fast. "Call 911," she said, to Martin.

"Why weren't you watching her?" Martin demanded. "This isn't my fault."

Miranda launched herself at Martin, grabbed her, and slammed her against a wall. "I want you to do two things," she said to the cowering Martin. "First, shut the hell up. Second. I want you to get on the phone, call 911, and get an ambulance here, *now*. Do it, or I swear to you, I'll rip out your fucking heart. Do it. Now."

She let Martin go. Martin goggled at her for a second, then grabbed the phone and called 911. Miranda got back down on the floor and kept up the mouth-to-mouth for another ten minutes, until the paramedics arrived and pulled her off.

What we didn't know is what happened between the time Miranda left and when she came back. The most logical sequence of events has Michelle, claustrophobic, getting up from the chair in a blind panic, accidentally running into the shelves, being knocked unconscious from the falling debris, and then suffocating when the latex covered her nostrils. It was the scenario that the Pomona police, in examining the scene and questioning both Miranda and Judy Martin, latched onto and were going forward with.

There was one small problem. Miranda said that she didn't recall seeing the breathing straws around Michelle when she was giving her mouth-to-mouth. This might mean nothing, of course: when you're busily trying to save someone's life, you're not going to take the time to notice all the minutiae around you. But it might also mean that the breathing straws came out earlier. And that opened up other possibilities.

For Miranda, who had to be physically restrained by the paramedics from killing Judy Martin, the answer was simple: Martin's slipshod preparation had allowed the breathing straws to fall out. Michelle, frantic, reached for them, got up to get help, collided with the shelves, and got brained. I also thought Miranda may have suspected Martin of pulling the straws herself, as misplaced revenge against her estranged husband's favorite actress, but that was a little far-fetched for me.

My own suspicions were also far-fetched, but not nearly enough for my own comfort: I thought that Michelle, in her depressed state, might have pulled the straws herself, in a melodramatic and not-too-well-thought-out suicide attempt. Either she expected Miranda to come back and panicked when Miranda didn't arrive on cue, or she was sincere, and halfway through realized that suffocation was a nasty way to go. Either way, that's when she got up out of the chair.

And that's when I think her autosuggestion kicked in, knocking her out just in time to crash into the shelves. The only good thing I could possibly see out of this scenario was that she was already out of it when she was hit by the can of latex. She would have felt no pain.

No matter how you sliced it, however, Michelle was lying in a hospital bed, respirator down her throat.

I arrived over an hour after Miranda called; when I announced on the set that I had to take Joshua with me, I had to deal with both threats and begging on the part of the crew. I told them if they could do the scene in exactly five minutes, I would wait. In the meantime, I called Carl's office and told Marcella to have him call me as soon as possible. After that, there was no one else to call; Michelle had been an only child, and both her parents were dead. She wasn't married. As far as I knew, I was the person on the planet closest to her. At that moment, that struck me as the saddest thing I'd ever heard.

Joshua pegged the scene in one take, and immediately bounded towards my Honda; we screeched off without a good-bye and raced to the 210, got to the 10 by way of the 605, and then sat in evening rush hour traffic for forty-five minutes. Carl called; I filled him in on the situation, and he said he'd make some phone calls. I had no idea what that meant, but it made me feel better. I eventually got off the 10 and made it to the Pomona Valley Hospital on surface streets, quicker than if I had stayed on the freeway.

I understood the power of Carl's phone calls when I saw a man in a suit looking for me in the emergency area.

"Tom Stein?" he said.

"Yes," I said.

"I'm Mike Mizuhara," he said, extending his hand. I shook it. "Chief of staff for Pomona Valley."

"Where is Michelle?" I asked.

"She's in ICU right now; I'll take you to her immediately. But we have to do something with your dog," he pointed to Joshua.

"What? Oh. I'm sorry," I said. "I almost forgot he was with me."

"No problem," Mizuhara said. "Why don't we take him to my office? He can wait there." We headed toward his office.

"Has the press arrived yet?" I asked. I had been surprised not to see any reporters in the emergency room; news of these sorts of things usually got around quickly.

"No press so far," Mizuhara said. "The paramedics didn't know who it was because she had a whole bunch of stuff . . . latex? . . . all over her face when she came in. The doctors working on her either didn't recognize her or didn't care who she was when they got all of it off her. Then I got a call from Carl about it. We've got her registered under Jane Doe at the moment. She arrived just after a shift change. The next shift change is at 2 a.m. With any luck, we should be able to keep this quiet until morning. By that time, our press folks will be ready. Carl also wanted me to let you know he's on his way himself as soon as he can. He's asked us to clear a space for his helicopter in our parking lot."

"Carl is amazing," I said.

"Sure is," Mizuhara said. "But then, I owe him one. He gave my son a job at Century Pictures just before he left. Now my son is vice-president in charge of development. I never thought he'd ever get a job. Carl can use me any time. Here's the office," he opened the door.

I walked Joshua inside; Joshua gave me a significant look that I knew meant that he had something to say to me. I asked Mizuhara to give me a minute to reassure my dog and then bent down.

"What?" I said.

"Try to get me in to see Michelle at some point," Joshua said. "I can scan her if you want. Find out what really happened, at least."

"Thanks, Joshua," I said, and got up to go.

"Will he be okay in there?" Mizuhara asked.

"Sure," I said. "Don't worry. He's house-trained. Let's go see Michelle."

Michelle was on the third floor, in a private room in ICU. Miranda was waiting in the hallway; she rushed to me when she saw me coming.

"Oh, Tom," she said. "I'm so sorry. This is my fault. I'm sorry."

"Shhh," I said. "It's not anyone's fault. It's alright."

"Actually, Miss Escalon saved her life," Mizuhara said. "From what I understand, her mouth-to-mouth kept Miss Beck alive until the paramedics got there."

"Hear that?" I said, to Miranda. "You're a lifesaver for sure. I think that deserves another raise, don't you?"

Miranda gave a little laugh and then started crying again. I hugged her.

I spent a few minutes with Miranda, getting her version of events, and then went with Mizuhara to see Michelle. She was the only patient in a semi-private room with three beds. Her head was bandaged; the sounds in the room were of a heart monitor and the sound of a respirator inflating and deflating. It was a terrible thing.

The door opened and a tall man in a lab coat came through.

"Tom, this is Dr. Paul Adams," Mizuhara said. "He's the one that worked on Michelle."

We shook hands. "How is she?" I asked.

"She's not good," Adams said. "We don't know how long she was without oxygen, but we think she went right up to the limit—five or six minutes. Her heart activity is fine, but we haven't been able to get her to breathe on her own. Her brain activity is very low; I think it's very likely she's probably suffered some permanent brain damage. She's in a comatose state now. I think we can expect her to come out of it at some point, and then we can judge the extent of her brain injuries."

" 'At some point,' " I said. "What does that mean?"

"Hard to say," Adams said. "She could come out of it later today, or it could be weeks. It just depends. The concussion she got," he pointed to the bandage, "doesn't help any, although it's actually the least of her problems; it was fairly superficial. In and of itself, it would have knocked her out, but she would have come out of it with nothing more than a bump and maybe some stitches. It was the lack of oxygen to the brain that's the real problem. If you don't mind me asking, what the hell was she doing with latex all over her face?"

"They were making a mask of her face for a movie," I said.

"So that's how they do it," Adams said. "Well, I'm no expert on these things, but I think they might want to find another way to do it from here on out. That mask of hers just about killed her."

"Dr. Adams," I said. "This may be offensive, but I hope you won't be going to the press with any of this."

"You're right, it *is* offensive," Adams said. "But I understand your concern. The staff that worked with me all understand that it's more important for Miss Beck to recover than it is to be shown on *Inside Edition* with a tube down her throat."

"Thanks," I said.

"Of course," Adams said, and looked back at Michelle. "Don't expect too much from her over the next couple of days," he said. "But if you can, talk to her. Let her hear familiar voices. That helps as often as not. If she has any family, you should contact them and see if they can come as well."

"I'm afraid she has no family," I said. "Although she has a dog. Would it be okay to bring him in to see her?"

"I'd really rather not," Adams said. "It's a question of hygiene. Also of state law. Unless it's a guide dog, of course." We shook hands again and he departed.

"I have to join Dr. Adams," Mizuhara said. "Carl should be arriving any minute now and we want to be there to meet him." We shook hands as well, and he left.

I stayed in the room, staring at Michelle. Miranda was in the hall, feeling guilty about Michelle's situation, but if anyone had to shoulder the blame, I felt it should be me. If I had gone with her rather than Miranda, this might not have happened. Michelle and I would be on our way to Mondo Chicken, her to sulk in her oriental chicken salad, and me doing my best to cheer her up. It occurred to me that if no one was closer to Michelle than me, than the reverse was also probably true as well. I couldn't think of anyone I was closer to than her. Except possibly Miranda, who I had managed to drag into this mess as well.

I sighed to myself, and rested my head back against the wall. I had really managed to screw this one up.

After a few minutes, there was a knock on the door. Miranda poked her head through. "Carl is here," she said.

I went out to see Carl, Mizuhara and Adams chatting about something or other. Carl turned to me when he saw me. "Tom," he said, shaking my shoulder. "I'm terribly sorry. But you did right to call me. Mike and I go back a ways."

"So I heard," I said. "Los Angeles really is a small town."

"Yes it is," Carl said. "Tom, Mike and I were trying to decide what we should do next. My first inclination is to move Michelle closer, perhaps to Cedars, but Mike and Dr. Adams think she's best off here."

"If it's a question of the quality of care . . ." Dr. Adams began.

"No, not at all," Carl said. "But in the next twenty-four hours you're going to be dealing with things you've never had to deal with before. Photographers posing as maintenance workers and nurses. Fan vigils. Reporters trying to interview everyone down to the cafeteria staff. It's a mess."

"We've managed to keep the lid on it so far," Mizuhara said. "And I think Dr. Adams will agree with me when I say that the best thing for the patient is continuity of care. Additionally, I'm not comfortable with moving her now. She's stable at the moment but she's certainly not out of the woods."

"We'd probably cause more of a commotion moving her than just keeping her here, anyway," Adams said.

"Tom?" Carl said. "What do you want to do?"

"I don't think I'm really qualified to answer that," I said.

All three of them stared at me for a minute. I suddenly became very uncomfortable.

"What?" I asked.

"You don't know, do you?" Carl said.

"Know what?" I said, looking at Carl, then Adams, and then Mizuhara.

"Tom, we had her insurance send over her information," Mizuhara said. "Discreetly, of course; I handled the request myself. Most people have someone listed who has the right to make medical decisions for them if they are unable to make the decisions themselves. Usually it's a relative or spouse or a longtime companion."

"Sure," I said. I'd filled out insurance forms in my own time; if anything ever happened to me, my mother would have to decide whether to unplug me or not.

"Well, Miss Beck doesn't have any of those," Mizuhara said.

"All right," I said. "So?"

"Tom," Carl said. "The person who Michelle authorized to make medical decisions for her is you."

I found a chair and sat down.

"You really didn't know?" Adams asked.

I shook my head. "No. No, I didn't."

"I'm sorry," Adams said. "It's a hard job to have."

"Tom," Carl said, again. "What do you want to do?"

I covered my face with my hands and just sat there for a few minutes, awash in guilt and grief. I felt my actions had put Michelle here to begin with; now I was being asked to make decisions that could affect the rest of her life. I was going to need a really good cry when this was all over.

But not right now. I put my hands down in my lap.

"We'll keep her here," I said.

Now if I could just figure the rest of it out.

The leak, of course, was as impossible to track as it was inevitable to occur. Sometime after the 2 a.m. shift change, one of the janitors or nurses or doctors hit the phones, waking up friends and relatives because, after all, how often does the hottest female star in the United States come into your hospital in a coma? At 3:35 in the morning, one of these friends or relatives called KOST-FM and requested to hear "Your Eyes Tell Me," the hit theme song from *Summertime Blues,* because she heard Michelle Beck had died. After the song played, another listener called in to say no, she wasn't dead, but she was in a coma, and she had heard that Michelle's corneas were slated to be given to Marlee Matlin, who was, after all, deaf.

KOST happened to be the favorite morning radio station of Curt McLachlan, KABC's morning news director, who was, at

3:35, getting into his car to head to work. The first thing he did was switch off "Your Eyes Tell Me," because it was, by any objective standard, the single worst pop song of the decade. The second thing he did was get on the car phone with his counterpart at *Good Morning America,* which, at 6:37 Eastern Time, was just a few minutes away from air. GMA's news director screamed at the video morgue to pull up clips of Michelle, and at some poor, groggy intern, nineteen years old and two days into her stint of slave labor, to ready a blurb for the hosts to announce on the air. Once McLachlan got off the phone with *Good Morning America,* he called his own assignment editor out of a sound sleep and told him to get working on a package. He flipped on the radio just in time to hear about the corneas going to Marlee Matlin. This prompted another round of phone calls.

News of Michelle's death and/or coma hit the airwaves at 7:03 Eastern, 4:03 Pacific. The folks at GMA had the presence of mind to stress that the report was from unconfirmed "radio sources." It hardly mattered. Newspaper and magazine entertainment editors up and down the Eastern seaboard of the United States leapt from their breakfasts and called reporters at home, hollering their demand for verification. It was the biggest potential young star death since Heath Ledger slept his life away.

My phone first rang at 4:13 a.m. It was the gossip columnist from the *New York Daily News,* looking for verification. I hung up on her and disconnected my phone. Less than a minute later, my cell phone rang. I turned it off and then realized my other cell phone was lost in the woods where Joshua had left it. I reconnected my home phone, which immediately started ringing; I picked up the receiver, dropped it back in the cradle, and then picked up again almost instantly, before it had a chance to ring again. I called Miranda, apologized to her for waking her up, and told her to meet me in the office. Then I called Carl, who, as it happened, was already up and on the phone.

"I have *The New York Times* on call-waiting, Tom," he said. "They said they couldn't reach you directly."

"I disconnected my phone," I said. My own call-waiting was going off like mad, making the phone sound like a Geiger counter.

"Good man," Carl said. "These guys are nothing but a pain in the ass. I'm fending them off for now. What do you want to do?"

"I was going to ask you that same question," I said.

"Right now, we don't do anything," Carl said. "I've got to call Mike and make sure they're ready for the onslaught—it's going to hit earlier than we expected. You'll need to make a statement, though; let's schedule it for noon and have no comments from anyone until then. Are you planning to go into the office right now?"

"I was, yes," I said.

"Don't. The fact that you're in the office at four-thirty in the morning will only verify the situation. Get in at your usual time. And be ready for the reporters. See you at eight, Tom," Carl said, and then hung up, presumably to yell at the reporter that had the temerity to wake him up at home. I called Miranda as she was getting out the door; she sounded grateful for the reprieve.

At Pomona Valley, Carl's promised onslaught had already begun. The hospital switchboard was lighting up with calls from reporters who were calling every Los Angeles–area hospital trying to find the one that was treating Michelle. This was followed by calls from fans looking for the same thing. These in turn were followed by both fans and reporters who had found out that Pomona Valley was in fact the hospital they wanted; the reporters were invoking the First Amendment, and the fans their right to know about their favorite star. These were followed by fans and reporters posing as family members. As Michelle had no living family, this didn't get them very far.

Credit where credit is due: Mike Mizuhara was as good as his word. He had the ICU ward sealed off; everyone who stepped off the elevator or out of the stairwell was greeted by a Pomona city cop, who had a printed list. On the list was the name and, more importantly, the photograph, of every doctor, nurse, and staff member who had access to the third floor. Anyone who showed up on the third floor without permission was quickly and efficiently arrested for trespassing.

By 8 a.m., more than a dozen people, posing as doctors, nurses, or staff, were in the pokey. A couple of them, from the tabloids, tried to bribe the officers. The officers were not amused; they had integrity, and besides, Mike Mizuhara had informed them that any bribe would be matched, plus ten percent; I later learned that Carl, who had bankrolled this effort, ended up shelling out nearly $25,000. The would-be bribers ended up in the pokey like everyone else, their money confiscated as evidence.

One amateur video guy, hoping to sell his tape to the afternoon tabloid shows, simply got on the elevator and, when the door opened on the third floor, sprinted down the hall, yodeling, waving his video camera wildly in hopes that a frame or two would later show Michelle in her bed. He was surprised when the cop stationed at the stairwell popped up in front of him. He was even more surprised when the cop shot him with a taser. He was given his props for the attempt, but went to the slammer anyway.

When it became clear that no one was getting onto the
third floor, more drastic measures were attempted: four people
were arrested when they tried to trip the fire alarms to cause an
evacuation—three by pulling the fire alarm, one by setting fire
to that morning's edition of the *Inland Daily Bulletin* and waving it at the smoke alarm. He was caught by an orderly's flying
tackle; the tackle cracked his skull on the floor. He was treated
for concussion on the spot, and then transferred to the county
jail infirmary.

As Carl suggested, I went into work at the usual time. I
took Joshua with me, at his insistence. "I want to do something
for you," he said, though he wouldn't explain what. On the
way in, I flipped through the radio stations. Nearly all the radio
stations were talking about Michelle; on one, the DJ was la-
menting the fact that Michelle's possible death brought down
the number of people on Earth worth screwing. On another
radio station, a caller had noted proudly that he had uploaded
the faked picture of the three-way between Michelle, George
Clooney and Lindsay Lohan onto every single pornographic
blog and newsgroup as a "tribute."

The entrance to Lupo Associates was swarmed with reporters, camera operators, and sound men. As I parked I saw Jim Van
Doren near the periphery of the crowd, scanning the parking
lot for my car; he spotted it and started moving towards it.
Some of the more alert camera operators followed him; within
seconds a stampede was coming toward my car.

"Oh, shit," I said.

"Let me out of the car," Joshua said. "Then follow me. Get
ready to run."

I hopped out of the car and let Joshua out. Joshua hit the
ground running and hurled himself at the oncoming swarm,

snarling and baring his fangs. There was chaos as members of the press retreated, screaming, from Joshua's full frontal assault; suddenly a path miraculously appeared through them. I set out at a sprint. Reporters, torn between being bitten by an angry dog and getting their story, hollered questions at me as they retreated; their sound people desperately swung their boom mikes towards me to catch my response. At least one of the boom mikes connected with a camera operator. I heard a crunch as a $75,000 video camera hit the ground but didn't stay to watch.

Joshua snarled one last snarl, then raced towards the agency entrance, getting there at the same time as I did. We were met at the door by Miranda, who unlocked it just long enough to let us through, and then pushed it shut again the second we were inside.

I turned around, expecting to see the reporters pressed up against the glass, shouting questions. Instead, there was a riot going on in the parking lot. Apparently the cameraman who got whacked by the boom mike had decided to take the cost of the damage out of the mike operator's hide. A couple of people were trying to separate the two; the rest, drawn into the melee, were content to start swinging. There's something deeply satisfying about watching some of the most over-paid reporters in the country slugging each other, pulling each other's hair, and kneeing each other in the groin.

"Tom, you should have been a movie star," Miranda said. "You sure know how to make a hell of an entrance."

"It's not me that did all that," I said, still looking at the crowd. "You can thank my furry friend Joshua over there."

Off to the side of the riot, Jim Van Doren leaned against a car. He looked at the fight, then turned to look at me. Then he saluted. What a kidder.

"Did you do that, Joshua?" Miranda said, in that voice you use with dogs. "What a good dog!"

Joshua barked happily.

I spoke to the press at noon, like we had planned. Carl had flown in Mike Mizuhara and Dr. Adams from Pomona Valley; all four of us were standing at a podium that had been put in front of the agency's entrance. Slightly off to one side, Miranda sat, petting Joshua, who sat attentively, waiting for a reporter to get too far out of line. I was told that the press announcement was being carried live on three of the local stations and also on the E! Channel. For some reason, I found this profoundly irritating.

Precisely at noon, I stepped up to the podium, tapped the microphone to make sure it was on, and got out my prepared statement.

"Good afternoon," I said, because at thirty seconds past noon, it was. "Since early this morning, the media has been filled with rumors concerning the well-being of my client Michelle Beck. It has come time to answer these rumors with the facts.

"First, and most important—Michelle Beck is not dead, nor is she near death. Rumors of her death have been irresponsibly spread; let them end here.

"Second, yesterday, at about 4 p.m., Miss Beck was involved in an accident during preproduction work on *Earth Resurrected*. The accident caused her to be suffocated; first aid was administered at the scene, and Miss Beck was then taken to Pomona Valley Hospital, where she remains now.

"Miss Beck has not regained consciousness since the accident, nor is there a timetable for her to do so. After I am done, Dr. Adams, who treated Michelle when she came in, and Dr. Mizuhara, the chief of staff of Pomona Valley, will give a brief medical up-date on Miss Beck's condition and will answer questions that re-late to her medical condition.

"Those of us who know her are praying for her recovery and hope that her fans worldwide will also do so. However, we ask that you do not attempt to visit her; she needs rest and quiet. Pomona Valley Hospital and the Pomona Police Depart-ment will not hesitate to arrest and prosecute any unauthorized attempts to visit Miss Beck. Please respect this request: it's in Miss Beck's best interests.

"Pomona Valley has also requested me to ask fans and ad-mirers to stop sending flowers and fruit baskets—their waiting room is clogged and after this point they will just be thrown out. If you feel you must do something, please write a check to the Pomona Valley Hospital general fund. I know that Michelle would greatly prefer that to flowers—these people are helping her and they deserve all our support."

I folded up the prepared statement and asked if there were questions. Obviously, there were.

"What will happen to Michelle if she doesn't emerge from her coma?" asked the reporter from *Entertainment Weekly*. "Will she stay on a respirator or will she eventually be disconnected?"

"We haven't even thought about that yet," I said. "Nor have the doctors at Pomona Valley given us any indication that's where things are going. Until we know her medical situation a little better, it would be premature to think about it."

"Who is the one that will eventually make that decision?" asked the anchor of *Inside Story*. "Her parents or some other relative?"

"Michelle's parents passed away a couple of years ago," I said, "and she has no other family. When I got to the hospital, I was told that I was the person to whom she entrusted her emergency medical decisions. So I suppose if that decision has to be made, I'll be the one to make it."

This answer caused a mild stir. I pointed to the reporter from the *Los Angeles Times*, but before she could ask her question, someone in the back hollered a question.

"Do you think it's appropriate for you to make that decision?"

Everyone's head swiveled around. It was Jim Van Doren, of course.

"Excuse me?" I said.

"I said, do you feel it's appropriate for you to be the one that makes that decision? Yes, you're her agent, but recently, there's been some question about your own work and the way you've treated some of your clients. Do you really think it's wise for you to be the one who makes this life-or-death decision?"

Over to the side of me, I could hear Joshua growling lowly. I knew how he felt.

"Listen," I said. "I never *asked* to be the one Michelle gave this responsibility to. Drs. Adams and Mizuhara can tell you how surprised I was when I was told about it. Would I have wanted this responsibility? No. Will I refuse it now? No."

"Uh-huh," Van Doren said. "Are you the beneficiary of her estate?"

"What?" I said.

"I'm just thinking here," Van Doren said. "If you're the person she trusts with her life, you're probably the person that'd benefit from her death. She just got $12 million for *Earth Resurrected*; that's a lot. So are you the beneficiary? Or will that be a surprise, too?"

The crowd of reporters erupted. I just stood there, blinking, stunned that Van Doren could just casually imply that I was a crazed murderer. On the other hand, he was driving me insane, and if he'd been in reach, I probably could have killed him right there. Van Doren just stood there, with a little smile that said *gotcha*.

I was still gripping the side of the podium when Carl tapped me and gently dislodged me from where I was standing. Miranda came up to me and pulled me back away. Joshua looked up at me worriedly. I heard Carl speaking to the reporters—"Let's try to keep our eye on the ball, here . . ." he began—and then wheeled around into the building.

I stormed into my office and went to my office closet. Miranda came in about a second afterwards, followed by Joshua.

"What are you doing?" Miranda asked.

"Tony Baltz got me a set of golf clubs last Christmas," I said, rummaging. "I'm going to take one and put a divot in Van Doren's head. What do you think? The five iron? Or maybe the nine. Or the putter, right between the eyes."

"I don't think that would be very helpful," Miranda said.

"Oh, I think it would," I said. I emerged with the seven iron in my hand. "It would make me feel a lot better."

"Only for a minute," Miranda said. "But I have to warn you, prison is just one long bummer."

I burst into tears. No one was more surprised than I. Miranda rushed over and held me, returning the favor from the day before, when I had done the same for her.

"I'm sorry," I said. "It's not every day that I'm accused of murdering my client."

"Oh, shut up," Miranda said gently, cupping my face in her hand. "You didn't kill her, did you?"

"Of course not," I said.

"Well, then," Miranda said. "Don't let it bother you. Tom, you did more for Michelle than anyone else ever would have. You're a good man, Tom. Everybody knows it. I know it. You're a good man."

I kissed Miranda. No one was more surprised than I.

"I'm sorry," I said. "I don't know what I'm thinking."

"Oh, shut up," Miranda said, and kissed me back.

After a couple of minutes of this, Joshua whined, which I think is doggie equivalent of clearing one's throat to remind others you are there.

"Spectator," I said.

"He's a dog," Miranda said "He doesn't care."

"You'd be surprised," I said.

The situation became academic a second later, when there was a knock. Miranda and I disentangled ourselves as Carl came through the door.

"I've got Mike and Adams at the podium now," he said. "Are you all right?"

"I'm severely pissed off, but other than that, I'm fine," I said.

"Be prepared to be pissed off a little more," Carl said. "Brad Turnow's on his way over."

My brain fuzzed a second before I realized he was talking about the producer of *Earth Resurrected*. "Oh, Christ, what a pain," I said.

Miranda looked at me and then at Carl. "What does Brad want?" she asked.

"His money back," I said.

"His star is in a coma," Carl said. "He's going to have to get someone else to play the part. He'll figure that, since Michelle is laid up, it's only fair he should get his money back."

"What a jerk," Miranda said.

"Do you want any backup?" Carl said, to me. "We could gang up on him."

"No," I said. "It's all right. I can handle him."

"That's what I like to hear," Carl said. "Kick his ass a couple of times. He'll be here at 1:15. That leaves you two about an hour to smooch."

I think I blushed; Miranda, who is made of sterner stuff, merely smiled. "Mr. Lupo, with all due respect to your position, that's just none of your damned business," she said.

"On the contrary," Carl said, smiling back. "I didn't get where I am today by not noticing these sorts of things. Come on, Joshua," he said, motioning to the dog. "Whether it's my business or not, I know when I'm not wanted."

"It's a terrible thing that happened to Michelle," Brad said, stating the obvious.

"Yes, it is," I said.

"I mean, my God," Brad said. "I'd hate for it to happen to me."

My eyes flicked over to the clock on my phone. For five minutes now, Brad had been finding new and not-so-exciting ways to restate the obvious point that Michelle was in a world of hurt. I was giving him another minute before I worked him over with a golf club.

The question was whether Brad would be missed. Somehow I doubted it. Up until *Murdered Earth*, Brad was a distinctly lower-rung producer, cranking out cheesy, low-production-value science fiction and adventure epics that would just about break even in the theaters and then eke out a profit in the video store afterlife: the sort of films you make when you're either on your way up or down the Hollywood food chain, but never when you're anywhere near the top. *Murdered Earth* was the exception because for once, Brad managed to get lucky with a star who was breaking into the stratosphere. That was Michelle, of course; the studio estimated that Michelle's presence in the film added $55 million to the $85 million domestic take. Having seen *Murdered Earth,* I personally gave Michelle credit for another ten million or so.

But with a hit movie under his belt, Brad was now a mid-rung producer looking to move up the ladder a little more. *Earth Resurrected* was going to do it for him, or so he thought. Now that Michelle was down and his production suddenly air-braking into oblivion, Brad wanted to do what he could before the whole thing derailed and sent him crashing back down into the ranks of a straight-to-video producer. Which meant getting someone else for the part and trying to recoup on his losses.

If I were in his position, I'd probably try to do something like what he was doing. Of course, I wouldn't have given Michelle $12 million, either. Be that as it may, I could sympathize with his situation. The problem was, he was about to try to screw my client. Sympathize or not, there's no way I was going to allow that.

"Look, I'll tell you why I'm here," Brad said.

"I'd appreciate that," I said.

"It's terrible what's happened to Michelle," Brad said again. Below his view, I was groping for the seven-iron. "But it also creates a real problem for *Earth Resurrected.* Tom, we're just about ready to roll, and we can't wait too much longer. Hell, we've already got the special effects crews working on some scenes, and the second unit's out shooting."

I sat there silently, waiting for Brad to continue. He wanted me to be openly sympathetic to his plight, which I was not willing to do. After a few seconds of waiting for me to say something, he went on.

"The real problem is Allen Green," Brad said. "In our contract, we committed to a start date, and if we miss that start date by more than a week, he can walk, with his full paycheck. Pay or Play. That's twenty million, shot right down the tubes. The start date's in ten days, Tom. Even if Michelle comes out of her coma today, she's not going to be ready to go in ten days. You know that."

Again, I said nothing. Why make it easy?

Finally, Brad said what he came to say. "We have to replace Michelle, Tom. I'm sorry, but we can't wait."

"The reason you paid $12 million for her was because you thought she was indispensable," I said. "I don't see how that's changed. She's a lot more indispensable than Allen Green. She's the only person who'll have been in both films."

"She *was* indispensable," Brad said. "Don't get me wrong, Tom, I want her to be in the film. But she's in a coma! And everybody knows it."

The subtext here: since everyone knows Michelle's in a coma, no one will actually expect her to be in the sequel anymore. It can be used as an excuse to replace her without anyone complaining. It's a fair enough assessment, although it left unanswered the question of who would go see the sequel, good excuse or not, if the reason that over two-thirds of the audience went to see the original wasn't there anymore.

"If you're going to replace her, you must have someone lined up already, Brad," I said.

"We do," he said.

"Gee," I said. "That was fast. Michelle hasn't been in a coma a whole day yet."

Brad flushed at that one. "I told you, we're under some time pressure here," he said.

"You did," I agreed. "Who is it?"

"Charlene Mayfield," Brad said. "You've heard of her?"

I had, barely. Charlene was a clone of Michelle, which is not saying all that much, as blonde, perky types are fairly endemic in these here parts. Charlene played a waitress on one of those sitcoms that act as sacrificial offerings against other networks' far more popular shows and are thus canceled after six or thirteen episodes; if you weren't actually in the business, you'd probably have no idea who she is.

"She's going to be great," Brad said. "I think she'll be able to step right into the part. Not that she could ever truly replace Michelle, of course," he added hastily.

"Of course," I said.

"So," Brad said. "Are there any problems? You understand where we're coming from?"

"No, I have no problems," I said. "You're on a tight schedule, I understand."

Brad smiled. "That's really great to hear, Tom. I knew you would understand."

"Thanks," I said.

"There is one other issue," Brad said.

"Shoot," I said.

"It's about Michelle's salary."

"What about it?"

"Well, seeing as Michelle is no longer on the film, there's some question about salary disbursement," Brad said.

"What question?" I said. "You already mailed me the check.

I've already handed it over to our accountants to be processed. It's *been* disbursed, so I don't see how there could be a question about it."

"Well, that's just it," Brad said, uncomfortably. "I think you can see what I'm getting at here."

"I'm afraid I can't," I said. "You'd better spell it out for me, Brad."

He squirmed. It was fun to watch.

"Look," he said. "We'd like you to return the salary."

"Oh, is that all?" I said. "Heck. That's easy. The answer is no."

"What?"

"No."

"No?"

"What part of that two-letter word don't you understand, Brad?" I asked. "Was it the vowel that threw you, or the consonant?"

"God damn it, Tom," Brad said. "This isn't a joke. You can't just expect us to walk away from $12 million."

"I can," I said. "I do. You hired Michelle for a job. Now, through no fault of her own, you have decided you want someone else in the role. I'm fine with that. But inasmuch as Michelle did nothing to warrant her dismissal, I don't see how you could begrudge her her salary as severance pay."

"Jesus Christ," Brad said. "The girl's in a fucking coma!"

"Yes, she is," I said. "One that was brought about by the negligence of one of your crew members."

"That's not true," Brad said. "That woman worked for Featured Creatures."

"Which worked for you," I said. "You hired them, Brad. The legal line of responsibility goes right back to you."

"I think that could be argued," Brad said.

"You could try," I said. "It'll take you about two years to get a court date. In the meantime, I'm sure our legal department could probably hold up the start of your production a couple of weeks. Maybe a month, if we have to."

"You're a real son of a bitch," Brad said.

"Hey," I said. "I'm not the one trying to screw someone in a coma."

Brad decided to try another tactic. "Tom, look. It's not a matter of me not wanting to do right by Michelle. You know I want to."

"That's good to hear, Brad," I said.

"But now we're paying two actresses for the same part. We have to have some economies of scale going on here."

"So you're paying Charlene Mayfield $12 million?" I asked.

"Well, of course not that much," Brad said. "But we're paying her quite a bit."

"How much?" I asked.

"Well, I can't really discuss it," Brad said.

"Hmmm." I said. I buzzed Miranda. "Miranda, how much is Charlene Mayfield getting for *Earth Resurrected?*" I asked.

"Two hundred seventy-five thousand dollars," Miranda said. "According to her agent, who I just called."

"Really," I said. "Do we know if she's making any gross points?"

"Of course she isn't," Miranda said. "Although she's apparently getting a point on the net."

Net points are a promise of the percentage of profits the film makes, should it ever make it into the black; as opposed to gross points, which are a straight percentage of the film's haul at the box office. Since studio bookkeeping is such that even a film that makes a quarter of a billion dollars in domestic box office can run deeply into the red, net points are rarely if ever given—they're what you're given if you're gullible, stupid, or the screenwriter.

"A whole point on the net," I said, looking directly at Brad.

"That's right," Miranda said. "That'll be worth at least a case or two of Fresca." I thanked her and signed her off.

"Wow, Brad, $275 thousand," I said. "Aren't you the generous one. That's nearly as much as you're going to pay for your second-unit catering. Good thing I had Miranda listen in on the conversation and double-check that salary for us."

"That was a dirty trick," Brad said.

"It's not dirty, it's called looking out for my client's well-being."

"Is it about your percentage?" Brad said. "Because if it is, I'm willing to deal. What if I said you could keep your ten percent, clear? No questions."

I rubbed my forehead. It was barely 1:30, and I was tired already.

"Look, Brad," I said. "What say we cut the shit, because I'm having a really bad day, and you're not making it any better."

Brad blinked. "All right."

"Good," I said. "The fact of the matter is, you're not getting the twelve million back. The way I figure it, since you are the one who indirectly put her into the coma, it's the very least you can do. It's possible that if we took it to court, you might get that money back. But in the meantime you will have tanked your entire movie production. What is it budgeted at? Eighty million? Ninety million?"

"Eighty-three million, counting salaries." Brad just about spat the word *salaries*.

"Eighty-three million against twelve million is a bad bet any day, Brad. And that's not counting the money you're going to throw down the lawyer hole. *Our* lawyers are on staff. *We* don't pay them any extra. And, of course, we're not even talking about the countersuits we'll throw back at you for negligence and violation of contract. Not to mention the *other* suits that will be filed against you by the studio and your other investors if you close down production. Make no mistake, Brad, you're going to get fucked. You won't be able to sit for a year."

Brad bristled, which is exactly what I wanted him to do. I'd gotten into the sensitive area where males feel threatened and will make stupid, macho statements just so they'll feel their balls are still attached. I was hoping that Brad would grope for his testicles.

Sure enough, he did. "Don't you threaten me, you little asshole," Brad said. "If you want a court fight, I'll give it to you. You'll spend so much time giving depositions you'll forget what the sun looks like. Don't think I don't have what it takes to win this."

"I don't doubt that you'd try, Brad. But let me scope out a scenario for you. You go to court to snatch money away from an actor who your own negligence has managed to put in a coma. You tank the film you're working on to do it. Let's say that somehow you manage to win. Fine. You get your twelve million back, and you go back to your offices to get ready to do another movie . . . *and no one will work with you.*"

Brad's eyebrows knitted. "What do you mean?"

"I mean no one will ever work with you again. Actors won't want to work with you, because you've given the clear signal that you don't give a shit about them. Agents won't want to work with you, because they'll never be sure you won't try to dick their clients around. Studios won't want to work with you because you'll have made it clear that you value your pride over their money. Which is not an attitude they want to know about. *You will never work in this town again. Never.*"

Brad looked like he'd been kicked in the balls. Which, in a way, he had. "You don't know that for sure," he said.

I leaned forward in my chair, over my desk, close to Brad's ear. "Try me," I whispered.

I sat back. Brad sat there, stunned, for a good minute. Then he got up, spun out of his chair, stalked around the office a couple of times, sat back down, and started gnawing on his thumb.

"Fuck!" he finally said.

It was over. I won.

Now was the time to get him back to our side. "Brad," I said. "You don't *want* to have the money back. You think you do right now because you're cheap and you're in a panic. But it's penny wise and pound foolish. In the long run, you're going to look good by letting Michelle keep it."

Brad smirked. "Somehow I doubt that," he said.

"Such little faith," I said. "Try this one on: today, as you may or may not know, I was casually accused of setting up my client for her accident."

"I watched that in the office, right before I called," Brad said. "What an asshole."

"You have no idea," I said. "What if we say that I set up this meeting in a panic, and begged you to take the twelve million back? That way, from my point of view, any suspicion would be off of me, because I'd have no financial reason to off my client."

Brad looked at me strangely. "This benefits you, but I'm waiting to see how it benefits me."

"It benefits you, Brad, because you angrily refuse to accept the money back. How dare I assume that just because Michelle is in a coma, that'd you'd snatch the money back. We can say that in addition to refusing the money, you demanded that if Michelle didn't recover, that I donate the money to brain trauma research. Say, fund a professorship at UCLA Medical School or some such."

"What *were* you going to do with the money, if you don't mind me asking?"

I gestured to the heavens with my hands. "Damn it, Brad. I don't *know* that she left me her money. Even if she did, I sure as hell don't want it. If it got given to me, that's probably what I'd do with it. Yes, that's what I would do. But my point here is—this idea came from *you*. You look good because you took a stand for Michelle."

"And you throw the scent off of yourself."

"There is that added benefit, yes."

Brad thought about it. "And you'll say that this is what happened?"

"No, Brad," I said. "This *is* what happened. At least, as I remember it."

Brad smiled, even though I'm sure it hurt to do it. "You sure are a piece of work, Tom. All right, keep the twelve."

"And her gross points."

"Oh, come *on*, Tom," Brad said. "Stop with the kicking."

"Tell you what," I said. "I'll drop our twelve gross points if you give Charlene Mayfield six."

"What do you care?" Brad said. "She's not even your client."

"Brad, you moron," I said. "They're not from *me*. They're from *you*. Remember the concept: Make Brad Look Good."

"Oh. All right."

"Great," I said, leaned back and closed my eyes. I was getting a headache. When I opened them again, Brad was still sitting there, looking pensive.

"Something on your mind, Brad?" I asked.

"Hmmm? No, just thinking about the accident. It's a terrible thing, you know."

"I know," I said. "We've been through this."

"No, I know," Brad said. "I was just thinking about why we were having the mask made in the first place."

"You were going to have her head explode, or something, I thought," I said.

"Well, not really that," Brad said. "It's for this scene in the film where the alien overlord is trying to get control of Michelle's body—we were going to have the overlord stick his tentacles in her mouth and ears as a way to get to her brain. Really disgusting, of course—eyeballs popping and mouth really huge and all that. Obviously we couldn't do any of those effects with Michelle's real face."

"Glad that you recognize that, Brad."

"We could have used digital effects, but those things are expensive if you want them to look good," he said, apparently oblivious to the fact that his latex mask had, in fact, just cost him $12 million. He grinned suddenly, a rueful grin. "You know, I could have used that alien overlord right about now."

"What do you mean?" I said.

"Oh, nothing," Brad said, waving me off. "I was just free-associating. If our alien overlord was real, then it wouldn't matter if Michelle was in a coma or not. He'd just suck her brain out, plop himself in, and do the part himself. No one would know any better. Michelle's not exactly Meryl Streep. Would have saved me money, anyway."

Brad caught a look at my face. "Jesus, Tom," he said. "I'm sorry. That was probably not the nicest thing I could have said right about now. Sorry if I just upset you. You all right?"

"I'm fine," I said. "I'm sorry, Brad. I just had a thought myself."

CHAPTER
Sixteen

The door to the third floor of Pomona Valley Hospital opened, and I was confronted by the face of Officer Bob Ramos.

"Hi, Mr. Stein," he said.

"Hi, Bob," I said.

"Nice dog you have there," Officer Ramos said.

Joshua did his best stupid dog grin.

"Not my dog, it's Michelle's," I said. "I thought he might help bring her out of it. You know."

"Sure," Ramos said. "I guess we can pretty safely say you don't want Dr. Adams to know about it, right?"

"Right," I agreed. "I'm not visiting at two in the morning just because I'm not sleepy."

"Got it," Ramos said.

"By the way," I said. "I've got something for you." I pulled out a CD that I'd been carrying under my arm.

Ramos took it. "What is this?"

"You mentioned that your daughter was a fan of Tea Reader's," I said. "So I thought she might like to have an autographed copy of the CD. See, look, it's even made out to 'Maria.'" I didn't tell Ramos that the CD had in fact been autographed by Miranda. The chances of Tea Reader herself doing me a favor these days were slim and fast approaching none.

"Well, that was really nice of you to do that," Ramos said. "My little girl is going to be thrilled right out of her socks. You're a real stand-up guy, Mr. Stein."

"It's nothing," I said. "Glad to do it. Is anyone else in with Michelle?"

"I've been here since midnight and no one's come through except for the nurse," Ramos said. "You might check with Officer Gardner. She's over at the stairs. Been there since eleven."

"That's all right," I said. "I'm just going to pop in for a couple of minutes. You'll let me know if the nurse comes by again?"

"Sure," Ramos said. "I'll make a lot of noise. Give you enough time to hide the dog in the can."

"Thanks, Bob," I said, and then headed down the hall with Joshua.

The door to Michelle's room had been left open. Inside, a cone of light illuminated Michelle, whose bed had been positioned so she was reclining rather than lying down directly. The rest of the room was dark, and the other two beds in the room, still empty, had their curtains closed around them. I closed the door, and then went over to Michelle. She was unchanged: comatose and on a respirator. I felt a fresh wave of guilt.

"Tom," Joshua said. "I can't do anything from down here."

"Do you want to get on the bed?" I asked.

"No, that'd be mighty uncomfortable," Joshua said. "Grab me one of those visitor's chairs and put it near the head of the bed, please."

There was one near the bed on my side; I wheeled it around to Joshua's side, to avoid him accidentally knocking over the IV. He asked me to turn it around so that the back faced the bed; when I had done so, he jumped up on the chair and propped himself up on the back of the chair, putting himself on a level with the bed.

"That'll probably be close enough," Joshua said.

"Are you going to be able to reach her?" I asked.

"Sure," Joshua said. "Ralph's body is totally gone now, you know. It's all me. I can make tendrils now. It still helps to be close, of course. Now I have to figure out where to enter her head—she's got so many tubes in her. I think I'll go through the ears. This is going to take a couple of minutes, so don't talk to me for a few. I'm going to have to concentrate."

With that, Joshua made sure he was securely positioned, and closed his eyes. Then his face disappeared. His snout elongated and became the transparent goo that Yherajks were usually made of. It looked like a glass elephant trunk. The trunk waved in the air for a second, as if tasting the air, and then made its way to Michelle's head. An inch above her face, the trunk split in two; each tendril wandered casually over to an ear, then covered it. Michelle looked like she was wearing headphones that were attached to a headless dog.

The scene was so surreal that I lapsed into mute gawking. It took Joshua to bring me out of it.

"Tom," he said, "I think we have company."

"What?" I said.

"Turn around."

I did. Miranda stood there, a book in her hands. Behind her, the curtain was pulled back from one of the vacant beds. Miranda was looking past me, at the scene of Joshua and Michelle. Her eyes were wide and black, and she had the expression you get when you're seeing something horrifying and you hope you're dreaming.

"Miranda," I said.

Miranda glanced over at me, not really seeing me at first. Then I could almost hear her brain *click* as to who I was, where she was, and that she, in fact, was not dreaming. She opened her mouth and took a sharp intake of breath. In one more second, I knew, it would come out as the loudest scream I had ever heard.

I leapt at her. I clamped my hand over her mouth and turned her around. Then I picked her up and sprinted to the bathroom with her, kicking, in my arms.

Behind me, I heard Joshua say, in a conversational tone of voice, "If she screams, we're fucked, Tom. Calm her down." The conversational tone of voice was simply so that it couldn't be heard outside the room—Joshua's voice was as tense as I'd ever heard it. As I shoved Miranda into the bathroom, I caught a whiff of something rotten and realized that Joshua *was* screaming—just in his own language. I closed the bathroom door behind me, locked it, and hit the light switch to start the fan.

In shoving her into the bathroom, I had accidentally pushed Miranda into the sink. Her aborted scream went out of her with a *whuff*; her book went flying. She reeled sideways, colliding with the tub. I reached for her to help her regain her balance; Miranda grabbed me, ducked her head down, and launched herself into my abdomen. It felt like I had been hit by a cannonball, and the impact slammed me up against the door— I felt myself bounce off of it. I couldn't breathe and went down to the tiles.

Miranda was now pushing me away from the door, trying to unlock it. I lurched up from the floor, grabbed her around the waist, and pulled her to the floor with me. On her way down, Miranda cracked me in the eye with her elbow. There was a mushrooming sensation of pain behind my eyeball; I was pretty sure I was going to be blinded for life. But I held on, rolled over on top of Miranda, pinned her arms with my legs, and used my weight to pin her down. Miranda opened her mouth to scream again. I reached down to cover her mouth. Her head dodged sideways and then flicked back; she caught the side of my hand in her mouth and bit down, hard. I had to bite the side of my cheek to keep from screaming myself.

"Miranda," I said, gritting my teeth. "This is *really* beginning to hurt."

Miranda let go of my hand; I pulled it up and started shaking it in pain.

"Thank you."

"Get off of me, *now*," Miranda said.

"I will," I said. "But you have to promise me not to scream."

"Tom, I want to know what the *fuck* that thing was out there."

"That's good," I said. "Because I want to tell you. Now I just need you to promise me you're not going to run screaming. Okay?"

Miranda nodded her assent. I gladly collapsed off of her and leaned my back against the door, clutching my hand. I could feel the blood; I wasn't yet mentally prepared to look at it and see the carnage. Miranda got up slowly, never taking her eyes off me, and perched on the tub; she was preparing to make a hole through me if she had to in order to escape. I had been lucky to catch her by surprise. In a real fight, she could have sent me to the hospital. Fortunately, we were already there.

"Explain," she said.

"Remember Joshua?" I said.

"The dog?" she said.

"No, the other Joshua," I said. "Well, actually, yes, the dog Joshua, too. They're both the same person."

Miranda looked at me very dangerously. I held my hand up.

"Start over," I said, took a second and then started again. "You remember that secret project Carl has me doing."

"Yes."

"The project is about aliens. Space aliens. They had contacted Carl. He wanted me to find a way to introduce them to the world. That thing out there is one of them."

"Joshua," Miranda said.

"Yes," I said. "He was an alien first, and then he took over the body of a dog named Ralph. Long story."

"What is it doing to Michelle?" Miranda asked.

"He's scanning her brain," I said. "Trying to see if she's ever coming out of the coma."

Miranda shook her head violently. "This doesn't make any sense."

I laughed, weakly. "If you have a more rational explanation, Miranda, I'd love to hear it." I finally got up enough courage to look at my hand. It was covered in blood; Miranda looked to have ripped out a fairly large chunk.

Miranda noticed it too. "My God, Tom, you're bleeding," she said.

"I know," I said. "I think I have a black eye, too. Our first fight. Remind me never to piss you off again."

Miranda came off the tub, helped me up, and walked me over to the sink. She turned on the water and put my hand under it; I just about jumped out my skin from the pain.

"Sorry," Miranda said. "Sorry about everything, Tom. I just didn't know what was going on. I still don't."

"What were you doing here, Miranda?" I asked. "The officer at the front said no one was here."

Miranda shrugged and started soaping the wound, which hurt like you wouldn't believe. "Dr. Adams said that we should talk to her, that it might help bring her back out. I figured I would come read to her. I brought *Alice in Wonderland,* if you can believe it. I got here about eight. Around eleven I got tired. It was a long day. I didn't think anyone would mind if I took a nap."

The blood had been pretty much washed away; with it gone the wound appeared much less severe than it had seemed. Miranda grabbed a washcloth from the rack near the tub, folded it once, and pressed it over the wound.

"Hold it there for a while," she said. "It doesn't look that bad. I don't think you'll need stitches."

"That's a relief," I said. "It would have been a little difficult to explain how it happened." It was an attempt at humor, but Miranda wasn't biting. So to speak.

"Tom," she said. "You said that he was scanning her brain."

"That's right," I said.

"What happens then?" she asked.

"Well, if it looks like she'll come out of it, he'll do what he can to help her. He's got the experiences of thousands of his people, Miranda. One of them has to have been a doctor or a scientist that could make guesses on how to do that."

"What if she has permanent damage, Tom? What if she's never going to come out of the coma?"

I took a deep breath. "Then I'm going to ask Joshua to inhabit her body."

Miranda drew back. *"What?"* she said, rather too loudly.

"Keep it down," I said.

"Keep it *down*?" Miranda said. "We're talking about Michelle's life, and now that thing wants to take it so he can have the body? Don't you have a problem with that?"

"Miranda," I said. "If Michelle's never coming out of the coma, she's *already* dead. Brain dead, at least, with her body kept alive by a machine. She's gone. And if that's the case, then there's an opportunity to make her death at least have some meaning, an opportunity for something historic."

"It's body snatching," Miranda said.

"Not any more than organ donation," I said. "Look, Miranda, the Yherajk—"

"The what?"

"The people who Joshua comes from," I said. "They're called the Yherajk. In their natural form, they look like Jell-O globs. People will be terrified of them. But if they could see them in human form first, it would make it easier. We need a Trojan horse, Miranda. Something that will allow the Yherajk to make it through the door of human consciousness without terrifying humanity half out of its brain. Think how you just felt out there; now multiply that by six billion. We need a Trojan horse."

"The Trojan horse wasn't so great for the Trojans," Miranda said.

"It's just an analogy," I said.

"How do you know Joshua won't just say she's not coming

out the coma, so he can get control of the body?" Miranda asked.

"Because he doesn't know I'm going to ask him to do it," I said. "This isn't his idea, Miranda. It's mine."

Miranda slumped back down onto the tub and pressed both hands against her head, as if to keep it from exploding. "I think I'm in shock," she said. "I can't feel anything. I don't know what to make of what you're saying to me."

I knelt down until I was at her level and took her hand. "If you were in shock, you wouldn't know you were in shock, Miranda," I said. "I think you're going to be just fine. Listen, I know how sudden this feels. When Carl introduced me to Joshua, it was the same thing—just threw me right into the deep end. He trusted me to be able to swim. I trust you to be able to swim, Miranda. And I'm going to need you to help me from here on out. I've had to deal with this thing by myself— Carl gave it to me because he couldn't be seen handling it, and I couldn't get help from anyone else. Now you know. I need you to help me. I need you, Miranda. Okay?"

"Oh, God, Tom," Miranda said. "If I knew the job was going to be this tough, I would have asked for more up front."

"Hey," I said. "I already got you two raises in the last few weeks. Don't push it."

Miranda laughed that time. She had a very nice laugh.

"Good to see you're both alive," Joshua said, as we returned to the bed. "I was worried there for a while. It sounded like a cat got caught in a dryer."

"We got it worked out," I said.

"Good thing, too," Joshua said. "Because from the look of it, Tom, she kicked your ass."

"I pulled my punches," I said.

"I'm sure you did," Joshua said, dryly. "Hello, Miranda. Sorry about the surprise. I'm afraid you're not seeing me at my best. I really do look nicer with a head. But then, really, don't we all."

"Hello, Joshua," Miranda said. "I hope you don't mind if it takes me a little while to get used to this all."

"No problem," Joshua said. "Personally, I'm glad you're in on the secret. Tom could use a better brain than the one he's got."

"Enough with the insults," I said. "Have you found anything?"

"I'm afraid I have," Joshua said. "I have bad news and worse news. Do you have a preference for which you want to hear first?"

My heart sank. Miranda reached over and took my hand. "Might as well tell me the worse news," I said.

"She's gone, Tom," Joshua said, bluntly. "From what I can tell, large chunks of her brain had already died before Miranda got to her. She was down a long time. It's pretty obvious, actually; I'm surprised that the doctors here haven't already told you. They probably want to do a couple more CAT scans to be sure. But *I'm* sure. It's a mess in here. I'm sorry, Tom. I really am."

"Isn't there anything you can do?" Miranda said. "Tom said that you have the experience of doctors and scientists. Can't you do anything?"

"It's not a question of expertise, it's a question of raw materials," Joshua said. "Michelle's brain is severely damaged, and the damage affects a wide range of functions. It's not like a stroke, where the damage is localized, and the brain might find some way to route around the damage. Here, if I was to try to route around damage, I'd only come across more damage. They're never going to get her lungs pumping again on their own, and from where I'm at, most of the parts of the brain that control things like her liver and kidneys look to be nonfunctioning. I'd expect that in another day or so, you'll be told they expect liver and renal failure within a few days. I'm sorry, Miranda. If I could do something, I would. But there's nothing *to* do."

"What parts of her brain *do* work?" I asked.

"Well, her heart's still pumping, so that tells you something," Joshua said. "Her digestive tract is fine, not counting the liver or kidneys, which I've already spoken about. Her auditory centers are working—"

"She can hear?" I asked.

"That's not what I said," Joshua said. "The parts of her brain that process sound are still doing that. But the parts of the brain that *interpret* sound aren't. Sound is going into the microphone, but it's not being recorded, if you know what I mean."

"What about *her*?" Miranda said. "You're talking about her body processes. What about her? Her personality? Her memories? Those things?"

"Like everything else," Joshua said. "Some parts are there, some aren't. Most of her recent memories are here; I'd say the last couple of weeks for sure. After that, it gets spotty. Of course, that could just have been the way her mind worked, anyway. You humans remember some things better than others. But as to her personality—well, let's just say that if we managed to somehow get the rest of her brain working, and she came out of it, she wouldn't be the Michelle you remember."

"What would she be?" I asked.

"Psychotic," Joshua said. "Frankly I doubt that she would comprehend the world anymore. It would just be some terrifying blur to her."

"So she's dead," I said.

"She—Michelle—is dead *now*," Joshua said. "This body, on a respirator, will last about another week. Best estimate. I'm going to disconnect from her now, Tom, if you don't mind. The scenery in here is starting to make me depressed."

About a minute later Joshua was completely reconstituted as a dog. He leapt down from the chair and padded over to us.

"Is anyone else hungry?" he said. "I don't know what it is, but ever since I melded with Ralph, every time I'm depressed I just want to eat."

"Hold that thought for a second, Joshua," I said. "I have a question for you."

Joshua sat. "All right, what is it?"

"You're positive that Michelle is gone and that the body will be dead within a week."

"Pretty much," he said. "I'm sorry about that for you."

"Joshua, why don't you use her body?" I said.

Joshua looked perplexed. "Come again?"

"She's dead," I said. "And you could use her body. You would finally be able to walk around and interact with humans. Michelle was famous. You'd already have a high profile. You could finally be a true intermediary between our species. Michelle's gone, we know that. But here's an opportunity."

"Tom," Joshua said, slowly. "I know you think that what you're suggesting is a good idea. From where you're standing, maybe it looks that way. But it's not. I can't take Michelle's body."

Beside me, I could feel Miranda nearly collapse with relief. Despite what I told her, she must have still harbored the worry that Joshua was simply waiting to snatch Michelle's body. Now that he was rejecting the offer, Miranda could believe that he was genuine and honest in his intentions. I, however, was merely confused.

"I don't follow," I said. "*Can't* take Michelle's body? Or *won't* take Michelle's body?"

"Either," Joshua said. "Both. Can't and won't."

"Why not?" I asked.

"Tom, Michelle is brain-damaged. Even if I could inhabit her body, I couldn't control it or keep it alive. I need an at least nominally functioning brain to do that. Michelle doesn't have that any more. It'd be like trying to drive a car without a steering wheel."

"But that's just temporary," I said. "You have Ralph's appearance now, but there's none of Ralph's body in you anymore."

"That's true," Joshua said. "But Ralph's brain was in one piece when I inhabited him. I had time to learn how to be a dog. I don't have that here."

"That's the *can't*," I said. "And maybe we can find some way around that. What's the *won't*?"

"The *won't* is that Michelle didn't give me permission to inhabit her body or transfer her personality," Joshua said. "That's incredibly important, Tom. Otherwise it's tantamount to causing soul death. I won't do that. It goes against everything that a Yherajk stands for, ethically."

"You didn't get explicit go-ahead from Ralph, and yet you inhabited his body," I said.

"But I *felt* that Ralph wanted me to," Joshua said. "It's hard to explain. And at the very least, Ralph was my friend, my very good friend. I knew better what he wanted than I would Michelle, who I didn't know at all."

"It's what *I* want," I said. "And Michelle gave me permission to make decisions on her behalf."

"Not this decision," Joshua said.

"You don't know that," I said, almost accusingly.

Joshua sighed. "Actually, Tom, yes, I do."

"What do you mean?" I said.

"Remember when I asked you if you wanted the bad news or the worse news?" Joshua said. "Well, the worse news is that she's gone. But the bad news was, she did it to herself."

"What?" Miranda asked.

"I saw it," Joshua said, turning to Miranda "Her last memory. After you left, Miranda. Michelle pulled the breathing straws out and closed the latex over her nostrils. Then she waited to suffocate. She committed suicide."

Joshua turned back to me. "Right or wrong, Michelle chose to end her life, Tom. And that's why I can't take her body, no matter what you say. Her decision was to die. And I can't take that decision away from her. Neither can you. No one can."

CHAPTER
Seventeen

Carl opened his door and squinted out at us. "This had better be good," he said.

It was not quite 4 a.m.

"It is," I assured him.

Carl tightened his bathrobe and turned away from the door. "Fine. Stop hanging around on my doorstep, then. The cops around here arrest anyone who's not in a house or in a car."

Joshua, Miranda and I walked into the house. Carl had lumbered off towards his kitchen. When we caught up to him, he was stuffing coffee into a filter.

"All I can say is that you're lucky Elise is in Sacramento," he said. "She would have pepper-sprayed first, asked questions later." He shoved the filter into the coffee maker and flipped the switch to start brewing. He turned around, and finally got a good look at me.

"God, Tom," he said. "Who did that to you?"

"I did," Miranda said.

"That was quick," Carl said. "Most couples don't get to the hitting stage until after the wedding."

"Carl," I said.

"All right," he said. "What is it?"

"We need some moral guidance," I said.

Carl laughed. "Tom, I'm an *agent*," he said. He stopped laughing when he realized that no one else was. "Go on," he said, grumpily.

I explained the events of the evening; discovering Michelle's condition, my body-switching suggestion, Joshua's refusal. Joshua and I had argued about it for another hour after that point, stopping just long enough to be booted out of the room by the nurse, who gave me a lecture for bringing a dog into the ICU. Joshua and I continued the argument in the parking lot, neither of us giving any ground to the other, before Miranda suggested that we bring Carl into the discussion. Miranda had meant for us to bring it up in the morning, but Joshua and I decided it needed to be dealt with at that moment. We drove to Carl's place, Joshua riding with Miranda to keep us from killing each other.

By the end of the recount, the coffee was ready. Carl got down three cups, poured, and gave me and Miranda both a cup. After a moment's reflection, he pulled down a bowl, filled it with coffee, and set it down in front of Joshua.

"This is an interesting philosophical debate," Carl said. "But I'm still not sure what you want out of me."

"Easy," Joshua said. "We want you to pick a side. I'd prefer you pick mine."

"Joshua, this isn't a bar bet," Carl said, irritably. "It's not a matter of choosing sides. And if I sided with Tom, I doubt you'd do what he's asking of you, anyway."

"You're right," Joshua said. "I guess we woke you up for nothing. We should be leaving. Thanks for the coffee."

"Sit, Joshua," Carl said.

"Hey," Joshua said. "That's not funny."

"Tom," he said, turning to me. "You realize if Joshua is right about how Michelle died, he's also right in his position of not bringing her back."

"Why?" I said. "Carl, Michelle is gone. She doesn't need the body any more. And we can use it. You know this makes sense."

Beside me, Miranda gave a shudder and set her coffee down on the countertop.

"Something wrong?" Carl said.

"I'm sorry," Miranda said. "I understand where Tom's coming from, but the thought of having Joshua inside Michelle's body gives me the creeps. All I can see in my head is Michelle as a zombie. It just feels wrong in my gut." She glanced at me, then glanced away. "I'm sorry, Tom. But that's the way I feel."

"Go with that feeling," Joshua said.

"Oh, shut up," I said to Joshua.

"Christ," Carl said. "You two are worse than kids in a back seat. Tom, if Michelle wanted to die, then let her die. All of her. Michelle's body *is* Michelle. Unlike Joshua's people, our souls, if we have them, appear permanently attached to our body. Michelle has her right to die, not to be shuffled around like a puppet."

"Yes. Right. Thank you," Joshua said.

"You're welcome," Carl said, and then slurped at his coffee. "But I'm not on your side, either."

"What do you mean?" Joshua said.

"Joshua, let me ask you a question," Carl said. "What would you do if you discovered that Michelle had actually wanted to live?"

"She didn't," Joshua said. "I saw the memory of her pulling the tubes out myself. It was a conscious, active act. It couldn't have happened by accident."

"That may be," Carl said. "But that's not relevant to the question I'm asking."

"Sure it is," Joshua said. "Because that's what happened."

"Fine," Carl said. "Hypothetically, then. If you were to come across a situation that was a near duplicate of our Michelle's situation, with the only variation being that the person in the coma had wanted to live, would you inhabit her body, if asked by someone in Tom's situation?"

"No," Joshua said, "because that hypothetical person would still have severe brain damage, which would mean I could never control that body."

"Let's take as a given that some way could be found around that."

"That's a mighty big given," Joshua said.

"That's the magic of hypotheticals, Joshua," Carl said. "You can make the givens as big as you need them. Now stop stalling and answer the question."

"I don't know what I'd do," Joshua said. "Even if the situation fulfilled all the conditions you described, there's still this huge grayness to it. There's no way I could make the decision and feel absolutely sure I was morally in the right. If I was wrong, I'd be branded a murderer by the Yherajk."

"Even if we had urged you to do it?" Carl said.

"Carl, with all due respect, you're not a Yherajk," Joshua said. "You don't fully understand the implications of what you'd be asking. It's just not in your frame of reference."

"But you have my thoughts and memories in you," Carl said. "They're human thoughts. You should be able to know whether or not I, at least, understand the implications."

"Yes, but *I'm* not human," Joshua said. "There's a chance I could misread what's there, just as much as you could misread us."

"You'll admit to the potential for error?" Carl said.

"Well, shucks, Carl," Joshua said. "Nobody's perfect."

"So, theoretically, if there was some way that you could know that it was morally kosher, that you could somehow control the body and that Michelle had actually wanted to live, you could inhabit the body."

"Yes," Joshua said. "Throw me a sparkler and a kazoo, and I'd sing 'Yankee Doodle' while I was doing it, too."

"Well, then," Carl said. "Your problems are solved."

Joshua turned to me. "Tom, did you just follow that last turn of logic?"

"Not at all," I said. "You've managed to lose both me and Joshua, Carl."

"I got it," Miranda said.

"Ah," Carl said. "The smart one finally speaks. Would you please enlighten our little boys, Miranda?"

"Joshua, you just said what you needed in order to feel comfortable with what Tom is asking you to do," Miranda said. "Now all you have to do is do it."

"I said nothing of the sort," Joshua said.

"Yes you did," Miranda said. "You have three conditions: that you know it's moral, that you know it's technically possible, and that you know Michelle wanted to live."

"But we were dealing in hypotheticals," Joshua said. "I don't know why I have to keep bringing this up, but Michelle killed herself. She wanted to die."

"We don't know that," Carl said.

"Carl," Joshua said. "I *saw* the playback."

"But you said yourself a few moments ago there was a potential for error," Carl said. "You said that there was a chance you could misinterpret emotions and motivations."

"Pulling out your air supply is pretty straightforward action, Carl," Joshua said.

"The *action* is. What I'm interested in here is the emotion behind the action," Carl said. "Joshua, people act like they're killing themselves all the time around here. But a lot of them don't really want to die. They just like the attention they get afterwards. Or they don't truly comprehend that dying means death. Teenagers try to kill themselves all the time, because they want to see how people will react once they're gone. They don't make the connection that they won't be there to see the reaction."

"Michelle wasn't a teenager," Joshua said.

"No, but she was a movie star, which on the maturity scale is pretty close," Carl said. "She was twenty-five, worth millions, and people never told her no."

He pointed over to me. "Tom couldn't say no to her. He just tried to get her a part she had no business trying for, because he didn't want to say no to her."

I took that moment to pay especially close attention to my coffee cup. I could see where Carl was going, but it didn't make that last statement any less painful.

"When someone finally *did* say no to her, she got depressed and moody, and decided to make a statement. But that doesn't mean she really wanted to die," Carl said. He set his coffee cup down. "Now, if Michelle wanted to die, then we should let her die. Simple. But if she wanted to *live*, then, in a way, we can make that happen. Point is, we don't *know* what she wanted. We only have your version of the event."

"Then we have a stalemate," Joshua said. "Because I'm the only one that can get into her brain."

"No, you're not," Carl said. "You're just the only one on this planet."

Joshua and I exchanged looks again. Carl being inscrutable was really beginning to annoy me.

"What are you saying?" I said to Carl.

"We need a second opinion," Carl said. "Fortunately, we have a whole spaceship full of them."

"I don't want to take Joshua's side in this," I said, "but if we can't trust Joshua's take on Michelle's suicide, I don't see how getting another Yherajk's opinion is going to help anything."

"We don't need a Yherajk for the opinion," Carl said. "We need one to act as a conduit. Yherajk can connect into our nervous systems; that much is obvious, since Joshua looked at Michelle's, and my memories were downloaded to the entire ship's community. Now we just need it to go the other way, to let a human look at the memory. And I have just the Yherajk to do it."

The light suddenly went on in my head. "Gwedif," I said.

"Bingo," Carl said. "He's done it before, and, as it happens, he is the only Yherajk around that wasn't one of Joshua's parents. As far as these things go, he's the most objective party."

"I'm not following any of this anymore," Miranda said.

"I'll explain it later," I said. "Promise."

"I'm waiting to hear how you're going to get an alien through security at Pomona Valley Hospital," Joshua said. "We're fresh out of dog bodies."

"If Mohammed can't go to the mountain, the mountain will go to Mohammed," Carl said. "We can't bring Gwedif to Michelle. So we'll take Michelle to Gwedif."

"Go to the spaceship?" I asked.

"Of course," Joshua smirked. "That's *so* much easier."

"Joshua, it's the only way," Carl said. "Think about it. Suppose we find that you *were* in error. That solves one of our problems. But then we have two other issues to deal with: trying to find a way you can successfully inhabit Michelle's body, and making sure it's morally right to do it. We need to confer with the other Yherajk on each of these. She has to go to the *Ionar*."

"How do you suggest we get Michelle there?" Joshua asked. "We won't even be able to get her out of Pomona Valley. They've got tabloid reporters covering all the exits, Carl. They're going to know if we try to move Michelle."

"Let me worry about getting Michelle out of the hospital," Carl said. "You worry about arranging the rest of the trip."

Joshua sat there for a minute, considering. "All right," he said, finally. "I still have problems with this, but I'll get in touch with the *Ionar*. We'll see what they have to say up there." He padded off towards Carl's study.

"Where is he going?" Miranda asked.

"To the computer," Carl said. "I set up an America Online account for him and the *Ionar*. It's a nonconspicuous way for them to communicate."

"How does the *Ionar* sign on?" I asked.

"Well, it's a hell of a long-distance call," Carl said.

The e-mail response from the *Ionar* was brief. *You idiots,* it said. *You were supposed to* solve *problems, not* make *them. Haul her up here.*

Here's how you get one of the most popular actresses in the United States out of a hospital without anyone noticing.

First, you let it leak that your actress is going to be moved. This is a simple matter of having the appropriate doctor causally mention the fact to one of the nursing staff. From there it spreads like an airborne virus. From the staff, it logically goes to the press; despite Mike Mizuhara's best efforts, some of his staff was in the pocket of the tabloids. It's not just the custodial staff, either—you'd be surprised at what a cardiac surgeon pulling down $300 thousand a year will do for an extra thousand bucks. It was time to let this blatant self-interest work for us.

At 9 p.m., an ambulance pulls up to the emergency entrance of Pomona Valley. Nearly as soon as it pulls up, someone is hustled into it on a stretcher. The stretcher is effectively blocked from view by a clutch of burly orderlies and doctors—only the briefest of flashes show the blonde hair that give those watching (and taping) a clue as to whom it might be. The ambulance pulls away, with much slamming of doors, flashing of lights, and wailing of sirens, followed by a caravan of hastily-gotten-into cars. Two of these cars are in a slight fender bender as they rush out of the parking lot; neither driver bothers to stop as they speed after the receding ambulance.

That's the decoy ambulance.

Roughly twenty minutes later, a medical helicopter screams overhead, dropping dramatically into the Pomona Valley parking lot, as Pomona Valley has no helipad. The doors to the emergency entrance burst open, and a stretcher races to the helicopter, orderlies and doctors in a full sprint. On the way, a woman's arm slips off the stretcher and dangles, her IV tube fluttering with the speed of the stretcher's journey. As the stretcher approaches the helicopter, the side doors launch open; in one unbelievably smooth motion the stretcher is lifted into the helicopter and the doors slammed shut.

The helicopter is lifting off even as the ducking orderlies scurry away, its final destination telegraphed, perhaps, by the lettering on the tail of the copter: Cedars Sinai Medical Center. This time, a smaller contingent of cars flies out of the parking lot, their drivers fiddling with their scanners in an attempt to grab the frequency the helicopter is on, or yammering on cellular phones, trying to contact the editor at the home office whose job it is to listen to the scanners.

That's the decoy medical helicopter.

The next ambulance ambles in ten minutes later. This time around, there's no mad rush; the press has been rousted out of the blinds, so now Michelle can be taken to her destination safely, securely, and at sane speeds. Only two orderlies and one doctor accompany the stretcher to the ambulance. In a few minutes she's in; the doctor confers briefly with the paramedics, then walks away as they step back into their rig and drive away, no lights, no sirens, and proceed normally toward the 10 freeway. Only one car, bearing one smart, experienced reporter, follows. Patience is a virtue—it shall be rewarded.

That's the second decoy ambulance.

The real ambulance rolls in, lights flashing but no siren, as the other ambulance exits. The orderlies and the doctor, heading back into the hospital, turn around. Inside this ambulance is a man who appears to be having a stroke; the doctor does a quick assessment as the paramedics unload the patient, and rushes him through the emergency door. As the door opens on one side, it opens on the other, and another stretcher pops out and into the back of the ambulance, just like that. There's only two orderlies this time—me and Miranda. We go in the ambulance with the stretcher. The paramedics close the doors behind us.

Mike Mizuhara and Dr. Adams were, of course, adamantly against moving Michelle. By now they knew she was never coming out of the coma, and were pressing us to let them do what they could to make her comfortable, to see out the process that had begun at their hospital. Dr. Adams in particular was bitter about my decision to move Michelle; he relented only after I had promised that he would be able to actively consult with the doctors that were continuing her care. It was a lie, of course, since the doctors continuing her care were 50,000 miles away in orbit and not doctors in any conventional sense of the word. But that's not really something I could discuss without a long explanation, or without being committed to psychiatric observation by Dr. Adams.

The ambulance pulled away and got on the 10 heading east. Two miles later it exited, drove behind an Albertson's supermarket, and stopped. That was where the paramedics got out. Their cars were stashed there. They weren't paramedics; they were out-of-work actors with emergency medical training. Where Carl found two actors with that combination of talents in less than a day, I have no earthly idea. That's why he's the boss.

As it was, one of them was hesitant to leave Michelle. She took the time to check her respirator's function and to make sure we knew what to do if it malfunctioned. I assured her that we would be fine.

"Ted and I talked up front on the way here," she said. "Both of us would be happy to take her all the way to where she's going. We won't tell a soul. We just want to make sure she gets there in one piece."

"I believe you, and thanks," I said. "But that's really not possible."

She sighed and looked at Michelle. "Look at her," she said. "You know, a week ago, I would have done just about anything to be where she was. Now, I'd bet she'd do anything to be where I am. It's kind of funny, isn't it? Funny ironic, not funny ha-ha."

"It is," I said. "What's your name?"

"Shelia Thompson," she said.

"Shelia, if you don't mind me asking, what are you and Ted getting out this?"

"I don't know what Ted is getting," she said. "I never met him before, actually. I'm getting a part on a pilot. I don't have to audition—do not pass go, do not collect $200, just go straight to acting. I've actually read the pilot. It's a medical drama, of all things. It's not bad. It might even have a chance to get on TV somewhere. It seemed like a smart move."

"You're not sure now?"

She shrugged. "It feels like I'm walking over Michelle Beck to do it. It's not what I expected. I hope that doesn't sound ungrateful."

"It doesn't," I said. "Listen, I never do this. But do you have an agent?"

"No."

"In a week, give me a call at Lupo Associates. My name is Tom Stein."

"I will give you a call, but not about acting," Shelia said. "I want to know what happens to Michelle. It's going to be hanging over me until I find out. And if I find out she died, I'm going to feel partly responsible. So you'll tell me. Fair enough?"

"Fair enough," I said, and shook her hand. "Try not to worry, Shelia. Michelle's going to be all right. Really."

She smiled a little smile and walked away to her car.

Miranda stayed in the back with Michelle. I got in the front and got behind the wheel. Joshua was already in the front with me, having driven over with the actor-paramedics.

"You would think these things would be roomier in the front," Joshua said. "But they're not. I spent the last hour squashed down in the footwell. The woman paramedic had to keep her feet under her."

"I just met her," I said. "She seemed nice."

"She was," Joshua said. "The other guy, on the other hand, was a real jerk. Talked about his acting all the way over, and kept hitting on the woman. I nearly ripped out his throat with my teeth. Only the fact that he was driving kept me from doing it."

"It's good that you think these things out," I said, starting the ambulance.

"Thanks," Joshua said. "One of us has to."

"What is that supposed to mean?" I said.

"Tom," Joshua said. "If we can't bring Michelle back, what are you going to do? You can't just take her back to Pomona Valley, you know. And you can't drop her off anywhere else. And if she dies, people are going to want to know the circumstances. What are you going to do? You don't have a backup plan."

"What are you talking about," I said, turning out of the Albertson's parking lot and towards the 10. "Of course I have a backup plan."

"Really," Joshua said. "Why don't you share your backup plan with your studio audience, Tom."

"Sure," I said. "If this doesn't work, I'll be fresh out of ideas. We'll have failed. The Yherajk will have to go back. By way of compensation, you can take us back with you."

"I like it," Joshua said. "It's desperate and half-baked, but with a certain pathetic charm."

"Thanks," I said. "I just thought it up."

"I'm wondering what Miranda might think of it," Joshua said.

"Shhhh," I said. "I'm saving it for a surprise."

We got on the 10 and headed east to the 15, towards Baker.

"*I* can't see a damned thing," I said.

"That's the point, Tom," Joshua said. "If you can't see anything, no one else is going to see anything, either. Now shut up and turn left . . . now."

I swerved left onto an unpaved road that I would have missed if Joshua hadn't pointed it out. The ambulance bounced as it slipped into the ruts left behind by years of ranchers' trucks.

"Could you try to drive a little more carefully?" Miranda yelled, from the back. "I don't want to think what this is trip is doing to Michelle."

"It's not exactly paved road, Miranda," I shouted back. "We left that world behind about a half-hour ago. I'm going as carefully as I can."

The ambulance descended as I hit a ditch that wasn't there two seconds before.

"I think I just trashed the shocks," I said to Joshua.

"Tom! *Carefully!*" Miranda yelled.

"Sorry!" I yelled back. "Are we there yet?" I asked Joshua.

"No," Joshua said.

"Are we there yet?" I said.

"No."

"Are we there yet?"

"No."

"Are we there yet?"

"Yes," Joshua said. "Stop the car."

I stopped the ambulance.

"Thank God," Miranda said, from the back.

"I can't see anything," I said.

"You've said that before," Joshua said.

"Well, it's still true," I said.

"There's nothing to see," Joshua said. "They're not here yet."

"When are they getting here?" I asked.

"What time is it?" Joshua asked.

I looked at my watch.

There was a very large *whump*. The ground rattled. A wave of dust pelted the ambulance.

"Just after midnight," I said.

"Well, then, they should be here," Joshua said. "And there they are."

The cube was exactly as Carl had described it—black, featureless, nondescript in every way except that it had just dropped out of space into the middle of nowhere.

Miranda stopped her hovering over Michelle long enough to peer out from the back. "*That's* our ride?" she said.

"It doesn't look like much, I know," Joshua said. "But it gets incredible mileage."

"Do we just drive into it?" I asked.

"Yep," Joshua said.

I started the ambulance and inched it forward, cutting the fifty yards separating it from the cube. Then we were inside.

"When do we leave?" I said.

"In just a minute, I'd expect," Joshua said. "Here, let me out. I've got to go help pilot this thing."

I opened my door and got out, followed by Joshua. Joshua went over to the overhanging ledge on the other side of the cube, where the pilots were; a portion of the ledge descended and allowed him to get on. I went to the back of the ambulance and opened the doors. Miranda peered out at me.

I nodded at Michelle. "How is she doing?"

"Fine, I suppose," Miranda said. "She hasn't moved or done anything since we got in the ambulance, so all things considered, I guess that's good."

"How are you doing?"

"I'm all right," Miranda said. "Actually, I think this cube is helping. If it looked like an actual spaceship, I think I might be freaking out a lot more. How long are we going to be gone?"

"I don't know," I said. "Carl was gone less than a day when he went."

"We should have packed a lunch," Miranda said. "I'm hungry already."

"I've got gum," I said.

"Hey," Miranda said. "Do you hear that?"

I stopped and listened. Not far away, and getting closer, was the sound of a car.

"Joshua!" I yelled, moving away from the ambulance. "We need to leave! Now!"

The side of the cube tore open. A dirty white Escort shot through the hole, swerving. It was heading directly towards me. I froze, which was probably not the smartest thing I could have done.

The driver of the Escort hit the brakes just in time to keep from squashing me like a bug. Then he turned off his engine, undid his seatbelt, and got out of the car. There was a small grinding sound as the automatic shoulder belt moved forward.

"Sorry about that," the driver said. "I didn't expect anyone would be standing right in front of my car."

"What in fuck's name are you doing here?" I said.

"Getting my story," he said. "What's *your* excuse?"

It was Van Doren, of course.

CHAPTER
Eighteen

"Joshua," I hollered. "We have to stop."

Joshua poked his head over the ledge and looked down. "It's too late," he said. "We're already off."

"Can we throw him out anyway?" I asked.

"Now, there's a thought," Joshua said. "But the answer is no."

"Pity," I said.

"It's the problem with being a civilized species," Joshua agreed. "No convenient falls from a great height."

"Hey," Van Doren said. "That dog is talking."

Joshua laughed. "You think that's weird, wait about a half hour. It's going to be a long night, pal." He stepped back out of sight.

Van Doren turned back to me. "What's going on?"

"I'm interested in hearing what *you* think is going on," I

said. "And as long as you're talking, how you managed to follow us here."

"I got word that you were moving Michelle today," Van Doren said. "I considered staking out the hospital, but I decided to stake you out instead. I figured that no matter where Michelle was going, you'd have to go there, too, sooner or later. You weren't in the office this morning, so I went to your house, where I saw your car. And waited. At about four, you and Miranda left your house in your car. What's up with that, by the way?"

By this time Miranda had made it over to where we were. "None of your business, creep," she said.

"Sorry," Van Doren said, mildly. "Professional curiosity."

"I doubt the 'professional' part," Miranda said.

"Yow. Feisty," Van Doren said.

"Tom," Miranda said. "Don't worry about kicking him out of this thing. I'm going to rip his teeny little heart out myself."

"Works for me," I said.

Van Doren looked at us both uncertainly and then continued. "You two went to Lupo Associates from there, and then spent about an hour there before heading to Pomona Valley. A couple more hours passed before you guys had the parade of ambulances."

"Why didn't you fall for it?"

"Because I was following *you,*" Van Doren said to me. "None of those people rushing out with stretchers looked like you. Or like her, for that matter. As it was, I just barely saw you when you did sneak out. That was a pretty tricky operation."

"Not tricky enough, obviously," Miranda said.

"Well, I'm more motivated than most," Van Doren said. "I followed your ambulance to that parking lot and then waited to see what you did next. A couple minutes later you guys got back on the freeway, and from there it was just a matter of not calling your attention to me. I've gotten a little better at that since the last time I tailed you, Tom."

"I still don't see how you followed us out when we went on the dirt roads," I said. "There was no one else out there with us. I'd have seen your car."

"I followed you quite a ways back," Van Doren said. "And I killed my lights."

He pointed to his car. His parking lights and brake lights were shattered and broken. His headlights were fine, but then he could just turn those off.

"Nice," I admitted.

"Yeah, well, it'll probably be the last time they let me use a company car, anyway," Van Doren said. "I just about wrecked it on these dirt roads. Between that and having this car towed from when you kidnapped me, Tom, they're not going to give me the keys again."

"You're breaking my heart," I said.

"That's how I followed you here. As to where *here* is, and what's going on, I have no clue. I assumed this building was some sort of weird clinic."

"Building?" Miranda said.

"Didn't you feel the thump, Van Doren?" I said. "You didn't see this thing before you got to it?"

"I felt a tremor, sure," Van Doren said, slightly confused. "So? This is southern California. We have tremors all the time. It didn't feel like it was close by. And no, I didn't see this place. It's *black*. I saw your tail lights disappear and I just followed you in."

"It didn't strike you as odd, the way you came in?" I said.

"I came in the same way you did," Van Doren said.

"Wow," Miranda said. "You're just totally clueless, Van Doren."

"Thanks for the vote of confidence," Van Doren said.

"She doesn't mean it as an insult," I said. "She means it literally."

"I'm not following you," Van Doren said.

"Joshua," I called.

"Yo." He poked his head over again.

"I'd like to show our friend here exactly where we are," I said.

"No problem," Joshua said.

The cube disappeared. The Earth hovered below us, the moon off to one side.

Jim Van Doren screamed higher than I had ever heard a grown man scream before.

"I think we have some sedatives back in the ambulance," Miranda said, after we had Joshua retint the cube.

"Nah," I said. "He maintained bladder control. He'll be fine."

Van Doren leaned on the side of his Escort. For some reason he had a death grip on his radio antenna. "Holy shit," he said.

"I remember having that very same reaction once," I said.

"Are we really in space?" he asked.

"Oh, yes," I said.

"What the hell is going on?" Van Doren asked.

"Jim, remember that time in my car, when you asked me to tell you what I was up to?"

"Sort of," Van Doren said. "I'm not thinking too well at the moment."

"Try," I said. "It'll help."

Van Doren closed his eyes to concentrate. "You told me that you were doing something with space aliens," he said.

"Right," I said.

"I thought you were just being an asshole," he said.

"Just goes to show," I said.

He pointed over to Joshua's ledge. "And the dog is an alien."

"Mostly. It's sort of a long story," I said.

Van Doren's mind was working furiously now. "Is . . ." he began, looked towards the ambulance, and then back at Miranda and me. "Michelle Beck's an alien, isn't she? Something's happened to her and now you have to take her back to the mothership?"

Miranda giggled. Van Doren scowled. "I'm sorry," Miranda said. "I think the word 'mothership' did it to me."

"Well?" he said, to me. "Is Michelle Beck an alien?"

"No," I said. "At least, not yet."

"Not yet?" Van Doren said. "What does that mean? Are they going to assimilate her into their collective?"

Miranda burst out laughing.

"What?" Van Doren was shouting now.

It was a second before Miranda could catch herself. Then she gently touched Van Doren's arm.

"Jim, you've got to stop watching so much science fiction," she said. "It's making you talk funny."

"Ha ha ha," Van Doren said, peevishly, and pulled away. "Look, I'm just trying to figure out what's going on."

I considered Van Doren for a moment, trying to decide what I was going to do with him. Joking aside, murdering him wasn't an option. But he now knew more about the existence of the Yherajk than anyone outside of me, Miranda, and Carl, and that could be dangerous to us. I was loyal to Carl and Joshua, and Miranda was loyal to me, but Van Doren wasn't loyal to any of us. Certainly not to me. Quite the opposite, in fact, since in the last few weeks he'd been doing his damnedest to cut my career out from under me.

Well, I thought. *Time to change all of that.*

"Jim, why do you work for *The Biz*?" I asked.

"What?" he said. "What does that have to do with anything?"

"I'm just wondering," I said. "You make no bones that it's a shitty little magazine, and that you're doing shitty little jobs on it. But you're still there. Why?"

"I don't know if you've noticed this, but journalism is not exactly a rapidly expanding profession," Van Doren said. "Particularly in Los Angeles, where you basically have to put a gun to people's heads to make them read."

"You could always move," I said.

"What, and miss all this?"

"I'm serious," I said.

"So am I," Van Doren said. "Would you want to be an agent in Omaha, Tom?"

"No, but that's not where my business is," I said.

"Well, neither is mine," Van Doren said. "I write about the entertainment world. Have to be here to do that. I'm writing for a magazine that's near the ass end of that world, I admit that. But you have to start somewhere. Think of it as the journalism equivalent of working on a straight-to-video flick."

"Why write about entertainment?" I asked. "Really, who gives a shit about it? It's not really important. It's not real news. You're just wasting your time and talent, such as it is."

"Nice cheap shot," Van Doren said.

"I try," I said.

"And you're wrong," Van Doren said. "It's not a waste. You're so stuck in the belly of the beast that you don't notice it, but our entertainment is the single most successful export America has."

"Shucks," I said. "And all this time I thought our most successful export was democracy. Guess that was just another lie I learned in school. I hear evolution's kind of a crock, too."

"Look," Van Doren said. "Other countries pass laws requiring that their movie theaters, television networks, and radio stations have to play a certain percentage of homegrown entertainment. Because if they didn't, Hollywood would wipe it all out. We're not a world leader because we have nuclear missiles and submarines. We are because we have *Bugs Bunny and Friends*. Our planet is what Hollywood has made it."

"Planet Hollywood," I said. "Catchy."

"I thought you might like it," Van Doren said.

"But that's a stupid argument," I said. "The only people who believe that Hollywood sets political agendas are nuts on the left who are scared of action figures, and nuts on the right who are scared of nipples."

"Who's talking politics?" Van Doren said. "We're talking about how people around our world want their world to *be*. And the world they want it to be like is the one they see in our films, and in our TV shows and hear in our music. That's power. Hollywood, that's where the world culture starts. If someone wanted to address the world today, he wouldn't do it from Washington, or Moscow, or London. He'd do it from Hollywood. *That's* why I work in LA, Tom."

"Sure," I said. "And as a bonus, you get to meet stars."

"Well," Van Doren admitted, "There *is* that too."

"Joshua," I said. "You wouldn't happen to have been listening to this little diatribe, would you?"

"As it happens," Joshua said, from his perch. "I've been hanging on every word."

"Does it sound familiar to you?"

"A little," Joshua said. "Of course, I said it better."

"Jim," I said, turning back to Van Doren. "I have a proposition for you."

"Do you, now?" Van Doren said, and leaned back on his car. "This is going to be good."

"I don't suppose you can guess why I, of all people, am the one that knows about these aliens."

"It's a stumper, yes," Van Doren said.

"It's because I'm their agent."

"Their *what*?" Van Doren said.

"I'm their agent," I said. "In one of those bizarre and strange coincidences, Jim, their outlook on things is remarkably similar to yours: if you want to get the attention of the world, you have to go through Hollywood. So they decided to hire an agent. I'm him. As such, I'm authorized to make deals for them."

"Wow," Van Doren said. "How do you collect your fee?"

"After this is all done, I get New Zealand," I said. "Now, are you going to shut up and let me tell you what I have in mind?"

"By all means," Van Doren said.

"This offer stands for the next ten minutes. After that, you're out. No second chances or second thoughts. Are we clear?"

"Sure," Van Doren said.

"Here's the deal," I said. "You get the story. Exclusive."

"What story?" Van Doren said. "Your story? I have that already."

"*This* story," I said. "The first contact between humanity

and an intelligence from another world. It's the single most important story in the history of the planet, Jim. And you'll be the only one who's in on it from the start. The only one who knows the whole story. Everyone else will have the reaction story. You'll be the one who gets to tell the world how it happened and what it all means."

"Jesus," Van Doren said, after a minute. "You don't screw around, do you?"

"Not when it's business, Jim."

"What's the catch?"

"The catch is this: Drop your stories on me and Michelle. Quit *The Biz*. And keep your silence until we're ready to make our debut."

"When is that going to be?"

"I don't know yet," I said. "We're still working it out. It could be tomorrow, or it could be years. But whatever it is, not a peep out of you until then. Not even a hint of a peep."

"What happens if I refuse?" Van Doren asked.

"Nothing," I said. "Except that you won't be able to get off this ship while we're off doing what we're doing. In fact, you'll be sent back as soon as we get there."

"Without your car," Joshua said. "Have fun hiking back to the 15."

"What's to stop me from filing a story when I get back?" Van Doren said.

"Nothing at all," I said. "You can tell anyone you like. In fact, I encourage you to, since there's probably not a quicker and easier way for your credibility to get squashed than for you to run around saying that Michelle Beck is an alien."

"So she *is* an alien," Van Doren said.

"Jim," I said. "Stay focused, here."

"I *am* focused," he said. "I'm just trying to make sure I have the story right."

"Then you're in?"

"Are you kidding?" Van Doren said. "You're offering me the biggest story ever in the universe, and you're asking me if I *want* it? Are you that dumb?"

"It's not actually the biggest story ever in the universe," Joshua said. "Just in this little corner of it."

"Close enough for me," Van Doren said, and turned back to me. "You've got a deal, Tom."

We shook on it. Chalk one up for our side.

"You all right with this, Joshua?" I asked.

"Well, the only thing I've seen of his is that piece he wrote about you," Joshua said. "It was kind of lousy."

"I can do better," Van Doren said.

"Lord, I hope so," Joshua said.

"I don't suppose you could tell me now how much this gig pays," Van Doren said, to me.

"Don't worry about it," Miranda said. "Tom's easy to score a raise off of."

One of the Yherajk meeting us in the hangar pointed at Van Doren as the cube melted away. "Who is that?" it asked.

Van Doren pointed back. "*What* is that?"

"That's what my people normally look like," Joshua said.

"Yeeeg," Van Doren said. "I like the dog suit better."

"This is Jim Van Doren," Joshua said. "He was a stowaway."

"A stowaway? Arrrgh," The Yherajk said. "Ye'll be walking the plank come morning, laddie. Arrrgh."

"This is really not what I expected out of an alien race," Van Doren said to me.

"You get used to it," I said.

The Yherajk slimed his way over to me and extended a tentacle. "You must be Tom. I am Gwedif."

I took the tentacle. "It's nice to finally meet you, Gwedif. I've heard a lot about you. I'm sorry we have to meet in these extreme circumstances."

"Extreme? You have no idea," Gwedif said. "No one around here has been able to talk about anything else. The air stinks of shouting. That reminds me." A smell like a wet, mildewed rug erupted from Gwedif; one of the other Yherajk immediately set off towards the door. "Now that we have an extra human, we need another set of nose plugs."

Gwedif moved the tendril to Miranda. "This is Miranda, I assume," he said.

"Hi," Miranda said. She didn't make an attempt to shake the proffered tendril. "You'll have to excuse me," she said. "This is the first time I've seen one of you in your natural state."

"Of course," Gwedif said. "I look pretty ooky. But I'm a really nice guy once you get to know me."

"I'm sure you are," Miranda said.

Gwedif next considered Van Doren. "How did you happen?" he said.

"I'm a journalist," Van Doren said. "I was following a story."

"I'd say you caught it," Gwedif remarked. "What do you think of us aliens so far?"

"You remind me of the headcheese at a smorgasbord," Van Doren said.

"Is he always like this?" Gwedif said to Joshua.

"We don't know. He was sort of a last-minute addition," Joshua said.

"Usually he's worse," I said.

"Hmmmmm," Gwedif said. "You know, headcheese man, you and I are sort of in the same line of work."

"Nuts," Van Doren said, smiling. "And they promised me I'd have an exclusive on the story."

"I'm sure we can collaborate," Gwedif said.

The noseplug Yherajk had returned with three pairs of noseplugs. We each fitted them in. Then he joined the other Yherajk at the ambulance and lowered Michelle's stretcher onto the floor. I went over to her stretcher and checked the battery on the portable respirator. It was three-quarters drained.

"We'd better get moving on this thing," I said.

"What are we doing now, anyway?" Van Doren wanted to know.

"Nobody tell him anything yet," I said. I looked at Van Doren. "Sorry, Jim. Hold your horses a couple more minutes." I looked over to Gwedif. "Jim doesn't know exactly why we're here. I think that's something that could be useful for what we need to do."

"Yes, you're right," Gwedif said. "How about that, headcheese man. You might come in useful after all. We won't install the plank until tomorrow."

"How long are you going to call me 'headcheese man'?" Van Doren said.

"Oh, I don't know," Gwedif said. "It just has such a nice ring to it. Now, follow me, please, all of you. We're going to the meeting chamber."

The corridors were as low as Carl promised. Van Doren,

the tallest of us, suffered the greatest from the low ceilings and lower gravity, bumping his head and cursing. Here and there Yherajk crossed our path, but mostly stayed out of our way as we headed towards the meeting chamber.

Gwedif pulled up to me as we walked. "I wish we had more time," he said. "This happened with Carl, too. Barely time for introductions, and then off to decide the fate of our peoples. If nothing else, we've learned that you humans thrive on crisis."

"Anything worth doing is worth doing at a fevered pitch," I said.

"I don't know about *that*," Gwedif said. "I think the first place I'll go when I visit your planet—really visit your planet, I mean, not that little trip I took earlier—I think I'll go visit a monastery. Those people seem to have the right idea. Slow, meditative spiritual contemplation."

"I think most of the monasteries these days are either making chant CDs or boutique wines," I said.

"Really?" Gwedif said. "Well, hell. What is it with you people, anyway?"

Before I could answer, we got to the meeting chamber. Gwedif touched the door, and we went inside.

Inside, a double-tiered low riser had been constructed, on which lay several Yherajk. I suspected the tier was for our benefit, not the Yherajk's, so that we could see who we were speaking to. The Yherajk who brought Michelle's stretcher in set the wheel locks and left. I went and stood next to Michelle. Miranda joined me; Joshua walked over to one side and sat, his eyes closed. Van Doren stood between Joshua and the stretcher, looking lost.

"Will you be speaking for your group?" Gwedif asked me.

"I will," I said.

"Very well. Today's meeting is a little smaller than the one

Carl endured, for which your nostrils will no doubt be thankful," Gwedif said to us all. "Rather than a shipwide meeting, we have convened the ship's senior officers. Tom, you may be familiar with our ientcio—" The Yherajk on the far left raised a tendril—"who, of all Yherajk, is our leader."

"I have indeed heard him spoken of, in the highest terms," I said. "I hope he is well at this moment in the journey."

"Oooh, nice," Gwedif said. "You must have paid attention to whatever Carl told you. The ientcio returns your respects and welcomes you to the ship." Gwedif then introduced the rest of the officer complement, about twenty in all. I didn't bother trying to remember them all; I concentrated on Gwedif and the ientcio.

"Joshua has already given us his version of your request, and his issues with it." Gwedif said.

"When did he do that?" I said.

"Just now," Joshua said, and turned to me. "I used High Speech, Tom. One nicely pungent fart gets it all across."

"I'm glad my noseplugs were in," I said.

"You don't know how true that is," Joshua said.

"Now that Joshua has given his report, the ientcio would like to hear your request from you, and hopes you will be willing to answer some questions as well," Gwedif said.

"Of course." I said.

"Please begin whenever you are ready."

"All right," I said. I closed my eyes, said a little prayer to whomever might be listening, and opened my eyes. Then I began.

"*The* human you see in this stretcher is named Michelle Beck," I said, motioning to Michelle. "I was her agent, and also her friend. We were probably each other's best friends, though I don't think either of us realized it. As her agent, I helped to make her one of the most well-known actresses in Hollywood—people everywhere recognize her face.

"A few days ago, Michelle suffered severe and irreversible brain damage due to lack of oxygen to her brain. My friend is now for all purposes dead. Her body is being kept alive through the use of this respirator, but it will not sustain her body for much longer. Soon her body will be as dead as her mind already is.

"I mourn the passing of my friend, more than I can express. As I said, I don't think I appreciated what she meant to me when she was alive. Michelle was a good person—good in heart and in intention, which I think counts for something. I could be wrong. But I think it does.

"As much as I mourn Michelle, I see an opportunity in her passing, an opportunity that I think gives her death, which was as banal and meaningless as any death could be, some resonance. I have been asked by Carl Lupo to find a way to introduce the Yherajk to humanity, so that humanity can accept you as the friendly race you are, rather than for the terrifying creatures you appear to be.

"It occurs to me that one way to do this—perhaps the best way—is to have Joshua inhabit Michelle's body. To *be* Michelle. Michelle is already known around the world. That much of the battle is already fought. What we can do now is to raise Michelle's profile even further, and give her a worldwide platform to be the spokesperson for the Yherajk. She can be the most effective bridge between our two peoples—someone that humans know and who is not only nonthreatening, but the focus of admiration. She can be the human face of an inhuman race—the Trojan horse, if you will, that gets the Yherajk through the gate of humanity's fears.

"Joshua has several issues with inhabiting the body. The most objectionable of these has to do with her manner of death—not the actual moment itself, but the events leading up to it. Before any other issues can be raised, this one must be dealt with. We have to have a clear accounting of her death. That being the case, I'm asking that a Yherajk other than Joshua connect to Michelle's mind, and acting as a conduit, send the memory into the brain of a human. This would allow us to see more perfectly what Michelle was thinking in those last moments.

"Without this information, this opportunity for our peoples could be gone forever. And, as importantly for me, my friend, who I did not value as I should have in life, will be gone as well."

I bowed my head, and put my hand over my eyes. I didn't mean to choke myself up as much as I did. But saying how much someone means to you jackhammers into your head the fact of whether you mean it or not. I had meant it. I didn't realize how much.

"That was a very noble speech," Gwedif said, after a minute. "But we must hurry. Are you ready to answer questions?"

"Yes," I said, clearing my throat. "I'm ready."

"Very well. The ientcio will speak for the officers, and I of course will speak for him."

"All right."

"The ientcio wants to know what you think happened in those last minutes of your friend's life."

"If the ientcio will allow it," I said, "I'd rather hold off on that question, for reasons that I'll get into in just a minute. But

I can say that, being a human, I suspect that the situation was not as clear-cut as Joshua saw it. Joshua was looking at Michelle's actions, but perhaps not her state of mind."

"What gives you the right to make this decision for your friend?"

"She gave me the right, if she were incapacitated such as she is, to make medical decisions for her. I believe this qualifies me to take this action."

"What will you do if we refuse your request, or if the results are such that Joshua is not able to inhabit your friend's body?"

"I don't know," I said. "I don't really have a backup plan."

"That's not very wise," Gwedif said.

"No, it's not," I agreed. "But giving her a chance here is better than her having no chance back on Earth."

"You realize that if Joshua inhabits your friend's body, your friend will still be dead."

"I understand that. At the same time, Joshua has told me that he has retained the memories and some of the personality traits of Ralph, the dog whose body he inhabited, and those traits are still with him even now. My hope would be that some of who Michelle was might still remain after Joshua inhabits her body. However, even if doesn't work out that way, from the practical purposes of having Joshua inhabit Michelle's body, it won't matter."

"It occurs to the ientcio that you might be proposing having Joshua inhabit your friend's body merely out of convenience."

I blinked. "I'm not sure I follow that," I said.

"You said that this course of action may be the best way to introduce the Yherajk to humanity."

"Right," I said.

"What are some other courses of action?"

"I didn't come up with any others that were as good as this one, I'm afraid," I said.

"That's what the ientcio means," Gwedif said. "This is, you'll admit, a rather extreme course, and your pressing for it may simply be a way to keep you from admitting that you couldn't figure out a more conventional or at least sane way of introducing the Yherajk to your people. How is the memory of your friend well served by what might be your instinct to save your own skin?"

I flushed. "I wouldn't deny that having Joshua in Michelle's body would keep me from having to admit total defeat," I said. "But with all due respect to the ientcio, if he or the rest of you had wanted to do this conventionally, you should have just dropped a cube down on the steps of the White House and gone in for the tour. This is an extreme course, yes. But it will give a Yherajk a chance to live as a human, to be a human. Joshua has human memories, but that's not enough. It's like watching a documentary of a war. You can watch it a thousand times, but you still can't say you've fought. If you want to understand humans, you have to *be* one. Here's a chance."

"Wouldn't her family know that your friend has changed?"

"She has no family," I said. "The only person who would have been close enough to note the change would have been me. And maybe her hairdresser. I don't know."

"You say that a Yherajk could send the memory to another human being, so they might see it. Which Yherajk? Which human?"

"The Yherajk would be Gwedif," I said. "He's worked with humans before, and he's the only Yherajk on the ship who didn't parent Joshua, so that makes him more impartial than any other Yherajk might be. As for the human, I had originally thought I could do it, but I'm biased towards my argument. So it would have to have been Miranda. Miranda is morally opposed to the idea of Joshua inhabiting Michelle's body, but I trust her not to let her own opinion color what she would experience in the memory. But now, as it turns out, we've happened to pick up someone who is totally unbiased, since he doesn't know the specifics of Michelle's event. So the human who sees the memory should be Jim Van Doren."

"What?" Van Doren said.

"You're the man," I said, "who gets to read Michelle Beck's mind."

"How do I do that?" Van Doren said.

"I'm going to stick tendrils into your skull," Gwedif said.

"Is it going to hurt?"

"Not if you're nice to me from now on," Gwedif said, sweetly.

"Tom, you never told me that I was going to get probed," Van Doren said.

"It's not really a probe," I said. "Come on, Jim. You wanted to get the story straight, anyway."

"Is this seriously necessary?" Van Doren said.

"Yes, it is," I said. "Honestly. What you experience now could change the course of the world."

"It sounds so hackneyed when you put it that way," Van Doren said.

"It's hackneyed, but it's true," I said.

Van Doren turned to Gwedif. "Promise me my brain isn't going to end up in a jar," he said.

"It will stay safe and snug in your chubby little skull," Gwedif said. "I promise. You'll be fine."

"God, what have I gotten myself into?" Van Doren said. "All right. Fine. Whatever."

"The ientcio has a question for Jim Van Doren," Gwedif said.

"Okay," Van Doren said. "What?"

"Tom feels it would be appropriate for Joshua to inhabit Michelle Beck's body. Miranda does not. The ientcio wishes to know what you think about Joshua inhabiting this human body."

"Well, it would take her off my list of people to date," Van Doren said. "Other than that, I don't know."

"The senior officers will now debate the issue and render a decision," Gwedif said. "You may notice the room getting smellier for a few minutes."

It did. By the time they were finished, my eyes were watering. Miranda had to sit down. Van Doren was standing his ground, but just barely.

"The senior officers have decided to allow me to probe Michelle and transmit the memories to Jim Van Doren," Gwedif said.

"Good," I said. "Another minute of discussion and my sinus cavities would have imploded."

"It was not a unanimous vote," Gwedif said. "There was a lot of shouting."

"What do I do now?" Van Doren wanted to know.

Gwedif had him sit next to the stretcher and explained Van

Doren's options—Gwedif could go through his nose, which was the most efficient way, but the most uncomfortable, or through the ears, which was less efficient but least uncomfortable. Van Doren chose the ears.

"What am I going to be looking at?" Van Doren asked me, as Gwedif was preparing Michelle.

"You're going to be looking at the last moments of her life," I said. "The ones just before she goes into the coma."

"What am I looking *for*?"

"Don't look for anything," I said. "That's the whole point of you doing this: you don't know what to look for. Just let us know what you're experiencing."

"Will I be able to tell you as it happens?"

"How should I know?" I said. "I've never done this before, either."

"Man, your alien dog was right," Van Doren said. "This *is* the weirdest night of my life."

Gwedif slopped onto his ears before he could say another word.

"*What* are you seeing?" I asked Van Doren.

"I'm seeing your ugly face, Tom," Van Doren said.

"Try closing your eyes," I suggested.

Van Doren did. "This is so *very* odd," he said, finally. "I'm seeing some woman pouring goop over my face. I'm feeling the goop. What is this stuff?"

"Try sensing it for yourself," Gwedif suggested. "Just like you would your own memory."

Silence for a moment.

"It's latex," Van Doren said. "I'm getting a latex mask done for this stupid movie I'm doing. The woman who's putting the mask on me is a real bitch. A minute ago she tried to make Miranda leave. Miranda stood up to her, and she's talking to her now about something else."

Silence for another moment.

"Now the woman is sticking straws up my nose," Van Doren said. "It hurts, the way she's doing it, but I don't say anything because I just want to get this over with. I'm more depressed than I've ever been in my life. Hmmm. That's odd."

"What's odd?" I say.

"The way Michelle is experiencing that," Van Doren said. "She *is* depressed. Really, really depressed. But she's trying to make herself more depressed than she is."

"Why?" I ask.

"I don't know . . ." Van Doren trailed off for a minute. Then he said, "I think it's because she feels stupid. The audition earlier in the day went incredibly badly because she had prepared the wrong scene and because she fainted because of her treatment, whatever that means. She knows these things are her fault, and they were stupid little things. I think she'd rather be depressed than feel stupid. Yes, that's exactly what it is."

Silence again.

"My face is completely covered now. Miranda is telling me she has to go. I don't want her to go, because I don't want to be left alone. But I can hear the pain in her voice. I think she ate a bad burrito. I feel sorry for her; my lunch was fine. I let her go.

"Now I'm just sitting here, thinking, trying to make myself more depressed. But it's not working. I'm replaying the earlier audition in my head and I'm looking stupider each time I replay the memory. And now, to top it all off, I'm sitting in Pomona with straws sticking out of my nose, for a part that I got because someone wanted to fuck me a couple years back. I'm disgusted with myself. I yank out the straws, and fling them away. I'll just sit here and die with goo on my face."

There it was.

I looked at Joshua, who was sitting there, a sad doggie look on his face. He was right. He wasn't happy about it, but he was right. I bit the inside of my cheek until it bled. I was in a jumble of emotions. Sad for Michelle, who chose a stupid, stupid way to end her life. Angry at myself for believing that Michelle couldn't, wouldn't try to kill herself, and for taking her body so far away from where it should be. Fearful, because now I didn't know what I was going to do about Michelle. Or myself. Where could I take her to die? To finally die?

Miranda was sobbing quietly next to me. I reached over to her and held her. All she had to deal with was simple grief. I almost envied her. Which made me feel worse.

"Oh, this is stupid," Van Doren said.

"What?" I said.

"This is stupid," Van Doren repeated. "Now I can't breathe. I try exhaling really hard to blow the latex out of my nose but the goo keeps dripping down. I need those stupid straws. Now I'm going to have to get up and crawl around to find those damned things. Without messing up my mask, if possible, so I don't have to do this ever again. I try to get up out of my chair while keeping my face in the same position. I get up and start walking around, feeling for things. I bump into the side of something. I trip. Now I'm trying to keep my balance. It's not

working. I crash into something backwards. I can hear and feel
stuff falling behind me. Now nothing's making sense—there's a
flash of brightness and a ringing in my ears. I fall down. I realize I'm bleeding from the back of my head. Something must
have dropped on my head. I'm dizzy. I can't get up. I feel sleepy.
I guess I really *am* going to die. This really sucks."

CHAPTER
Nineteen

The response was immediate. Seconds after Van Doren's recounting of Michelle's last memory, the room erupted in a smell that can truly only be described as utterly fucking rank.

Somewhere in the smell-processing centers of my brain, my olfactory nerves handed in their resignations; Miranda moaned, turned away, and threw up. Van Doren, still connected to Gwedif, appeared unaffected. Later I found out Gwedif had suppressed his olfactory sense. Lucky bastard.

"Uh oh," Joshua said. "Now we've done it."

I leaned over Miranda and tried to help her. "Jesus, Joshua," I said, perhaps redundantly. "What's happening?"

"Remember what Gwedif said about the vote not being unanimous?" Joshua asked.

"Yeah," I said. "So?"

"Well, actually, it was. The senior officers were all against having Gwedif probe Michelle. All of them."

"What? So why did we go ahead?" I said.

Gwedif piped in. "The ientcio overruled them, Tom. On the grounds that it was important to see how accurate Joshua's interpretation of the event was, not because of your arguments. He said he was confident that Joshua's version was the correct one, and that it would only be polite to fulfill your request, as you are our friend and partner."

"He did this as a *favor?*" I was suddenly and uncontrollably outraged. "Hey, fuck him. And fuck *you* for going along with it, Gwedif. I'm not interested in favors for the sake of appearances. I'm trying to offer your fucking people what you said you want."

"Tom, please," Gwedif said. He voice sounded strained; I wondered how much of it was actual strain he was allowing me to hear, and how much was playacting, since the voice was an artificial way for him to communicate. "You don't know what's been going on around here."

"Enlighten me," I said.

"The senior officers aren't the only ones who are opposed to the idea of allowing Joshua to take control of your friend's body. Nearly everyone on the ship is. The taboo against inhabiting a thinking being against its will is extremely strong for Yherajk. It's entrenched in our culture in ways you can't appreciate."

"It's worth about five or six of the Ten Commandments," Joshua said.

"That's a flip way of putting it, but yes," Gwedif agreed. "And now you come and want us to throw aside all that entrenched thought, Tom. Frankly, there's a large group of Yherajk on this ship who think your request may be proof that humans aren't ethically developed enough for us to be involved with at all. They want to call this all off."

"But it's not as if Michelle is alive," I said. "She's brain dead. Dead."

"We don't *have* brains, Tom," Gwedif said. " 'Brain dead' is not a concept that has a direct translation. It doesn't come across to us. For Yherajk, there is body death, which doesn't necessarily mean the death of the personality. And there's soul death, which doesn't necessarily mean the death of the body. But if a Yherajk inhabits the body of another Yherajk, its because he's caused the soul death of the other. Murder, Tom. This looks and feels like murder to us."

"But she's *gone*," I said, almost plaintively.

"It's a distinction without difference," Gwedif said, quietly. "At least, for most of us. That's why the ientcio had to say that he was being polite."

"Huh?" I said.

"Christ, Tom, you can be dense sometimes," Joshua said, irritably. "The *only* way that the ientcio could get the rest of the senior officers to go along was by saying that we ought to honor your request for the sake of politeness. The senior officers went along with it because they had expected my version of the events to play out. Now that it didn't, they've got a whole new thing to think about. And *you've* got your foot in the proverbial door."

I took a minute to let what Joshua said sink in. "Wow," I said, finally. "They must not be very happy with you at the moment, Joshua."

"They're not," Joshua said. "Screw 'em. They were being provincial about it."

"But you were against it, too," I reminded him.

"Sure," Joshua said. "I'm still not entirely thrilled about the idea, to tell you the truth. But now I know that Michelle didn't really want to die. That helps. And also, you're right. This would probably be the best way for the Yherajk to meet humanity."

"I'm glad you've come around," I said.

"Don't get cocky," Joshua said. His tongue rolled out of his doggy mouth.

"What happens now?" I asked Gwedif.

"Now we argue," Gwedif said. "We have to see if the senior officers can wrap their minds around the concept of human death. Once we've done that, we might get them to see the wisdom of having Joshua inhabit this body. It could take some time."

"Hope you brought a good book with you," Joshua said.

Miranda, who had been slumped at my side, moved. "Do we need to be here for this?" she said. "If they yell anymore, I may have to barf up a lung."

"I'm sorry," Gwedif said. "You're right. No, you don't have to be here. This is something the officers will have to hash out for themselves. I can take you back to your car, if you like."

"I have to pee," Van Doren said, coming out of his daze. Gwedif disconnected; Van Doren's nose immediately scrunched up in disgust.

"I thought I told you to go before we left," Joshua said. "Now you're just going to have to hold it."

"Really?" Van Doren said.

"No, not really," Joshua said. "Hmmmm. We don't really have bathrooms, though. Let's go see if we can find you a secluded corner or something."

Joshua and Van Doren went off to find a bathroom substi-
tute; Gwedif, Miranda and I headed back to the ambulance.
Miranda opened the back and crawled onto the stretcher there.
Gwedif took his leave of us, promising news as soon as it happened.

I got into the back of the ambulance with Miranda and started
rummaging around. "I thought I saw water around here somewhere," I said. "Though it might have been plasma. I'm not sure."

"If you find it, give me some," Miranda said. "I've got the
great taste of vomit in my mouth and I want it out."

"Water or plasma?" I asked.

"At this point I really don't care," she said. She rolled on her
back and covered her eyes with her arm. "God. What a bizarre
day."

"So what do you think of the Yherajk?" I said. "Everything you ever wanted in an alien civilization and more?"

"They're fascinating," Miranda said, languidly. "An entire
people, amazingly technologically and ethically advanced, all
in desperate need of Dr. Scholl's foot deodorizers. Where's that
water?"

"Here," I said, handing her the bottle I found. "This is
clear, at the very least."

"Good enough," she said. She propped herself up on her
elbow and took a slug. Then she offered the bottle to me. "Want
some?"

"What, after you put your vomit-coated mouth on it? I don't
think so," I said. "Besides, I don't know where you've been."

"Yes you do."

"Well, over the last twenty-four hours or so, yes," I said. "But
before that, it's all one big, scary, dangerous blank. Twenty-seven
years worth of blank. Yikes."

"You're silly," Miranda said. "All my time is spent at work. When I'm not at work, I'm at home. No mystery there." She patted the stretcher. "Come take a nap with me."

"I think I should stay awake," I said. "Gwedif might come back."

"Tom, it smelled so bad in there that I threw up," Miranda said. "I think it will be a while."

"There's not enough room on that stretcher for both of us," I said.

"Don't be a baby," Miranda said. "I don't bite."

"I'm bitterly disappointed to hear that."

"Get me sometime when I'm not so tired," Miranda said.

I maneuvered onto the stretcher.

"See," Miranda said. "That wasn't so bad."

"I've got a metal rail in my back," I said.

"It builds character," Miranda said.

"Just what I need now," I said. "Character. Oh, great. I've got the extra arm."

"What?" Miranda said.

"When two people are in the same bed together, there's always an arm that gets in the way. It's this one."

"We're not in bed," Miranda said. "We're in a stretcher."

"Same concept," I said. "Even more so, in fact."

"Well, move it."

"Where?"

"Here."

"Here? That doesn't help."

"Here, then."

"If I keep it here, my entire arm will fall asleep. Ouch. No."

"You *are* a baby," Miranda. "How about here?"

"Wow," I said. "That *is* comfortable. How did you do that?"

"Hush," Miranda said. "I should have some secrets."

We were asleep in seconds.

We woke when Van Doren pulled open the doors of the ambulance. "Rise and shine, sleepyheads," he said, rather too cheerily.

Miranda grabbed at the water bottle and chucked it half-heartedly at Van Doren. "Die screaming," she said.

"Remind me not to be around you in the morning," Van Doren said.

"I don't think you'll need to worry about that one," Miranda said.

"Sorry to wake you guys up, but the senior officers have come to a decision and they want you guys to come," Van Doren said.

"A decision?" I said. "How long have we been asleep?"

"About six hours," Van Doren said.

"Six hours? Jesus, Jim," I struggled to get up without putting an elbow into Miranda. "Michelle's portable respirator only had a quarter charge in it."

"Relax," Van Doren said. "They recharged the battery."

"How did they do that?" I asked.

"These people use their technology to travel trillions of miles, and you ask how they can recharge a battery," Van Doren said. "Sometimes you're just not too bright."

"What have you been doing all this time?" Miranda asked Van Doren.

Van Doren puffed himself up, mock pridefully. "While you two were wasting time sleeping, I wandered around this place. Not bad. Although I have to say if we ever plan any joint human-Yherajk spaceship, they're going to have to come up with taller passageways. The top of my head is bruised. Enough chatter. I was sent to get you. They'll be annoyed with me if I show up by myself."

"Go on without me," Miranda said. "I'll just stay here and nap a little longer."

"No can do," Van Doren said. "They specifically asked for you to come, Miranda."

Miranda sat up when she heard this. "Why?"

"Do I look like I can interpret their smell language?" Van Doren said. "They didn't give me reasons. They just asked for both of you. Now, as Tom once said to me, less talk. More walk. Get up."

When we got to the meeting room, it was much less stench-filled than when we left it. Still, the residue of the hours-long debate wafted in the air of the room, like the echoes after a rally; it smelled like the lion cage at the zoo after a particularly large meal had been consumed.

"Tom, Miranda, Jim," Gwedif said, as we entered. "Welcome back."

"Thank you, Gwedif," I said. "It smells much better in here now."

"It got worse before it got better," Gwedif confided. "At some points it was so thick in here that we had to stop to clear the air."

"We use that expression, too," I said.

"Yes, but you don't mean it literally," Gwedif said.

Joshua, who had been conferring with one of the Yherajk, trotted over and spoke to Gwedif. "Got the last-minute objection ironed out," he said. "We're ready."

"Very well," Gwedif said. "Should you speak or should I?"

"It's your show, big man," Joshua said. "Far be it from me to steal your thunder."

"All right, then," Gwedif said, and wafted out a not-too-obnoxious odor. The Yherajk on the risers, who had been clustered in groups, broke out of the groups and arrayed themselves in their formal positions. When they had gotten to their places, Gwedif spoke to us.

"The ientcio wishes me to inform you that after much debate, the senior officers have decided, at this juncture, to withdraw all opposition on moral ground to Joshua's inhabitation of your friend's body," he said. "Be aware that this does *not* mean that the senior officers have fully resolved the overarching philosophical and ethical issues at hand. Far from it, in fact. Be that as it may, the senior officers have come to agree that what is moral and ethical for Yherajk may not have an exact analogue for humanity, and that this is likely to be one of those issues where the analogue does not exist. If nothing else comes of this, you may at least have the consolation that you've introduced a new philosophical issue for the Yherajk to argue about for at least a century or two."

"I didn't mean to cause trouble," I said, looking at the Yherajk that I assumed was the ientcio. "You have to believe that I meant well."

"The ientcio says he understands that you humans have a phrase—'The road to Hell is paved with good intentions.' He suggests that this may be a case where that phrase might apply."

"Possibly," I said. "But we also have another phrase, 'You have to go through Hell before you get to Heaven.' It might also apply."

"The ientcio agrees that it might indeed," Gwedif said.

"I can't believe you just quoted a Steve Miller tune to the leader of an alien race," Van Doren, standing next to me, muttered under his breath.

"Shut up," I muttered back. "It worked."

"With the ethical issues in this case tabled at least for the moment, we have one final issue to confront," Gwedif said. "But there is a complication. It involves one of you."

"Which one?" I asked.

"Before I can answer that, I have to request something," Gwedif said. "We have to ask something of one of you. That person must answer a question, and that answer must be truthful, arrived at without coercion from the other two of you. There's a number of ways that we could do this, but the most convenient would simply be for the one of you asked the question to answer it without conferring with others."

"How would you do that?" I asked.

"We'd ask the other two of you to step away and turn around."

"Kind of low-tech, isn't it?" Van Doren asked.

"You'd prefer electrodes or something?" Gwedif said, breaking formality for just a second.

"Well, no," Van Doren admitted.

"Then I suggest we do it my way," Gwedif said. "Will you all agree to this?"

We all nodded our assent.

"The person is Miranda," Gwedif said.

"Crap," Miranda sighed. "It figures."

"Tom, Jim, please turn around and step back," Gwedif said. "Please listen, but do nothing else."

We did as we were told.

"Now, Miranda," we heard Gwedif said. "As I'm sure you know, your friend Michelle's mind is severely damaged. Even if Joshua were to attempt to inhabit the body, he would not be able to control it, because of the severity of the brain damage."

"I understand that," I heard Miranda say.

"Normally, this would be the end of the issue," Gwedif said. "But Joshua has suggested another avenue that we have never explored. Simply put, it involves removing Michelle's remaining personal memories, then replacing the damaged brain, and using a template of another, similar brain to control Michelle's body."

"My brain," Miranda said.

"That's right," Gwedif said. "By examining how your brain functions and handles body operation, it's possible that Joshua might be able to train his own body to mimic your total brain function, and then use those functions to handle Michelle."

"Will that really work?" Miranda asked.

"We don't know. There are several issues that complicate matters. The first, of course, is whether Joshua can successfully map your brain at all, well enough to have that map control a human body. The second issue is whether the way your brain handles your body is at all similar to the way Michelle's brain handled hers. There are bound to be subtle differences, and possibly some that are not so subtle. The advantage would be that it would help give Joshua an even better idea of what it is to be human. It's also the only idea we've come up with that has a chance, however small, of succeeding."

"Why can't you use Tom's brain or Jim's brain as a model?" Miranda asked. "They're human, too."

"Yes, but they're men," Gwedif said. "On the level of bodily function, this presents obvious problems, since men and women are physically sexually differentiated. Tom's brain or Jim's brain aren't prepared, for example, to handle something like menstruation."

"*There's* a comment that works on a whole bunch of levels," Miranda said.

"I'll bet," Gwedif said. "Beyond the physical issues, men and women also have different cognitive structure to their brains—they use different parts of their brains to handle the same tasks. They're different enough that it would just make sense to use a woman's brain if we can. In a way, it's very lucky that you found out about Joshua; otherwise the chances of success for this idea would be even lower than they already are."

"How would you make a template of my brain?" Miranda asked. "Would you do what you did with Jim?"

"It's going to be quite a bit more involved than that, I'm afraid," Gwedif said. "Joshua would literally have to go swimming in your brain, examining each part of it, discovering how it functions and how it relates to every other part. He did this to some extent with Ralph, the dog whose body he inhabited, but in that case he had a couple of weeks to do it, and it was a fairly organic process. This will be much quicker and more invasive. There is some potential for injury on your part. We feel that it is small, but we would be remiss not to bring it up."

"What happens to Michelle's brain?" Miranda said. "I mean, the one that's in there right now?"

"I suppose we'd get rid of it," Gwedif said. "It serves no further purpose at that point. It's already terribly damaged, and if we can't get this to work, your friend Michelle will be dead regardless."

"That's terrible," Miranda said, and I could hear a trace of bitterness in her voice. "She deserves better than to have her brain, or any part of her, just thrown in the trash. Any of us do."

"I understand," Gwedif said. "And we're all very aware of your opposition to having Joshua inhabit the body. That's why we need to ask you, without input from Tom or Jim, whether you would do this. You will possibly be risking your own life and your own brain for something that is not likely to work. If it does not, your friend will certainly die. If it does, your friend is still dead and another person will have taken her place. This is your decision, Miranda. It can be made by no one but you."

I suddenly felt my hand taken up by Miranda's. "It's funny," she said. "I understand why you don't want me to ask Tom or Jim about it. I know how much this means to Tom. I don't know what it means to Jim, but if I had to guess, I'd say that he'd agree with Tom. But I think that either of them would tell me to make up my own mind. I'm sure of it, in fact."

I squeezed Miranda's hand fiercely. She squeezed it back briefly, and then let it go.

"I have a few more questions," Miranda said.

"Of course," Gwedif said.

"If Joshua goes into my brain, will he be making a copy of *me*?"

"I'll answer that," I heard Joshua say. "Miranda, no. I don't have any interest in things like your memories, just the way your brain handles your body."

"But who I am isn't just my memories, it's how I see the world," Miranda said. "Part of that's got to be how my brain works."

"Well, yes," Joshua said. "But, remember that your brain pattern is going to be overlaid onto my personality as it is now, and that Michelle's memories will also be in the mix. The end result is going to be something that's part you, part me, and part Michelle. And part Ralph the dog, now that I think about it. It's going to be a wild time inside *that* skull, let me tell you."

"How much of Michelle is going to be in there?" Miranda asked.

"I haven't decided yet," Joshua said. "I have to see what works and what doesn't."

"You have to promise me that you have as much of Michelle in there as possible," Miranda said. "And not just memories, Joshua. Anything of her that can be salvaged."

"I don't know if I can do that," Joshua said. "It may make it more difficult to inhabit the body."

"I don't care," Miranda said. "If you need me to do this, you have to live with my conditions. That's my condition. You and I don't belong in that body, Joshua. She does. I want as much of her in there as can be there. Or we have no deal."

"You understand that what you're asking may put you yourself at additional risk," Gwedif said. "Joshua will have to spend more time integrating your brain with what remains of her brain. The longer he has to be in your brain, the more dangerous it is for you."

"I figured as much," Miranda said. "But it's important to me. And it's the only way I'll do it."

"Are you sure?" Joshua asked.

"I am," Miranda said.

"All right," Joshua said. "I'll do it your way."

"Then I'll do it," Miranda.

It was only after I relaxed that I realized I was tense. I turned around.

"When do we start?" Miranda asked Joshua

"As soon as you're ready," Joshua said. "You might want to have that extra stretcher from the ambulance to rest on, though. It's going to be a long, drawn out process."

"I'll make arrangements," Gwedif said, and slid away to do

so. Joshua stepped back to the risers, apparently to confer with the senior officers. I went to Miranda, who stood there, looking drained.

"You're a star," I told her.

She smiled wanly. "I bet you say that to all the girls," she said.

"Sure," I said. "But I really mean it this time."

Miranda laughed a little, and then rested her head on my shoulder and cried just a little bit as well. Van Doren, who had been watching us, decided this was a good time to stare at a far wall. "Oh, Tom," Miranda said, finally. "I don't have the slightest idea what I'm doing."

"You'll be fine," I said. "You'll be just fine. I'll stay with you, if you want."

"And have you see me with aliens digging into my skull?" Miranda smiled more widely and wiped her eyes, clearing away the film of tears. "I don't think so, Tom. I don't think we're at that point in our relationship yet."

"I guess that's true," I said. "Most couples would save the alien probe scene until at least the tenth anniversary. You know, to add some zip to a stale relationship. We're just way ahead on that curve."

Miranda placed her hand on my cheek. "Tom," she said, not unkindly. "Right now, that's nowhere as funny as you think it is."

Miranda, Michelle and Joshua wheeled away towards the Yherajk medical area, shapeless Yherajk pooling on the sides of the stretchers, pulling it along. Van Doren and I looked at each other. We had no idea what to do with ourselves now. Gwedif, who remained with us, offered a full tour. I accepted, and Van

Doren tagged along, apparently excited at the idea of actually understanding what it was he was looking at this time.

The rest of the ship was as visually unappealing as what we had already seen: corridor and rooms carved out of the stone of the asteroid, smoothed over and filled with the Yherajks' equipment. For all intents and purposes, we could have been at a science lab anywhere on the planet—everything functional, none of it aesthetically pleasing.

Gwedif, who was trying to keep us distracted from our concern about Miranda and Michelle, acknowledged that for us the ship might not be tremendously exciting to look at. That's the problem with our species having different primary sensory organs, he said. It's really fascinating to smell, he assured us. Of course, most of the smells on the ship would make us pass out from their potency if we didn't have noseplugs. Which Gwedif also admitted put a damper on the wonder of the ship.

The one area of the ship that I found the most interesting was what Gwedif labeled as the art gallery, with the tivis that Gwedif described to Carl. Like everything else on the ship, the tivis weren't much to look at—they looked like shallow bowls left on the floor, with blackened crusts of something surrounded by wires. Gwedif steered us to one, suggested we sit down to get closer to the tivis, and then slid a tendril into a slot on the floor near the tivis.

The tivis immediately started to warm up; the wires were apparently heating elements. Through my noseplugs, I smelled something acrid, but I was also immediately overwhelmed by a sense of wistfulness, with overtones of happiness but the slightest bit of regret. It was the feeling you get when you see an old girlfriend, realize that she's a wonderful person, and that you were kind of an idiot to let her go, even if you're happily married now. I mentioned this (without the drama) to Gwedif.

"It worked, then," Gwedif said. "Tivis work by stimulating certain emotions through smells. This one," he pointed to the one we were at, "is actually fairly crude—it's just one primary emotion with only a couple of emotional harmonics. Any of us could have made it, actually. It's the tivis equivalent of a paint-by-numbers. Some of our tivis masters can create works of incredible emotional depth, layering emotion on emotion in unexpected combinations. You can get really worked up over a good tivis."

"I'll bet," I said. "These could go over real big on Earth. You need to introduce me to some of the Yherajk who make these."

"Looking for clients already?" Gwedif said.

"I've already got all of you as clients, Gwedif," I said. "Now I just need to find out which ones of you need individual attention."

We sampled a few more tivis before I got restless and wanted to return to the ambulance. If I was going to be worried, I wanted to be worried near something familiar. Van Doren came with me. We hung around the ambulance for an hour before Van Doren fished through the glove compartment and unearthed a pack of cards. We played gin. Van Doren kicked my ass; he apparently didn't believe in or understand the concept of a friendly game of cards. After I got sick of cards, I grabbed a blanket out of the ambulance, spread it out on the floor of the hangar, and willed myself into another nap.

I was awakened this time by someone sticking their toe in my side. I swatted at the leg. It jabbed, harder.

"Wake up," someone said. It was Michelle's voice.

I spun up, whacking my head on the ambulance as I struggled to get up. Michelle stood before me, naked. There was a crooked and slightly sardonic grin on her face. Never in all the years that I knew her had she ever had an expression like that. Sardonicism would have been a little much to ask out of Michelle.

"Joshua?" I asked.

"You were expecting maybe Winston Churchill?" Joshua said. "By the way, I think you might as well start calling me Michelle. There are very few people who look like this," she motioned to her body, "who would be called Joshua."

"All right . . . Michelle," I said.

Van Doren came over and frankly stared at Michelle's naked form. "Wow," he said. "I may have to revise that comment about taking you off my list of women to date."

"Back off, jerky," Michelle said.

"I just can't win," Van Doren complained.

"I guess we can say the transfer was a success," I said.

"It was easier than I thought," Michelle said. "It helped that Gwedif had rummaged around through a human brain before. When I first suggested the idea of going into Miranda's brain, he shared his knowledge with me so I didn't have to fly completely blind. And Miranda was very open as well. Between the two of them, we made some remarkable progress."

"Where is Miranda?" I asked.

"She's sleeping," Michelle said. "The experience took a lot out of her."

"Is she all right?" I said. "I mean, no damage to her?"

"Other than fatigue, no, none," Michelle said. "Though you might give her a few days off when we get back. Let her rest up."

"She can take the rest of the year off," I said.

"Give her a raise, too," Michelle said. "Hazard pay."

"Pretty soon she'll be making more than I do," I said.

"And about time, don't you think," Michelle said.

"How much of you is you?" Van Doren asked Michelle.

"Which me are you talking about?" Michelle said. "Joshua, Michelle, or Miranda?"

"Michelle, for starters."

"There's actually quite a bit of who Michelle was in here," Michelle said. "Miranda's insistence on that matter made me take a look at the whole picture again. It took more time to get it all in, but now I agree with Miranda. It was the right thing to do. Now, I *did* do some judicious editing. Miranda's natively smarter and has more common sense than Michelle. In those matters, I had a tendency to model the template towards Miranda than Michelle. And at the end of it, everything that was Joshua is in here too, although a lot of it is being subsumed by the parts from Miranda and Michelle. I'm much more human than I was before. And yet I retain all my endearing qualities from before. Truly, a perfect being."

"And modest, too," Van Doren said.

"Feh on you," Michelle said. "I'm going to remember that comment when the revolution comes."

The door to the hangar opened and a stretcher wheeled out, pulled along by Yherajk. Miranda lay on it. She smiled and waved as her stretcher was pulled up to where we stood.

"You ought to be sleeping," Michelle said, severely.

"You ought to be dressed," Miranda said.

"That hospital gown was so *not* me," Michelle said. "I've retained Michelle's fashion sense."

"I urged her to rest, but she insisted on coming back here," Gwedif said. He was one of the Yherajk pulling the stretcher.

"How are you?" I asked.

"I'm fine," Miranda insisted. "I feel like my sinuses were used as a bypass for the 405, but that's over with. Now I want to go home. It's been fun having an alien probe, really, but I have plants to water and a cat to feed. I've already missed two feedings. I miss one more, and I get classified as food myself."

"Is she well enough to move?" I asked Michelle.

"She's fine," Michelle said. "But I still think she needs some more rest."

"I can sleep on the way down," Miranda said.

"Good luck with *that*," Michelle said.

"Don't make me get huffy," Miranda threatened. "Besides, we have to go back. You need to be outfitted, Michelle."

"That's true," Michelle admitted. "There is much shopping to be done. We should head back immediately. Stores are about to open."

"Do we all have to go back?" Van Doren said. We all turned to him. He shifted, slightly uncomfortable. "If no one minds, I'd like to stay here for a while."

"Why?" I asked.

"If my job is to be the storyteller for this little venture of ours, then it stands to reason that I should spend time getting to know the Yherajk," Van Doren said. "I think Gwedif and I could stand to spend a little more time together. I want to get this story right, Tom. Besides, it's not like I have anything going on back on Earth. I don't even have a cat. And this way you're guaranteed that I'm out of your hair."

"Gwedif?" Michelle asked.

"I don't mind," Gwedif said. "It could be valuable, in fact. It could be helpful in figuring out what we need to do to make the *Ionar* more friendly to humans."

"Start with air freshener," Van Doren suggested.

"Watch it," Gwedif said.

We said our good-byes to Van Doren and Gwedif. Miranda, still in her stretcher, lay in the back; Michelle, still naked, stayed in back with her. Two Yherajk pilots arrived and positioned themselves; in a moment a platform formed beneath them and a transport cube began taking shape. Behind the wheel, I waved again at Gwedif and Van Doren. Then the cube wall slid higher, obscuring the view.

Michelle poked her head up to the front. "Well, you did it," she said. "You got me into this body. You've made me a human. What are we going to do now?"

"It depends," I said. "How well do you think you can act?"

Michelle snorted. "Better than I could before, that's for sure."

"Well, then," I said. "I have a plan."

CHAPTER
Twenty

"Tom," Roland Lanois said, stepping out of his office. "What an unexpected pleasure." His intonation stressed *unexpected* slightly more than it emphasized *pleasure*.

"Roland," I said. "Sorry about the sudden visit. But I have a proposition that I think you'll be interested in, and I thought you'd want to hear about it immediately."

"I'm afraid that you've picked a rather hectic time to drop by," Roland said. "I have a five o'clock, and it's already a quarter of five."

"I only need five minutes," I said. "I'll be long gone before your five o'clock."

Roland grinned. "Tom, you are so unlike other agents. I actually *believe* that you only need five minutes. Very well, then," he motioned into his office with his hand. "The clock is ticking."

"Here's what I came here for," I said, after Roland had closed his office door behind us. "I've got a deal for you on the Kordus material."

"That's excellent," Roland said, taking a seat at his desk. "I hope your price is not too steep. We'll be doing this story on a shoestring."

"Oh, I think you'll be able to afford it," I said. "You can have the rights to excerpt any of Krzysztof's writing at no cost."

Roland sat, silent. "That's impossibly generous," he said, finally. His intonation this time stressed *impossibly* more than *generous*.

"I spoke to the Kordus family," I said. "I showed them the script. They love it. Moreover, they are well acquainted with your work and trust that you will do a brilliant job. They feel that if giving you the rights at no cost will help this script make it to the screen, it's worth it. They expect that the additional book royalties that will be generated through the exposure of the work in the film will offset any loss they take giving you permission to use the work. They're taking the long view. Of course, they will want your permission to use artwork from the film to help promote the book reissues."

"Yes, of course," Roland said. "Of course. Tom, we'd be happy to do that. And you must thank the Kordus family for me, profusely. This is a true gift."

"Well, yes and no," I said. "There is one thing you have to do for me first."

"What is that?" Roland said.

"Give Michelle Beck another reading for *Hard Memories*."

"Um-hmmmm," Roland said. "That might be difficult."

"Why is that?" I said.

"Well, to begin with, I understand that she is currently in a coma."

"She was," I said. "She got better."

"Better?" Roland blinked. "How does one get *better* out of a coma?"

"We took her to an exclusive clinic where we tried some experimental therapies," I said. "She's fine, really."

"Experimental therapies."

"Very experimental. You wouldn't believe how experimental."

Roland continued to look dubious. "If you say so," he said. "However, there is the more pressing issue that Avika Spiegelman is dead set against Michelle for the role. I don't think that there's anything that could be done to change her mind. And without her consent, nothing happens."

"Let Michelle worry about that," I said. "All you have to do is get Avika to come here for another reading."

"She won't come if she knows it's Michelle who is having the reading."

"Surprise her," I suggested.

"I'd rather not," Roland said. "Tom, you don't understand how close I am to losing this project to begin with. If Ms. Spiegelman shows up with Michelle here, I will be well and truly screwed."

"Roland, you're well and truly screwed anyway," I said. "You don't have an actress. None of the actresses who could carry this film are available. You have slightly under two weeks to cast this thing, if I'm correct. If you blow it now, you're only losing something that's already lost. This is in fact your last chance to *save* the project. All Michelle wants is a second reading, Roland. That's it. You really have nothing to lose."

"Except possibly my professional reputation," Roland said. "It might be cheaper just to pay cash for the Kordus rights."

"All right, Roland," I said. "You force me to bring out my big gun."

"I can't wait, Tom," Roland said. "Are you going to suggest Pamela Anderson in a supporting role?"

"How much would it take for you to produce the Kordus film?"

"The Kordus film?" Roland said. "I did a preliminary budget not long ago. My first estimate is about twelve million. Possibly less if I film entirely in Poland."

"How would you finance it?" I asked.

"I'm still thinking about that," Roland said. "I have a nice arrangement with BBC, which will finance three and a half million on the front end in exchange for broadcast rights in the UK. The CBC will kick in just under a million and a half for Canadian rights. I might be able to extort financing out of the French if I hire enough French nationals to work on the film. Miramax or Weinstein might be worth a few million, although with these sorts of properties, they tend to purchase distribution rights on the back end rather than up front."

"But no matter what, you end up a couple of million dollars short," I said.

"That's the drama of making small, serious films," Roland said.

"Here's the big gun," I said. "Get as much financing as you can from your usual sources, and whatever your shortfall, Michelle will cover it. Whatever it is."

"What if I get less financing than I expect for the Kordus project? Or none at all?"

"Then Michelle will bankroll the entire production cost," I said. "Though I think we should reasonably expect you to make the effort to line up other financing as well. But no matter what, you get the money from Michelle if you need it. It's solid."

"And all I have to do is give Michelle another reading," Roland said.

"That's right. If Michelle dazzles, then you get to make *Hard Memories* and then go with the Kordus story. If not, you can get to work on the Kordus picture right away. No lost time. You win either way."

"Christ, Tom," Roland said. "You sure know how to pack your five minutes."

"You know me," I said. "Always go for the dramatic gesture."

"When do you want your reading?" Roland asked.

"Give me three days," I said. "I need that much time to prepare Michelle."

"Tom," Roland said. "I appreciate your offer, and Michelle's as well. But I have to tell you I suspect that three days is not going to be enough time for Michelle to get herself up to the level she needs to be to convince Avika Spiegelman."

"I think you'll be surprised," I said. "Michelle's accident changed a lot of things. In some ways she's a whole other person."

"*I* still don't know why I'm going to Arizona," Michelle said.

"You're going there because I asked you to," I said.

"Remind me not to listen to you when you ask me to jump off a cliff." Michelle said.

"Arizona is not so bad," I said. "It has some lovely scenery."

"Are we going to visit any?" Michelle asked.

"No," I said. "But you can look out the window."

Our chartered jet was descending into Sky Harbor International Airport.

"Let me take a different tack," Michelle said. "Why did you want me to go to Arizona?"

"Because there's someone here I want you to meet. Someone I think will make a difference in your reading tomorrow."

"Oh, yes, *that*," Michelle said. "The one you gave me so much time to prepare for. Thanks."

"You said you still retained Michelle's memories of the script and her reading," I said.

"I did," Michelle said. "But Tom, just because she read it doesn't mean she *understood* it. It was not as much reading as staring at the page and waiting for the sentences to come into focus. Michelle was a nice person, but she really was in over her head."

Our jet was now sliding over the runway. We landed with a small bump and much squealing of tires.

"Thank God," Michelle said. "I'm afraid of flying."

"You were never afraid of flying before," I said. "And you weren't scared when we were dropping into the atmosphere in a cube at Mach 20."

"Welcome to the new me," Michelle said. "And I trust Yherajk technology a lot more than I trust yours. Now get me the hell off of this plane. I have to go kiss the ground."

A limo driver was waiting for us as we exited the plane. We went through the crowd rapidly, before anyone could recognize Michelle, and were in the limo and on our way in a matter of minutes.

I rolled up the barrier between us and the driver almost immediately. "How flexible are you?" I asked.

"Why?" Michelle asked. "You looking for excitement in the back of a limo?"

"No," I said. "What I mean to say is, can you generate any tendrils or tentacles?"

"Sure," Michelle said. "It's not like when I was in Ralph and I was stuck in his digestive system. I've got Michelle's whole head undergoing transformation. See, look." Michelle's eyes suddenly bulged, dropped out of her eye sockets, and began swinging around.

"That's the most disgusting thing I think I've ever seen," I said.

"Now you know what I'm going to be doing for Halloween," Michelle said.

"Can you make the tendrils any smaller?" I asked.

"Of course," Michelle answered. "I can make them invisible, if you like."

"I would like," I said. "I think you may need them where we're going."

"Where *are* we going?" Michelle asked again.

"We'll be there soon enough," I said.

Less than half hour later, we were there.

"The Beth Israel Retirement Home," Michelle said, reading the stone sign out front of the facility. "Tom, I realize that Hollywood stops hiring actresses after a certain age, but this is ridiculous."

"Hyuck, hyuck, hyuck," I said. "Come with me." We went inside.

The nurse at the reception desk wasted no time looking at me, preferring to look at Michelle instead.

"Aren't you Michelle Beck?" She asked.

"I'm not Michelle Beck," Michelle said. "But I play her on TV."

"Excuse me," I said, drawing the nurse's attention to me. "I made an appointment to see Sarah Rosenthal. I'm Tom Stein, her grandson."

"I'm sorry," The nurse said, snapping out of her celebrity stupor. "Of course. She's just woken up from a nap, so she should be quite alert. It's good of you to visit. We've heard a lot about you. Your mother comes in quite frequently, you know."

"I knew that," I said. "Since I was in town, I thought I might come for a visit as well."

"That's very sweet of you," the nurse said. She glanced over at Michelle. "Are you two together?"

"For the first ten percent, yes," Michelle said. The nurse looked slightly confused. Below the nurse's view, I stepped onto Michelle's toes. Hard.

"Yes, we're together," I said.

"Follow me," The nurse got up and motioned towards the corridor.

Sarah Rosenthal, my grandmother, was in her wheelchair, staring out her window. The nurse knocked on the open doorway to get her attention. My grandmother turned, recognized me, and broke into a wide grin. Her teeth were in. I went over to give her a hug; the nurse excused herself. Michelle stood in the door, attentive but uncertain.

"I didn't know your grandmother was still alive," Michelle said.

"She is," I said, crouching down and holding my grandmother's hand. "But I don't see her very much. She retired down here while I was still in elementary school. We'd see each other at high holidays and during the summer, but not very much beyond that. Grandmama was a very independent soul. She had a stroke not long after my father died, which took away her power of speech; my mother came down to be closer to her."

My grandmother peered over at Michelle and motioned her over. Michelle came over; Grandmama held out her other hand, and Michelle gave her hand. Grandmama shook it in welcome, and then turned it over. Then she looked at me.

"What is she doing?" Michelle asked.

"She's looking for an engagement ring," I said. "Grandmama's been pushing me to get married since I was about thirteen." I turned back to my grandmother. "Michelle's just a client, Grandmama," I said. "But you'll be happy to know I have a nice girlfriend now. Very nice."

"She's a little like me," Michelle said, to my grandmother.

"I'll bring her down next time," I said. "Okay?"

Grandmama nodded in agreement, and then patted Michelle's hand, as if to say, *I'm sure you're a very nice girl, anyway.*

"Michelle, would you close the door?" I said.

Michelle went to close the door; then she came back over.

"*Now* will you tell me what we're doing here?" she asked.

"My grandmother wasn't born here in the U.S.," I said. "She was born and lived the first part of her life in Germany. She was a teenager when Hitler came to power. She was a newlywed when she and most of her family were sent to the camps."

"My God," Michelle said. "I'm terribly sorry."

"Grandmama came to the U.S. after the war, married again, and had a child late in life," I said. "My mother. And now we've come to the end of what I know of the story," I looked over to Michelle. "Grandmama would never talk much about her life before the U.S. to my mother, and of course my mother never did talk about it much with me. I'm hoping I can get her to share her experiences with you."

"Now I see," Michelle said.

My grandmother looked over to me, confused.

"Grandmama," I said. "I haven't gone over the bend. I know you can't talk. This is hard to explain, but Michelle has a way of talking without talking. I know your memories are painful, and that you don't share about them for a reason. But Michelle wants to know what your memories are, if you'll share them. It will help her understand many things about our lives, and our history. It would mean a lot to me if you would share your memories with her."

Michelle got down on her knee and took Grandmama's other hand again. "See what I'm doing now?" Michelle said, holding grandmama's hand lightly. "This is all I'd have to do. Just sit with you for a little while. You wouldn't even have to think about those things, if you didn't want to, Sarah. All we'd have to do is sit together."

My grandmother looked at Michelle, and then at me. She smiled, gently slid her hand out of mine, put it to her temple, and made a corkscrew motion.

I laughed. "I know. We both sound nuts. They're going to be hauling us both off sometime soon. But in the meantime, will you help us?"

My grandmother looked me and at Michelle. Michelle she patted on hand. Then she lightly tapped my shoulder, and pointed at the door. I looked at her quizzically.

"I think she's saying she's willing to do it, but she doesn't want you around," Michelle said. "Maybe she had a reason for not telling the story to your mother or you, Tom. She doesn't want to run the risk of you hearing it."

Grandmama nodded her head vigorously and patted Michelle's hand again.

"Out you go," Michelle said.

I stood up. "How long will you need?" I asked Michelle.

"An hour, maybe two," she said. "If you can manage it, I'd prefer that we weren't disturbed. I want to get this all at one time."

"I'll do what I can."

"Thanks, Tom," Michelle looked up at me briefly, and then back to Grandmama. "Now, shoo. Sarah and I are going to have a conversation."

Twice a nurse came by to check on things. Twice I sent her away, the second time bribing her with the promise of an autograph by Michelle. The nurse left behind her clipboard and her pen as insurance. I hoped it didn't contain serious information about any of the other folks in the retirement home.

Three hours after she began, Michelle opened the door to my grandmother's room and came out. She touched my arm distractedly, and then propped herself against the corridor wall. She looked exhausted.

"Here," I said, handing her the clipboard. "I promised the nurse an autograph if she would go away."

Michelle took the clipboard and stared at it like it was some sort of strange animal.

"Michelle," I said. "You okay?"

"I'm fine," she said, taking the pen from the top of the clipboard and scratching her name on the piece of paper it contained. "I'm just very tired."

"How is Grandmama?" I asked.

"She's nodded off in her chair," Michelle said, handing the clipboard back to me. "You should have the nurse put her to bed."

"I will," I said. "Did you get what you need?"

For the first time, Michelle looked directly at me. Her eyes were startling; they were the eyes of someone who had walked through the coals of Hell and came through them, but not unscathed, not without wounds.

"Your grandmother is a remarkable woman, Tom," she said. "Remember that. Don't ever forget it."

Then she lapsed into silence. We didn't talk again that day.

"*What* the hell is *she* doing here?" Avika Spiegelman said, referring to Michelle.

Roland had taken my advice and surprised Avika, saying only that he found an "interesting" actress that he thought might pull off the role. The withering glare she was now carpet bombing Roland with made me understand why he had been reluctant to go along with my scheme to begin with.

"We never got a full reading the first time," Roland said, holding his ground with aplomb. "I felt Miss Beck deserved that much before we rejected her out of hand."

"Roland, she *fainted* at the last reading," Avika seethed. "And a good thing too, since she was clearly incapable of the reading to begin with. I can't believe you would be wasting your time with her now, considering how little time you have left with this property."

Michelle, who sat in front of the video camera, just as she had at the last reading, had a smirk on her face that did not indicate she was taking Avika's insults seriously. Positioned as I was on the couch, I was getting the full panoramic view: Michelle's smirk, Roland's aplomb, Avika's seething. This was going to be a fun reading.

"Boy, it's swell to see you again too, Ms. Spiegelman," Michelle said.

Avika regarded Michelle coolly. "Aren't you supposed to be in a coma?" she said.

"I got over it," Michelle said. "Which, apparently, is more than you can say."

"You planning to faint again?" Avika said.

"I won't if you won't," Michelle said. "Do we have a deal?"

"Fat chance," Avika said, and turned to Roland. "I'm leaving now, Roland." She turned to leave.

"Bitch," Michelle said.

Avika froze. Very slowly, she turned around.

"*What* did you just say?" She spat at Michelle.

"You heard me perfectly well," Michelle said, leaning back in her chair with an air of supreme relaxation. "I called you a bitch. I was going to call you a raging bitch, but then I thought, why give you the courtesy of a modifier? You're just a bitch, plain and simple."

Avika looked like the top of her head was going to pop off. She turned to me. "Tom, do you always let your clients insult the people who can give them the roles they want?"

"Hey," I said. "I'm just here for the show."

"I'm not calling anyone who will give me a role a bitch," Michelle said. "Clearly, you have no intention of giving me the role. As far as I can see, the only reason I'm calling you a bitch is because that is what you so obviously are."

"I don't need to be insulted by you," Avika said.

"Well, you need to be insulted by *someone*," Michelle said. "And it looks like I'm the only one here with enough interest in you to do it. Sort of sad, really."

"Listen, you little shit," Avika said. "You don't even deserve to *read* for this part, much less play it."

"Well then, we're equal," Michelle said, "since you don't deserve to make that decision."

"I'm her *niece*," Avika said.

"You're her third cousin, twice removed," Michelle said. "I checked. And your only qualification is that you're tangentially related. All you're interested in is appearances. I don't fit your notion of who your sainted aunt was, so I'm out."

"You're nothing like my aunt," Avika said.

"I'd say I'm a lot like your aunt. Your aunt spent a lot of her time flying in the face of ignorant morons who decided the world was one way and there was no other way the world could be. As far as I can tell, I'm doing the same right now. I'm more like your aunt than *you* are."

"How dare you say that?" Avika hissed. "You can't even *act*."

Michelle smiled. "Neither could your aunt, bitch."

Roland, who had been observing the exchange between Michelle and Avika with an increasing expression of horror, glanced over at me with an expression that loosely translated to *Get me out of here*. I shrugged. There was nothing to do now but to ride this one out.

Michelle got up, grabbed a script, and walked over to Avika. "I'll tell you what, Avika," Michelle said. "I'll admit I could be wrong about you being a bitch. I'm entirely convinced you are, but it is within the realm of possibility that I'm wrong. But the only way you can prove it is to admit *you* might be wrong about me not being able to do the part."

Michelle slapped the script on Avika's chest. "The only way you're going to do *that* is to let me read. Come on, Avika. It can't hurt."

"I don't have to prove anything to you," Avika said, grabbing the script.

"Sure you do," Michelle said, turning around and heading back to her seat. "Because there's one difference between you and me, Avika. You see, I couldn't give a shit that you think I can't act. But it's clear that it bothers you that I think you're a bitch."

"Hardly," Avika said.

"Really?" Michelle said, sitting down. "Then why are you still here?"

Avika's mouth dropped open. Roland, a strapping man, looked like he wanted to curl up into a fetal ball.

"Come on, people," Michelle said. "Let's shit or get off the pot. Read me or don't, but let's make a decision."

Roland snapped out of it before Avika could utter another word. "What scene would you like, Miss Beck?"

"Your choice," Michelle said. "I really did memorize the script this time."

"The whole script?" Roland said.

"Sure, why not?" Michelle said, and glanced over to me mischievously. "Elvis did it."

Avika flipped the script open and read. " 'How dare you tell me what I can and cannot do?' " Avika said. " 'You are my wife, not my master.' "

" 'I am your master's instrument, Josef,' " Michelle said, the words ripping out of her with an intensity that took us all by surprise. " 'Go on the *Judenrat* and you turn your back on your people and your God. And you turn your back on me. For I *am* your wife, Josef. But cooperate with the Germans and *we are not married*. You will be as dead to me now as you will be soon enough by the hands of the Germans.' "

There was dead silence. We all stared in disbelief. Even me.

Michelle smiled sweetly. "Got your attention, didn't I?" she said.

Avika opened the script at random and quoted line after line. Line after line was responded to with the sort of stunning display of acting that you get to see one or twice in a lifetime. It was flabbergasting. It was impossible. It was the most incredible acting experience I'd ever seen. And it was just a line reading. We were all beginning to wonder what was going to happen once Michelle actually started acting for the record.

After an hour, Avika dropped the script at her feet. "I wouldn't have believed it," she said, simply.

"I know you wouldn't," Michelle said, as simply. "And I thank you, Avika, my friend, for finally letting me show you."

Avika burst into tears and headed towards Michelle. Michelle burst into her own tears and met Avika halfway. They stood in the middle of the room, crying hysterically. Roland and I looked over at each other. Both of us had these incredibly smug smiles on our face.

We were in business.

CHAPTER
Twenty-One

*A*montage of the next year, as told through headlines:

Daily Variety, **March 5**
MICHELLE BECK VOWS "HARD MEMORIES"

Michelle Beck, wasting no time after her near-death experience during the pre-production of Earth Resurrected, *signed today to star in* Hard Memories, *a biopic of civil rights activist and Holocaust survivor Rachel Spiegelman. Spiegelman became famous for her association with Martin Luther King during the late 50s and early 60s. Hard Memories is to be directed by Roland Lanois, and produced by Lanois in association with the Spiegelman family. Compensation package was not discussed, though with a total budget of less than $18 million, Beck is undoubtedly taking much less than the $12.5 million she scored for the ill-fated* Earth Resurrected. *Filming in the Czech Republic and*

Alabama is expected to begin in April for an Oscar-look release date of December 19th in New York and Los Angeles.

Beck is repped by Tom Stein of Lupo Associates.

Los Angeles Times Calendar Section, March 11
Jewish Groups Protest Casting of "Promises."
Decry casting of Michelle Beck as "stunt";
producers, family stand firm behind their star.

BEVERLY HILLS—Michelle Beck is 25. Blonde. Blue eyed. Gentile. Rachel Spiegelman was brown haired. Brown eyed. Jewish. And at the height of her notoriety, she was well into her fifties.

So how did Michelle Beck get the call to play Spiegelman, noted civil-rights lawyer and Holocaust survivor, in the upcoming Roland Lanois–directed biographical film Hard Memories? *It's a question that several Hollywood Jewish groups would like to have answered.*

One of these groups, the Jewish Actors Association, went so far as to place a full-page ad in film industry trade magazine Variety *on Friday, decrying the movie as "stunt casting" and calling upon director Lanois and the Spiegelman family to drop Beck for a more suitable actress.*

"It's not about Miss Beck being Jewish or not," said Avi Linden, communications director for the JAA. "What bothers us is the fact that here is someone who is so clearly cast for box office purposes. She's made $300 million in her last two films, and that's what the producers are looking at—not how truthful the casting is to reality. The fact is, there are dozens of actresses, Jew and gentile, who are more suited to the role."

Roland Lanois, the Oscar-nominated director and producer, acknowledges that his selection of Beck was bound to be controversial.

"We understand that this casting is not intuitive at first blush," he said, noting that Beck was not the first choice, landing the role only after

actress Ellen Merlow dropped the role to take on a television series. "We ourselves were hesitant at first. All we can say at this point is that it was Michelle's performance, not any other consideration, that got her the role."

Avika Spiegelman, spokesperson for the Spiegelman family, which had unusual veto rights on the casting of the role, issued a terse press release. "Michelle Beck is the best person for the role, period," the release said. "She has the full support of the Spiegelman family."

Entertainment Weekly, March 17
Comebacks We're Not Looking Forward To

. . . . .

3. Jim Carrey: *Cast as a poodle in a live action flick. Insert your own "It's gonna be a dog" joke here.*

4. Michelle Beck: *25-year-old beach babe cast as serious, 50ish civil rights crusader. The makeup artist is an automatic Oscar nominee.*

5. Roseanne's "Comeback" Album: *Stop her before she sings the Star-Spangled Banner!*

. . . . .

Variety, March 24
A SEAT AT SOMETHING SPECIAL

BEVERLY HILLS—The atmosphere was electric at the Fine Arts theatre on Wilshire Boulevard, but not for the usual reasons. On Saturday night, the Fine Arts was the scene, not of a movie, but of an unprecedented SRO reading of Hard Memories, the film made controversial by the casting of Michelle Beck in the central role of civil rights activist and Holocaust survivor Rachel Spiegelman. The guest list for the reading included the cream of the film industry and several members of the Jewish groups that had criticized Beck's casting. It was a tough crowd, and Hard Memories director-producer Roland Lanois knew it.

"If I were in their shoes, I would have the same reaction that they have had. Absolutely. No doubt," Lanois said prior to the reading. *"What this is about is helping them into* our *shoes. I think they're going to be surprised."* Beck, in the center of the storm, waded into the crowd before the reading, thanking folks for coming and chatting directly with those who had opposed her casting, as if to show there were no hard feelings. At 8:30, Beck, costar and noted legit theater star David Grunwald, and Lanois and producer Avika Spiegelman sat up front on simple stools and read the script, Beck as Rachel Spiegelman, the other three trading off the other roles. By 9, there were already tears. At 10:30, when the reading was finished, Beck and her crew were treated to an ovation the likes of which I have not seen in many a year. It was a tough crowd, but Beck won them over in spectacular fashion. Next up: the audience at large . . .

Hollywood Reporter, April 30
Young Ankles Lupo Associates

Elliot Young, star of the mid-rated ABC series Pacific Rim, has dropped agent Ben Fleck of Lupo Associates in what insiders call an acrimonious split. Young was apparently disappointed in Fleck's inability to transfer Young's moderate television stardom into a film career.

"Fleck had come in promising Elliot the moon," said Pacific Rim director Don Bolling. "Then he of course experienced trouble delivering. Elliot dropped him and, I think, rightly so."

Young is currently being repped by Paula Richter of Artists Associated.

Daily Variety, May 22
DISH: MERLOW'S FURLOUGH FROM 'GOOD HELP'

Dish hears that the already legendarily tense set of Good Help Is Hard to Find has had the tension cranked up another notch, when two-time-Oscar-winner-turned-would-be-sitcom-comedienne Ellen Merlow jetted back to her Connecticut horse farm during the middle of taping, placing the show in jeopardy of making its series debut September 9th. This latest flare-up follows last month's standoff between Merlow and costar Garrison Lanham (who played Weezix, the alien butler) that resulted in Lanham's replacement by Bronson Pinchot, and by last week's mass crew walkout, protesting their treatment by Merlow and her entourage. The Dish hears that Merlow's latest act might have placed her in violation of her $20 million contract, giving exasperated producers Jan and Steven White the excuse they need to bounce her from the show. . . .

Daily Variety, **June 16**
MILESTONES

Tom Stein, *29, of La Canada married* **Miranda Escalon,** *28, of Manhattan Beach, on Saturday, June 14th at the Vivian Webb Chapel in Claremont. He is an agent at Lupo Associates. She is also an agent, newly promoted, at the same firm. Stein's best man was Lupo boss Carl Lupo; Escalon's maid of honor was Michelle Beck, who flew in from the Czech Republic for the wedding. . . .*

Ad in Daily Variety and Hollywood Reporter, *July 10*

Lanois Productions
and
Century Films

Are proud to announce the completion of principal photography on

HARD MEMORIES

Starring Michelle Beck and David Grunwald

Written by Connie Reiser & Larry Card
Directed and Produced by Roland Lanois

LIMITED RELEASE: DECEMBER 19 IN NEW YORK
AND LOS ANGELES
WIDE RELEASE JANUARY 16

Entertainment Weekly, August 8
Stingless 'Scorpion'
Mindless Summer Explode-Fest Rings Hollow

. . . *Inquiring minds want to know: In this utter loss of a movie, does anything work? Well, the explosions are pretty. Apologists may note the presence of Michelle Beck, whose upcoming performance in* Hard Memories *is one of the most intensely awaited of the Oscar season. Maybe some of that alleged intensity rubs off here? No such luck. This Michelle Beck, at least, is scene decoration, hardly onscreen before her helicopter is blown out of the sky by a preposterous string of coincidences. Don't worry, this revelation won't ruin the plot for you: there'd have to have been a plot at all for that to happen.*

Rating: **D**

Daily Variety, August 11
'SCORPION' VENOMOUS TO COMPETITION
$49.7M takes tops BO report; 'Gold Master' takes
silver at $16.2M

Scorpion's Tail *proves that some films are critic-proof; the widely panned action flick stung the competition with a $49.7 million take, injecting a boost in the severely lagging summer box office . . .*

Entertainment Weekly, September 22
OSCAR WATCH

. . . Oscar-nominated director-producer Roland Lanois (The Green Fields) may have another contender on his hands with Hard Memories. *Insiders at a Century Pictures rough cut screening say the film caused notoriously thick-skinned Century head Lewis Schon to cry into his trademark Goobers. Of special note is Michelle Beck's performance, which those at the screening labeled "revelatory." Century's marketing department is already getting in high gear for the Award season. . . .*

The Arizona Republic, September 25
Obituaries

Sarah Rosenthal, *of Scottsdale, of complications from a stroke, at 3:15 pm, September 23rd. Mrs. Rosenthal was born in Hamburg, Germany on April 3, 1922 and emigrated to the United States in December of 1945. She is survived by daughter Elaine Stein, also of Scottsdale, and grandson Thomas Stein, of La Canada, Ca.*

The Chicago Sun-Times, October 8
Hollywood Star, Agents to Endow U of C Chair

CHICAGO—*The University of Chicago, normally the most staid of places, received a little Hollywood sparkle on Tuesday as Michelle Beck, star of the smash hit* Summertime Blues, *and the upcoming* Hard Memories, *arrived on campus to announce a $3 million gift to endow a chair in Holocaust Studies.*

Speaking in the University's cavernous Mandel Hall, Beck alluded to her experience working on the Holocaust drama Hard Memories *as a motivating factor in the gift.*

"We must not be so worried about history repeating itself as simply rubbing itself out of existence," she said. "Each year that passes rubs off a little more of the memory. This is a way to keep the memories fresh, and to refresh the story for each generation of students that walks through these halls."

The chair, formally known as the Sarah Rosenthal and Daniel Stein Chair for Holocaust Studies and Jewish History, will be filled the next year, following a nationwide search. The chair is named for Sarah Rosenthal, a survivor of the Holocaust, and her son-in-law Daniel Stein, a graduate of the university.

Besides Beck, other endowers of the chair include Carl Lupo, CEO of Lupo Associates, a talent agency in Los Angeles, and Tom and Miranda Stein, also agents at Lupo Associates. Tom Stein is the son of Daniel Stein.

Entertainment Weekly, November 17
WINTER MOVIE PREVIEW
December—Hard Memories

What a difference a year can make. Last year at this time, no one would have predicted that Michelle Beck, of all people, would be whispered as the front-runner for the Best Actress Oscar. Best Beach Bunny, maybe. Best Actress, no way.

One year later, though, Beck's performance in Hard Memories is the talk of the town—even with those who haven't seen the performance yet. They talk of the protests when Beck was cast in the role. They talk of the now-mythologized reading at the Fine Arts theater which quelled all complaint. They talk about Century Pictures prez Lewis Schon blubbering uncontrollably into his snack food. Some theorize her miraculous recovery from her coma earlier this year did something unexpected—kicked her acting centers into gear, perhaps. . . .

Washington Post, December 13
Michelle Beck, Resurrected

Michelle Beck nearly died in February when a freak accident during the ramp-up to *Earth Resurrected* sent her spiraling into a coma. Since then she's been in the center

of the Hollywood storm with her new film *Hard Memories*. Beck just doesn't know how not to get in trouble.

To begin, Michelle Beck sympathized with the people who hated her getting Hard Memories.

"Who are we kidding?" she says. "The woman is an icon, Jewish, older, and intellectual. I'm not any of those things. I don't think I would have cast me, and if I had, I'd probably have claimed temporary insanity afterwards."

But a funny thing happened on the way to the flogging: Michelle Beck stood up to the critics and turned them around. Now the actress, just turned 26, looks like the closest thing to a lock in the Best Actress race. All it took was one reading.

"Arrrgh, the reading," Beck says, and scrunches up her face. "It's becoming like Woodstock, you know. Everybody who was actually physically in Los Angeles says they were there that night. I mean, come on! What does the Fine Arts sit? 300? 400 at most."

Beck leans forward as if to confide. "The fact was I was terrible that night. I was nervous as hell—I just about spotted my panties in fright. I would have been happy just to get out of there alive."

Instead, she got a thunderous ovation. Not bad for a woman who a month earlier was in a coma, hooked up to life support.

"Yes, yes, yes," Beck waves off the coma story. "You want to know what the coma was like? It was dark, mostly. That's it. I didn't see God when I was in my coma. I didn't even see Elvis. And when I came out of it, nothing had changed—most people forget that I had read for Hard Memories *before I went into the coma. It wasn't like I came out of it with a gift. I was just following the plan I had set for myself long before."* . . .

Daily Variety, **December 16**
Review: Hard Memories

It's been a rumor for so long it's become almost mythical—Michelle

Beck's transformation from beach blonde to serious actress with her role in Hard Memories. *Her performance has been so built up for so long that it's finally a relief to have seen it, and to be able to say that it's everything it has been claimed to be—and even more, if that's possible. Guided by Roland Lanois' sure directorial hand, Beck hands in a performance that not only rockets her to the top of the Oscar nomination list, but perhaps also into the first rank of our nation's actresses. Following what is sure to be a record-breaking limited engagement, this picture should do solid business in wide release, possibly flirting with the $100 million mark if public opinion gets behind it. . . .*

New York Times, December 20
"Hard Memories," "Pocket Change" Lead Golden Globe Nominations

Hard Memories, *the story of Jewish civil rights activist Rachel Spiegelman, led the pack at the Golden Globe nominations Friday, garnering seven nominations, including Best Picture (drama) and Best Actress. The Tom Hanks comedy* Pocket Change *followed, with six nominations, including Best Picture (Comedy or Musical) and Best Actor.*

The Golden Globes, given by the Hollywood Foreign Press Association, are less prestigious than the Academy Awards, but are often viewed as a bellwether for that more prestigious award. The Academy Awards are to be announced January 20th.

NBC-TV will broadcast the Golden Globes ceremony January 18.

Los Angeles Times, January 5
Hard Memories Takes Top Critics Prize
The Roland Lanois film narrowly beats *Dust and the Moon;* Beck wins second Best Actress award

NEW YORK—After a particularly contentious voting process, Hard Memories *beat the Vietnamese film* Dust and the Moon *to win the best film award from the National Society of Film Critics on Sunday. The award joins the Best Picture citation awarded by the Los Angeles Film Society; The New York Film Circle gave its award to* Dust and the Moon.

Michelle Beck, whose narrow loss to Eleni Natavsaya of the Russian film Wolfhounds *with the Los Angeles critics precluded an expected sweep of the critics awards, nevertheless garnered her second Best Actress award from the National Critics. . . .*

Daily Variety, January 19
"HARD MEMORIES" COMPLETES NEAR-SWEEP AT GOLDEN GLOBES
Biopic Wins Best Picture, Actress, Supporting Actor, three others; 'Pocket Change' Wins Best Comedy

Los Angeles Times, January 19
Hard Memories Rises to the Top

In tandem with its Best Picture and Best Actress win at the Golden Globes, Hard Memories *opened strongly in its first weekend of wide release, with $21.4 million at the box office. The week's other new release, Walt Disney's* Natty Bumppo, *did poorly with its core children's audience, grossing only $3.1 million . . .*

Daily Variety, January 21
"PROMISES" MAKES GOOD WITH EIGHT NOMINATIONS
Best Picture, Director, Actress and Screenplay nods; Hanks nominated for 'Pocket Change.'

(inset)

Nominations for Hard Memories:
Best Picture: *Roland Lanois, Avika Spiegelman, producers*
Best Director: *Roland Lanois*

Best Actress: *Michelle Beck*

Best Screenplay (Adapted): *Connie Reiser & Larry Card, from the book* Hard Memories *by Rachel Spiegelman*

Best Cinematography: *Januz Kandinsky*

Best Score (Dramatic): *Julian Ruiz*

Best Editing: *Roland Lanois, Cynthia Peal*

Best Makeup: *Nguyen Trinh*

Daily Variety, **February 4**
OSCAR NOTES

Best Actress Nominee Michelle Beck will join the Oscar broadcast as an announcer, director Lars Giles said today. Ms. Beck will introduce the fifth and final Best Picture clip, to be shown just after the Best Actress award is to be announced. The Oscars will be broadcast on ABC-TV February 23 starting at 6 pm Pacific . . .

"Stop squirming," Miranda said.

"I can't help myself," I said. "Michelle's my first client to get nominated for an Oscar. I'm nervous."

"Is that the only reason?" Miranda said.

"Well, no," I said. "But that's the reason I'm going public with. Also, my cummerbund itches."

Miranda and I were at the Academy Awards.

We weren't in the good seats, of course. The good seats are saved for the nominees, their guests, other really big stars, and studio heads. Carl Lupo had a good seat. Michelle had a good seat. Our seats were in the back of the balcony. Miranda brought a pair of opera glasses. We needed them. At least we weren't as bad off as Van Doren. He was stuck in the press room. "It's like a cattle pen," he told me, "except that instead of cows mooing next to you, you have Roger Ebert."

Things were going well for *Hard Memories;* so far it had won Best Makeup, Best Cinematography and Best Editing (the last of which greatly relieved Roland—at least he wouldn't be going home empty-handed). Best Score got away, which I thought was fair; Julian's score was good but not all *that* good.

"It's time for the screenplay awards," Miranda said.

Best Original Screenplay first. Keanu Reeves read off the nominations, which struck me as mildly ironic. The winner was Ed Fletcher, who wrote *Pocket Change.* Ed, hyped up on too much caffeine and nicotine, started on an extended riff about Nietzsche. The orchestra leader, clearly not impressed, cut him off after thirty seconds.

"Good call," Miranda said, as Ed was manhandled off the stage.

"Well, you know," I said. "It's probably the only time he'll be in front of a billion people," I said. "You can see why he might get a little excited."

"All the more reason to get him off the air quickly," Miranda said. "I'd hate to go through life with people pointing at me and saying, 'Hey, aren't you the idiot that made a fool of yourself on the Oscar show?' Rob Lowe has never lived down that dance with Snow White, you know."

Keanu was back, mangling names for the Best Adapted Screenplay. He appeared to give himself a papercut opening the envelope. Sucking on his finger, he announced the winners: Connie Reiser & Larry Card, *Hard Memories.*

"Bingo," I said.

"Four for five," Miranda said. "We're not doing too bad. I think Michelle actually has a chance."

"Oh, God," I said. "I wish you hadn't said that, Miranda. My stomach just dropped down the Mariana Trench."

Miranda patted my hand. "Relax, Tom," she said. "It's been covered, remember. Even if she doesn't win Best Actress, she'll be on stage right after to show the *Hard Memories* nomination clip. It'll be fine."

"I know, I know," I said. "But it's not optimal, you know. It would be better if she won."

"Duh," Miranda said. "But, unfortunately, we couldn't bribe the accountants from Price Waterhouse. We'll just have to hope the voters don't decide to give it to Meryl Streep again."

"Meryl Streep," I muttered. "She oughta be disqualified from future nominations."

Miranda patted my hand again. "Tom, you're just so cute when you're agitated."

Last year's Best Actor winner stepped on the stage to announce the Best Actress award.

"He wears a wig," I said to Miranda. "I hear it's one of those ones with the snap-on titanium screws."

"Oh, hush," Miranda said.

The usual lame patter, then he stared intently into the teleprompter to read names. They started with Michelle's. They ended with Meryl's. Alphabetical order works that way, I suppose.

Miranda's hand found mine again. She squeezed it so tight I thought a bone might pop. I would have complained, but I was squeezing hers just as hard. Our mutual pain was so intense that we barely heard our former Best Actor begin *and the Oscar goes to* . . .

"Michelle Beck."

We heard that part.

The room erupted into applause and a standing ovation. They loved her. It was her moment. They had no idea just how true it was.

Michelle stood up. She was sitting next to Carl Lupo. Carl stood up with her, kissed her on the cheek. He was crying. Only four other people in the building knew exactly why.

Michelle made her way to the podium like a queen. She was wearing a golden dress of a design that no one had ever seen before. Joan Rivers had asked her about it out on the red carpet before the show. Michelle responded that the designer was no one that anyone around here would know. Joan remarked that it fit Michelle like a second skin. Others agreed. They had no idea how true that was, either.

Michelle accepted her award and a peck from the former Best Actor. Then she plopped the Oscar down on the podium and, beaming, waited for the applause to die down. It took a while. Then she began to speak.

"Oh God," Miranda said. "This is really it."

"Before I do anything else," Michelle said, "I need to thank one person, my agent, Tom Stein. He's way up there in the balcony. Hi, Tom!" She waved enthusiastically, which got a big laugh. I waved back.

"Shut up and get to it before the orchestra cuts you off," I muttered under my breath.

"Tom's probably muttering at me to get to it before the orchestra cuts me off," Michelle said. "He always did look out for me.

"This award means more to me than you could ever know," Michelle continued. "It's not just my award. It's the award of Rachel Spiegelman, who saw hatred of the demonized 'other' destroy her world, and dedicated the rest of her life to making sure that we saw men, all men, as brothers, regardless of their color or their creed.

"It belongs to Avika Spiegelman, who looked beyond my

physical appearance to allow me to take the role of a lifetime. It belongs to those who initially protested my getting this role, because they came and gave me a chance to perform it, and realized that while I did not match Rachel's appearance, I would try to match her heart. Over and over again, I have seen people of all stripes look beyond the appearance, look beyond the otherness, and see what it was that truly connected us all.

"And now I'm wondering if you, all of you, every one of the billion people worldwide who are watching this show, can take one more step.

"You see," Michelle said, "I am not who you think I am. I am not *what* you think I am. This face is a mask. This body is a pose. Who I am and what I am is something you have never experienced before."

At this point, people had begun to start whispering. Some of them were worried that Michelle was about to launch into some odd New Age screed about togetherness. Still others began to wonder if Michelle was going to use this worldwide podium to announce she was a lesbian or a Scientologist. But some noticed that the bottom of Michelle's dress had suddenly gone crystal clear. And so, for that matter, had Michelle's legs.

"I'm wondering," Michelle said. "This award tells me that you believe I have reached into myself and touched some fundamental humanity, some common bond that ties us all together. But could I reach into myself and find this fundamental humanity if I were not human?"

By now it was unmistakable; from toe to armpit, Michelle had gone totally clear.

"What if I told you that that which makes you fundamentally human is something that you share with another people, a people so different from you that they might appear strange or frightening at first glance. A people who might terrify you from appearance alone. Could you make the jump, and understand that inside, they are not so different at all?"

Michelle was now completely clear. As if she had been replaced by an indescribably delicate and beautiful figurine of hand-blown, iridescent glass. She moved away from the podium and stood in full view of a billion speechless members of the human race.

When she spoke again, her voice rang out, amplified not by electronics but by her own crystalline body.

"Could you accept that another people, so unlike you, and yet not unlike you at all, would offer you their hand in friendship? Because, my friends, we are here."

We never did find out who won Best Picture that year.

CHAPTER
Twenty-Two

On the whole, people took it rather well. The only place that rioted was North Korea.

The fact that an alien had managed to sneak past humanity, pose as a superstar, and win the Best Actress Oscar had the desired affect of showing the world that the Yherajk were an essentially benign race—after all, if they had been a warlike people, they could have overrun us with their spaceships, or at the very least have fielded a football team and tried to win the Super Bowl instead. Winning the Best Actress Oscar was the most nonthreatening, yet high exposure, way to introduce one species to another.

The other point that came across was the point Michelle made in her speech—despite the differences, we were in many ways just the same. Michelle wouldn't have been awarded the

Oscar if she had not been able to create such a believable performance as a woman and a human. It was only afterwards, after all, that people realized she wasn't human.

Michelle made it easy for most of humanity by meeting them halfway; although she remained transparent, she also retained Michelle's body shape rather than reverting to the basic Yherajk shapelessness (or smell). She did her job as a true bridge between our peoples—clearly alien, and yet, human enough for most people to accept her.

The only unpleasant thing about Michelle winning the Oscar came later, when some academy members petitioned to have Michelle disqualified as the Best Actress winner. Their rationale was that not only was she not really a human, there was no way to determine that she was, in fact, female.

The academy voted down the proposal in the interests of interspecies peace. Michelle kept her Oscar.

Roland, who never discovered if he had won Best Director or Best Picture, consoled himself with his Best Editing Oscar, and the fact that Michelle's alien status gave *Hard Memories* the Oscar Bump of the ages. By the end of its run, *Hard Memories* grossed half a billion domestic and another billion and a half foreign. Before video and cable. Roland, whose gross points were now worth $300 million, went on to make the Krzysztof Kordus film without Michelle's money. He paid for it himself out of petty cash.

Roland wasn't the only one raking in the fame and fortune. The day after Michelle unveiled, Jim Van Doren walked into the offices of *The New York Times* and plopped down a story about life on the Yherajk spaceship. It was picked up by every newspaper on the planet; shortly thereafter, Van Doren received an $8 million advance for a book on Human-Yherajk relations, which, as it happened, he'd already cowritten with Gwedif. It was rushed into print so fast that the glue was still wet when the books hit the stores. It stayed at the top of the bestseller lists for the rest of the year. It's still there now. You wouldn't believe what he gets in speaking fees these days. I don't and I'm his agent.

Beyond Michelle, however, the Yherajk decided it was best if they stayed in their ship for a little longer. They realized the value of having Michelle, for the short run, be the contact between our peoples. The rest of the Yherajk went the go-slow route, answering e-mail from scientists, politicians and common people alike, and communicating with the world through their Web site, letting leak, bit by bit, information about the Yherajk's true nature and appearance. By the time the majority of the Yherajk land on Earth, humanity will have had enough time to absorb the fact of their differences.

Of course, humanity was still impatient. Fortunately, patience is a Yherajk trait. *Soon enough*, they said, *we will come visit your planet, and you will be invited to our spaceship. And then our peoples will truly learn all we can from each other.*

Governments and self-appointed ambassadors sent e-mail back towards the *Ionar*, saying *When? When can we visit?*

You'll have to check with our agent, the Yherajk invariably signaled back.

Which leads back to me, sitting in my office, with my headset on, lightly bouncing a blue racquetball off the pane of my office window. Talking to my most important client, who was, and still is, and will probably always be, Michelle.

"I don't see why I have go to Venezuela," Michelle was saying to me.

"Because you've been to Peru, Brazil, Chile, and Paraguay,"

I said. "The Venezuelans are a little touchy about their place in the South American hierarchy of nations. Throw them a bone, Michelle. Don't make them the only South American country on the block without a visit from an Oscar-winning alien. They have enough troubles as it is."

"When are the rest of the Yherajk going to come down?" Michelle wanted to know. "There's two thousand of us, you know. Wouldn't hurt to have some of *them* pitch in."

"Jim says the human quarters are just about ready on the *Ionar*," I said. "When they're ready, we'll start inviting folks up and bringing other Yherajk down. It'll be soon, I promise."

"You said that a month ago, Tom."

"You can't rush these things, Michelle. These things take as long as they take."

"Which reminds me," Michelle said. "How long until Miranda pops?"

"If she hasn't gone into labor in about a week, our doctor wants to induce," I said. "Miranda has her own opinions on that one."

"I don't doubt that," Michelle said. "Pick out any names yet?"

"We have," I said. "Michelle if it's a girl, Joshua if it's a boy."

"Well, shucks," Michelle said. "I'm touched. I may cry."

"You don't have tear ducts anymore," I said.

"I'll make them especially for this purpose," Michelle said.

Brandon, my new assistant, popped his head through the door. "It's him, on line three," he said.

I nodded and shooed him out of the room. "Listen, Michelle, I have to go. I have a three o'clock with Carl, but before I do that I have to take this call I've got coming in. Where are you now, anyway?"

"I'm somewhere over the Midwest," Michelle said. "I'll be in Chicago in about an hour. I can't believe you have me going to a science fiction convention."

"Hey," I said. "It won't be so bad. Jim is going to be there. And besides, these people are your core constituency. Give 'em a thrill."

"Oh, I will," Michelle said. "Wait till you see what I have planned for the masquerade." She clicked off.

I looked at my watch. 2:55. Five more minutes. If I took this call, I ran the risk of being late to my meeting with Carl, which would be bad.

Oh, what the hell, I thought. Might as well live dangerously. I flicked the button on line three.

"Hello, Mr. President," I said.

The ball went *thock* as it hit the window.